AURORA: INVASION

Book #6 of the Black Eagle Force series
Book #2 of the Aurora series

AURORA: INVASION

BY

KEN FARMER
&
BUCK STIENKE

Cover by Ken Farmer

THE AUTHORS

Ken Farmer – After proudly serving his country as a US Marine, Ken attended Stephen F. Austin State University on a full football scholarship, receiving his Bachelors Degree in Business and Speech & Drama. Ken quickly discovered his love for acting when he starred as a cowboy in a Dairy Queen commercial when he was raising registered Beefmaster cattle and Quarter Horses at his ranch in East Texas. Ken has over 41 years as a professional actor, with memorable roles *Silverado, Friday Night Lights, The Newton Boys* and *Uncommon Valor*. He was the spokesman for Wolf Brand Chili for eight years. Ken was a professional and celebrity Team Penner for over twenty years—twice penning at the National Finals—and participated in the Ben Johnson Pro-Celebrity Rodeos until Ben's death in '96. Ken now lives near Gainesville, TX, where he continues to write novels.

Ken wrote a screenplay back in the '80s, *The Tumbleweed Wagon*. He and his writing partner, Buck Stienke adapted it to a historical fiction western, *THE NATIONS*—a Finalist for the Elmer Kelton Award. They released the sequel, *HAUNTED FALLS*—winner of the Laramie Award for Best Action Western, 2013—in June of 2013. *HELL HOLE* was the third in the Bass Reeves saga written by Ken alone.

Buck and Ken have completed ten novels to date together including the westerns. *BLACK EAGLE FORCE: Eye of the Storm, BLACK EAGLE FORCE: Sacred Mountain, Return of the Starfighter, BLACK EAGLE FORCE: Blood Ivory, BLOOD BROTHERS* with Doran Ingrham and lastly, *BLACK EAGLE FORCE: Fourth Reich, THE NATIONS* and *HAUNTED FALLS*.

Buck Stienke is a native Texan originally from Houston. He spent many of his formative years in the Texas hill country, and lived on the LBJ ranch when Lyndon Johnson was president.

His love of almost all things Texan extends to movies, books as well as music. He's an accomplished guitarist and singer / songwriter. In fact, a country song he wrote inspired this novel. Buck has an extensive knowledge of guns, modern gunsmithing and ballistics.

Buck and his writing partner, Ken Farmer, have published ten novels to date. Six have been from a series of best-selling BLACK EAGLE FORCE Military/Techno novels : *Eye of the Storm, Sacred Mountain, Return of the Starfighter, Blood Ivory, Blood Brothers.* They also wrote a pair of historical fiction westerns: *The Nations* and *Haunted Falls* (Laramie Award winner - 2013). *Devil's Canyon* was Buck's first solo effort.

ISBN-13: - 978-0-9904389-4-6 - Paper
ISBN-10: - 0-9904389-4-5
ISBN-13: - 978-0-9904389-5-3 - E
ISBN-10: - 0990438953
Copyright 2014 by Timber Creek Press. All rights reserved.

Timber Creek Press
Imprint of Timber Creek Productions, LLC
312 N. Commerce St.
Gainesville, Texas

ACKNOWLEDGMENT

The authors gratefully acknowledges Loree Lough, T.C. Miller, Alex Cord, and Doran Ingrham for their invaluable help in proofing and editing this novel.

Contact Us:
Published by: Timber Creek Press
timbercreekpresss@yahoo.com
www.timbercreekpress.net
Twitter: @pagact
Facebook Book Page:
www.facebook.com/TimberCreekPress
214-533-4964

DEDICATION

AURORA: INVASION is dedicated to all writers of Science Fiction and their tireless efforts to keep the wonderful genera alive. Special kudos go out to E. E. "Doc" Smith, Gene Rodenberry, Jules Verne, Issac Asimov, Edgar Rice Burroughs, the father of SyFy, H. G. Wells and especially to the genius of Nikola Tesla. Much of what we see as science fiction when it was written, soon becomes science fact.

First printing - 9/12/2014

HISTORICAL FICTION WESTERN

THE NATIONS by Ken Farmer and Buck Stienke
www.tinyurl.com/the-nations-Bass
HAUNTED FALLS by Ken Farmer and Buck Stienke
www.tinyurl.com/haunted-falls-Bass
HELL HOLE by Ken Farmer
www.tinyurl.com/hell-hole-Bass3
DEVIL'S CANYON by Buck Stienke
http://tinyurl.com/devils-canyon-B

WESTERN ROMANCE

SURRENDERED by Peggy Patrick
http://tinyurl.com/Surrendered-I
SURRENDERED II by Peggy Patrick
http://tinyurl.com/Surrendered-2
SURRENDERED III by Peggy Patrick

Coming Soon

MILITARY ACTION/TECHNO
BLACK STAR BAY by T.C. Miller

HISTORICAL FICTION WESTERN
ACROSS the RED by Ken Farmer & Buck Stienke
Book four of the Bass Reeves Saga

TIMBER CREEK PRESS

CHAPTER ONE

LAGRANGIAN POINT 2

"This cannot be!" The telepathic blast caused Lucy's copilot to physically turn.

"What is it, Annuna?"

"Notify Mauler 612-B Excalibur of a warp distortion between SEL2 and the Tellus satellite, Darron."

"Impossible! We've never been able to open a singularity this close to a planet's orbit," he replied as he sent the notification when he looked at the display screen of the area between their stable point in space over a million miles outside the orbit of Earth's moon.

"Apparently the Reptoids have made some significant advances." One after another, giant iridescent green egg-shaped domed craft emerged from the disturbance in the very fabric of space. *"They are an entirely new type of craft for them,"* sent Annuna.

"And size."

"They are armed transports."

A fleet of twenty silver Tyranian triangle fighters swarmed like angry bees from the surface of the dark side of Earth's moon and streaked for the half dozen Reptoid craft.

Outside the Mars orbit, a large distortion shimmered and four huge Tyranian *Mauler* battlecruisers emerged one at a time and flashed to encompass the green vessels in their deadly cone of annihilation with the fighters. Each silver interstellar craft was over a mile long and three-quarters of a mile wide.

This time it was different. The new Reptoid ships from the Alpha Draconis system were unaffected by the massive tractor beams from the great silver ships and the purple beams of pure energy only caused their screens to flare into the red.

"They have a new type of shield! Our beams are ineffective," projected the commander of *Mauler* 612-B.

"Their force fields are cycling through the spectrum faster than we can adapt," said the gray science officer telepathically from his station.

"Launch a barrage of Thorium torpedoes."

"Aye." The combat officer's tiny gray hands flashed over his touch screen and a dozen of the ultra-deadly missiles sped toward the nearest green craft. Thousands of miles before they reached their target, the torpedoes exploded simultaneously, briefly lighting up that section of space between the Lagrangian Point 2 and the Moon like mini-suns. *"No effect...they were eliminated by some type of extreme range screen unknown to us."*

"Send for two more squadrons," ordered Lucy. *"They'll have to use concentrated fire."*
"Aye, Captain."

Within moments, two more groups of four of the giant *Mauler* battlecrusiers emerged from the worm hole. The twelve triangle super ships were able to encircle the Reptoid vessels in the cone of annihilation. The swarm of tiny fighters joined in the formation and simultaneously began a centrally coordinated pounding with massive annihilating purple beams of pure energy from their projectors.

"Don't waste power trying to use your tractor beams or torpedoes, just put everything you have into your force beams," sent the commander of 612-B *Excalibur*, to the rest of the fleet.

The very ether itself vibrated with the concentrated ravening beams from the massed Tyranian ships and the gargantuan pulsed green lasers—some over a mile wide—pounded back at the silver ships. Six of the *Maulers* focused on one of the green dreadnaughts and slowly her force fields flared to violet, and then to incandescence. She vaporized into a greenish cloud in the cold vacuum of space.

Three of the Reptoid ships targeted one of the mile long Tyranian *Maulers* with their massive beams and the silver triangle flared through the visible spectrum and literally dissolved into nothingness from the combined power of the lasers.

One after another of the tiny silver fighters winked out of existence at just the touch of one of the deadly green pulses from the giant ships.

"Our projectors are overheating!" beamed a combat officer.

"Let them! Increase power, the Reptoids must not escape," answered the commander.

It was the last order she ever gave as her *Mauler* disintegrated into the void.

Another of the giant green egg-shaped ships flared into vapor along with ten more Tyranian fighters.

"Activate the cloaking device on my signal," ordered Klsth—the Supreme Commander of the Reptoid fleet—in what sounded like a series of consonants and clicks emitting from his snakelike head with alligator jaws. It sat directly on top of his square scaly green torso with four eyes on short articulating stalks—each capable of directing one of its four tentacle arms independently—while two elephantine legs supported his nine foot tall massive body. One of his eyes curled toward his operations officer. "Mark."

"They disappeared, Annuna!" beamed Darron.

"I know." She stared at her visaplate, empty except for the surviving Tyranian ships and scattered debris.

Their observation position at the SEL-2 Lagrangian Point gave them a perfect view of the region of the Sol solar system where the latest battle with the evil Reptoids took place. *They cloaked and are headed to Tellus…*

WHISKY RIVER CLUB
Cross Timbers County

Dave Alexander's band was playing western swing to a packed crowd. Several couples were decked out in their best cowboy finery and were two-stepping around the powdered mica dusted dance floor.

Detective Darrell Ulysses Bone—known as just 'Bone' to friends and foe alike—Captain St. John and Inspector Loraine Rodriquez were seated at a table near the dancers with longneck beers sitting atop paper coasters.

"We'll, it's about time we heard some decent music. Dave and his boys are good, aren't they, kiddies?" commented Bone.

"I think so. They have a sound like Bob Wills and the Texas Playboys…"

"They do, don't they, Captain. I just wish I could dance like that," observed Loraine.

"That can be arranged. I'll even waive my usual fee for you," said the 6' 8" detective.

"You're kidding, right?…I thought you played football."

"Of course he did. That's what caused all the brain damage that we have to deal with," said St. John.

Bone saw the somewhat incredulous expression on his partner's face and roared with laughter. "You don't know much about football, do you, Loraine? Linebackers are always practicing fancy footwork…Pass coverage, stunts and chasing down little bitty runnin' backs…They used to call me twinkle toes."

"Right…Twink." The raven-haired beauty grinned. "Maybe after the next beer you can show me. I've got to make a visit to the little girls room."

"I'll go get us another round," offered St. John.

Bone stood and watched as they walked away, glanced around, took a silver dollar out of his pants pocket and a tube of Super Glue from a shirt pocket. He pulled off the cap and applied a couple of dabs to the coin and then put the glue away.

Looking around again, he took a couple of steps onto the dance floor, bent over as if he was brushing dust from his boots and surreptitiously placed the coin—glue side down—on the floor, stepped on it for a few seconds and then slowly walked back to the table.

Loraine returned from the ladies room at the same time St. John walked up with three beers. Bone got back to his feet and pulled out her chair.

"And I thought chivalry was dead."

"Actually I needed more room for my feet."

"Why does that not surprise me? You could use those them for pontoons."

"Har, har."

She grabbed the back of the chair as Bone pushed it under her.

"What? Think I might jerk it out from under you?"

"You? Now why would I think that?" She rolled her eyes.

Bone palmed a few rubber bands from his shirt pocket as he sat back down.

An unsuspecting club patron spotted the coin on the floor and bent over to try to pick it up.

Bone held the longneck in his left hand and extended his thumb, looping the rubber band over it. He pretended to take a swig from the bottle as he pointed his index finger and let loose with his thumb. The rubber band struck the cowboy wearing tight fitting Wranglers on the butt.

Bone had turned his head away from the targeted victim and set the beer back on the table with a wry grin on his face.

The embarrassed cowboy looked around and walked away rubbing his butt.

"You're not going to make fun of me on the dance floor are you?" asked the very attractive Hispanic cop.

"Moi? You're my partner…I'm serious about this dancin', or as Muhammad Ali used to say…'I float like a buttterfly'."

While he conned Loraine, he surreptitiously reloaded as another victim—Tonya Parker, a pretty twenty-five year old redheaded girl in skin tight Cruel Girl jeans—bent over to pick up the silver dollar.

Bone's rubber band found its mark on her heart-shaped rear. She jumped as if stung by a bee and wheeled around to see a couple dancing nearby. She assumed an old ex-boyfriend, Todd Farr, had pinched her as he danced by and slapped him hard enough for him to lose his hat.

"Jerk!"

He was speechless, but his girlfriend, Shelly, reacted to the slap with one of her own to Tonya.

"Slut! Keep your paws off my man!"

Tonya swung back at Shelly, missed and connected with Todd's jaw, knocking him on his tail.

Choruses of "FIGHT!" started echoing across the floor as the band got distracted and stopped playing in a disjointed manner.

The two girls grabbed each other by the hair and both fell to the floor. A friend of Tonya's came over and broke a bottle of beer over Todd's head just as he was getting up. He goofily spun slowly and sank back to the floor. The whole dance hall erupted into a fight.

"Oh, damn…You had something to do with this, Bone… Don't know how, but I know you did," St. John accused.

"I resemble that remark, Cap'n... You know, Pard, this might not be the best time to take a dance lesson…I expect we'd better boogie."

Bone nodded at his captain, pulled Loraine to her feet, shoved a couple of brawlers out of the way and the three made their way to the door as the sounds of sirens could be heard in the distance.

BONE'S RANCH HOUSE
Cross, Texas

Just a few miles outside of town, sited on a full section of open rolling pastureland mixed with a couple of spring-fed creeks—lined with towering cypress and cottonwood trees—sat a large one hundred year old dog-run style house. Nearby, a red barn, a shed and a hand-dug well were the only other structures visible. Light from a wide screen plasma TV flickered though the shear curtains covering the windowpanes of the spacious living room.

Bone stretched out his big frame in a custom-made saddle leather recliner. He was decked out in his usual weekend garb—a well-worn Marine Corps workout T shirt, red with a gold eagle, globe and anchor emblem on the front, dark gray drawstring shorts and running shoes.

"Thanks for inviting me to have a beer with ya'll," his godfather, Padrino, said without bothering to look up. He occupied a similar, but smaller chair, and had a wall-mounted reading light turned on as he eagerly dug into his passion for historical fiction books.

"You probably wouldn't have enjoyed it anyway. Pretty boring evening, all told…Dammit, I knew the Rangers screwed up big time when they let Nellie Cruz get away in the off season," Bone grumbled at the screen. "Look at that! He's kickin' their ass again…A two RBI triple to put us down by three with only one inning to go."

Padrino glanced up from reading *Haunted Falls* just in time to see the replay of the ball bouncing off the right field wall and rolling past the frazzled defender. Cruz had already rounded first and was almost to second base by the time the right fielder got his hand on the ball and tried to make the throw to the infield. He glanced over to his young friend, saw the anguished look and grinned. "Another foot and it would have been a Jimmy-Jack."

"Morons...I could manage that team better than him." Bone got up and grabbed another Shiner Bock from the fridge when the gold and blue bracelet on his right wrist began to buzz.

A yellow and cream colored pit bull that had been sleeping beside the coffee table raised his head at the familiar noise.

"Lucy's coming to see us, isn't she, Tyrin?"

The dog's tail thumped the carpet rapidly as he seemed to smile. "Woof."

The air shimmered for a second as holographic image of a small woman appeared before them in the middle of the room. Standing only 4' 11", she was clad in a skintight suit of a shiny semi-metallic gray material, with gloves that matched and a smooth seamless helmet featuring large almond-shaped black lenses. She removed the headgear and shook her predominantly brown hair that was cut in a short pixie style and streaked with gray. Her eyes reflected a deep concern.

"Hey, Lucy, good to see you again," the muscular off-duty detective said. "Something's bothering you, I can tell..."

"Indeed it is. Our old enemies, the Reptoids are back...and we couldn't stop them all this time."

10

"I'll get my gun."

"I'm afraid it's going to take a lot more than that, Bone..." the hologram countered. "...We lost several ships already. They have developed some new weapons...plus a whole new class of armed transport, about the size of a domed football stadium.

"They are far too big and powerful for our fighters to handle individually and our Mauler cruisers cannot use their Thorium weapons or energy beams inside your atmosphere."

"Why not?" Padrino asked.

"They are designed for interstellar battles. Inside your atmosphere here, the effect would be similar to a gigantic electromagnetic pulse...Your species would suffer greatly."

"You mean like a nuclear EMP? Knocking out the entire power grid simultaneously?" Bone questioned.

She shook her head. "I'm afraid not...Many times worse than that. The gamma radiation alone would kill most of the life forms on the side of the planet directly exposed to the blast. All of your electrically powered devices and computers would cease to function...What would be left of the human race would be abruptly returned to the 18th century, but without the animal power to survive those conditions."

"I hate it when that happens...What can we do?"

"We believe four of the new Reptoid ships are cloaked inside your thermosphere. For our part, we are developing new defensive shields to counteract their advancements and constructing a smaller class of combat craft between our fighters and Maulers that can operate inside your atmosphere...But that will take a little time."

Bone nodded and glanced at Padrino. "I see. What did they come here for? More enriched uranium fuel like the last time?"

Lucy shook her head. "If only that were the case...Unfortunately, they are on a hunt for food on a interstellar scale. Protein makes up almost ninety percent of their diet...They are here harvesting."

Padrino and Bone shared another look. The elder shaman was thunderstruck by the realization of her words. She read his thoughts as quickly as he formulated them. *They want us!*

"Our best bet is to utilize the resources available through your best special operations organization. Luckily, they are close by," she said.

"Lucy, I'm not following you...Who is close by?" Bone asked.

"The Black Eagle Force. You were wearing one of their hats when I first met you."

"Oh that...Almost forgot. Hate to break it to you, but the BEF is fiction...Like Area 51, you know?"

"Sometimes, the truth is better hidden in plain sight. No one would believe an ultra top secret base lies buried underneath the North Texas Regional Airport in Grayson, County...Or that an alien was living on a ranch outside of Cross, Texas for over a hundred years." She winked.

"Holy moly," Bone said as he swallowed hard. "You mean they actually *do* exist?"

"They do indeed. Our scouts have monitored them for the last few years when we first detected third and fourth order wave spikes from some of their weaponry."

"Like you were telling us about before you were rescued…What about the fifth order wave?" asked Padrino.

"They've been following your Nicola Tesla's work and you are very close."

"I'll get my truck," Bone said.

"There's no need for that…We've got a much faster means of getting us there…If you'll recall?"

"Oh, yeah, that."

Bone and Lucy shimmered and disappeared. The wiry, white haired Viet Nam veteran got a wry grin on his face, picked his book back up and casually returned to the story.

NORTH TEXAS REGIONAL AIRPORT
BEF Underground Headquarters

On the west side of the field once known as Perrin AFB—until it closed in the 1970s—stood a series of former Air Defense Command hangars that were used to house the F-102 *Delta Daggers*. Burgeoning airspace requirements for the newly created DFW International Airport helped the USAF make the decision to close the base and it reverted to local civilian ownership. After several years of standing idle, the weather-beaten white elephants were purchased by a company calling itself Warbirds Restoration, Inc.

The new owners set about the task of converting the facilities to its stated purpose—painting, servicing and restoring WWII fighters and bombers for the well-heeled aficionados of such expensive big boy toys. WRI had gathered a stellar reputation as the go-to group for the Commemorative Air Force and others actually wanting to fly the old birds with radial and Rolls-Royce V-12 Merlin engines. They actually made money doing such aviation work, but the whole operation was a clever way to disguise the real operation underground.

Over eight and one-half acres of subterranean aircraft parking, storage, command center, offices and secret training facilities of a clandestine group had been built to house President Ronald Reagan's brainchild—the Black Eagle Force.

It was conceived as a quick reaction force to solve militarily any number of critical problems that confronted the United States without constraints of artificial Rules of Engagement, the Posse Comitatus Act of 1878—or interference from politicians.

Its members consisted of the cream of the crop of Above Tier One warfighters, pilots, elite Special Ops units, technicians and support personnel from every branch of the service and a smattering of civilian geniuses who did things no one else could.

The BEF operated under the direct control of the Secretary of Defense and was funded out of the black ops budget that also created and managed Area 51 and built the SR-71 *Blackbird* spy plane, developed the F-117 *Nighthawk* and the B-2 *Spirit* stealth bomber.

Over the years the BEF had grown and was expanded to include operational control of four fighter squadrons—two operating modified F-15 *Eagle* and two equipped with F/A18 *Super Hornets*—also modified—in addition to their deadly *Black Eagle* VTOL squadrons. All of the fighter units were supported by two giant C-5M Super Galaxy transport that had been modified to serve as armed airborne carriers.

Inside the rather spartan office—for a three hundred-million dollar a year organization—BEF CEO Dare Phillips was reviewing the status reports of the latest upgrades to the team's fourth generation fighter aircraft. He was a retired Marine Colonel that went by the call sign "Iron Horse" when he flew Super Cobra's in combat in Iraq. Fit and trim at age fifty, Dare stood 6' 1" and still kept his salt-and-pepper hair cropped short—almost short enough for corps regulations.

He saw movement over the top of his laptop screen that startled him. *What the hell?* A huge guy in a Marine crimson and gold PT shirt and shorts stood in front of him holding a beer—with a puzzled look on his face. Dare swore that there was no way the man could have walked in the door without his seeing or hearing him. He had just appeared out of thin air.

"How the hell did you get in here…and who are you?" Dare demanded as he got to his feet.

Bone looked around nervously and took a swig of his bottle. "Damn if I know! She said she would get us here quicker." He turned around. "Lucy? Lucy, you here?"

Dare stared at his uninvited guest and reverted back to his military upbringing. "Marine…this is a secure facility and I've never seen your face before…You better start coming up with some answers…and I'm not in the mood to play games. I asked you once…Who are you?"

"The name's Bone, mister and I know this gonna sound crazy, but my friend, Lucy…she's from the planet Tyrin…she says the Reptoids have broken through and are gonna start harvesting humans and we need to get the Black Eagle Force to try to stop 'em before millions of us get eaten," he said in a rapid staccato of words.

"You're right…it sounds crazy. Are you drunk? Now how the hell did you get in here and who told you about the Black Eagle Force?" Dare reached for the intercom. "Tom, I need some Raptors down here for security."

Bone glanced down at the brass nameplate affixed to an oaken base, flanked by two chromed 50BMG rounds. "Colonel Phillips…Darrell Bone, Marine Force Recon, inactive…I'm not drunk…Sir, like I said, I was contacted by this alien friend of mine and I she had me beamed in to notify you guys of the danger."

He looked around the office. "She's, uh, supposed to be here as well, but something must have gone wrong. She's, uh, Lucy, or Annuna…and she's up in her little fighter UFO watching out for us…I mean the earth, but she's way out there and…"

Dare shook his head and held up his hand. "Whoa there, big fellow…Stop. Have a seat, relax. Security will be here in a couple minutes to escort you out."

Bone looked around at the two chairs facing the desk and slid down into one. "This ain't the way to stop those Reptoid bastards. Hell, I wouldn't believe me if I hadn't shot a couple of those ugly mother…uh, four-armed creatures myself."

Tom Tallman's voice came over the intercom. "Bad Poole, Widowmaker Baker, report to Dare's office on the double."

16

Bone took another sip of his beer as he heard running down the corridor outside. *Joy. Just what I need. I hope those jerks don't try to tase me.*

Dare looked at the size of the man in his office. *Damn. I hope he doesn't get violent. Aw, hell...I hope Bad and Widowmaker are enough to handle him.*

There was a shimmer in the air next to Bone as Lucy appeared, but not in holographic form. She was still dressed in her gray space suit and carried the helmet under her right arm. Dare jumped back, startled again.

Widowmaker reached the doorway just in time to see her materialize. "Holy crap! How the hell did you do that, lady?"

"Lucy! Tell these guys what you told me. A man can't get any respect around here. He thinks I'm nutty as a fruitcake." Bone stood up. "Colonel, this is my friend Lucy I was talking about."

The diminutive Tyranian extended her gloved hand. "Mister Phillips, I understand you are the Chief Executive Officer of the Black Eagle Force. Is that correct?"

He stood there with his mouth agape for a second before he reached out and took her tiny hand. "Uh, yes, ma'am. Dare Phillips at your service."

"Archimedies?"

He glanced over at a grinning Bad and Widowmaker. "Yes, ma'am...but my people call me Dare."

"Of course."

"Lucy, what took you so long? I didn't know you were just gonna beam me over here from Cross."

"Unanticipated technical glitches. Nothing is perfect you know. I had to first transfer to our Mauler orbiting outside your thermosphere. They had a slight problem with their transporter. It may have been battle damage from the Reptoid's weaponry."

"Mauler?" Dare looked even more puzzled.

"You might term it an interstellar battleship."

"Ah, I see...Uh, have a seat miss Lucy...Do you mind if I call you Lucy?"

She sat down next the 285 pound detective, making her look even smaller than she actually was. "No, please. Call me Lucy if you like...I'm rather used to it now. My real name is Annuna and I'm from the planet Tyrin in what you call the Orion system."

"Mister Bone mentioned that..."

"See? Told you I'm not drunk." Bone grinned.

"Dare, we have followed your technical progress closely and need assistance from your Black Eagle Force immediately. You have unique capabilities that I believe may prove very valuable...Perhaps it would help if Blaze Hermann and Gears Formby could join us...There is much to do and very little time before the Reptoid's begin to process their captives."

How the blazes do they know so much about us? "He mentioned that term, Reptoids. Who or what are they and what threat do they pose to America?"

Her pixie-like face turned cold at the thought. "Not just America, Mister Phillips...but your entire world...They are a most disgusting race of creatures from the star system Alpha Draconis. They do not produce much, except for machines of

18

war. All the resources and food they need, they prefer to take by force. They are very powerful beasts physically as their planet's gravity is several times that of Tellus...your Earth.

"They possess cloaking devices, and can project holograms around themselves changing their appearance. Many of your ancient cultures have known them as shape shifters."

"But why are they coming here now and why have we never heard of them before?" Dare inquired.

Bone spoke up, "Sir, Lucy's race...the Sumerians called them the Anunnaki...have watched and protected earth for millennia...they even provided our original human DNA. I happened to have run into her a while back and helped her get back with her people...These Reptoids are really bad dudes and absolutely ruthless...They kill women and children and never think twice about it. The worse part is they look at the human species as food...Cattle, if you will."

Widowmaker and Poole exchanged glances.

Dare sat back and tried to wrap his mind around all that he had heard. He leaned over and tapped the intercom once again. "Tom, I'd like Blaze, Gears, Heater and all other key personnel to join me in the conference room...ASAP."

***

CHAPTER TWO

EARTH'S THERMOSPHERE
SOUTH POLE

"What is the time required to repair the damage to our vessels?" asked Supreme Commander Klsth.

"At least four revolutions of this puny planet, Sire. The concentrated Tyranian energy beams not only partially penetrated our new multiphased shields, but our power reserves were severely depleted," replied chief engineer, Slkph, who was identical in appearance to the others, but almost twenty percent larger.

"If we could disengage the cloaking device, we would be able to recharge our accumulators much quicker," stated Sub-Commander Prlk.

AURORA: INVASION

The four remaining *T-Cruisers* were holding stationary over the south pole at nearly 300 miles above its icy surface. They used the concentration of the earth's magnetic field at its southern apex to recharge their new type of power accumulators. The scaly creatures had reverse-engineered the ability of a captured Aldebaran vessel to draw on cosmic energy as a power source, eliminating the need to carry large supplies of Uranium-237.

"No! It is better to disengage the shields than the cloak. If the Grays cannot find us, we do not need the protection...What is the status of our T-Cruisers and protein dehydrator processors?" asked Klsth of the fleet science officer Krpld.

All the commanders of the four transport ships had gathered in the commander's office on board the flag ship, T-233. The conference area was permeated with the atmosphere closely approximating that of lizard being's home planet, Draco—oxygen based, but with a high percentage of chlorine as ClO^2 or chlorine dioxide—a yellow-green gas.

"All suffered some degree of damage, but nothing that cannot be repaired in the time allotted, Supreme Commander...We will, however, need an additional cycle to replenish our source of ClO^2 which we can obtain from the amazingly abundant supply of NaCl or sodium chloride on this world."

Klsth nodded his four eye stalks in agreement. "When all necessary procedures are complete, we will disburse to the four most populous areas of Tellus and begin the harvest. I surmise the Tyranians will eventually devise a solution to our new multiphased shields that not only are more resistive to their energy projectors, but also are able to shear off from their tractor beams. They will seek to engage us again…It is not my intention to be here when they come…and believe me they will come."

He waved his four tentacle-like appendages about and pointed to the cloud-ensconced blue globe on the giant visaplate. "Even with our reduced number of T-Cruisers, we should be able to harvest one to two billion of the puny little beings available on this insignificant world. That will give us a more than ample food source for the foreseeable future."

CONFERENCE ROOM
BEF Headquarters

Once the key personnel had assembled, Dare introduced Lucy and Bone and asked the team members to identify themselves along with their area of expertise. When Blaze Hermann did so, Lucy's eyes sparkled as the gorgeous redhead with piercing green eyes simply said, "Engineering."

"You are so much more than that, young lady," Lucy said with a slight smile. "Your brain function is extraordinarily developed for your species. I sensed that as you postulated the functionality of the lens in my helmet…Here, have a closer look." She pushed the flexible uniform hood across the cherry wood table.

Blaze blushed slightly as she picked it up and handled it carefully. *Gosh it's so light. Not carbon fiber, far too flexible for that...I wonder if it's a spin-off from graphene. But there are no seams whatsoever. How is it made?* She looked across the table at Lucy. The words *three dimensional printing at the atomic level* flowed across her consciousness as Lucy smiled, but said nothing. Blaze's eyes grew wider. *Did you just think that to me? Telepathy?*

Lucy nodded and then turned to hear Gears Formby say, "Aircraft Commander, Mama Bird and engineering."

"Partsman" Meadows identified himself as the head of maintenance, followed by James "Hollywood" Stewart—F-15 Wing Commander, Maria "Double D" Williams—F-18A Wing Commander, Mike "Cowboy" Hermann—VTOL *Eagle* Flight Commander, and the two local *Raptor* team leaders, Leroy "Bad" Poole and Sean "Widowmaker" Baker.

The last BEF key person to speak was seated between Dare and Bone. He was a tall, retired USAF brigadier general with a handsome face and gray at his temples.

"I'm Heater McElhenny, Chief Operating Officer...Lucy I suggest we turn this over to you and you can bring us up to speed."

"Thank you, Heater." She opened a nearly invisible pocket in the thigh of her skintight—formfitting space suit—withdrawing a credit card sized device and laying it on the table. Lucy touched a flush button on the end and a small blue light began to emanate from the center of the unit. She closed her eyes and pictured the image of a Reptoid as she maintained contact.

A holographic life-sized three dimensional image of the hideous creature materialized in only a second. Blaze gasped as did several other members of the BEF.

"Holy crap!" exclaimed Widowmaker. "Look at the size of that thing!"

"There is nothing holy about them, I can assure you, Mister Baker. With four eyes, mounted on those articulating stalks as they are, it is almost impossible to sneak up on one when they are in a defensive mode or engaged in hunting."

"And four arms, too...If that's what you call those things. I'm not gonna try to go hand-to-hand with one either," Poole added.

"No kiddin'," Bone said quickly. "Plus they have a disruptor type of ray weapon like the Romulans and Klingons on Star Trek that will flat out incinerate your ass with one hit...Hell, they took out a couple of squad cars from the sheriff's department over in Cross Timbers County. I recovered one of 'em from the first one I killed."

"How did you survive the encounter?" Dare asked.

"He missed...My partner Loraine and I didn't."

"Oorah," Widowmaker said with a grin.

"The thing is, didn't know they were aliens. See, they looked like some regular guys who were harassing my friend here. Loraine and I snuck up and got the drop on 'em. Ol' ugly tried to tag me with this tube-like thing, but Loraine triple tapped him with her 1911A, while I dropped and rolled...Came up shooting and also triple tapped his butt with my 500 Smith."

"Their shield technology is based upon energy beam and pulse laser weapons," said Lucy. "His solid copper projectiles easily defeated the force field surrounding their holographic projection."

"Solid copper?" asked Heater.

"Barnes 275 grain hollowpoints at 1,688 feet per second in the Cor-Bon load," Blaze said before she became slightly self-conscious. "I, uh, read about it when they first came out a few years ago."

"She's got a photographic memory, to go along with her two doctorates," Dare said with a grin.

"Impressive," Bone replied. "Unless they changed since we tangled, even a .45 ACP can penetrate their ship's hulls. Loraine and I double-teamed again and their ship blew up as it climbed into the upper atmosphere."

"Why didn't you report…" Dare asked, and then abruptly halted himself and shook his head. "Dumb question…You figured you guys would be treated exactly like I just treated you when you appeared in my office…Right?"

"Pretty much. We had one more encounter with those jackalopes, but the Feds showed up and whisked the body away. They made us sign nondisclosure agreements or they would have locked us up."

"Don't worry about that. Water under the bridge, besides we trump those guys," Heater said. "What about their ships?"

Lucy touched the projector again. The creature hologram shrunk and disappeared. Again, she closed her eyes and the armed transporter craft appeared. "It's about the size of Cowboy

Stadium…including the parking area…in your Arlington. Very powerful weapons, new shields…we are working on counteracting…and the ability to cloak itself."

"Jesus," Hollywood said. "It would take a lot of 20 MM rounds to do much damage to something that huge. Even an AMRAAM would be like bear huntin' with a .25 auto."

"Ripple fired slammer's could probably cause multiple hull breaches," Double D said with conviction.

"They were able to destroy our Thorium torpedoes before they reached their targets. It's possible they have a new type of targeting laser…However, that was in the vacuum of outer space at great distances. We don't know what would happen in the close confines of your atmosphere."

"Lucy, how low do those ships have to come to collect their prey?"

"We are not exactly sure. We've only seen the *results* of their raids and never actually seen them in action. Up to now, we've been fairly successful at keeping them at bay. Generally, Draconian technology is inferior to ours. If they have transporter beam technology…like we used to get here…it will likely not be as powerful and therefore, they will have to descend to within a few thousand feet of the surface."

"If that's the case, we can use our particle beam weapons from our C-5M Super Galaxies, and the G2 coil guns on the M600s and 800s," Gears said enthusiastically. "The only problem is their cloaking device. It's probably different than the Nazi's used on their Horton 429s we encountered in South America."

"How were you able to detect their cloaks?" Lucy asked.

"Electromagnetic disruptions associated with the Tesla third and fourth order waves as well as heat distortions. We measured those…"

"And computed their future position using the super computers aboard Mama Bird…" Blaze jumped in.

"Then…correcting for the speed of light and the particle beam distance to travel, made some adjustments and…viola! Got some direct hits…" Gears continued.

"Which in turn, forced them to discontinue the use of their cloak. I switched off our Lizard device and engaged them in good old one v one aerial combat. They had some killer kind of EMP ray weapon, but never got a nose-on solution to take a shot.

"Like your friend Bone said, they missed…I didn't." Hollywood crossed his arms and sat back contemplating the air battle he won.

"I see," Lucy said. "Those German flying wing fighters were very maneuverable and rather hard to see against the Bolivian jungle below. Excellent use of the vertical. You'll have to tell me how your coil gun functions…I could see the blue plasma trails of the hypersonic projectiles."

Hollywood's chin dropped as he stared at Lucy. *How did she know?*

"Annuna," Blaze said.

Lucy turned to lock eyes with the resident Ph.D. in Electrical Engineering and Physics. Blaze said nothing, but obviously was thinking very hard.

Dare saw a slight vertical furrow form in her usually smooth forehead. *What's going on? She only does that when she's really concentrating hard.*

After a few seconds, Blaze closed her eyes, and placed her right hand to her forehead. "Ahhh…something's giving me a headache."

"I'm so sorry, my child. I should know better than that. You're not ready for that much information at one time," Lucy said. She turned to Bone. "Go help her with her headache, please."

"Me? What do you want me to do?"

Do what you did for the Aldebarian woman. Use your hands one on each temple…Concentrate. The thoughts came to him without a word being spoken.

"Okay, since you put it that way." He pushed back from the table and walked around to where Blaze sat. "Pardon me, Miss. I won't hurt you." Standing behind her, he placed the tips of his fingers on her temples and his massive thumbs almost touched together on the top of her head. He took in a deep breath and closed his eyes.

Dare watched closely as a faint blue glow appeared between his fingers and a look of contentment crossed over Blaze's face as her pain went away.

Bone released his touch. "Better?"

"Amazing…The pain is gone and I still remember all Annuna taught me."

The big man moved back to his seat as Lucy spoke up, "My apologies to you all. My people have evolved far enough to communicate telepathically. It's rude to do so when others cannot be part the conversation. I know better and I'm sorry."

"What did he do?" Blaze asked.

"He gave you some of his life force energy...to help compensate for the mental overload I put you through."

"And now I've got a headache," Bone said.

"Finish your beer." Lucy smiled. "You'll start to feel better...I guarantee."

"Now that's the kind of doctor's orders I can live with." He tipped the longneck back and drained it.

Dare turned to Tom. "Get the SecDef on secure video. He's got to be involved in this."

"Yes, sir." Tallman got to his feet, went to a control panel and keyed in a code. The ten foot concave curved plasma screen on the wall came to life with the seal of the Secretary of Defense.

After a short moment, Secretary Jack "Burner" Stewart appeared sitting behind his desk in the Pentagon.

"Is there a problem, Dare?"

In front of him on his desk was a model of a F-104 *Starfighter*—in all black. Over his shoulder was a life-sized painting of Joe Rosenthal's famous photo of the United States flag raising on Iwo Jima.

EARTH'S THERMOSPHERE
SOUTH POLE

Chief engineer, Slkph, waddled into the command center of B-233 on his two short, but very thick legs. "Supreme Commander, I regret to inform you, but four of our ten buss bars were burned out in the attack. Please forgive my dalliance in reporting."

"We lose four buss bars and you are just now telling me!" Klsth thundered. "Fool!"

He raised one of his tentacles—one with a silver tube attached. A green beam shot out and caught Slkph just below his snake-shaped head. His entire massive body glowed green briefly and dissolved into a wispy green vapor.

"Sub-Commander Prlk, elevate assistant chief engineer Rdllt to replace this idiot. Have him send a Death Globe as a scout ship...we must locate sufficient quantities of AU-79 to replace the four buss bars. Without all ten functioning, we will not be able to fully catalyze and charge our accumulators.

"Right away, Sire."

A metallic green thirty foot diameter globe slowly rose from its launch tube on top of the T-233. Once clear of the massive mother ship in her position some 300 miles above East Antarctica, the craft shot NNE.

"Our scanners show a sizable deposit of refined Au-79 along celestial longitude 28.189444399999957 at latitude 25.8602778. The images collected by T-233 show a large flat-topped structure overlaid with an elemental scan placing the Au-79 in the NW quadrant," said co-pilot Qrts.

"We are there," said pilot Mrrst. "We will hover just above the plotted location of the largest supply and create an opening in the top of the structure to extract the metal."

"I will prepare the reception chamber."

"We must decloak in order to activate the laser and transporter. Make haste before we are seen by the natives or possibly Tyranian scout ships. But, I severely doubt these primitives have any weapons that would pose a threat to us."

"I understand."

The inertialess drive enabled the globular craft to stop instantly from its Mach 8 speed and hover twenty feet from the roof of the South African Mint Company. Mrrst calculated the depth inside the building and programed a low-level laser to burn through the roof and all the way to the steel-lined vault in the basement.

"What in God's name is that? One second there was nothing and the next there is a shiny green ball…just floating above the roof!" said a secretary in a third floor office across the Old Johannesburg Road from the mint in Centurion, South Africa. She motioned her boss to look out the large window on the west side of his office. "Do you see that?"

He spun his chair around. "Jesus! I do indeed, Clair…I think we're witnessing a bona fide UFO." He keyed for the company operator on his desk phone. "Ruth, this Dean Harmse, get me Archie Martin, please, at AFB Waterkloof…Hurry."

"General Martin here. How can I help you Dean?"

"Archie, you may not believe this, but you know me...I'm not prone to hallucinations. There is a UFO hovering a couple hundred feet above the mint across the road...Round as a basketball and about ten meters in diameter."

"Details, Harmse, details."

"My secretary saw it first. It suddenly appeared...you know, like it just materialized and is hovering there...Wait a second! There's a green beam, two meters across that just emitted from the base of the globe...Now there's smoke coming from the top of the building...Archie? Archie, you there?" He looked at Clair. "I'll be damned. He either thought I was nuts and hung up on me...or it scared the hell out of him and he's scrambling fighters."

NORTH TEXAS REGIONAL AIRPORT
GRAYSON COUNTY, TEXAS

Jill McElhenny Hermann glanced over her right shoulder at the other three F-15 *Eagles* in echelon formation. *Looking good, you guys.* The four matte-black fighters with no external marking whatsoever were descending though 4,000' MSL six miles southwest of the airport.

An ATC controller from Fort Worth center came on frequency, "Echo one-five flight, radar services terminated. Squawk twelve hundred, contact Grayson tower on two-thirty-three point seven."

The new pilot who had taken the offer to join the BEF when contacted by the SecDef, a former USAF Fighter Weapons School instructor named Tex Richards, replied quickly, "Echo One-five flight squawking VFR and going to tower. Good Day…Flight button two."

The other pilots responded with their position as they reached for the comm control switch. "Two, Three, Four."

"Grayson tower, Echo one-five flight…seven miles out for an overhead to three-five right with information Oscar"

"Echo flight, Grayson tower, roger. You are cleared for the approach to three-five right. Altimeter now three-zero-zero-one. Expect landing clearance on final."

Tex read back the altimeter and began the final decent to the pattern altitude, leveling off at 1,500' AGL and slowing to 250 KIAS. As they approached the two north south runways, he rolled smoothly into a 45 degree left bank—one matched by the other veteran fighter jocks as if they were tied together by some invisible wires. Midway down the runway, Tex broke quickly to a steep left bank, leaving the formation as he pulled the throttles to idle and extended the speed brake.

His wingmen followed his lead in three second increments, turning back south as they slowed and extended their landing gear. Tex looked over his left shoulder as he lined up with the yellow chevrons painted in the overrun. When the hash lines were pointed directly at his *Eagle*, he knew from experience that he was exactly forty-five degrees past the end of the runway. He executed a descending left turn back to the north and rolled wings level as the tower radioed the *cleared to land* call.

Jill, in the rear instructor's seat, monitored the action as he put the bird down smoothly on the left side of the runway, only 200 feet past the numbers. "Nicely done, Tex."

His wingman touched down on the right side of the asphalt just about the time Tex deployed his drag chute and applied light to moderate brake pressure. With only 8,000 feet of runway, North Texas Regional did not allow much aerodynamic braking.

The four pulled in front of the southernmost Warbird Restoration hangar and shut down line abreast as the ground crew—in their powder blue jumpsuits—gave hand signals, chocked the main tires and positioned crew ladders.

Jill unstrapped, slipped off her black helmet and stashed it in the padded bag she had stowed beside her seat.

One of the crew chiefs scrambled up the ladder and took the helmet bag from her. "Jill, you did get the word about the key personnel staff meeting, didn't you?"

"Sure did, thanks. That's why we didn't do any touch and goes." She stepped onto the ladder and leaned forward to speak to Tex. "Hey, good sortie...Gotta run...We'll debrief after I'm through."

"Fine...I can use a shower anyway, Lucky. See you downstairs."

The other instructor pilot in the flight was the commander of the second BEF *Eagle* squadron, Bob "Flash" Peterman. Like Tex, he was a seasoned Air Force combat pilot, but he had joined the clandestine group after he retired and already had two big missions with them under his belt.

"What's up? Gotta any ideas?" he asked Jill as they rode the elevator to the lower level.

"Not a clue. Dare usually sets these up a week or so in advance, to allow personnel that are off duty time to plan for them. Let's just pop in." She laughed. "It's not like they never smelled sweaty flight suits before."

The forty-five year old former colonel chuckled and lines around his blue eyes crinkled at her comment. He was an Air Force Academy graduate, as was she—but slightly stockier build as he had played quarterback back in high school. He stood slightly over six feet, barely taller than the gorgeous blonde who walked beside him.

Her hair was considerably damp from the air combat training mission over the Fort Hood MOA. Jill's ponytail hung like more like a golden rat's tail over her black survival vest as they made their way past the operations desk and to the conference room. She rapped twice and opened the metal door. "Sorry we're late. Knocked it off as soon as we…"

The sight of the Reptoid armed transporter hologram floating above the table gave her pause.

"Have a seat, please. We're filling in Burner with the details that we presently know," Dare said.

Lucy glanced first at Jill, and then at Bob. She smiled and nodded. *What a close knit organization. She's married to Mike Herman over there and is Heater's daughter. The pilot who calls himself Flash is long time friends with the Secretary of Defense...Interesting.*

"Oh, our new friends are Lucy and Bone...Just so you know," Heater said as the two latecomers took their seats.

Jill waved and smiled, but it did little to hide her obvious confusion.

Bone waved back. "Nice to meet you guys."

What the hell is that thing? Peterman wondered, looking at the alien hologram. He glanced at the tiny woman seated next to the big guy in the Maine Corps T shirt. *You know, that almost looks like a space...Crap! Is that a helmet on the table? Who are these people?*

Lucy stood up and pointed to the Reptoid craft. "Our analysts have been able to pinpoint the pulse laser weapon articulating lens to this area of the ship. Images recorded during the battle showed at least six stations per side, for a total of twelve.

"It is assumed there is a deck associated with the with the armament, but we have no direct knowledge of this craft's maximum combat capability, other than the fact than we lost two of our battle cruisers and dozens of fighters like the one I fly."

"Did your people destroy any of them?" Burner asked.

"Yes, two confirmed with probable battle damage on the remaining four. Their shields were much improved over the last century and our tractor beams proved ineffective."

"How big are those things?" Flash inquired.

"About the size of Cowboy Stadium…plus," Hollywood replied.

"Sorry I asked."

"Any idea about the location of their bridge or command center?" Blaze asked.

Lucy shook her head. "Sorry, but no…Note that there are no windows or portals on the exterior. I expect it to be near the top, here." She pointed at a slight dome. It's the only place where one could see in all directions."

"Except they used cameras and virtual windows," said Gears.

"As you do in your shop? That's a valid point."

"The Reptoids have cloaking ability and you do not?" Dare asked.

"We have the capability, only have found little need for it…until now, unfortunately…Bone would you kindly demonstrate it for us?"

"Sure thing, Lucy…Guys this handy dandy bracelet allows a person to generate a screen of invisibility for three feet around themselves. It works like this…" He tapped a sequence of symbols on the turquoise and gold bracelet on his left wrist. He shimmered and disappeared.

Bad and Widowmaker exchanged glances.

"Beats our Lizard system all to hell," Bad said.

"It lasts about an hour," Lucy added.

37

Bone suddenly reappeared with a big grin on his face. "Pretty cool, huh?"

"If you are invisible, how can you see the bracelet?" Mike asked.

"Inside the field, you can see yourself and you can see out, but they can't see you." Bone replied. "Oh, one other thing…it's not a zone of force shield, it's a *light refraction screen*. You can shoot through it. I used my fifty cal and popped a perp that tried to napalm Lucy's house…Jackwagon never knew what hit him."

"You do that a lot?" asked Widowmaker.

"Only if they don't cease and desist when I ask them nicely."

"May I ask why do you carry a fifty caliber?" inquired Heater.

"'Cause they don't make a sixty," Bone replied dryly. He winked at Dare, who simply smiled and shook his head.

"Kinda like this guy," Bad whispered to Sean.

***

CHAPTER THREE

AFB MAKHADO
LOUIS TRICHARDT, SOUTH AFRICA

Each Saab JAS 39 *Griffin* was connected to its own power cart that the pair of crew chiefs had started as soon as they had arrived on the hardstands. Four other mechanics were ripping the rectangular red engine inlet and pitot tube protective covers from the alert aircraft.

Two South African Air Force fighter pilots from 2 Squadron raced from their alert crew rest facilities located beside the concrete revetments only seconds behind the mechanics.

They scrambled up the crew ladders placed on the right side of the fuselage, slid into the seats and began strapping in. The gyros stabilized and the lightweight fighter's avionics systems came to life. The crew chiefs assisted the pilots in connecting to the ejection seats and insured the comm and oxygen systems were secure before they raced down and removed the ladders.

South Africa owned only twenty-six of the modern little single engine warbirds—designed to be multi-role air-to-air, ground attack and recconaissance—that were continuously rotated from active duty to short-term storage due to lack of funds. Only a handful were ever operational at any one time.

Lieutenant Jayden Kotze gave the universal signal to start engines to his crew chief. The enlisted man leaned over to insure all personnel were clear behind the Volvo RM12 exhaust and spun his upright index finger in rapid circles.

My God, I hope we remembered everything he thought as the turbine began to wind up. Lack of money for training made a real 'this is no drill' fighter scramble a thing fraught with all manner of self doubt.

Captain Nicholas Veermak in the other *Griffin* found himself almost hyperventilating at the thought of engaging a real UFO, but his commanding general had made the launch call himself and was insistent the men get airborne ASAP. He signaled for the chocks to be pulled as the starter disengaged and the aircraft hydraulics system came up to the green band. He slammed the stick left and right, getting a confirmation of the flight control response from a visual check of the canards and the crew chief monitoring the routine sequence from the outside. He closed the clamshell canopy and pushed the throttle up.

"Lion zero-five, flight of two, taxi."

The ground controller responded immediately, "Lion zero-five flight, Makhado ground, roger. Cleared for immediate takeoff. Fly runway heading...Climb and maintain five thousand."

BEF HEADQUARTERS
Conference Room

"As I understand the situation, Lucy, your people do not know exactly where the hostile ships are or where they will initiate there first...uh, *harvesting* operation, as you put it. Is that correct?" SecDef Burner Stewart asked.

"Yes, Mister Secretary. We are aware that your Black Eagle Force was able to detect a low level fourth order wave distortion in those Nazi flying wings. That is a capability we Tyranians have been unable to match, as of yet...We can only detect fourth order sharp spikes in the ether, like from your weapons.

"My commander has authorized me to make this extraordinary contact with your team...something that is not usually authorized under our law."

"You mean to say...there are prohibitions against helping us directly?"

"Interference with the natural evolutionary process of a species is not taken lightly. Our intergalactic alliances do not...in most cases...permit us to choose sides. Helping one culture gain advantage over others is a very dangerous thing to do and might have disastrous results."

Burner nodded. "We see that often in the political arena. It's called the *law of unintended consequences*...I believe they called it *The Prime Directive* on Star Trek."

"Star Trek?"

"A popular SciFy television and movie series on here on Earth...Go on, please."

Lucy smiled. "Of course...The threat here is worldwide...not just to a single race or political belief. In fact, we on Tyrin are also vulnerable to these abominable creatures. Their evolution is ongoing...and their appetite for our type of protein is insatiable." She paused for a moment and looked around the room. All eyes were upon her.

"I may as well be completely frank with you. Our culture is an old one...over several millions of your Earth years have passed since we evolved to our current form. Our scientists believe our species has essentially stopped evolving...as the Tyranian genome has not changed appreciably in the last 500,000 years. We lack an infusion of new genes and heretofore hybridization has not been applicable."

Mike spoke up quickly, "Like with cattle? We crossbred Shorthorn, Hereford and Brahma to create a new breed called Beefmasters that outperforms any of the parent ones down in south Texas...The result is called hybrid vigor."

"That's an excellent example. The last two times we infused our DNA into the homo sapien species...which is Latin for 'wise man', by the way...was around 100,000 years ago, then finally 10,000 years ago at the end of your last ice age...which gave you your most recent major leap forward," she continued. "We have closely monitored your progress through the millennia...Today, I had the great honor to meet what may well be the first human who has evolved past *us* and hopefully will enable both planets to survive these marauding reptiles."

Her statement caused an instant buzz among the key personnel.

Dare sensed the meeting was at the verge of losing its focus on the task at hand. "Settle down, people...please. Lucy, can you give us a hint as to whom you are referring?"

Lucy's face broke into broad smile and her eyes twinkled. "She does not really need an introduction. It's your girlfriend...Blaze Hermann...For all intents and purposes...the new Eve."

The brilliant redhead felt all eyes fall upon her and her cheeks turned a rosy pink. She glanced at Lucy and then across the table at her older brother. Mike grinned, nodded and give her a thumbs-up sign.

She turned to Dare and shrugged. He gave her an air kiss and flashed a big smile.

Up in DC, Burner sat back in his chair. *Wow...I always knew she was something special, but evolved to a new level? That is something, now.*

"Lucy, I am going make a command decision as Secretary of Defense. We have to keep a lid on this, and I mean a tight one. I will give the full resources of the US military to support the

BEF, but there can be *no* outside press leaks whatsoever…Am I quite clear?"

"Absolutely, sir. News of an actual alien invasion would panic the masses and could kill tens of millions even before the Reptoids attack."

"Our community organizer in the White House and his dipstick VP can't be trusted for two seconds. They just cannot wait to get in front of the cameras and spill the beans." Burner sighed. "It appears they have no sense of *COMSEC* at all. If the Reptoids monitor satellite TV transmissions, those two idiots would telegraph our every move and possibly insure our defeat."

"I agree. We must be covert, diligent and move very quickly. I suggest we relocate our operational command to your Eagle Nest facility, particularly when our Annihilator is complete," she said.

"Annihilator?"

"Our newest vessel, designed to counterbalance the Reptoid's advance in craft and weaponry."

"How many months will that take to build?" Burner asked.

Lucy chuckled. "Our people are already well underway with the construction, using a technology similar to your three dimensional printing…only only a much grander scale. The ship was conceived, input into the design computer telepathically and the multiple high-speed projectors went to work. Atom by atom and molecule by molecule, the first one is presently being laid down and will be operational in three days."

AURORA: INVASION

"Everything? Wires, weapons, bulkheads, power plants?" Blaze blurted. "Oh, my God…"

"Yes, interior and exterior…simultaneously. I will share our latest shield and weaponry technology and work with you and Gears to learn how you detected the German's cloaking device.

"My Mauler in orbit will hopefully be able to pinpoint the Reptoid's location once they start moving and allow us to intercept them."

Burner listened closely. "Dare, I'm going to sign off now. I'm feeling rather useless like a true rear echelon type at this moment. You've got the team in place and I'm always available to fill in if you need hands-on assistance…I'm serious about that…You have the conn."

"I appreciate that Burner. I'll keep you advised on where we stand."

True to his word, the link to the Pentagon went dark. Dare took in a deep breath and slowly let it out. "You heard the man, people. The ball's in our court…If you need help, ask for it. Don't waste any energy on power point presentations…We don't have time for that kind of crap."

Lucy leaned forward. "Ladies and gentlemen, we can transport you to Eagle Nest. No need to spend time flying back and forth."

"How about our gear?" Bad asked.

"We can take care of that, too," she replied. "It's going to be a lot different than you are used to…I would imagine. It might take a while to get adjusted to the concept of teleportation."

"Give us a few minutes to get ourselves organized, please. See, we are used to having the complete upper deck of the C-5s pre-positioned with all of our anticipated mission gear," Dare said.

"If that's what you're comfortable with, then leave it as it is...We'll transport the entire ship."

"You can do that?" Bone asked.

She gave him a look and then grinned. "Do you really think the Egyptians built the pyramids, block by block?...Do you?"

"Any chance you can drop me by the ranch? I could use a change of clothes and get my gear."

"Yes, we need to pick up Padrino for his empathy skills and your partner, Loraine."

"Cool, I was hoping you'd say that. She watches my back, plus she helped me take down the first Reptoid...actually she fired the first shot."

"I knew that when you rode back to the house after your encounter."

"How...Oh, never mind."

"Besides, Loraine has a skill you are not aware of that we need."

"Really? What?"

Lucy grinned again. "You'll see."

AIRSPACE OVER SOUTH AFRICA

The two *Griffin* fighters accelerated through 25,000 feet at Mach 1.8—banking in between some puffy cumulous clouds

46

dancing in the middle altitudes of the early South African winter sky. Captain Nicholas Veermak glanced over at his wingman flying line abreast in a tactical spread formation some 100 feet off his right wingtip. He checked the full color moving map display and selected the 300 Km range bar. Magenta concentric circles appeared, overlaying the topo chart and he could easily see the town of Pretoria at the top of the display.

Using a roller ball controller, Veermak placed the cursor atop the suburb of Centurion where the South African mint was located. *Shit. Almost three hundred kilometers.* He thumbed to a *time en route* display based upon the aircraft's current speed and distance. *Nine minutes? Got to push it up. Should be in missile range in eight...*

He eased back on the stick and allowed the aircraft to accelerate to its limit of Mach 2 and then continued their climb to FL 500—leaving the white clouds far below them as the sky above darkened to a deep blue-black.

Lieutenant Jayden Kotze tweaked his PS-05/A pulse-doppler X-band multi-mode radar but got no hits. *Damn it. Still too far.*

Developed by Ericsson and GEC-Marconi, the unit was capable of picking up returns out to 120 miles or 200 kilometers.

Nicholas checked his fuel gages as the flight approached the halfway point. The JAS 39 normally had a combat radius of 800 kilometers, but that distance did not envision a burner climb to 50,000 feet. Both drop tanks were long dry and he considered jettisoning them. *Not unless we make contact. The colonel would have my ass for us wasting four tanks on a wild goose chase. We can always put it down at Swartkop if we have to.* He nosed the *Griffin* over and initiated their descent

"Possible radar contact twelve o'clock low, range 180 kilometers," Jayden called.

"Contact there, unknown rider...holding in a hover. Arming switches on," Veermak replied. His breathing rate began to pick up noticeably. In four years active duty service, he had only amassed slightly more than 320 hours total flying time—this was his first one in actual combat. He tried to swallow at the lump beginning to build in his throat, but the dryness of the pressure breathing the highly compressed oxygen mixed with ambient air made that an impossibility.

He lifted the red safety covers guarding the arming switches and toggled them to the *armed* position. At 2,204 Km/hr, the two fighters were closing on the UFO rapidly. Each of them was armed with four IRIS-T short-range German heat-seeker missiles. The small weapons had a maximum range of approximately 25 kilometers or about fifteen miles. The smallish HE warhead worked well on contact with fighters or helicopters and was roughly comparable to the American *Sidewinder,* but with higher ECM resistance and flare suppression. *What will they do an alien ship? Man, oh man. I wish we were packing AMRAAMs.*

SOUTH AFRICAN MINT COMPANY
Centurion

Workers ran for their lives as the roof and upper three concrete floors crumbled under the intense heat of the laser. Reinforcing rebar melted and dripped below onto the thick steel-lined vault located in the building's basement.

Water from the numerous fire sprinklers collected on the intermediate floors and cascaded down the smoldering hole, creating a hellish cloud of steam as the water made contact with both the hot concrete rubble and the greenish laser and hissed like giant snake. Contact with the cooler water caused the tortured concrete to further fracture and explode, sending fragments ricocheting across the rooms.

"How much longer, Qrts? We are highly vulnerable without our cloak and shields!" Mrrst said as he looked at the televised images from below the sphere. "Can you not increase power?"

"Captain, we must not be careless. Too much power and we will vaporize the Au-79 when the laser breeches the containment structure. I am almost though the ferrous plate now."

"I am ready with the transporter beam. Notify me when...stand by! Sensors detect we are being scanned by electronic pulse signals."

Qrts maneuvered one eye stalk to view the defense systems control screen to his right.

"Are they from a Tryranian vessel?" Mrsst asked.

"No. Much too basic for our old enemies. It would appear it is a primitive scanning device attempting to locate us by reflecting radio beams off our hull. They possess no pulse or energy weapons at all, apparently."

"How quaint…They have no idea how backward they are. Finish the job and I will get what we came for."

"As you command, Captain."

Fifty miles to the north, the two fighters separated by a quarter of a mile to press in their attacks simultaneously. Traveling at over twenty-five miles a minute, the pilots activated the warhead super-cooling step which enabled the missiles to be sensitive to minute heat differences at their full operating ranges.

"One minute out," Veermak announced as he flipped his weapons switch on the stick from guns to missiles. The seconds counted down as the *Griffins* streaked over the northern outskirts of Pretoria. *They are gonna raise hell about the sonic booms, but there's nothing I can do about it.* "Tally ho," he called as he picked up the green ball over the smoking building.

A warbling tone began to build in his helmet. "Tone! I got tone!" He squeezed the trigger twice in rapid succession. A pair of IRIS-T missiles roared off the rails—on from under each wing—and accelerated to Mach 3, leaving a wispy trail of white smoke behind them.

"Fox two, fox two!" he called as his wingman also fired a pair of the nine foot long weapons.

"Qrts, I believe these natives are attacking us…Interesting," the commander of the alien vessel said as their ship's sensors detected the incoming missiles.

"I will narrow the cutting beam and intensify it slightly," he replied. Using two of his upper eye stalks, he viewed the display visaplate and lifted one of his elephantine legs up and stepped slightly closer to the defensive systems panels. "Our shield cannot protect us, but the pulse projectors will." Using one of his four arms, he tapped a series of commands on the symbols dotting a keyboard-like protrusion.

On the circumference of the ship, a set of ports opened, exposing a pair of bulbous clear protrusions which bore more than a passing resemblance to the four eyes on the vile creatures' snakelike heads. Four brilliant green pulses of energy flashed out in a narrow fan.

Almost instantly, the incoming IRIS-T missiles detonated in rapid succession—still some twelve miles from the ship.

"There, almost done," Qrts said as the two inch thick steel vault succumbed to the intensified articulating laser beam that had cut a circular path around the periphery of the hole in the concrete. The red hot disk dropped fifteen feet onto a pile of gold bars set atop a heavy duty metal cart. It clanged noisily upon impact and spun crazily to the floor and finally came to rest as a stream of water poured down into the basement.

Quite pleased with his performance, Orts clacked his alligator-like jaws together several times rapidly.

"Step out of the way…I have work to do," the captain ordered. "And take care of those pests. Make yourself useful."

"As you command, my leader," Qrts replied. He moved to the defense panel and touched two of his lower tentacles to the control pad.

Ten miles out from the target, the SAAF pilots were dumfounded by the destruction of the heat seeking missiles.

"Lion flight, go to guns," ordered Captain Veermak.

"Two," acknowledged Jayden as he thumbed the selector on the stick. His HUD instantly transformed to a pipper for the Mauser Bk-27 revolver cannon, a lightweight single barreled weapon firing the 27x145 mm rounds at 3,600 feet per second.

Lieutenant Kotze rolled right and climbed back up to 10,000 feet as they had discussed en route. Both pilots would make their attacks in a forty-five degree supersonic dive to keep the collateral damage to a minimum, as the target was near highly populated areas surrounding the mint.

Boundary layer air separating over the canards and wings turned a milky white color as he cranked the stick aft and his G suit inflated to compensate for the eight G pitch-up. He grunted, panted quickly and tightened his abdominal muscles to keep his vision from fading to gray and then black.

In only seconds, the little Saab fighters zoomed back up through 10,000 feet, rolled inverted and initiated their strafing attacks. Kotze remembered he only had 120 of the HE rounds on board. *Got to make them count. Range four miles and closing.* The green countryside filled his visor and came up quickly. He centered the pipper's red dot on the iridescent green ball and cross checked the gun's radar ranging as the numbers counted down the meters to target in almost a blur.

Mrrst was happy with the telemetry from the transporter. He slid the control bar with his lower left tentacle as he guided the beam with his right. "Perfect. Commander Klsth will be most pleased with my performance." The transporter hummed.

In the mint basement, an entire pallet of gold bars and the heavy, solid wheeled cart upon which they lay, shimmered and disappeared.

Upstairs in the security office, the lone guard who had not abandoned his post in terror watched in amazement when the closed circuit video feed showed that one of the two-ton stacks of bullion simply vanished.

Captain Veermak watched the range to target rapidly roll through 3,000 meters. He began to squeeze the trigger on the fighter's stick as a brilliant green light emanated from the widest spot on the alien craft's circumference. The laser instantly grew in size and completely enveloped the *Griffin*. He never felt a thing.

A taxi driver two kilometers from the mint looked up as a bright flash, followed by a few seconds later by a thunderous clap that startled his passengers. Tiny bits of wreckage fluttered down.

"Driver! What was that? A bomb going off?"

"Don't think so. It was up in the sky, a big boom…" The cab was rocked by another blast from the sky, but this time from behind them. "Oh no…Another one! What do you think it could be?"

Mrrst didn't turn around. His upper left stalk rotated to view the tons of gold metal on the transporter pad. He nodded his snakelike head vigorously and a thick slimy mucous flew about as he snapped his jaws together in joy. *I will be promoted for sure after my supreme commander learns of my deeds.* "Engage the cloak and take us to the rendezvous point. I declare this mission a success."

BONE'S RANCH HOUSE

Padrino glanced up from his book as the big man materialized in the living room. "So, how was your trip?" he asked with his penchant for dry understatement.

"Absolutely crazy. I thought I was gonna get arrested for a while. We need to get…" He stopped in mid-sentence as he noted a pair of large soft-sided ballistic bags were already packed and lying near his jumbo-sized recliner. A smaller one next to them was Bone's range bag, his duty belt and 500 Smith & Wesson were laying on a fresh pair of black tactical BDUs. "How did you know?"

Padrino closed his book and set it on top of the smaller nylon bag. "Lucy filled me in during the meeting. I'm packed up as well. Captain St. John agreed to watch over Tyrin here for the duration."

"What did you tell him?"

"Nothing, really. I said you and I and your partner had to save the world and would be out of pocket for a few days."

"That's it? He bought it?"

"Uh huh. Said he wished he could go along…Some of us still have personal credibility."

Bone looked at him somewhat askance. "Was that a cut?"

"I don't know, was it?" Padrino said with a wry grin. "Get dressed…She wants us ready to go in fifteen minutes."

"But, I gotta talk to Loraine. She doesn't know what she's getting into."

"Lucy took care of everything. Relax."

"But I was right there all the time and she never called anybody."

Padrino tapped his index finger against his temple.

"You mean she…?"

"Yep. She just thinks it and suddenly we know."

"How does she do that?"

"Dunno…Magic? Maybe you should ask her."

"Think I will." Bone slipped his Marine workout T shirt over his head, tossed it in a pile with his running shoes and pulled on a clean black one. "Got plenty of skivvies and socks for me? I'd hate to run out."

Loraine materialized in the center of the room wearing black BDUs. She was in a relaxed sitting position with her hands exactly like they had been when she had been paying her monthly utility bill on line using a keyboard. She promptly fell back on her butt. "Ow."

A workout bag appeared beside her as she looked up at Padrino and then Bone. "Damn you, Bone! This is your fault."

"Me? What did I do?"

"You told her to do this."

"Did not."

"Did too."

"Hey, Pard, it was a surprise to me too."

"What if I had been in the bathroom?...You know, going potty?"

"Can't tell you how glad I am you weren't...New carpet."

She gritted her teeth. "I'm going to kill you, Bone."

"All right, that's enough, children. Lucy probably didn't have the time to go through normal protocol," said Padrino. "She's kind of busy, you know."

"I still don't understand why I'm even here."

"Lucy said you had a skill we needed to combat the Reptoids...That's all I know."

"What? What skill is she talking about?"

"Didn't say...I didn't ask. She probably thinks I need my partner." He grinned. "She knows we watch each other's backs."

"Now you try to butter me up."

"Anyway, don't get too comfortable...Lucy's crew is gonna beam us down or over to some place called Eagle Nest before long."

"But I do need to go potty...now."

"I'd wait if I were you."

"Eeek!" She squealed as the three of them shimmered and disappeared.

***

CHAPTER FOUR

CENTURION, SA

The sound of two massive back-to-back explosions in the sky overhead caused Dean Harmse to back away from the plate glass window, fearful that it would shatter and shower him and his secretary, Clair, with glass. *What the blazes was that?*

The thick panes shook from the noise of the unseen blasts, but held tight. He stepped back to the outside wall and stared at the green ball hovering over the South African Mint Company. Suddenly—it shimmered and simply vanished.

That can't be! How could a UFO just disappear? It was not even moving! He stepped back to his desk and lifted the phone. "Ruth, get me General Martin again!"

"General Martin, go ahead."

"Archie! It just vanished! One second it was here and the next it was gone!"

"What are you talking about? What was gone?"

"The UFO, the one I called you about! Did you send fighters? I heard several explosions…Two really big ones overhead. My windows rattled."

"Dean I don't know what you think you saw or heard, but it must have been a product of your imagination…My people tell me there was an electrical fire reported at the mint and then we had two of our aircraft on a routine training mission collide in midair near Pretoria…We are still trying to sort out what happened in that incident.

"But rumors of any UFO involvement are clearly wild speculation from your part. I would suggest you keep your comments to yourself. Sorry, but I have to go." The line went dead.

Dean glanced over at his secretary with look of shock and budding anger. "They covered it up! It hasn't been gone five minutes and already they are claiming it was nothing at all!"

EAGLE NEST BEF UNDERGROUND FACILITY
Webb County, Texas

Bone, Loraine and Padrino materialized in a hallway outside the comm center.

"That was different than when she transported us inside my truck," Padrino said. "Did it feel like a tickle to you guys?"

"More like a full body itch, if you ask me…not counting the cold…Brrr." Loraine replied.

"Guess I'm gettin' used to it," Bone bragged. "My fourth time, you know…Looks like this place is underground like the BEF facility over at Denison."

"Wonder where this Eagle Nest is?" asked Loraine.

A tall slender Raptor wearing black BDUs approached from the doorway leading to the communications and administration area.

"Hey, I'm Davy Crockett, Raptor Team Four leader. Dare asked me to show ya'll around. Here are your ID badges to get you in and out of the security doors above ground…Oh, and we're in south Texas, ma'am…Webb County to be precise." He handed the laminated photo IDs—3x5 color head shots with thumb prints hanging on a half inch thick heavy woven lanyard—to the each of new arrivals after checking the images.

"How did you get our pictures, not to say anything about the thumb prints?"

Davy just looked at Bone and grinned.

"Yeah. Never mind."

After the introductions were made, Loraine looked at her picture closely. She could see the corner of a familiar calendar in the upper edge of the ID. "That's a shot taken from my laptop inside my apartment! How the hell did you get that?"

Davy grinned. "We stole it from the NSA. Better than your driver's license one, isn't it?"

"Yeah, but that's still kinda creepy."

Bone looked at the back of his. An abbreviated summary version of his Marine Corps service record was imprinted thereon. "Jeez, you guys are fast."

"We have to be…any time, any where…actually the BEF's motto is Semper Paro Bellum."

"Always ready for war," Padrino said, translating the Latin.

"Correct, sir. Oh, by the way…Semper Fi, Bone." Davy said as he held out his fist. "Inactive Marine sniper and Force Recon as well. Semper Fi, Padrino."

Bone smiled broadly. "I knew there was something I liked about you." They bumped fists, and then Davy turned around.

"Leave your gear against the wall. I think you guys are gonna stay with Dare and the family up at the ranch house. We'll pick it up after I show you around the facilities."

First stop was to meet the Eagle Nest Operations Officer—retired USAF colonel Karl Richter. He had taken over mission commander slot aboard the C-5M *Super Galaxy* called *Sister Bird* from Heater McElhenny when Burner Stewart took the Secretary of Defense job and Heater became the BEF COO. Karl's background was in fighter bombers, particularly the F-105 *Thunderchief*—known to most folks as the *Thud*.

A while later, the new arrivals were shown the martial arts workout and adjoining weight rooms. A beautiful woman with jet black hair was dressed in a white Karate gi with a black belt—sparring with two much larger men and giving out more than she received. Her speed and skill was astonishing as she swept the feet from underneath one man and executed a spinning high kick to the other's face as he made a move to grab her. The kick resounded across the room. The male *Raptor* hit the mat and moaned. Raven stepped back, bowed to the two men, and then noticed Crockett with his three companions. *Hmm, big guy...Interesting.*

Bone and Loraine both winced. "Ya'll do full contact workouts?" she asked.

Davy nodded. "Usually...We find there's no substitute for actual contact. If our lives depend on a skill in the field, we don't back off much in training...But the boss does frown on broken bones...Reduces readiness, or some such bullshit like that, he said."

"She's good, isn't she Pard?" Bone asked.

"Not bad...bet I could take her with a little warmup."

"Really?" Dave asked.

"My little friend is a fifth degree black belt in Kung Fu," Bone said.

"You guys should get along great. Her name's Cathy Papadakis...we all call her Raven. She has a fifth in Kung Fu, also...Plus advanced belts in Karate, Kenpo and Aikido. She operates our micro drones for us." Davy held up his fingers about two inches apart.

"Rather small for combat aren't they?" Padrino asked.

"Well they're not weaponized…at least not yet. She can control two of 'em at once, you know…One with each hand… looking at a split screen…Beats me how."

"Maybe she has a dual personality," offered Bone.

"Nope, just one…All bad ass."

Bone glanced back over his shoulder and caught her looking back at him—she winked.

After viewing the team quarters and mess hall, Davy brought them back to the comm center. Bone grabbed up his and Loraine's bags and Crockett hefted Padrino's. They were waiting for the elevator to arrive at the lower level when Dare, Lucy, Blaze, Mike and Jill materialized in the hallway.

"Wow! That was something. Though we were in a deep freezer for a second there." Dare shook his head and looked up. "Oh, good. Glad to see you three made it here safely."

"Quite an operation you have here, Mister Phillips."

"Dare…Please call me Dare. You must be Loraine, Bone's partner." He extended his hand. "Welcome aboard."

"I'm his godfather…Folks just call me Padrino," the silver-haired shaman said as he stepped closer.

"Semper Fi, Archibald Cord…Padrino." Dare grinned and held out his fist.

Padrino cocked his head. "My, my, your outfit is thorough, I give you that."

"Have to be, sir, have to be."

Once everyone was introduced, the assembled group rode up four floors in a small side elevator to the hangar deck.

Bone glanced at the large metal trimmed concrete floor in the center of the hangar. "Is that what I think it is?"

Crockett followed his look. "Oh. Yep, aircraft carrier hydraulic elevator salvaged from USS *Valley Forge* when she was scrapped in '71. The one at home base is from *Oriskany,* the Mighty O. We keep our Black Eagle VTOLs below, bring 'em up to load in Mama or Sister Bird…We launch and recover in flight."

"You're kidding," said Loraine.

"No, ma'am, kid you not. Usually around ten or twelve thousand feet at 250 knots…Gets a bit hairy on occasion."

"You think?" commented Bone as he grinned and shook his head.

Davy helped load the bags in the back of a white Chevy Suburban with the Eagle Nest logo on the driver's door and the eight passengers departed for the three mile drive to the historic Eagle Nest Ranch House.

The SUV braked to a stop in front of the two story German style stone home facing the Rio Grande. There were two people on the wide, full width porch in rocking chairs—the woman with a glass of iced tea and the large gray-haired man nursing a Shiner Bock longneck. They set their drinks down and got to their feet. Both were dressed in jeans, boots and work shirts, his chambray, and her's a blue and white check.

"Oh, my God! Is that who I think it is?" said an astonished Loraine.

Davy grinned. "Yes, ma'am. Former President Annette Henry Thompson-Hermann. Eagle Nest was the southern White House when she was in office."

"Then that's her husband, Gunter Hermann," said Padrino. "He was in my platoon at Parris Island when I was a DI at the end of my last tour…One tough son of a gun."

They got out and walked up the flagstone path to the front porch. The stately, attractive auburn-haired woman stepped down the steps to greet them.

"Welcome to Eagle Nest. I'm…"

"Yes, ma'am, we know…Madam President," said Bone, somewhat embarrassed. "They call me Bone."

"Then just call me Annette, please. We don't stand on formality here…besides, that's history…I'm happy to say."

"Gunny? Gunny Cord?" exclaimed Gunter.

"Good to see you, Gunter, after all these years. Glad you made it out in one piece…Just call me Padrino now." He grinned and the two old comrades exchanged bear hugs.

"Permit me to introduce a couple other new friends you don't know," Dare said. "Lucy and Loraine…Annette and Gunter Hermann.

Annette shook hands with the diminutive alien first and was surprised by the visions of a far distant world, two suns and then a view of earth from outer space—a brilliant blue and white ball silhouetted against a black sky with billions of stars blanketing the void beyond. She gasped slightly but maintained her warm affable smile. "So pleased to have this opportunity, Lucy. Welcome to our home."

"The pleasure is mine, Annette. I only wish it were under different circumstances."

"As do I...We will have a chance to get acquainted over dinner." She pivoted slightly and took Loraine's hand. "I'm happy to meet you, too, Loraine. Dare tells me you're a police investigator."

"Yes, ma'am. Bone and I are partners and met Lucy some time back."

When he took Lucy's hand, Gunter had much the same experience with visions that Bone and Padrino had when they first met her, including visions of the fateful crash in back in 1897 at Aurora, Texas—he quivered just slightly. "Come on inside, everybody. Dinner's almost ready. We'll have the girls finish the salad and we'll be good to go."

Lucy smiled and accompanied the big rancher inside. The rest glanced at each other, and then followed along.

"I see where Carla gets her genetics after meeting you," Lucy said softly to Gunter as they headed to the dining room.

THE PLANET TYRIN

The two orange dwarf suns shown brightly in the lavender sky over the green and blue landscape—one appeared almost twenty percent larger than the other. This was because it was the primary star in the small three planet system at the far flung edge of the massive Orion Nebula nearest the Sol system. The smaller star was what was termed a wanderer, but had been part of the Tyrin system for over a billion years. In galactic terms, Tyrin—only slightly smaller than Earth—was one of her closest inhabitable neighbors at a little over thirty parsecs away. Both systems were located in the Orion–Cygnus Arm—over 10,000 light-years or 3,100 parsecs in length—of the Milky Way Galaxy.

The large crystal spired city housed the government of the race of small people the Sumerians had called the Anunnaki or *sky beings.* At the top of one of the clear glass buildings, the Supreme Council was in session. The slightly lavender light penetrating the interior of the room from outside was diffused by the polarized metallic glass-type material.

"Kanndol, what is the progress on our new Annihilator class vessel?" asked Ravalon—he was considerably taller than most Tyranians at almost six feet and wore a silver-white robe, belted at the waist with a deep purple sash.

His leonine mane and white flowing beard gave the leader of the High Council a very aristocratic appearance.

"Honored Overlord, we are almost two-thirds complete." He waved a tiny hand over a nearby glass wall and a scene from the Tyranian interstellar ship fabrication facility over twenty miles away, wavered and came into focus on a partially completed ship of the cosmos lying in her cradle. "Notice the thickness of the new skin," said the Chief Fabrication Officer.

The image enlarged and zoomed in on the edge of the silver material being formed. It was almost four feet in thickness, but the interior of the armor had the appearance of laced honeycomb. The thousands of computer programed gigantic projectors, controlled by fields and beams of force that surrounded the nine hundred foot long by six hundred foot wide combination space carrier and battlecruiser, were laying down molecule by molecule in 3-D fashion. Each pass of the projectors added micron-thick layers of the vessel and its equipment simultaneously.

"Once we solved the mechanics of combining aranak with that wondrous Graphene material from Tellus that Annuna had described to us, the fabrication has gone smoothly...We have named it araknene. Plus we have an unlimited source of carbon in our atmosphere."

"Rollân, do you have anything to add?"

The Chief of Science nodded. "We can now actually project our enhanced beams of pure force through the new multilevel fourth order shields by sequencing them on and off in micro-millisecond phases. Our protective screens themselves are almost impenetrable by any combination of fire the Reptoids can presently generate...and they are adjustable which makes them a weapon in and of itself."

"Explain, Rollân," said Ravalon.

"We have discovered that fourth order waves actually create another dimension when the maximum level of magnitude nine is accessed. The Reptoid shields are strictly multiphased fourth order, sixth magnitude and this sets up a condition of stasis in the particles composing the ether. The particles are comparatively widespread...If we had a fifth order projector, the rays and particles of the fifth order would pass through the fixed zone without retardation.

"Therefore a fifth order wave, being composed of what our scientists have termed *Dark Energy*…when activated to the highest level…will slice through any known zone of force by separating it at the subatomic level as if it did not exist at all. But, alas, a fifth order projector has not yet been devised. It may take another one or two hundred years."

"What are the drawbacks to a full zone of force?…There must be some," asked Fleet Commander Garrple.

"When fully activated, the zone of force is absolutely impenetrable by anything, including light in either direction…with the exception of thought waves which we now believe are of the sixth order and are, of course, instantaneous."

"Meaning we can project our faster than light thoughts, locate the enemy, bring our totally invisible ships in reasonably close proximity, flick the shield off and back on in your micro-milliseconds and effectively slice the Reptoid craft in pieces?"

"Theoretically…Yes…assuming we are able to locate fourth order cloaked vessels."

"I understand…How long until we can have the first squadron of six?" inquired Garrple.

"The first Annihilator will be finished and tested in two more cycles. Thereafter, we can complete each ship in three cycles."

"Make it so, Rollân," said Ravalon. "Annuna indicates she has enlisted a society known as the Black Eagle Force with unusual weapons and personnel, but she will need the first Annihilator for teleportation…quickly."

BLAZE'S LAB
Eagle Nest

"Interesting," Lucy said. She removed her safety glasses after the power had been turned off and the model aircraft in the Plexiglas cover reappeared. "You have managed to recreate the fourth order cloak the Nazis used on their flying wings and attack craft. Did you reverse engineer it from the wreckage?"

"No. We have not recovered the airframes as of yet, so we looked at the distortions the cloaks created and using some empirical data gathered by the sensors aboard Manta…tried to kick around ideas of what could break matter from the atomic level to its sub-atomic particles…" Blaze replied.

"Without the use of a supercollider, "Gears added. "A rather daunting task, I might add."

"I understand." Lucy smiled. "Don't get me wrong here…I think your work is outstanding. But, I do believe I can help your team with cloaking. You saw the bracelet that Bone demonstrated…We can supply the entire BEF with those and we even have the technology to create the same for your fleet of aircraft."

"Why did you not employ them on your fighters, carriers and cruisers?" Blaze asked.

"It seems rather foolish now, but, historically our technology has been vastly superior to that of the Reptoids. Our shields were stronger and their weapons could not defeat the heavy armor on the larger vessels. We ascertained that there was no

70

need to utilize invisibility cloaks on our combat craft, except for our small atmospheric scouts and fighters."

Gears grinned. "You know, that sounds a lot like our pacifists and isolationists here in American after World War I...and I would love to hear about your inertialess drive."

"The war to end all wars." Lucy's face turned slightly more somber. "I know...I lived here through all that...We'll get into our inertialess drive at another time."

"It must have been difficult, having to keep to yourself while you waited for a rescue mission," Blaze commented.

"I admit it was a bit lonely at times. I still miss my mate Garrin." She forced herself to smile once again and took a breath. "That was then and this is now, one of my neighbors liked to say. One other thing...just because I'm from a more advanced civilization, please do not assume that I know everything about everything. In many ways, I'm not so much different than you."

"How so?" Gears asked.

"First...I'm a fighter pilot and commander of my own squadron. That's what I know and how I think. I know a lot about technology and weapons, because I was trained in their use. But I'm not an engineer like you two.

"I can operate fantastic machines and do great things with them, but I cannot design them or delve into their quantum mechanics. You don't know how difficult it is for a fighter pilot to admit that." She laughed.

"Oh, I think we have a little idea about the ego thing," Gears said. "Some of our new hires have to be told to tone it down."

"Once they realize they are surrounded by the best of the best in their respective fields, they settle in after a while," Blaze said with a twinkle in her eye.

"And that allows the team to be stronger in the end…I would imagine."

"Right you are, Lucy. It does seem to help…Speaking of help, what can we do for your people? You have superior cloaking technology, but cannot find the Reptoid while they are cloaked?"

"I suppose we should go over the sensor settings you developed for tracking the Nazi flying wings. We'll have to send the data to the Mauler. From there, they can pass it through to the engineers on Tyrin via the worm hole."

"There's no way to communicate directly to your planet?"

"No, unfortunately. Transmission speed in subspace is slightly over 100 years each way."

"Bummer. I'd like to be able to ask them some questions," Blaze said.

"What I can do is have the Mauler at Lagrangian Point 2 beam down a communicator. It's like a cell phone and can scan and transmit images and even project holograms."

"Right. I remember you using it in the conference room. Does it have its own charger?"

Lucy shook her head. "Runs on cosmic energy or Millikan rays. It's permanently powered…at least in this portion of the galaxy."

BEF UNDERGROUND HQ
Eagle Nest

Bone and Loraine changed into their workout gear in the side-by-side locker rooms. She had chosen a skintight powder blue Lycra top and black yoga pants. He had a clean Marine Corps T shirt and his favorite charcoal gray drawstring shorts and running shoes. They headed down the hall to the workout facilities and met a couple of *Raptors* walking the other way. Loraine picked up on the strange looks the men gave her.

"Hey, Double D," one of them said as he passed.

Her eyes narrowed as she heard his comment. *Of all the nerve!*

She stopped and looked back over her shoulder.

"What's wrong, Pard?" he asked.

"Did you see how they looked at me? And what the short one said?"

"Guess I wasn't payin' attention. So much to think about."

"He called me Double D…How rude is that?"

"Maybe he never saw real hooters before…Good guess, though."

Loraine smacked him hard against his chest with the back of her hand.

"What? I didn't say anything…"

"Never mind," she said as another *Raptor* walked by.

"Hey, D…" he said. "You cut your hair or something?" The look on his face was one of slight confusion.

Loraine shook her head. *I'm getting a weird vibe about this place.*

They popped into the weight room where several other team members were already occupied on the various machines and a few were using free weights. The walls were lined with floor to ceiling mirrors and a rubber padded carpeted floor helped muffle the clang of the barbells and dumbells when they were set down.

"What's your pleasure, girl?" Bone asked.

"Think I'll try the elliptical to loosen…" She stopped in mid-sentence as a man helping a woman in a nearly identical outfit stepped away from a Nautilus lat machine and she saw the reflection the mirror. "Holy Christ. She's almost a dead ringer for me."

Bone looked in the direction his partner was so mesmerized. "Damn, Pard. You're right…Maybe she's a Reptoid. But that guy doesn't look much like me."

The muscular man working out with his spouse glanced over at the new arrivals and then back quickly at his wife. *What the hell?* He could see the confused look in their faces. He tossed the white hand towel over his shoulder and began to walk their way—he stuck out his hand. "Hey guys, I'm Mickey Williams…Gunter and Annette's son…Yesterday was one of my days off, and I ran down to Falcon Lake to do some fishin'…Sorry I missed you at dinner."

"Pleased to meet you," Bone said, taking his hand. "Excuse me, but do you know who that lady is?" He pointed at the other woman dressed in a blue top.

"That's my wife, Maria...flies the F-18A Super Hornet...call sign "Double D"...for some reason I never quite figured out." Mickey rolled his eyes, grinned and motioned them to follow.

Except for the different hair styles, Maria and Loraine could almost pass for twins. They excitedly compared backgrounds and interests while Mickey and Bone stepped to the side.

"My brother Mike caught the resemblance in the security screen before they made up the IDs," he said as they walked toward the free weights. "He wanted it to be a surprise, so he made Dad and Mom, and Blaze play along...The look on your face was priceless."

"Had me going, I can tell you. Loraine and I already had one run-in with the Reptoids when they chose to be clones of us as they rampaged around town. They were pissing folks off left and right, and everybody thought it was me and my partner!"

"I never had to face anything like that in the Secret Service, thank God. Tell you what...let's get back to the workout, and I'll buy lunch afterwards...Deal?"

"If you're waitin' on me, you're backin' up."

"You know, my grandmother on my father's side was a Rodriguez," Maria said as she set the resistance level on a stair climber.

"What was her father's name...Your great grandfather," asked Loraine.

"Armando."

"Get out!"

"You don't mean?"

"Armando Rodriguez…Born in…"

"Guadalajara."

"Oh, my God…Hello cuz."

Loraine and Maria hugged.

"Guess that makes us…"

"Third cousins."

They both squealed, grabbed each other's shoulders and started speaking Spanish.

Mike was spotting Bone on his ninth rep with 325 pounds on the olympic bar. "Come on, big guy. One more…get it…Push!" He looked over and saw his wife and Loraine jumping up and down. "What the…"

The bar slowly sagged to Bone's chest as his face turned red. "Sp…spot," he wheezed.

"Oh, shit. Sorry man." He assisted Bone as he pushed the weight to arms length and guided it back to the rack with a clang.

Bone took a deep breath, rubbed his chest and got to his feet. "Gotta pay attention, slick…What the hell were you looking at?"

"D and Loraine got somethin' goin'…Woop, here they come at a run. They look like long lost sisters or somethin'."

The girls ran up, their arms around each other's waists.

"Ya'll are not going to believe this, but…"

"Let me guess. You're cousins."

"Damn you, Bone! How'd you know?" Loraine put her hands on her hips. "You take the fun out of everything."

"Lucy said I was a receiver…and I think it's obvious you girls had to be related back along the line somewhere. I mean you both got…"

Loraine and D each whacked him on the shoulders.

"Damn you, Bone…gonna kill you!" they said simultaneously, and then looked at one another, broke out laughing and hugged.

"I think we're in deep do-do, Bone," Mickey whispered.

***

CHAPTER FIVE

BLAZE'S LAB
Eagle Nest

A small area on the metal work table near the center of the lab shimmered, and then a small device no larger than a smart phone materialized.

"Ah, here we are," said Lucy as she reached for it.

"It looks almost like my Galaxy 5, except just a touch thicker," commented Gears.

"The slight extra thickness is to allow for the cosmic energy accumulator…Right?"

"Blaze, you are growing by leaps and bounds. I think you are now able to get a data stream direct from me without my sending it. Outstanding."

"Well, not really. It just seemed logical, that's all."

"I don't think you're aware of receiving it." Lucy grinned as she picked up the communicator and keyed it on. "Darron, notify Rollân we are ready."

"Yes, Captain Annuna."

"Captain?"

"I was promoted when I returned."

An area in the center of the lab next to the table, shimmered and a hologram of a wizened, white-haired Tyranian in a pale lavender belted robe appeared. He was even smaller than Lucy. He bowed slightly.

"Rollân, Chief of Science at your service."

"Amazing, you look almost real, sir," said Gears.

"I assure you, I am real, Mister Formby...but, some thirty-one parsecs away. Our transmissions are only 1.232 rals delayed."

"Rals?" questioned Blaze.

"Within micro percentage points of your seconds. Tyrin's rotation is 23.1 of your hours. We call that increment of time a cycle and the equivalent of your sixty minutes is a zote...But, I have no objection to using your terminology."

"That'll keep it simple," said Gears.

"Rollân, they were able to locate the cloaked flying wings of the Nazis by triangulating the electromagnetic disruptions and heat distortion from three of their drones and computing the location from the data."

"Yes, that would be acceptable, but not functional in locating the denizens from Alpha Draconis...Their vessels do not radiate heat and even if they did, it would not be discernible through their level of fourth order screens."

"What about the electromagnetic disturbance in the ether itself?" asked Blaze.

"Ah, child, now there you may have something. However it would only indicate that it exists, not where it was...We did find something interesting in our analysis of the battle area between Lagrangian Point 2 and your satellite."

"What was that Rollân?" asked Lucy.

He glanced at her. "Traces of neutronium or what we term 'quark matter'."

"Neutronium?...A form of very dense matter made up of two bound forms of neutrons with no protons or electrons...Star material, it is believed," offered Blaze.

"I see what you mean about this Terrestrial, Annuna...You are correct, my dear. We now believe the Reptoids are using neutronium to catalyze their warp drive, fourth order mulitphased shields and enhanced cloaking screens which gives them a great advantage over their former status."

"Once our Science Society identified this new catalyst, we were able to synthesize it and named it Hadronium. The Reptoids apparently found the remnants of a dead star after it went nova and salvaged some material. They are not sufficiently scientifically advanced to create it. They only steal what they come across.

"Since we have progressed into the upper fourth order wave, this new material used in place of Thorium allows us to create weaponry and defense screens that are superior."

"Correct, Annuna. But we still don't have a method of actually finding a fourth order cloaked ship."

BEF CAFETERIA
Eagle Nest

Mickey led the way from the men's locker room down the hallway into the underground dining facility. Bone looked at the curved side walls.

"Interesting construction."

"The whole complex is modular. Built out of a type of plasticized waterproof composite with carbon fiber reinforcing rods…no metal…somewhat in the shape of Quonset huts with curved ceilings and all. Totally self-contained…They can withstand a direct nuclear hit, EMP, biological attacks, hurricanes, tornados, volcanos, earthquakes, floods, solar flares, meteorites and ground assaults."

"Damn! How far underground are we?" Bone exclaimed as they entered the mess hall.

Mickey pointed up. "The arched roof ten feet over our heads is one hundred feet below the surface…We've got some great cooks working down here. You should be able to find something that floats your boat."

"Thanks," Bone replied as he went through the serving line first and chose two portions of chicken fried steak and a large helping of mashed redskin potatoes made with the skins left on.

"You want gravy on the steaks?" the server asked.

"Hit me with your best shot...I'm still a growin' boy," he said with a big grin. "Those green beans look kinda good, too...and the biscuits...with a side bowl of that cream gravy."

"Takes a lot of calories to keep all those muscles churnin' and burnin'," Mickey said.

"I'm tellin' you," Bone agreed. "My partner is always giving me grief, but hell, she doesn't weigh a hundred and ten."

"Wait 'til you get married. Then the food police are there every meal...well, practically every meal."

"Heard that. Didn't evolve this far up the food chain to eat grass and leaves."

"Go pick us a out a table...I'm gonna have 'em cook me up a steak rare. Gals should be right behind us...after they dry their hair and touch up their makeup."

Bone swiped his ID card though the checkout as shown by the server who provided his Texas-sized glass of iced tea and moved to a square table near the curved back wall. He set the tray down and noticed the glass salt and pepper shakers in the center.

Looking around, he took hold of the salt and sprinkled it liberally on the potatoes. Bone unscrewed the stainless steel top off the shaker and then set it down carefully atop the glass dispenser and picked up the pepper.

A couple of minutes later, Mickey joined him and sat down.

"You said you went fishin' down on Falcon Reservoir? Aren't things still a little dicey with the cartels just across the lake these days…What with that guy gettin' shot off his jet ski, and all?" Bone asked.

"Actually the lake is not too busy because of the security issues, so the fishing's getting pretty good…Kinda hard on the marina's and mom and pop bait stores, though.

"The governor had the Department of Public Safety outfit a few cigarette boats with a half dozen M-60s and a passle of big-ass outboards. When the cartel types see them coming, they just move up or down river a few miles and lay low 'til the DPS guys are gone."

"What happens if you are there and the state guys aren't?"

"We have a little surprise for them," Mickey said with a smile. "I'll take ya'll up to the range after lunch. Blaze made up a nifty little carbine that I take with me. If I can see 'em…I can blow their ass into little bitty pieces. Not even enough to fill a shoe box."

"Friggin' awesome. Think I'm gonna like working with you guys."

"Hey, here they are. You girls are fast."

Both men stood up as Maria and Loraine sat down their trays, laden with two large cobb salads and grilled salmon filets.

"How nice of you to wait for us," Double D said.

"Always the gentleman, right, Pard?"

"Don't make me laugh," Loraine replied. "Never get between this man and a donut…It's worse than being caught in a buffalo stampede."

Mickey chuckled and reached for the salt shaker. He turned it upside down and the cap fell into his pile of french fries along with a full tablespoon of salt. "Crap! Must have just filled it and forgot to tighten back on."

Loraine shot a look at Bone.

"What?" he said in mock innocence.

"I know you did it...Only you would do something so mindless."

"My old M600 pilot...and now brother-in-law...would do that," Maria said.

" No harm, no foul," Mickey said. He screwed the top back on the shaker and scraped the excess salt away from his potatoes. "But remember, paybacks are hell." He winked across the table at Loraine.

She smiled and nodded.

BEF ARMORY

"Hey, Chris, I like to check out two G3 carbines to demo to our friends."

The former US Army Special Forces master sergeant pushed his chair back from his desk and got to his feet. "You bet, Mickey. How many mags do you need?"

"One each oughta do...A hundred and twenty rounds be more than enough."

Chris flipped on the lights to the darkened room behind him. He walked back into the vault, lined with almost every firearm in the US military arsenal—plus some not found anywhere else on earth.

Bone looked at the assembled hardware and whistled lowly. *What a neat toy box.*

The armorer returned carrying what appeared to be two Steyr AUG rifles. He laid them on the counter and stepped over to a wall-mounted recharging station and pulled two triangular batteries out of the slots. "They're ready to go. Log 'em to your account?"

"Yep. Thanks, see you in a few." Mickey picked up the two battery packs and handed one to each of the ladies and then grabbed the closed carbine and handed it to Bone.

"It's not a AUG…the barrel's too fat. What do you call this thing?"

"Blaze and Gears designed this bad boy. It's an electromagnetic coil rifle that shoots a ferromagnetic projectile at a user-selectable velocity of between seven and twelve thousand feet per second."

"Holy moly! Never heard of anything that fast."

"Even the great Bone can learn something," Loraine added.

"Bite me, princess…How does it work?"

"Without beating the physics to death, there are tiny little carbon fiber nanotubes wrapped around the inner barrel…all filled with superconducting mercury. The batteries supply electrons to the capacitors connected to the tubes and a computer sends signals to the coils which levitate the bullets, if you will, and push and pull them down the barrel."

Bone blinked and looked over the deadly weapon. "All without making contact with the bore, thus eliminating drag, friction and heat. The optical sight is also a laser range finder and ballistic computer that compensates for drop and wind drift..."

"I was just gonna say that," Mickey said. He looked curiously at the big man.

"I know," Bone said. "Man, it's gettin' freaky...I'm startin' to pick up people's thoughts."

"That is scary," Loraine said as she made a face. "Just hope they don't pick up yours."

He just grinned at her with a twinkle in his eyes.

Mickey continued, "The magazine carries sixty of the projectiles and they feed automatically up to the chamber after each shot. The slide control over here on the forearm sets the speed...back for slow, forward for fast." He winked at Bone. "Marine proof."

"You're funny GI...but, then again, looks ain't everything," Bone shot back. "Wait...what do you call poppin' some caps on a coil gun?"

"Lets go up topside and I'll show you."

BEF OUTDOOR RANGE

The thousand yard range had a number of earth camoed concrete buildings off to the side at the 100, 400 and 1,000 yard markers. A 40x10 foot concrete pad was poured at the firing line and a small building housed the target control mechanisms.

Mickey swept his ID badge across the electronic lock and opened the door. Once the laptop inside was turned on, he chose a couple of man-sized silhouettes at the 400 yard range and pressed enter.

A side door opened and two targets emerged on the track system and moved in front of the eight foot high berm.

"Pretty snazzy setup. Don't have to walk down there except to score 'em," Loraine said.

"Actually…" Mickey said.

"They have a closed circuit TV system to does that for us," Bone added. He shrugged.

"Well, alrighty, then," Mickey said. For the benefit of your partner, I'll show her how to install the battery." He popped open a cover on the buttstock. Inside was a slightly irregularly shaped triangular compartment exactly the same size as the battery. "Drop the power pack inside and snap the door shut. It only goes in one way."

"Marine proof," Loraine said with a slight smirk.

"Hey…I was a Marine aviator," Maria grumbled.

"My apologies, didn't know, cuz." Loraine sniffed.

"Moving on," Mickey continued. "Here's the on-off switch. Push this button to load the first round. Keep the muzzle pointed downrange, boys and girls…Remember, there isn't any body armor made that will save you from a misfire."

"Piece of cake," she said as she snapped the battery in place and locked the cover. "What about ear protection?"

"Don't need any…You'll see," Bone said.

"Safeties off, the range is hot. You may fire at will."

"I got the one on the left, Pard…Show me what you got."

She threw the carbine to her shoulder and placed the cross hairs in the ten ring over the heart on the target. Her finger barely touched the trigger when a strange sound emanated from the weapon.

Ponk.

A faint blue light was created as the hypersonic projectile ionized the air molecules from the friction. Dust kicked up almost instantly from the caliche berm behind the target.

Damn, she's quick, Bone thought as he saw the dust fly.

"A ten at four o'clock…two inches out," Mickey said.

Bone squeezed the trigger.

Ponk. Dust boiled up from the berm.

Christ! That was only about an eight ounce trigger pull.

"A nine at six o'clock. Five inches low."

Both shooters fired a dozen or more shots, peppering the ten rings.

"Nice shooting guys. Some of our Raptors may be asking you for instructions."

"Doubt that, D," Bone said. "These are bad…seriously bad."

"Mind if Maria and I take a couple rounds? Those Reptoids might get here sooner than we think."

"Be my guest," Bone said. "The heads are still clean."

The married BEF teammates took control of the two carbines. Each fired ten rounds at the life-sized noggins on the paper opponents.

"I knew you were joking about needing instruction. Look at that…ten head shots at 400 yards…each. Man that is some kind of shootin'," Bone said looking at the TV monitor. "How much penetration can you get with these gadgets?"

"Five or six feet in hard stone…like granite. Twenty to thirty feet in dirt and twenty-four inches of hardened armor is no problem at max," Double D said quickly. "What's impressive is the effect on human targets."

The images of rebel soldiers asulting the Presidential Estate in Kenya appeared in his mind from Maria. When the rounds impacted them, their bodies literally exploded. "Whoa! That's some serious ass whippin' there."

"That was with the thirty caliber six-barrel G2," she said. Almost wish I had it on the F-18."

"We usually have a beer or two…or three after range practice at Cross…I'm buyin'."

"Best idea I've heard all day, Bone."

"Great!…Now where?"

"Oh, we built a new open-air company lounge down on the banks of Becerro Creek where the old mill was. It's a clear water creek that runs into the Rio Grande…Got some history."

"Can't wait to hear it," said Loraine. "Long as I don't have to shoot a can of beer off of someone's head."

"Now that I've got to hear about, cuz."

EARTH'S THERMOSPHERE
SOUTH POLE

"Scout pilot, Mrsst, reporting, Fleet Commander."

"What amount of Au-79 did you obtain?"

"A small amount over 1,800 kilos, sir. It is being transferred to engineering for conversion to buss-bars. The 800 kilo excess is going into reserve storage."

"Excellent, Scout Patrol Leader Mrsst."

"Thank you, sir." *I knew I would be rewarded...Promoted to Patrol Leader, a well deserved honor.*

The tips of all four of his upper appendages briefly vibrated in pleasure—a movement not lost on Klsth.

"Take two four ship units back to that same land mass and fill your cargo bays with mammalian protein. Our food supply is running low for the fleet. I had anticipated we would be in harvesting mode by this time, but we need another of this puny world's revolutions to finish our repairs."

All four of Mrsst's tentacles extended straight overhead from his massive body in salute.

"As you command, Sire. We observed many four-legged creatures and numerous outlying collections of the two-legged creatures in our trip for the metal we obtained. Our larders will be filled in short order. We expect no difficulties from the backward weaponry of the humanoids."

GOVERNOR'S LOUNGE
Cross, Texas

Captain St. John and three of his off duty officers sat at a square table just off the small dance floor.

"Damn, kinda quiet without Bone and Loraine," commented Stella Johnson, a very attractive blond uniform officer.

"Speaking of, where are they?" asked Peach Presley, a good looking tall brunette technician from the Cross PD Forensics Lab.

"Padrino called me yesterday and said they would be gone a few days…something about saving the world." St. John took a sip of his Coors longneck.

"Oh, my God! Better check and make sure my insurance is paid up," commented patrolman Joel Newman.

"No, really, Captain, where are they?" inquired Stella.

"Not kidding, that's exactly what he said. Had to do with Lucy…Wanted me to take care of Tyrin and the horses."

"You mean he's out there at that big ranch by himself?"

"Well, Peach, if Bone and Padrino are both gone, I'd say Tyrin is alone out there. I went out and fed everybody before I came here…He's doin' fine."

"Like hell. I'm not goin' to leave that sweet thing out there all by his lonesome."

"Now just what do you intend on doing about it, miss bleeding heart?" said Joel.

"I'm going to stay out at the ranch until they get back, that's what, mister smart ass."

"Do what?"

"You heard me."

"I'll go too, Peach."

"Oh, bless your heart, Stella, that's so sweet."

"Actually not a bad idea, girls. Sure save me a lot of trips."

"Who's going to watch over ya'll?"

"Newman, if you'll recall, I beat the socks off of you at the range last time."

"I just had an off day."

"Anytime you want a rematch, Wild Bill, you let me know."

NIGEL, SOUTH AFRICA

Mrrst maneuvered the lead processing ship, known as a *Reaper*, into a position over a large feed lot in the small town southeast of Johannesburg. Another one of the 300 foot long scavenger vessels pulled along side his as the other six sausage-shaped monsters silently came to a hover over similar high-density cattle finishing operations in the nearby towns of Edenville, Stella and Frankfort.

The mid-afternoon sun was hot and the Afrikaner cattle—varying in color from a light tan to a deep cherry red—were bunched near the shade of several acacia trees near the back of the lot.

"Discontinue cloak. Initiate transporter beam on my command."

"Yes, Captain Mrrst," his systems operator Qrts replied. He used one tentacle to tap an icon on the control pad, as his four eye stalks independently monitored the external visual displays. "These large creatures must weigh close to 800 kilos apiece."

"I see that. And there are hundreds of them in close proximity to each other." His arms vibrated with excitement as his long jaws snapped together rapidly. "I may not wait for the desiccation units to dry them to leather. I will eat one raw for the taste sensation."

"Bah! Not me…all that blood and undigested vegetation inside. You are a barbarian, Captain," he said before he caught himself. "But I mean that in a good way, Scout Patrol Leader."

"Your comment will not be recorded in your personal file, Qrts…this time. Watch how you address me, underling. My wrath is second only to our most fearless leader." He scanned the herd of Afrikaner and spotted a mature bull that had past its time for breeding and was being fattened for ground beef. Its spreading horns were distinctive and went almost seven feet across. "That one! My taste buds are talking to me. Beam that one up first."

Orts followed his commands and a bright white light descended upon the bull—it vanished.

Mrrst made his way quickly to the cargo hold after the startled animal reappeared inside the processing ship. The *Reptoid* trudged across the deck and approached the wary creature. Using one tentacle on each of the bull's horns and one on either side of its jaw, he lifted its head up as the bull tried to back away from the hideous alien.

The animal's hooves slid on the slick deck floor and its strength was no match for a rapacious alien being used to five times as much gravity on its home planet.

Mrrst's jaws clamped down on the bull's throat and cut through hide, flesh and bone as the neck less Reptoid shook it like a dog with a new chew toy.

The bull's legs turned rubbery as a sickening crack resounded when the neck was severed. Frothy red blood spurted for several feet as Mrrst's snakelike head ripped a thirty pound chunk from the carcass and let the body crash to the deck with a thud. The crocodilian jaws flew open wide and the bloody morsel dropped into his waiting giant maw. With one long gurgling sound, the captain swallowed the still quivering flesh and then beat his four tentacles against his chest in a display of dominance.

Qrst rotated the one eye stalk he had employed in watching the gruesome incident on the visaplate and focused back to the task at hand. His body shivered at the thought of his captain being even slightly displeased with him.

He swept the beam over six steers and brought them aboard the craft at the same time. They were instantly moved into the large desiccators where all fluids were removed and ejected into the atmosphere. The remaining protein, mineralized tissue and bone were crushed into six inch thick flat sheets, cut into blocks twelve by twelve inches and transported into storage containers.

The other six ships stripped nearby feedlots in a similar fashion. A hundred black and white Nguni cattle were snatched up before the craft drifted to the next enclosure and began to transport the bellowing herd of Beefmasters aboard. Two lanky Zulu employees crouched in terror of the sight of the pair of alien craft hovering overhead.

One took off running and screaming in terror. His cousin followed close behind.

AURORA: INVASION

A young black man hired to clean the feed troughs, looked up when a brilliant white beam of light drifted across the nearly empty pen. He ducked back into a small open door at the base of a circular metal granary. Closing the door almost shut behind him, he held his breath as the light drifted closer and closer.

A series of small portals on the ship's exterior opened as the desiccators separated the fluids from the captured bodies of both the human and bovine cargo. Streams of a sticky reddish liquid cascaded down—mixing with the air as they fell—and spread out into a ring of putrid pink mist that covered the ground and a beat-up tan Toyota pickup.

The boy slammed the granary door completely closed and put his back against it. The heat and dust of the corrugated metal enclosure was oppressive and the stench from the terrifying scene he had just witnessed outside was overpowering. He bent over as his stomach cramped and projectile vomited until he had nothing else left to regurgitate at all.

After a time—he was unsure how long—he summoned up the courage to peek outside. The sky was clear and the feedlot was strangely silent. A swarm of black flies—normally content to feed upon the cattle—had settled to the ground and were feasting on the organic rain that stood in puddles all about.

He looked around and made his decision to make a run for it. A mile later, he stumbled into his family's modest frame house.

"Why are you not working?" his mother asked. "We can't afford for you to quit that job."

His eyes were still wide with fear and his body covered in sweat. The young man pointed back down the road. "Aliens! They are coming! They are coming!"

EAGLE NEST RANCH HOUSE

"...And that's how we found out that Loraine and I are cousins," Maria said with a big smile.

"Small world...isn't it?" Gunter observed. He took a sip of iced tea from the large thick-stemmed goblet.

"That's a nice story, honey, " Annette said. "We need to get some pictures for the family album, if you don't mind, Loraine."

She beamed. "It would be an honor. It's like finding a long, lost sister that you didn't know you had."

Maria grinned and nodded.

Mike, Mickey and Blaze shared a look. Only two years earlier, they had learned who had placed Mickey, the former head of the President's Secret Service detail, up for adoption as a child. They had been unaware, as had Gunter, that the baby boy was the result of a college romance between Annette Thompson and the Hermann patriarch. Slightly over thirty years later, she had broken the news to her old lover and together, they announced the truth, along with the news of their impending marriage.

Bone took a bite of the beef brisket, covered with the Eagle Nest Ranch commercial sauce. He savored the flavor for a second before he swallowed. "Mike, I gotta tell you...ya'll do a great job on that meat. And the sauce...man, I usually make my own, but I can't come close to this stuff."

"We appreciate that. I'll pass the good words over to Ralph down at the smokehouse."

Gunter nodded. "They do a killer job, that's for sure. Need some more cole slaw or potato salad? Got plenty."

"Nah. Thanks, but gotta save room for the dewberry cobbler. I smelled it cookin' when we walked in...Madam President..."

"Annette."

"Yes, ma'am...Annette. Why a woman who could cook like you ever went into politics is beyond me."

"Sometimes, I have to ask myself the same question." She laughed, as did Gunter.

"Well, big boy, Mickey said you got to check out Blaze's G3 carbine today. What did you think?" Mike asked.

"Mighty impressive...awesome piece of engineering." He looked down the table at Blaze. "You know I've been carrying around that fifty cal hand cannon for several years. Love the way it shoots, but good God...talk about loud..."

"Huh?" commented Loraine, cupping her hand behind one ear.

Bone laughed. "Did you and Gears ever think about making a handgun version?"

"No," Blaze replied. "The thought never actually crossed my mind. I looked at it more as a precision long range weapon...plus I never was really all that good with a handgun."

"She made the G1 as a coyote gun…it was her first coil weapon," Gunter added.

Bone glanced back at Blaze. A slight frown crossed her face. Suddenly, the images of two Mexican soldiers firing automatic weapons at the ranch house came flooding in as she remembered that fateful day.

He could see her memories clearly as if they were his—*the EoTech reticule floating in midair and the rogue corporal sweeping the M-4 carbine up toward the woman holding the highly modified Remington 700 rifle in the second story window. She pulled the trigger. Ponk! Blap! The man's body exploded like a bursting water balloon and his head popped up like a champagne cork, climbing almost thirty feet before it dropped down to the caliche drive between the house and the barn.*

The red dot inside a 65 mil ring slid over to the Mexican private firing an M-16. Ponk! Blap! His body disintegrated in a red mist, leaving only a bloody bone sticking out of a single boot. A third soldier—a lieutenant by his rank—took off and sprinted into the barn before she could get off a third round.

Whoa. That was just outside here. Bone nodded once to Blaze, acknowledging her traumatic ordeal.

She nodded back and then shrugged.

"Worked fine on the two-legged variety, I see."

"It was awesome, indeed," Mike added. He had not seen the impact directly, only the aftermath.

"I suppose a handgun would not be too difficult," Blaze said. "If I kept it a standard size, we could use existing holsters...It would just have a thicker barrel like the G3."

Bone agreed, "A combo U shaped battery pack with a stack of projectiles in the center could be replaced every thirty rounds or so."

"Right!" the brilliant redhead blurted. "I'll see what I can conjure up...Lucy, do the Tyranians use handguns?"

"No, we finally learned to settle our personal differences peaceably, thank goodness. We still have weapons, but rely on our vessels to do our fighting...particularly with the Reptoids. They are so much bigger and stronger than us...It's not prudent to be on the ground...one on one."

"I hear you," Bone said. "Besides...God made man, but Samuel Colt made them equal."

"I'm not so sure the Great Entity made the Reptoids. Not sure how that vile race came about." Lucy frowned and took a sip of tea.

Bone contemplated her statement, remembering she lost her mate to them over a hundred years before. The memories of his first encounter with the creatures came back to him in slow motion—*the blast of the disruptor beam narrowly missing him as Loraine fired her Kimber 1911 and he rolled up on one knee with his 500 Smith and Wesson blazing.*

"Dumbass!" he blurted. "Sorry, not ya'll...me."

"What is it?" Mickey asked.

"The disruptor! I captured a Reptoid weapon when my partner and I smoked that shape changing SOB! Can't believe I didn't think of it 'til now."

"It dissolves matter in a single blast?" Blaze asked.

"Did you see that cedar tree behind me?"

She nodded.

"Well, all I can say is if it wasn't for my catlike moves and my quick little trigger-happy partner, we would not be having this conversation."

"Where is the disruptor now?" Annette asked.

"Back at my ranch, in the gun safe. Lucy, you think we can go back and get it in the morning?"

"Of course. I don't see why not."

"Will our Raptors be up against that disruptor thing if we go man to man with the Reptoids?" Mickey asked.

"That is almost a certainty," Lucy said. "It would be nice to find a way to counteract or neutralize that infernal device."

***

CHAPTER SIX

BONE'S RANCH HOUSE
Cross, Texas

Peach stood next to the stove in the spacious turn of the century kitchen dropping bits of muenster cheese in the scrambled eggs cooking in the large black cast iron skillet. There was a plate of crispy bacon on the counter.

"Is the coffee ready?" came the call from Stella still in her bedroom down the hallway.

"Yes…Eggs are almost done, too. Best come get it while it's hot…Tyrin has his eyes on the bacon."

"I'm not dressed yet."

"What difference does it make?"

"Oh, yeah," Stella said as she made her way down the hall in her thong panties and black lace bra. "Does anything smell better than bacon cooking in the morning?"

Peach picked up the skillet with a hot pad and scraped the eggs into the platter beside the bacon with a long handled wooden spoon. She turned the electric stove—powered by Lucy's cold fusion generator—off, set the pan on a back burner to cool and bent over to give Tyrin a piece of bacon as Stella padded through the door, her bare feet made very little sound on the hardwood floor.

The air shimmered just behind Peach who was still in her white baby doll nighty—Bone materialized.

"Wow!"

Stella screamed. Peach spun around to see him standing less than three feet behind her staring at her butt. She screamed, too, and started whacking him about the head and shoulders with the spoon.

"Damn you, Bone!"

Stella grabbed a broom from the corner and joined in. "Bone, you did this on purpose!"

"I'm gonna knock a knot on your head Oral Roberts cain't take off."

"Ow, ow, ow…Hey, hey, ya'll cut it out."

Peach threw the spoon at him and grabbed a dish towel to cover her perky breasts that plainly showed through the thin summer cotton.

"I didn't see anything," he said as he caught the spoon in midair.

"Liar!" She opened a drawer and grabbed another towel for Stella and pitched it to her. "How did you get in here?"

Tyrin's tail wagged furiously as he danced happily on both front feet in front of the big man.

"Somethin's burnin'," he said.

"The toast!" Peach screamed, turned around, started to bend over to open the oven door, but caught herself and spun back with her rear to the counter. "You get it."

Bone grinned, grabbed a hot pad, opened the oven and slid out the cookie tray she had used to put the buttered bread on. He set it on top of the stove in between the burners. "Just like I like it...burnt and scraped like mama's," he said as he looked at the blackened toast.

"Now, I asked how you got here," Peach demanded.

"Can I have breakfast first?"

"No!" the girls said simultaneously.

"All right...I can only tell you that Lucy sent me to get something."

"What?" they said together again.

"Can't tell you."

"Oh, bull patties...Bless your heart, Bone, you would tell a fib when the truth would be a lot easier," said Peach.

"I'm not kiddin'."

"The captain said something about saving the world," countered Stella.

"Uh, well, yeah." He glanced at the platter on the counter. "Breakfast is gettin' cold."

"Damn you, Bone," the girls said as they backed out of the kitchen.

"We'll be right back…Keep your hands off the bacon," called Peach from down the hall.

He listened as they closed the door to their room, turned and headed out the other doorway to the den. Bone went to his large steel gun safe, punched in five numbers on the key pad and swung open the heavy door. He reached in, grabbed the pipe-like Reptoid disruptor, slipped it in a side pocket of his black BDU pants, closed and re-locked the safe.

He was leaning against the counter sipping on coffee from his special large white mug when the girls walked back into the kitchen. Each was wearing cutoffs and Cross PD gray tank tops.

"You ladies didn't have to change on my account…kinda liked you the way you were."

"Hush your mouth…Gonna kill you one of these days, Bone," snapped Stella as she reached for the broom.

He held up his hand. "Kings X."

The air in the center of the room shimmered and Lucy materialized wearing a formfitting silver jump suit. Both girls screamed again.

"I apologize for scaring you," she said as Tyrin was jumping straight up and down and then flopped over on his back at her feet. He wiggled all over as she knelt down and scratched his stomach. "He loves to have his belly rubbed."

His right hind leg beat a tattoo in the air. Bone pointed at his middle and grinned.

"In your dreams," said Stella.

"Bless your heart, Lucy, that's okay. I knew you could do that, but this is the first time we've seen it." Peach glanced over at Johnson, who nodded.

"Bone said he couldn't say what ya'll were doing."

"I know." Lucy grinned at Stella.

"Oh, right."

"It's probably better that we keep it that way."

"See?" said Bone as he pulled up a chair and sat down at the kitchen table. "I'm famished."

Lucy and Stella also pulled up chairs at the table.

"Guess it's a good thing I cooked plenty. The chickens have been workin' overtime," Peach said as she carried the platter to the table. "Sorry about the toast…It was Bone's fault…bless his little black heart."

"Well, at least I didn't have to stop by the store for a henway," he said as he broke a piece of bacon in half and shared it with Tyrin.

"What's a henway?" asked Stella as she raked a helping of eggs into her plate.

"Oh, 'bout three or four pounds. Wouldn't you say, Lucy?"

She giggled and almost choked on her coffee.

The little blond briefly looked puzzled, and then she slapped him across the shoulder with a dish towel. "Damn you, Bone."

"Well, thank you, Billy Sunday," Peach added as she re-filled Lucy's cup.

"Did you get what you came for, Bone?" asked Lucy.

"I'm good," he said as he shoveled in a forkful of eggs.

Peach and Stella exchanged questioning looks.

"Don't suppose..." Peach started to ask.

"Nope." He grinned and pointed. "You gonna eat the last piece of bacon?"

Lucy glanced at him. "I thought we ate at the ranch before we left."

"We did...Daddy always told me never turn down a meal...you never know when the next one's coming."

"Darrell Ulysses Bone, Human Vacuum." Stella laughed. "Kinda long for a name tag, doncha think?"

She and Peach bumped fists. Lucy merely shook her head.

"Come on, Bone," Stella said. "You can't keep us out in the dark forever..."

He dabbed his napkin at the last remnants of his second breakfast hanging on his chin, and then leaned in closer to the two eager girls. "Can ya'll keep a secret?" He carefully looked around the kitchen.

"Yeah!" they both chimed simultaneously as they smiled broadly.

"So can I," Bone whispered and stood up with his trademark grin planted firmly in place. "Sorry to eat and run. Thanks for the groceries...wait a sec. This is *my* house and those were *my* groceries...Never mind. Thanks for keepin' an eye on the pup and the caballós." He reached down and rubbed on Tyrin's head. "See you later, boy. Mind your aunties while I'm gone."

He woofed and his tail began to wag quickly, beating against the table leg like a drum.

Lucy pushed back from the table. "I take that as our cue to disappear." She tapped her new bracelet communicator. "We're ready, Darron."

They shimmered slightly and vanished.

BLAZE'S LAB
Eagle Nest

Padrino, Loraine and Blaze simultaneously turned when the air in the center of Blaze's newly enlarged lab shimmered and Bone and Lucy materialized. Gears looked up from his computer microscope.

"Lucy, you need to add some tinkley music to that transporter like on Star Trek," Blaze commented.

She laughed. "I suppose I'll have to find some time and watch that show sometime. Everyone seems to reference it."

"Star Trek: The Next Generation is *my* favorite," commented Blaze. "The reruns are on five times a week."

"If *you* like it, I'll certainly have to find some time to watch it," said Lucy.

"I enjoyed that one too. Ran for seven years…plus a couple of movies. Excellent franchise," added Loraine.

"Let's see what you brought us, Bone," said Gears.

He took the silver tube from his pocket and handed it to his godfather. "I've never fired the thing…Padrino has."

"Accidentally…The actuator seems to be in that slight depression." He held it up and pointed to a small area on the side of the tube.

"The Reptoids have claws on their two digits at the end of each tentacle. It looks like that trigger was made for the tip of one."

"Let's take it outside and test it, shall we?" recommended Gears.

"Not so fast. I need to set up some parameters and get together some different materials." Blaze started rummaging around some metal storage shelves. "Some titanium, carbon fiber rods, glass, stainless steel…and…" She pulled out her cell and keyed a number. "Ralph? Would you happen to have a couple of thawed whole chickens and a turkey laid out?…Great! Mind bringing them to my lab?…I really do appreciate it. Thanks."

"Whole chickens?" asked Bone. "Ah, never mind."

She grinned and nodded. "Grab that three foot piece of railroad tie over in the corner, would you, Bone. That was my original test target when I build the first coil gun." She laughed. "Who knew what it was going to lead to?"

Blaze pointed. "Padrino, there's an ultrahigh speed camera and tripod in that cabinet over there. Would you bring them, please?"

"Can do."

She headed to the door. "Oh, and might as well give it a try on some of our Dragonskin…"

"Dragonskin?" questioned Bone.

"It's our special lightweight armor for all BEF personnel when we go in combat." She grabbed a top off a wall hook.

"Uh, lightweight ain't gonna get it, little missy."

"Might be surprised…Well, we're off to see the wizard," said Blaze.

"Wizard?" questioned Loraine.

"Yeah, you know?…The wizard?" replied Bone as he lifted the heavy chunk of creosote impregnated wood to his shoulder.

She looked at him with her puzzled look. "No…Oh, why do I even ask?"

"You'll see."

"Are you and Bone like this all the time?" asked Lucy as they headed out the door.

"Usually…Unless he's home asleep…It doesn't faze me anymore. I just consider the source and ignore it."

She just shook her head. "Blaze, I'm taking Maria, Mike and Jill to BEF headquarters. I Promised them and Hollywood I'd brief the Black Eagle, F-15 and F-18 squadrons on Reptoid battle tactics. Don't worry about preparing a report, I will be linked with you…What you see, I will see."

"I'm still not quite used to that, but it sure simplifies things."

Lucy nodded, hugged her and tapped her bracelet.

Blaze led the procession to the range which was only fifty yards from the lab. Gears set up the camera at the side of the twenty-five yard berm while Bone set the piece of tie in front—Loraine and Blaze placed the other items.

A white Ford pickup with the Eagle Nest logo on the side braked to a stop in back of the firing line and Ralph—the manager of the commercial smokehouse—got out. He set a cardboard box from the truck on the shooter's bench. "Here you go, Blaze," he shouted. "Got to head back to the shop to finish that shipment for the Kroger Super Market chain."

She waved. "Thanks again, Ralph."

Back at the firing line, Gears said, "Padrino, why don't you take the honors? You've got the most experience."

He laughed. "Don't know if incinerating my favorite lamp qualifies as experience, but what do you want to shoot first?"

"We don't have any lamps handy, but let's start with that small cedar tree to the left side of the berm...Ready with the camera, Gears?"

"Standing by, Blaze. Anytime, just give me a countdown. I'll start recording at two."

"All right, we'll start on my countdown, Padrino. Three...two...one."

He pointed the device at the ten foot cedar, touched the trigger mechanism on the side of the tube and a green beam leapt at the tree. A greenish glow spread out like lightning from the trunk to the tips of all the branches and the tiniest of the prickly leaves. There was an audible hiss as the tree completely vaporized in a couple of milliseconds—leaving only a tendril of smoke curling up from the remains of the stump just barely sticking up above ground.

"That looks familiar," said Loraine.

"Holy sweet Jesus," remarked Gears as he looked up from the display screen on the camera.

NORTH TEXAS REGIONAL AIRPORT
BEF Underground Headquarters

Lucy, Maria, Jill and Mike materialized in the hallway near the operations desk. Double D crossed her arms and rubbed her forearms under her flight suit—Mike scratched at the back of his neck

"Dang, it tickles when we do that transporter thing...Does that happen every time?" Maria asked.

"Pretty much, but you'll get used to it," Lucy said.

"Dang sure quicker than flyin'," Cowboy added. "Thought I had a spider crawling on me for a minute. Everybody else in the briefing room?"

"All the squadron and flight commanders are inside, Mike. Just as you requested." The shift supervisor behind the operation desk motioned with her thumb down the hall.

"Good, thanks, Connie. Let's get this dog and pony show on the road," he replied.

Inside, James "Hollywood" Stewart sat near the head of the long table with the other commanders from the *Black Eagle*, F-15 and F/A-18 departments spread around on either side. The BEF COO, Heater McElhenny sat across from him. Lucy took a seat at the head of the table and set her smart phone-sized projector on the polished cherry wood veneer.

"I'll get right to it and try not to wander around too much in the brief. We'll start with an overview of how we plan to transport and deploy you, and then we'll discuss tactics and weaponry. This is not a one-way conversation, by the way. If you have something to say, I'd like to hear it."

Hollywood glanced up and down the table to see several heads nod.

Lucy closed her eyes. The device projected a three dimensional image of the *Annihilator*. "Here's out latest project...the first of six, named *Garrin* after my mate who was killed in 1897. It should clear the mooring docks on Tyrin sometime tomorrow...considerably bigger than your naval aircraft carriers, it should easily hold all of the BEF's assets simultaneously."

A murmur moved though the assembled warriors. She collected their thoughts instantly.

"Right...I know there is no takeoff or landing deck and most you are not current in your carrier quals." She smiled. "We'll beam you aboard, launch and bring you back the same way."

"A fully armed fighter or a Super Galaxy? You have the technology to do that?" Heater asked.

"Are you familiar with Project Blue Book?" she asked.

He nodded. "Vaguely…It was an old Air Force program to maintain the records of alien abduct…"

"Sometimes your pilots took…let's simply call them aggressive attitudes during our chance encounters. They were teleported before they could inflict damage or injury to us or our ships." She grinned. "But we always gave them back…"

"Mighty nice of you." Heater chuckled

"Some of you may question the rational behind tying up all your forces in a single vessel."

"The thought crossed my mind," Heater said quickly.

"We will not engage all of your resources at the same time. My engineers assure me that our newest shield technology will provide you with a measure of safety you cannot achieve on your own. They are also working on far more effective weapons and with assistance from Blaze and Gears, hope to be able to pinpoint the location of the cloaked Reptoid ships…Plus we will start to spread out as the additional superdreadnaught carriers arrive…assuming the battle is still going on."

"I am correct that their antigravity propulsion systems do not leave a heat signature?"

"Neither theirs nor ours do."

"How's that gonna affect our Sidewinders and Stingers?"

"We'll get into that in the tactical portion of the brief, Flash. I don't mean to put you off."

"Not a problem…I'm just trying to get my head around the idea of attacking those mile long monster ships and their fighters."

"I know where you are coming from…I may not look like it, but I'm a fighter pilot too, okay? So, moving on, Once the Annihilator arrives in orbit, we'll provision each of the C-5Ms, along with the Raptors and Black Eagles and beam them aboard, with replacement munitions. The squadrons of F-15s and F-18s will come next.

"When we are ready, the Annihilator will move into position to engage either the Reptilian transports or the harvesting vessels."

"What's the top-end speed on the Annihilator?" Jill inquired.

"In your atmosphere, about 9,000 miles per hour. Out in space, 300,000 kilometers per second…until we jump interstellar through a singularity or what you call a wormhole."

"Whoa," Maria said. "Makes the Super Hornet look like it's standing still."

"Hold on," Mike said. "Did you mean kilometers per hour?"

"No," Lucy replied. "We can get up to light speed when our inertialess drive is engaged in space and there's no way to calculate speed when we go to warp."

"My God, that's 671 million miles an hour."

"You did those calculations in you head…Almost instantaneously."

Mike stared back at her mischievous grin and began to blush slightly. Maria gave her brother-in-law's foot a playful kick under the table and arched one eyebrow.

"Mentioned inertialess drive. Just exactly what is that?" asked Dare.

"To make instantaneous stops, starts and those abrupt lateral or vertical movements most of you are probably familiar with from your UFO cable shows, we go inertialess or massless, if you will. Everything inside the field, including us has the same intrinsic kinetic energy and are therefore not affected by any type of acceleration."

"So you're saying no 'Gs'?" asked Jill.

"Exactly…"

Connie from the operations desk knocked on the conference room door. She moved to Heater and whispered in his ear, "Sir, Burner Stewart is on the line. He has some intel about possible alien activity in South Africa."

"Put him on Skype. This could be serious."

Lucy closed her eyes. The blue hologram of the *Annihilator* shrunk in size and vanished to a pinpoint that disappeared into the projecting device. Mike placed his hand on hers and recoiled slightly as her thoughts flooded into his consciousness. *We're not ready…*

RANGE
Eagle Nest

"Well that is interesting," Blaze said as they looked at the Titanium, glass, carbon rod, stainless steel and railroad tie. "Perfect holes the exact size of the internal diameter of the disruptor in each except the wood and it burned much of the area around the hole…but it completely disintegrated the tree."

"Let's try the chicken and turkey," suggested Bone.

"All that's left that we haven't shot, Blaze, except for the Dragonskin," said Gears.

Bone carried the carcasses down to the berm and set them up on some limestone rocks the size of washtubs.

When the big man cleared the area, Blaze gave the order, "Go to it, Padrino. One after the other."

He raised the tube as if he was pointing his finger and fired three times.

"I'll be darned," said Loraine.

"Each one disintegrated like the tree," said Gears.

"Now the coup de grâce," said Blaze.

"Beg pardon?"

"Our Dragonskin armor, Loraine."

"Ah, good idea."

Bone hung the black garment on a metal silhouette target downrange mounted on a truck tire. "Feels almost like a wet suit, except for those hard little plate-like things inside," he said as he walked back.

"It's titanium and ceramic plating like scales on an alligator gar sandwiched between multiple layers of Graphene…the strongest, most impenetrable substance we know of."

"Right."

"Fire away, Padrino," said Blaze.

He raised his hand and discharged the weapon in one smooth move. The top flashed and when the smoke cleared there was a singed area in the dead center of the material.

The entire group walked down to the berm to inspect the armor.

"Looky here, didn't go through, but it melted a four inch area of the steel plating behind it. You're dead meat any way you look at it," observed Bone.

"The Graphene and ceramic plating diffused the charge when it stopped the beam…Yep, right on, Bone," said Gears.

"Let's go back in the lab and look at the high speed recording…I think I know what it is," said Blaze. "Twenty-two Gigapixel-per-second and a speed greater than 22,000 frames-per-second at full 1Mpx resolution should enable us to observe the destruction at the cellular level and confirm my hypothesis."

"My God in heaven," said Gears as they played the footage back for the fifth time.

"Purely a killing weapon, although very dangerous against armor and vehicles, there is no surviving any kind of hit for anything organic…even inside Dragonskin. The energy charge, which is a combination of a laser and a concentrated microwave, follows the fluid, be it blood, water or sap and disintegrates the entire tissue at the cellular level," stated Blaze.

"Watching the beam hit one of those chickens was like watching a water balloon explode in slo-mo," added Loraine.

"Just never seen a one burn at the same time it exploded, though," added Bone.

"Got to figure out some type of shield or screen," said Gears.

"Or a way to neutralize the beam...if a way exists," said Blaze.

THE PENTAGON
Washington DC

SecDef Burner Stewart waited for the secured Skype connection to complete. He checked the video feed from the BEF conference room and noted the familiar faces he could trust. "Ladies and gentlemen, it would appear we have the first evidence of alien contact from the invading Reptoid fleet. The South African mint was, for all intents and purposes, raided and a sizable stack of gold bars taken without setting foot inside the building."

"How was that possible, Mister Secretary?"

"One security guard claims he saw the cart vanish into thin air. There is a large hole burned though the top of the building that our near earth orbit satellites confirm...although the South African government claims it was an electrical fire, strong enough to burn though several inches of steel and four feet of reinforced concrete, of course. Oh...all the security camera digital files are claimed to be missing as well."

"Let me guess...the backup computers crashed at the same time...just like the emails in the Lois Lerner IRS scandal," Heater replied.

"Looks like they are following the same script."

"Any witnesses?"

"Actually, yes. I'll let Captain Lowe fill you in. He's one of my aides. I put him on full time duty scanning the web for any mention of suspicious activity on any social media...Bob, Heater McElhenny, COO of the BEF. Tell 'em what you found."

"There was a lot of chatter and speculation about a series of noises...explosions actually...overhead of downtown Pretoria. Hundreds heard them. But they appeared to emanate several miles from where the alien ship was spotted."

"Captain, do you have any witnesses of the craft itself?" Lucy asked.

"Uh, yes, ma'am. Here's a video he posted on his Facebook page." Lowe turned to a laptop he had wirelessly linked to the Skype connection. He rolled a cursor over the play icon and left clicked it. The video began to roll.

"I'm Dean Harmse and you are looking across Old Johannesburg Road at the South African Mint. What appears to be a ball-shaped alien spacecraft is attacking the roof of the building. I can see smoke coming up from the top of the building...I apologize for the poor quality of the video, but it is several hundred meters from my office building and I don't have a tripod for my phone. Wait! The laser has cut off!"

Once the two minute video had finished, Lucy stood up. "Captain thank you for the work finding that clip. I would imagine it has been removed from Facebook, am I right?"

"Yes, ma'am. There are no traces of it and the gentleman who posted it has disappeared as well."

"That does not surprise me in the least. I can confirm what we saw was a Reptoid Death Globe scout ship. If I'm not mistaken, it fired its defensive weapons several times. You have to know what you are looking for, but I believe I saw its pulse weapons discharging to the right of the screen. Would that be in the same direction the explosion were heard?"

"Using Google maps of Mister Harmse's place of employment, that would be north and that corresponds with the sounds of multiple explosions in the sky."

"Burner, do the South Africans claim any of their fighters were destroyed?...Either by accident or unknown causes?" Hollywood asked.

"Two JAS 39 Griffins on a routine training mission were reported to have had a midair collision over Pretoria at the time in question."

"I think we can rule that out, judging from what we I saw on the video." Lucy shook her head. "Those pilots never had a chance. Even the Reptoid scout ships have enough firepower to knock out almost any conventional Terrestrial fighter they will come across."

"So where does that leave us, Lucy?" Heater asked.

"That leaves us the unconventional." She winked.

***

CHAPTER SEVEN

EAGLE NEST
BEF underground facility

Bone pulled up to the main hangar and parked the Ford Expedition in one of the spots outside. He and Loraine got out, quickly walked inside and took the elevator to the main level.

"What's your plan, girl? We got an hour and a half before lunch."

"Lunch? You just had a second breakfast...Lucy told me everything."

"I thought the food police were supposed to be off duty...'Sides, I'm gonna do a leg routine. Already did my upper body yesterday and wouldn't want to get out of sequence."

"Right. I'm thinkin' about doing some laps in the pool. I want to do some cardio and it's already getting a little too hot outside for a run."

"Good idea. You can never drown with those puppies inflated like they are…"

She instantly backhanded him across his chest. "Ow, you big dummy! See what you went and made me do? I coulda bruised my hand…Your pecs are already like iron."

"You should see my abs of steel…and tookus of titanium."

"Pass," she said, shaking her head. "Men…All alike."

"And that's why you love me. See you outside the cafeteria at noon, Pard."

After leaving the men's locker room, Bone made his way into the weight room, stretched a bit and then settled in on the leg press machine. He had worked up quickly to 1,000 pounds and fifteen reps and was glistening from the effort. Out of the corner of his eye, he caught a dark-haired beauty entering the room with a white towel around her neck. Her skintight yoga pants and V-neck Lycra top matched her jet black pony tail and accented her well proportioned toned physique. *Whoa, it's that Raven chick Davy told me about.*

She set up on a lat pull machine and adjusted the weight to 110 pounds before she sat down on the bench and fastened the strap across her thighs. Grabbing the chromed bar above, she proceeded to complete ten reps of front pull downs and stopped to increase the weight to 130.

Bone took a couple of furtive glances in the mirror and pretended to be not interested, but his imagination was already working overtime. *OMG. How do these guys find such hotties with special skills. I never saw anything like her in the Corps.*

He moved to the leg extension machine, and set up for 160 pounds. His quad muscles rippled as he flexed them and straightened his lower legs, while holding on to the twin handles on either side of the seat. Bone took another peek at Raven, checking out the definition of her upper body. *Nice. Seriously nice...Weapon's grade nice.*

He used his towel and wiped the perspiration off the vinyl covered padded bench and then moved to a leg curl machine to set up for some femoral bicep exercises. He slipped the pin into a slot at 100 pounds for warm up.

Raven had moved to the adjoining identical machine and was already in position face down on the bench. She slipped her ankles under the heavily padded crossbar and began to curl her lower legs up ninety degrees. The affect on Bone was immediate.

Try as he might, he couldn't take his eyes off her backside. The muscles on the back of her thighs drew up and accentuated the heart shape of her tiny waist and sculpted butt as it raised up slightly from the bench. *Incredible...Absolutely incredible.* He was so mesmerized that he forgot to breathe. His scan slowly drifted up her body and as it reached her head, she turned and locked eyes with him—sparking like twin black diamonds, they captivated him instantly.

She smiled.

He coughed, the oxygen in his lungs depleted.

"You okay?"

"Yeah, thanks…just a little dry," he lied.

"We've got bottled water in the fridge over there."

"Appreciate it. Think I will."

As he walked to the unit, she studied his every move and liked what she saw.

"Hey, want one?" he called back.

"Sure," she purred.

He returned with two bottles of local spring water. "Shall I open it?"

"Please," she said as she continued her reps.

He broke the seal and set the bottle down within her reach before he opened his and took a big swig.

"All better?" she asked.

"Uh, huh, sure is…Nice day to be working out."

"That it is." The Greek beauty finished her set of leg curls and sat up straddling the bench. "Thanks for the water." She leaned over and took a sip, wiping the excess off her teeth with the tip of her tongue.

She did not do that…Christ that's so damned sexy. He suddenly felt self conscious, something he almost never did.

"Darrell Bone, is that right?"

"Yeah, but friends can call me just Bone. You're Raven…at least that's what Crockett said."

"How tall are you? Six nine?"

"Only if I wear boots…otherwise I'm only six eight."

"And you have big hands and big feet…I noticed."

Bone grinned at what he considered a funny observation. "You know what they say about guys with big hands and big feet…Big gloves and big boots."

She laughed, her dazzling smile making him return one. "That's not the saying I was thinking of." She took another sip.

Bone chuckled and thought for a microsecond about not using his best icebreaker line. But, being true to his impulsive self, let it flow, "Hell, I don't have a little dick…Just looks little on me."

Raven yanked the bottle away as icy cold water spurted out of her nose. They both began laughing instantly. Bone handed her his towel.

"Sorry…couldn't help myself. Actually I'm impulse control challenged or so they keep tellin' me."

She tried to regain her composure and was fairly successful as she dried her legs and the bench.

"Didn't know you had a drinkin' problem."

She grinned back at him. "Me neither. Heard a lot of lines, but never heard that one before." She returned his towel and locked eyes with him. "Do you know Kung Fu?"

"Was he that bad guy in the Charlie Chan movies?"

"No, I mean martial arts…do you know any?"

He grinned. "Just jerkin' your chain…I knew what you meant. My partner's an advanced Kung Fu gal…I only know some Karate and Marine Corps street fighting techniques, plus a few things I worked out on my own…Suppose my motto has always been fight to win. I don't really care what they call it."

"Interesting…Would you be up for a little sparring?"

Bone's mind raced. *Wow. That came out of friggin'
nowhere, but I'd be a chump to pass it up.* "Sure. Try not to
break my nose, though. I kinda like the way it is now...'Course,
wouldn't be the first time."

"Deal." Raven extended her hand. Bone took it and helped
the young warrior to her feet.

BLAZE'S LAB
Eagle Nest

Blaze opened the front of a very futuristic looking machine that
was about the size of a clothes dryer and placed the Reptoid
disruptor on a glass plate in the center.

"What's that?" Padrino asked.

"It's my own special invention. You're familiar with a MRI
aren't you?"

"Of course."

"I call this an EMRT for Elemental Magnetic Resonance
Tomography."

"I thought MRIs were only for organic tissue."

"I figured that as long as the material wasn't ferrous, the
principle would remain the same...except it could be made
much more powerful. The medical units range upwards to
7T...Teslas. I made this to go up to 30T for inorganic matter
through multiplicating capacitors. Handy if I want to look inside
something to see how it works without disassembling it."

Padrino shook his head. "Amazing...You do think outside
the box, don't you?"

"That what Doctor Ortowski taught me at Rice University when I was working on my doctorates."

She smiled, pressed the start button and she, Padrino and Gears watched the monitor as the unit made multiple passes over the tube.

"Well that looks pretty simple. Small cosmic power source, a tiny piece of neutronium catalyst interacting with rodinium through an emerald crystal...reminds me of an arc light. The activator button moves the neutronium in close proximity between the crystal and the rodinium and creates a laser heterodyned with a concentrated microwave through the coign...ergo, a total disruptor for organic tissue."

"Or in simpler terms...Somewhat like putting an egg inside a microwave oven except it's directional via laser," Padrino observed.

"I thought I said that."

"The problem still remains...do we shield against it or neutralize it?" added Gears.

"Exactly...we do both," said Blaze.

Lucy materialized in the lab. "Well, did we make some progress, children?"

Padrino looked at her and grinned. "Haven't been called a child in a long time."

"You're all children to me."

EAGLE NEST
BEF underground facility

Bone and Raven stretched their legs and twisted their torsos to limber up. He watched her bend forward at the waist and bring her face almost in contact with her knees. *Damn. If she's that flexible, she can probably stand flat-footed and still kick my head. Gonna have to be quick to keep from gettin' my ass beat in a New York minute.*

"BEF rules," she said. "Full contact is allowed, but no dislocations or broken bones."

"Yeah, I hear Dare frowns on that." Bone took in a big breath and let it out. He took two steps back and bent over slightly at the waist. "Show me what you got."

"With pleasure." A wicked little grin crossed her face as she assumed a defensive posture and then took a couple of tiny shuffle steps closer to him on the balls of her feet.

Bone watched as she sized him up and then had a strange sensation. Thoughts of a left hand sword attack, followed by a hammer fist to his groin flashed into his consciousness. Suddenly, he realized he had read her mind as he instinctively moved to block her left hand with his right and brushed aside the low hammer fist. He followed through with a swift slap to her cheek—not meant to injure, but to transmit the short message *you left an opening there*.

Christ...he's fast as a rattlesnake. She danced left and then right, looking for her next move. Bone took a sharp snap kick at her thigh. She blocked it, stepped back a few inches and executed a high spin kick at his head.

He ducked, caught the oncoming foot with his right hand and swept her left leg from underneath her as his other hand flashed out and grabbed her closest arm. Bone spread his arms, easily lifting her off the mat and holding her suspended for a moment.

What the hell? Nobody has ever done that to me! Raven brought her left leg up and around in an attempt to kick free from his grasp, but the effort was already too late. He released her and her own torque caused her to roll and fall on her side. She bounced back to her feet and assumed a defensive posture. *Settle down girl. You got this guy.*

She took in a couple of quick breaths and then threw a flurry of punches at him. A couple even connected on his rock hard abs, but he showed no evidence of even feeling it.

Dammit! It's like David and Goliath in here. She tried a four move combination—twin hammer fists to the face and chest with a snap kick to the groin followed almost instantly by a roundhouse kick to the head.

Bone blocked the first three and ducked under the roundhouse, actually increasing her spin as he pushed her thigh past and thumping her on the forehead with his cocked middle finger as her upper body spun past at knee level.

Ow. How the hell did he do that? Nobody does that!

"You're telegraphing your kicks, darlin'. I can see it when you set up," Bone said.

"Bullshit. You're sandbagging me, I know it. What kind of title do you hold? You've got to have a black belt," she said as she danced to the side.

He could sense her growing frustration. "None…Really, it's not even a belt. A drawstring actually…and light gray." He glanced down at his workout shorts and lifted the bow.

Her lighting fast double back-fist smacked his jaw and staggered him slightly. She attempted to follow up with a side hand chop to the neck.

Bone recovered well enough to block it and spin her around with a rapid push-pull of his own on each of her shoulders. He snaked his right arm out and secured a naked choke hold across Raven's neck and thrust his hip out as he brought her feet off the ground. Flexing his forearm muscles, he raised her chin slightly and cut off the blood flow in both carotid arteries. Her body went limp in seconds.

He released the hold and eased her to the mat. Gazing at her, he rubbed the tender red spot on the side of his jaw. *Jesus. Salty little shit, I'll give you that.* He straddled her and sat down on her thighs and then grabbed each of her wrists and placed his forearms across hers. Bone was taking no chances about what she might do when she came to.

After a few seconds, Raven's eyes fluttered open. Her pupils dilated briefly and then returned to normal as the face of her opponent came into focus. She tried to move, but couldn't. "How long was I out?"

"Not long…Ten maybe fifteen seconds. Wanna continue?"

She pursed her lips and shook her head.

"You're not hurt are you?"

"Just my ego…I've never been beaten."

"Me neither…Let me help you up."

He moved to the side and knelt , as she sat up and stretched her neck left and right. They locked eyes again for a moment and both grinned like Cheshire cats.

"It just looks little on me," she said. "Love it…So big boy, Where you taking us for dinner?"

"Understand they serve a good steak over at The Mill. Even have a small dance floor under the stars."

"They do indeed. Pick me up at my quarters…Seven sharp."

"I can do that…Laterbye."

She watched him walk toward the men's locker room for a moment, and then she turned and headed to the lady's with a sly grin on her face.

Bone draped his towel around his neck and pushed through the door into the locker room. A wiry redheaded man approached him and stuck out his hand.

"Winston Chisholm III, former Airborne, everybody just calls me Trey. I'm Rav's partner. Never saw anybody best her before."

Bone looked down at the 5' 8" *Raptor*. "Are you kiddin', bub? She let me." He shook his head and laughed. "She could have turned me every which way but loose if she had wanted to."

"Man!…She must really like you. That's first too…We call her 'Nevermore'…behind her back, that is."

Bone raised his eyebrows and cocked his head to the side. "You don't say?"

"I do."

"Sumbitch." He began to whistle to himself as he got undressed for his shower.

NORTH TEXAS REGIONAL AIRPORT
BEF Underground Headquarters

Lucy materialized and proceeded to Dare's office. She knocked twice and stepped inside as he was discussing fighter crew assignments with Flash Peterman.

"Excuse me, gentlemen. I don't mean to intrude."

Dare got to his feet. "Not at all…We were just finishing up reviewing the training status on our new hires. What can we do for you?"

"I've been checking on the progress down at Eagle Nest with Blaze and Gears. Things are developing as I had hoped, but I do need to meet with Partsman Meadows. My people aboard the Excalibur must to be aware of the physical interface requirements needed to power and control the cloaks we're building for all your aircraft."

"Sure, I'll have Tom call him down." Dare made his request over the interphone.

"You named your cruiser after a King Arthur's sword?" Flash asked.

She laughed. "Actually, it's the other way around…Some of my associates visited him many years ago. The early English were awed by their weapons and considered them to be gods. We made his sword aboard Excalibur and he named it after our ship. My friends were quite taken with him."

"Open mouth, insert foot. Sorry...I can't seem to wrap my head around how old your civilization is compared to ours. We must be pretty backwards in your eyes."

"Nonsense, Flash. I see great things in you and your friends. Beyond that, I'm going to be out there fighting with you. This battle isn't won...not by a long shot."

Partsman knocked on the office door jamb. "Boss, you wanted to see me?"

Dare motioned him in. "Our friend does. You'll know what she needs."

The BEF's Chief of Maintenance stuck out his hand. "Afternoon, Lucy. Nice to see you again...How may I assist you?"

"My engineers will be fabricating the field generators for your vessel's cloaks aboard Excalibur. Without the use of cosmic ray accumulators, they will need to tie in to your ship's energy source as well as to the CRTs to display Reptoid threats."

"And turn the devices on and off, I surmise...I can get you all the schematics on a flash drive, but for actual installation, it would help of one of their tech guys could come down and see how we physically rack the black boxes and run the cables to the cockpit. We have G forces to contend with and induction interference constraints with fire and explosion possibilities vis a vis the fuel system...among other things.

She smiled. "That's why I'm the pilot and you're the mechanic. I will defer to your judgment. The best thing I can do is get the Science Officer and Chief of Maintenance down here for some hands-on examination of the issues."

"Sound like a plan to me."

On the hangar deck—many feet below the surface—two small figures cloaked in silver-gray flight suits materialized. One was slightly over five feet five and the other stood five two. Both removed their helmets. The taller one extended his hand to Partsman.

"Greetings, sir...I am Reddak, Chief of Science aboard Excalibur at your service. Annuna has explained our dilemma, I presume?"

"My pleasure to meet you, sir. My friends call me Partsman. Lucy, I mean Annuna, has told me of your plans." He turned to the other gentleman. "You must be my counterpart, the Chief of Maintenance."

"Indeed. I am called Doppek...May we see the first vessel? I am curious to see how your culture deals with electrical power."

"Follow me gentlemen."

Meadows led them a short distance across the spotlessly maintained light blue epoxy painted floor to a McDonnell Douglas F-15 Eagle. The large fighter's exterior paint had been covered with a dull black radar absorbing material with thousands of tiny aramid discs to absorb high PRF radar beams. "All of our aircraft use a twenty-eight volt DC system run through an inverter with an output of 115 volts AC power at 400 hertz." He reached up and pressed two flush-mounted latches on the side of the fuselage. A large access panel opened up and he raised it to a point where the two air-charged pistons kept it in the up position.

"Here's what we call the avionics service bay. These black boxes are air data computers, gyros for the pilot's instrument display and so forth." He pointed to the cable coming out of the back of one. "Data is transmitted from here up to the cockpit. Power comes in here." He pointed to a smaller single wire. He took a screwdriver out of his overalls and turned a dzus fastener 90 degrees opening up a small fastener. Grabbing a handle built into the black box, he slid it out a few inches.

Partsman reached behind the unit and unscrewed the quick couplers on the two cables. He pulled the whole unit out and turned it around for the Tyranians to see. "That's how the cables hook up and we can change out a bad or damaged box in seconds. Any new equipment you create should, ideally, be compatible with the rack lock mechanism and be able to interface directly with either the AC or DC bus systems, depending on which source of electricity you choose."

Doppek nodded. "Primitive, but logical layout. Are the aircraft consistent within their type?"

"That's a good question. Actually, there are many differences between the single seat and trainer model fighters and major differences between the VTOL variations. I took the liberty of making a sixteen gig flash drive with all the aircraft manuals, wiring diagrams, photographs and specifications of the various connectors. Will you have any trouble accessing this data?" He held up the thumb-sized unit for them to see. "I seriously doubt if you guys use a USB type port any more…"

Reddal and Doppek shared a look.

"We should be able to access it without problem," the Science Officer replied with a slight nod. "I would like to see the cockpit of this fighter. I am curious as to how your battle space is displayed in such as tiny area."

"Absolutely…Let me get this unit reattached and we'll get a set of crew stairs installed."

Forty-five minutes later, the trio had inspected the F-18, the C-5M, M200 *Hawk*, M600 *Black Eagle,* M800 *Condor* VTOLs and the *Manta* unmanned reconnaissance fighter. Reddak bowed slightly to Partsman.

"You have been most accommodating and obviously possess wealth of mechanical knowledge, making this visit most productive. We shall contact you shortly with the first prototype and see to its testing." Once again he extended his tiny hand.

"Thank ya'll for coming. I'm glad you've been on our side all this time…It really is an honor to be able to work with you." He shook each of the Tyranian's hands before they replaced their helmets and called to their battlecruiser for transport.

EARTH'S THERMOSPHERE
SOUTH POLE

"Fleet Commander Klsth, all of the harvested protein has been processed and packaged. Do you wish to distribute rations to the other ships?" asked Sub-Commander Prlk.

"Excellent idea, we should reward the fleet with a feast for this abominable wait while we finish our repairs. Has there been any activation of Tyranian vessels by our detector screens?"

"None, Sire. There is only one of their Maulers outside the orbit of the Tellurian satellite."

"Still licking their wounds, I would surmise...Good. You may tell the fleet to disengage the cloaking screens for the transport of the protein containers. Do not take anymore time than is required, as we are highly vulnerable with both shields and screens down. Maintain a high state of readiness with our detectors."

"As you wish, Fleet Commander," the monstrous Prlk replied as he turned and waddled out of the command center on his two tree-trunk thick legs.

SOUTHERN OCEAN
USS *ALVIN YORK*

The newest Zumwalt class stealth destroyer, USS *Alvin York* cruised some 550 nautical miles off the coast of Enderby Land. The new type greyhound of the sea strongly resembled the *Merrimac* ironclad of the Civil War. Her shape was designed to deflect radar returns away from enemy ships and aircraft. Inside her eighty foot wide beam, she could carry twenty long range missile in her Mk 57 cold launch system.

She was testing the US Navy's top secret satellite killer missile in a desolate area of Antarctic waters. A decades-old low earth orbit satellite was decaying into the outer reaches of the atmosphere and could pose a threat to thousands if it plummeted intact into an inhabited metropolitan area. Their maiden voyage mission was to intercept the six ton behemoth and destroy it, along with the forty-three pounds of enriched uranium enclosed inside the power source's nuclear reactor.

"Captain to the ops center. Captain to the ops center," blared the speaker on the ultramodern bridge.

"What in hell?" said Captain James Picard as he got up from his padded gray leather command chair and headed to the hatch between the bridge and the ops center. "What is it, Jonesie?" he asked of the PO3 manning the radar array screens.

"You may not believe this, sir, but I have four huge blips that just popped up three hundred miles directly overhead Antarctica in the thermosphere. Didn't come in...just suddenly appeared."

"Sure it's not an aberration or some type of inversion?"

"No, sir, way too high for that. They're actually at the outer edge of the atmosphere almost in the exosphere...outer space, sir...and they're stationary."

"Opinion, Mister Jones."

The black Petty Officer glanced about the room that resembled, in many ways, something that might have been designed by video gamers with its array of flat screen displays. "Sir, these are hard blips, each over a mile long and a half mile wide..."

"What? That can't be."

"Yes, sir, no question about it, they're that big and metallic. I, uh, well, sir...I think they're, uh...ET...You know? UFOs..."

"Captain, they're pinging us with something...don't know what it is, but it's something. Never seen it before," said PO2 Karen Wade.

Captain Picard turned to the PO1 manning the comm center. "Sound battle stations, Mister Knudson. Make ready tubes one through four of the Star Killers."

"Aye-aye, sir."

Knudson lifted the Plexiglas shield covering the large red button inset into the panel in front of him. The twenty-nine year old E-6 subconsciously took in a deep breath and pressed it, knowing that it was the first time the new ship had gone to that readiness state for real. Klaxons throughout the ship began sound simultaneously, sending the well-trained crew into frenzied motion.

High-Def digital cameras were already in place and had been recording essentially every inch of the operations center and bridge. Activation of the battle stations readiness state initiated a direct uplink to a geostationary MILSATCOM satellite that was part of the Global Information Grid in the TSAT Network Integration Group and sent the feed directly to the HQ US Fleet Force Command at Hampton Roads in Norfork, Virginia. TSAT allowed ultra-secure real-time communication throughout the entire worldwide US military satellite network. It was known basically as Battle Command-On-The-Move capability.

SECDEF STEWART'S OFFICE
Pentagon

Willamena "Bill" Parker, Executive Assistant to every Secretary of Defense since 1970, answered the incoming call from USFLTFORCOM headquarters. Her looks and demeanor reminded many people of Katharine Hepburn.

"Good afternoon, Secretary Stewart's office."

"Bill, Admiral Cooke. I have flash message for Burner."

"I'll connect you to the Secretary...Please hold." She pressed the key placing the Fleet Forces Commander on hold and then activated the intercom. "Sir, 'Blood and Guts' is on line one with a flash message."

"I've got it, Bill." *What the hell this time?* He reached over and lifted the receiver. "What's up, Percy?"

He knew the Admiral despised his given name, but he had been a constant pain in the ass for the former Chairman of the Joint Chiefs, Charger Valenti—one of the first conservative flag officers axed by the incoming president. Cooke had been promoted from Vice Admiral to four star Admiral when he was assigned to Norfolk.

"Mister Secretary, our first stealth destroyer, USS *Alvin York* went to battle stations, three minutes ago off Antarctica. There is something huge in at the edge of the atmosphere giving solid radar returns."

"How huge are you talking about?"

"Bigger than any thing known to exist on this world, Burner...I'm talking over a mile long...and there's four of them."

The former Air Force four star general's heart sank. *There's no time left.* "Send me the link to the live feed."

"Aye-aye, sir. You should be seeing what I'm seeing momentarily." Admiral Cooke turned to his technician. "You heard the man."

SOUTHERN OCEAN
USS *ALVIN YORK*

Captain Picard looked over the shoulder of the petty officer manning the radar. The four targets were still stationary. He turned to the weapons station controller.

"Commander Sanders, give me a lock on all four. Stand by."

"Aye-aye, sir." He tapped a command on his key board and using a roller ball, right clicked each bogie. A green box appeared around the individual returns, and then turned red when the lock was confirmed. "We have a lock on four, sir...range 312 to 318 miles."

"Very well."

Seconds passed before an intense sensor beam passed over the ship's position. A high pitched squeal came over the electronic warfare officer's headphones. He looked at his flat screen display and saw a huge spike at the right of the grid pattern.

"Sir! We have an unknown rider probing us with a high gigahertz radar beam. I don't recognize it as any one I'm...Jesus!" He yanked the headphones off as the tone went even higher and the amplitude almost defended him. "Ahh!

Dammit!" Ensign Swanson yelled as he pushed the headphones away.

"What is it? Swanson? What's happening?" Picard demanded.

"Not certain, sir, but I think they just locked on us!"

Picard wasted no time at all. "Sanders, fire one through four and ready another eight…Helm, flank speed, evasive action."

On the bow of the ship along both gunwales, four missiles gas generators inside the canisters lit off with a monstrous roar, lifting the deadly weapons up simultaneously past the square-covered hatches that kept them hermetically sealed from the harsh sea environment. Once well clear of the ship, the solid-fuel rocket motors ignited. In seconds the missiles blasted through Mach 5 accelerating straight up at the bogies. Thin white trails of smoke stretched heavenward until they were out of sight.

A sailor on the bridge watched the spectacle and crossed his fingers. "Go, baby, go."

***

CHAPTER EIGHT

SECDEF STEWART'S OFFICE
Pentagon

The silver-haired former fighter pilot watched as the MILSATCOM logo gave way to multiple live shots on his eighty-five inch screen that had just lowered down from the ceiling on the far wall across from his desk. There was a high orbit sat picture of USS *Alvin York* moving in an evasive pattern at high speed through the choppy Antarctic waters. Over twenty miles away, her maintenance and supply tender escort, the Oliver Hazard Perry class frigate, USS *Harold Baker*—named for his predecessor—was trying to keep pace.

Another shot inside his giant plasma unit showed the frenetic activity inside of the Operations Center on board the *Alvin York*. There were still four white smoke trails heading toward space visible above the ship from the satellite shot. Burner flipped up a control panel cover that was inside his top left hand drawer of his desk and keyed in three numbers. Ten seconds later, Tom Tallman at the BEF Ops center in Denison came on one of the eight screens in his giant multiplex wall unit.

"Tallman here, sir."

"Tom, get Dare and Heater, immediately."

"Yes, sir." He nodded and in three seconds, the view switched to the conference room of the underground facility. Dare, Heater and Lucy were just entering the door and took seats at the large walnut table.

"Activity, Burner?" asked the head of the Black Eagle Force.

"You could say that. Glad you're there too, Lucy…You can see what I see. This is real time. The *Alvin York* just fired Star Killer missiles at four giant unknowns in the thermosphere above the south pole and is presently taking evasive action."

EARTH'S THERMOSPHERE
SOUTH POLE

"Fleet Commander! A surface vessel is scanning us with some primitive electronic pulse signals," said Sub-Commander Prlk.

"Shields up!" commanded Klsth.

"Sir, over half of our protein is in transport mode, we will lose it if we raise shields."

"I said shields up, fool! Would you rather we be vulnerable to attack or loose part of our replaceable food supply?"

"The Tellus vessel has launched four projectiles at our position, Commander! One is targeted for each of our ships." said Weapons Officer Krrlp from his station.

"Knock them down, and then take out that impertinent insect of a Tellurian ship that dared to fire on us."

"It is very small and difficult to track, Sire. We can not lock our pulse projector on its position. Apparently they are using some type of physical cloaking, plus they are moving erratically."

"Did I ask its size or position, Krrlp? I said take it out!"

SOUTHERN OCEAN
USS *ALVIN YORK*

At thirty-five knots, the *Alvin York* was almost thirty knots below its classified top speed. The twin screws beneath the hull spun quickly up to their maximum revs and soon the bow was cutting through the choppy Southern Ocean waters sending icy spray in a deep V shape as the vessel tried to evade whatever retribution the monster alien ships far above would inevitably send down.

The ship heeled almost forty degrees to starboard, nearly putting her gunwale into the frothy waters. Fourteen foot swells broke over the needle-like prow as she rolled out of the pre-programmed evasive pattern.

Winds were already at a steady forty knots and the entire section of the ocean was covered with whitecaps as the top of the green waves tore off.

"Captain, we have first stage separation," Commander Sanders reported. "Second stage ignition is a go across the board." He watched as the hypersonic missiles accelerated past Mach 11 in the thinner air.

"Keep me advised," he replied. Picard spun to speak to the Electronic Warfare Officer. "Swanson, how's it coming?"

"Sir, I have run through every jamming routine we've got, but they keep modulating their freqs and coming back at us. I'm not certain they can maintain a lock...they seem to be sweeping for us because the beam amplitude keeps varying."

"I'm thinking the random course changes and stealth are working...somewhat. Keep at it."

Video feed from the warheads initiated automatically once the missiles passed 100 miles, but the mile-long targets were just tiny specks. The aptly named *Star Killers* kept accelerating to their maximum design speed of 25,000 miles per hour—almost 7 miles per second—fast enough to overcome the Earth's gravitational pull.

Just aft of the radar and guidance package in the nose cones, the warhead itself consisted of a small cylinder of highly explosive Duo-C-8 compound—a vast upgrade of the old reliable C-4. The purpose of it was to disperse the surrounding rods of one of the densest materials known to man—depleted uranium. Fifteen of the half-inch thick, three foot long rods would transfer the immense kinetic energy of the warhead into whatever it hit.

"Range one hundred miles, Captain. We have visual."

"Holy crap. Look at those, those…"

EARTH'S THERMOSPHERE
SOUTH POLE

Three of the Reptoid ships vanished when their cloaks engaged. On the bridge of the fourth, Captain Brzll had delayed implementation to allow the full transport of his ship's intended cargo of processed protein slabs.

His subordinate trembled as he watched the visaplates showing the approaching missile. He turned one of his four eyes around to gaze at the most rotund of all the Reptoids. "Captain, Fleet Commander Klsth ordered us to initiate the shields…"

"Silence!" he thundered as his upper left tentacle lashed out—the razor-sharp claw on the end of one of the two finger-like appendages caught one of the junior officer's offending eyes and severed it cleanly—stalk and all. It flew across the bridge and thwacked against a bulkhead before it fell quivering at the feet of the ship's navigator and blinked twice.

"We need only ten more *drdtz* and the shipment will be complete. I didn't come this far to go home empty. Never question my judgment again! We have nothing to fear from these backward natives."

"No, Sire," replied the chastened subordinate. He tried to staunch the flow of his gray bodily fluid with one of his tentacles, but it dripped down his scaly trunk and pooled between his legs.

Three of the eye stalks of the navigator swiveled around the room, and then one of his four tentacles flicked out, grabbed the apple-sized eye and stalk from the deck and slipped between his massive tooth-lined jaws. A single smack and it disappeared down its giant maw.

SOUTHERN OCEAN
USS *ALVIN YORK*

"Three of the targets have disappeared!"

Captain Picard leaned over Petty Officer Jones to confirm his radar screen only showed a single alien blip. "Crap. Where did they go?"

Up on the visual feed from four missiles, three of the screens showed only the blackness of space with a sprinkling of tiny stars in the background—the fourth ship was only fifty miles away and was clearly seen rapidly getting larger in the frame. Three bright green spots abruptly appeared on the screens where the cloaked ships were supposed to be. The spots flared to full screen and then instantly they all went blank.

"What the hell was that?" Picard asked. "Did they detonate prematurely?"

"Negative, Captain. Something just took them out. One is still running though...Impact in three...two...one."

CONFERENCE ROOM
BEF Headquarters

The room was rapidly filling up since Dare, Heater and Lucy had entered. Partsman, Widowmaker and Bad were taking their seats—all eyes were fixated on the giant concave screen with the multiple views.

"Jesus, that damn ship can move...Oh, beg pardon, ma'am," Widowmaker apologized to Lucy.

"Perfectly all right, young man." She looked back up at the screen as the camera feed from the three missiles went to empty space. "Oh, dear, they got their screens back up."

"One didn't," observed Dare as the giant craft got larger and larger in the frame until they could see the actual green lambent surface and the aperture of the transporter on the bottom—if only briefly. The picture flashed bright white and then black as the missile detonated. "Will that one missile take it down, Lucy?"

"I seriously doubt it, but we can hope it hit a vital area."

"Partsman, hit the Eagle Nest relay. They should be watching this, too," said Heater.

Meadows nodded and a small screen within a screen opened in the lower right hand corner showing Blaze, Gears, Bone and Loraine had just joined the viewing at the ranch.

Farmer & Stienke

**EARTH'S THERMOSPHERE
SOUTH POLE**

The *Star Killer* fuse detonated a few milliseconds before contact, sending the uranium rods tumbling and blasting through the *T-Cruiser's* outer hull. The giant ship shuddered from the impact as they ripped and demolished everything in their path. Two of the rods passed completely through, flipping end over end back out into the cold vacuum of space on the top side.

"Shields up! Damage report!" Captain Brzll bellowed as he flapped all his tentacles up and down.

Buzzers and flashing blue lights on the bridge control panels announced the significant devastation the missile had inflicted.

"Hull breaches on lower level and on level one. Shields and cloak generators destroyed, accumulator numbers three and four...damage reported. Transporter off line, pulse generators available at sixty percent and sixteen dead," the maintenance officer cringed when he finished his summary.

**SOUTHERN OCEAN
USS *ALVIN YORK***

"Direct hit on target remaining!" Commander Sanders yelled.

A roar of applause broke out in the ops center.

"Donnie, give me eight more...ripple fire. Take that big son of a bitch down!"

150

"You got it, sir." He pressed the launch buttons on the already prepped Mk 37 canisters in half-second intervals. Doors covering the VLS tubes on either side of the ship's bow snapped open in response—one after another in sequence—the cold launch systems blasted the thirty foot long missiles from their protective cocoons. Once clear of the ship, the red and blue avengers streaked skyward in a series of blinding flashes. "Missiles away. Telemetry looks good."

Two hundred yards off the port bow, a brilliant flash of green light from above impacted the water. In a few milliseconds 1,000,000 gallons of water were vaporized by an incredibly powerful laser pulse from the outer reaches of the atmosphere. A huge cloud of stream formed almost instantly and rolled across the surface with the howling winds.

"Holy crap!" One of the seamen on watch on the bridge yelled out. "Cap'n! You need to see this!"

Picard hustled forward. "What is it?" He turned to see the cloud drift away behind them through the bridge window. Another laser beam stuck four hundred yards dead astern, with the same effect. "Jesus! That beam had to be a thousand feet across!"

The automated helm control rolled the ship hard to port. The captain grabbed onto a nav display table to keep his feet. The ship wallowed a bit as she turned across the wind and took the swells at an oblique angle. Several times the stern lifted high enough to partially cavitate the huge twin screws driven by the giant electric motors, causing the asymmetric torque load on the propeller shafts to send vibrations straight to the keel beam.

"Son of a bitch!" Picard muttered as the entire ship shook with the chatter.

CONFERENCE ROOM
BEF Headquarters

"*Alvin York* just launched eight more Killers! Oorah!" shouted Dare.

The room erupted in cheers.

"Go get 'em, Navy!" yelled Bad Poole.

Then all eyes focused on the satellite view of the new destroyer.

"Oh, goodness, the remaining three Reptoid ships are targeting your vessel with their pulse lasers."

"Can they take a partial hit from one of those, Lucy?"

"Not at all, Dare. Those weapons took out two of our Maulers and they had shields."

"Any chance your new ships could get here in time?" asked Heater.

She just shook her head. "Our Mauler is on the opposite side of the planet from your south pole and at Lagrangian Point 2. They cannot actually detect the Reptoid vessels due to the inclination of the earth. We could easily reach their ships with our energy beams if we were in a position to see them, but the enemy is far too close to the atmosphere of Tellus to make that feasible. We could literally burn away much of the ozone layer in your southern hemisphere or possibly even set the entire atmosphere on fire. It's a case of having weaponry too powerful for the situation." She looked up at the Eagle Nest screen. "Blaze, have you and Gears had any breakthroughs?"

"We've hit a stone wall right now, Lucy."

SOUTHERN OCEAN
USS *ALVIN YORK*

Captain Picard glanced back at the ship's stern to see another monstrous green flash impact the ocean five hundred yards astern, causing a geyser of superheated salt water steam to blast up and form a half mile wide mushroom cloud.

The ship's wake, a churning light blue zigzag line in the tortured dark waters stretched back for miles between a dozen similar smoke-like formations. His mind raced back to history classes he had taken at Annapolis. *Smoke screens. They used them to hide behind. It's worth a chance.* He pushed away from the navigation table and stepped back into the ops center.

"Helm! Hard to port, heading two one zero!"

"Aye-aye, Captain."

The ship rolled into a max performance turn as he overrode the programmed evasive maneuver.

Jim Picard glanced over at the eight screens showing live video of the sole visible target. Bright green flashes appeared from the blackness nearby. "Donnie, launch two missiles at each of those invisible sons of bitches that are shooting at us."

"Captain, those Star Killers are radar guided. I can't shoot at them if we don't have radar contact."

"Can't you do manual guidance? Anything?"

"Not until the missile is out past one hundred miles."

Picard checked the distance to target on the first of the eight missiles the ship had ripple fired. *Less than a hundred miles to go.* A thunderous laser pulse blast tore into the sea three hundred yards off the starboard side.

"Give me six missiles at the remaining target...take over manually, and then aim at their laser pulses...Can you do that?"

"I'll do my best, sir." Sanders knew the system had impulse jets to make minor corrections once the guidance fins became ineffective in the upper atmosphere. He had even done so with one missile in the simulator.

His hands directed the roller ball over the damaged Reptoid ship. He locked it up and launched six missiles on a half second separation, not wanting to take the chance of any two colliding in flight.

"Sir, it would really help if I had two more sets of hands for the other missiles."

Picard glanced over and gave orders. "OD, you're one and CPO Barker, you're the other. Take a seat at those monitors and follow Donnie's orders to the letter. Clear?"

"Aye-aye, sir," came the joint reply.

EARTH'S THERMOSPHERE
SOUTH POLE

Weapons Officer Krrlp noted the incoming missiles that rapidly approached the fourth *T-Cruiser*. "Fleet Commander, the Tellurian missiles are almost upon Captain Brzll's ship."

"Let it be a lesson to those who defy my orders. Our shields will protect us. I want that pesky little craft below sunk! Do I have to remove you from duty and do it myself?"

"No, Sire. We are getting closer ever time we fire," he replied.

On the partially disabled fourth vessel, things were much different.

"Shields up! I demand it!" Brzll screamed. His tentacles flailed nervously as the ship's weapons officer counted down the time to impact.

One after, another the eight warheads detonated—sending their deadly payload of depleted uranium rods rampaging though the uncloaked vessel. At 40,000 feet per second, they sliced through almost anything they contacted without slowing down appreciably. One exited the bridge floor directly between Captain Brzll's legs. His bodily fluids sprayed the overhead with a fine gray mist. The only thing left of him were a few scattered teeth and eight tentacle claws.

The ship immediately began to roll as its navigation control panel exploded. Life support systems went next and the huge craft began venting its noxious yellow-green atmosphere into outer space. Those Reptoids nearest the narrow breaches in the hull were sucked out into the vacuum as the ship's artificial environment failed to maintain pressure. Once the inertialess drive went off-line, the earth's gravitational force took over.

Slowly at first, the green transport ship drifted out of formation. It began to accelerate as it fell in cold silence toward the white ice cap of the Antarctic over three hundred miles below.

SOUTHERN OCEAN
USS *ALVIN YORK*

"She's losing altitude, Captain! I think we got her!" Sanders hollered.

"Now, see if you gentlemen can hit the cloaked ones...We know where they are now!" He turned to the helmsman. "Come right ten degrees. Get us under those damned clouds."

Two more monster laser pulses slammed into the sea only a few hundred feet either side of the ship.

EAGLE NEST
Conference Room

Blaze watched intently as the video feed continued. "It's coming down! Look at the range to target display!"

"You're right. They must have knocked out the inertialess drive," Gears said. "Sixteen feet per second squared."

"What's that?" Loraine whispered to Padrino.

"Acceleration of earth's gravity…in a near vacuum."

Raven came in and took a seat. "What's goin on?"

"Our stealth missile destroyer is dukin' it out with the Reptoids down near the south pole," Bone replied without taking his eyes off the screens.

"How are they doing?"

"Looks like they got one and are still shooting. Got six birds flying…hold it…Wow, look! The missiles have veered off course out into empty space."

"No…They're steering them manually to where those green pulses are originating. That's where the cloaked ships are," Blaze said.

"How far are the missiles from the enemy?" Loraine asked.

Gears pointed to a screen from Commander Sander's station. "One fifty or less. Go baby go!"

Blaze got a look on her face that relayed her extreme concentration.

Lucy glanced at the screen from Eagle Nest and saw the furrows forming on the young redhead's forehead, nodded and smiled.

SOUTHERN OCEAN
USS *ALVIN YORK*

The cloud of cooled steam began to sink and form a dense fog bank. The Antarctic horizon rapidly disappeared as the destroyer slashed though the oncoming waves and the icy spray drifted past the bridge.

Twenty seconds. Come on, dammit. Another four hundred yards. Captain Picard glanced up through a tiny portal in the overhead of the bridge.

There was a huge flash of green and the entire ship was circumambiented—she vanished in a millisecond. A geyser of sea water steam went up from where the mighty ship had been.

CONFERENCE ROOM
BEF Eagle Nest

A piercing high-pitched squeal blasted out of the speakers and all of the monitors went dark, except for the six headed for the cloaked alien ships and the live satellite feed from the Southern Ocean—with the view from BEF headquarters. In an instant the room was deathly silent.

"Oh, my God," Blaze gasped as she lifted her hand to her mouth.

"What happened?" Loraine leaned over to Bone.

He shook his head. "A direct hit…They were so damned close to hiding."

Raven reached over and took his hand. She had tears in her eyes. He placed his other hand on hers and then wrapped his arm around her quivering body and pulled her close.

Blaze leaned in closer to the big screen. "We still have telemetry from six of those Star Killer missiles. It looks as if the Reptoids stopped firing."

AURORA: INVASION

BEF HEADQUARTERS
Conference Room

Lucy had also noticed the bright green pulses were no longer emanating from the inky blackness. "It is reasonable to assume that they monitored the radar search frequencies and ECM transmissions of the *Alvin York*. Once she was destroyed they saw no reason to keep firing. They used up a tremendous amount to power in knocking her out."

"What is their source of energy?" Bone asked. "I remember when they came to Cross looking for plutonium."

"These ships are much more advanced that those older scout ships…Judging from where they were holding above the south pole, I have to believe that they were utilizing your planet's magnetic line of flux to collect cosmic rays," Lucy commented.

"Of course! The lines of flux concentrate the rays and bombard the poles. They must have developed a system similar to your Tyranian accumulators," Blaze commented.

"It takes a lot of cosmic energy to make a laser pulse like the ones we saw," Gears said.

"Almost immeasurable amounts, actually," Lucy replied. "Those Reptoids will have to maintain position around one of the poles for some time to completely recharge their transport ships. The smaller harvestor ships, known as Reapers, and the Death Globes will still be a threat."

159

Blaze looked over at the one of the other monitors. Suddenly, the feed of the star speckled empty sky went blank and was replaced by a single Greek letter *Delta*. "Wait a second! The proximity fuse didn't go off because of the Reptoid cloak, but the backup contact fuse did! Hey, there's another one and another..."

Both conference rooms exploded with a huge cheer as five of the six *Star Killers* made contact. The last one—the only weapon that didn't strike its target showed a small explosion off to the edge of the viewing frame before it streaked past the three cloaked ships and began its long voyage out of the solar system.

SECDEF STEWART'S OFFICE
Pentagon

"Admiral Cooke on one again, sir."

Burner took one last look at the slowly dissipating cloud of steam that was formerly USS *Alvin York* on his big screen, and then punched his intercom. "Thanks, Bill." He switched to line one. "Stewart."

"Guess you saw?"

"I did." He struggled to keep his voice from breaking. *On my watch, dammit to hell.*

"At least we got one of the bastards and may have done some damage on the others."

"Small consolation."

"Guess I better put a call into Chairman Parsons and break the news."

"You'll do no such thing."

"Excuse me, sir?"

"I didn't stutter, Percy."

"Mister Secretary, we just lost a three and a half billion dollar first class ship of the line and one hundred and thirty-six patriotic Americans…I have to make a report to the Joint Chiefs."

"You do and you'll be a God damned ensign by Saturday…is that clear?"

There was an extended silence on the other end and then: "Don't suppose you care to tell me what's going on?"

"Not at this time BG. I just know it's vital we keep this from that gutless wonder in the White House…and General Parsons at the Pentagon is not much better."

"Well, I can agree with that…on both parts. Parsons couldn't shine Valenti's shoes and we're on the same page with our so-called commander-in-chief…God help us."

"Give me forty-eight hours and you'll get a complete briefing or none of us will be here."

"Jesus H. Christ! You're not kidding are you, Burner?"

"Not hardly, BG, not hardly."

"You're gonna owe me big time, you know that."

"I know…Just one last thing."

"And that would be?"

"If you still know how to pray…now would be a good time."

***

CHAPTER NINE

EARTH'S THERMOSPHERE
SOUTH POLE

"Damage report!" thundered Fleet Commander Klsth as the blue lights flashed on the bridge. "Turn off that infernal buzzer. I cannot think with all that noise!" He spun around, his four tentacles lashing out in a semicircle.

The other Reptoids gave him a wide berth in his fit of rage. He turned back to his weapons operator who was busy silencing the various warnings.

"Krrlp! How could you let this happen? I directed you to engage the shields and destroy that fly-spec of a boat. You allowed their minuscule little toys damage three of my ships!"

"Sire, I followed your order explicitly…All the officers know the punishment for disobeying any directive."

"Are you mocking me? I should take your head off!" He drew back two tentacles and extended his claws menacingly.

Krrlp's rearmost two eyes grew wide and followed every movement of his Fleet Commander's extremities. "Your plan was an excellent one, Sire. No one knew that this inferior species that infests Tellus was capable of any weapon that could penetrate our shields. Our knowledge of them is far from complete. The Emperor cannot hold you personally responsible for failures in our military intelligence community."

Mention of the Emperor gave Klsth pause. He knew full well the wrath of the eleven foot tall leader of the Reptoid planet Draco orbiting Thuban—a white giant star, 250 times more luminous than Sol—in the Alpha Draconis system had a mercurial temper that left its own bloody swath through the ranks of former fleet officers and commanders. The brilliant thought of pinning the major tactical setback in their plans on a subordinate seemed to lose its luster.

"Indeed, it is so…Damage report and be quick about it."

Knowing that his quick thinking had likely saved his life, Krrlp ran through the list of damages.

Klsth seethed. "How can a warhead no bigger than my leg have caused so much destruction? Inconceivable!" He turned to the head of maintenance. "You, Krrk! When will we be back to 100%?"

The smallish—standing just under seven feet tall—technician brought all four of his appendages to his sides in a reptilian version of coming to attention. "Sire, one of our Reaper vessels was so badly damaged, it will only be useable as spare parts. Three Death Globe scout fighters were likewise rendered out of commission for an extended time. Our pulse projector is damaged, but my men report that repairs should take no longer than one cycle of Tellus. Exterior hull breaches were small and the adjoining decks were all sealed off using standard protocols. Only five crew members were sacrificed when their atmosphere vented to space before we secured the connecting bulkheads and plugged the floors or ceilings in the affected decks."

"When will you be able to effect repairs to the outer hull?"

"One half cycle should be more than enough time for the EVAs. Our replicator is off-line, but the other two remaining T-Cruiser mother ships can handle any fabrication of hull plates. We may have to use a Death Globe to ferry parts back and forth. The transporter on Captain Lssps' ship is, unfortunately, permanently disabled. Only one of the Tellurian missiles struck his ship, but the damage was to critical components."

Fleet Commander Klsth snapped his massive jaws open and closed twice and then let out a blood curdling roar. Krrk stepped back fearful that he would become a casualty as a result of being the bearer of bad news.

Klsth waved his tentacles toward an elevator to the bridge as his eyes grew bigger than softballs. "What are you doing standing around here talking? Get to work!"

Krrk bent forward a the waist and waddled away as quickly as his stubby legs could carry him.

Slowly tumbling due to the asymmetrically loaded cargo of compressed beef and human protein, the stricken *T-Cruiser* once commanded by Captain Brzll accelerated though Mach 4 in the mesosphere as the outer surface began to heat up significantly. The nose lowered slightly and the hull glowed a cherry red.

Inside the mile long vessel, the bodies of the suffocated crew—bloated and blacked from exposure to the cold vacuum—tumbled from the floor to the wall and then to the ceilings of the craft, like macabre monster dolls.

At twenty-five miles up, the *T-Cruiser* reached its maximum speed, Mach 5, and plunged like a flaming arrow through the stratosphere for the center of the most desolate continent on Earth. It screamed downward in a perfectly vertical free fall, blasted almost instantly through the two mile thick ice cap and finally buried itself in bedrock a mile below the ice.

Shock from the impact registered on seismographs across the globe and caused an avalanche of shattered ice to tumble down the impact shaft and bury the crushed remains of the alien warship for all time.

UNITED STATES SEISMIC STATION
McMurdo Station, Antarctica

The largest research station on the continent was operated through the United States Antarctic Program, a branch of the National Science Foundation and included a seismic module.

The base had been established in 1951 and housed over 1,258 residents.

Kellie Cunningham, the head of the geology team at McMurdo got up from her chair where she had been taking her turn monitoring the seismometer unit. She stretched her arms over her head, and then bent over and touched the palms of her hands to the floor. "Got to go to the gym after my shift...getting stiff."

"Yeah, noticed," said her field geologist, Mark, with a grin.

"Going to refresh my coffee. Need any?"

"I'm good."

She walked over to the coffee bar at the side of the small building and started pouring the strong black brew into her brown US Geology Survey insulated cup. The building shook and the floor seemed to rise, and then fall back down. She staggered, spilled some of the hot coffee on the back of her hand. "Ow! Damn!" She set the pot back on the burner, kissed the coffee off her knuckles and scurried over to join Mark, already at the seismometer.

"Holy cow! Eight point six on the Richter," he read from the graph.

"Not an earthquake. Must have been a meteor."

"Too big for a meteor...I'd say asteroid."

"That's going to break off some big chunks from the ice shelf," observed Kellie. "Better put out an iceberg alert."

CONFERENCE ROOM
BEF Eagle Nest

"I've got an idea," Blaze said as her face softened. "If we make the assumption that the mother ships must remain in the general vicinity of one of the poles and the airspace over the north pole is under direct surveillance by the Mauler *Excalibur*, we eliminate the need to search the northern hemisphere...at least initially."

Gears agreed, "But that still leaves us with a huge area...Antarctica is a big place."

"Five point four million square miles, give or take," she replied. The Pacific coast lies slightly over seventy degrees latitude and the Atlantic is only a few degrees farther south."

Mike shook his head. "That's only four thousand, one hundred and fifty two miles across...Piece of cake, sis."

She shot him a look. "Hold on...I haven't told you my idea yet."

He shrugged. "Speak, mighty priestess of the great unknown, we're listening."

"Jerk...Remember when we used drones with missiles to simulate the F-16s and lured the Chinese J-20s to engage us off the west coast?"

"Sure," Jill replied. "They were decoys equipped to simulate the radar signature of the Falcons...Worked like a champ."

"Right. If we used a drone to ping the Reptoid mother ships, they would likely fire at them, giving their positions away. That would give us the chance to engage them."

"With what? You do know they are over 300 miles up?"

"Oh, yeah…But it could work on the Reaper ships and those little scouts. They come within range of our fighters."

"That's true, but they will not be holding in the polar magnetic flux," Jill said quickly. "There's nothing for them to harvest down on the south pole…except a few thousand scientists spread out across the continent and a couple dozen penguins. I would bet they go for a higher concentration of humans or animals."

"India, Indonesia, Malaysia, Argentina, Brazil, South Africa," Bone added.

"The Congo, Peru, and China, if they go that far north," said Loraine.

Blaze nodded. "Oh, my God…What about a world cup soccer match? They could knock off 200,000 in one place."

"Holy crap. I hadn't thought about that," Bone said. "Some concerts pull together a hundred thousand or more and what about beaches?…They would all be sitting ducks."

Heater McElhenny nodded. "Guys, we obviously have our work cut out for us. Put your heads together and see what you can come up with."

Lucy suddenly materialized in the conference room in the chair next to Raven. The young drone operator started at the unexpected arrival.

"Lucy, I wish you had some kind of warning signal…like to have scared me to death."

She patted Raven on the arm. "I'm sorry my dear, but I think my place is here with you people…Blaze, your idea of radar emitting drones may be of use. Until we come up with a means to detect the cloaked ships, a secondary means of engagement is better than none."

"I'll check our inventory and see how many of those decoy missiles we still have," Gears said.

"Good idea," Lucy agreed. "We only need one."

"I was thinking more like 250. Each fighter will need at least five…Oh yeah, then another twenty for the Manta fleet and any other drone platforms."

Lucy smiled. "I understand…just get me the one and I'll have my people aboard Excalibur replicate whatever we need."

"Why can't I get my head around that capability? I suppose because no place on earth can do it yet."

"I expect your species will find a way soon." Lucy's smile faded. "That is, assuming you can survive the next few days."

THE MILL BAR AND GRILL
Eagle Nest

The summer sun had set over the Rio Grande as Bone and Raven sat on the outdoor patio watching the fireflies dart to and fro and put on their own light show.

"Ready for another?" he asked.

She looked at the empty glass. "Why the hell not? Silver Patron, rocks, with salt and lime.

"You got it." He turned to the shapely waitress who was taking orders from a couple of *Raptors* at nearby table. "Sally…two more top shelf margaritas on the rocks, all the way."

The blonde nodded as she headed back to the bar. "Yes sir, right away."

"Tell me about your little spybot things. What can they do?"

Her eyes lit up. "The babies I call Heckle and Jeckle...after the cartoon magpie characters, you know? They're a sophisticated class of MEMD...sorry...Micro Electronic Mechanical Devices. "

"I'm with you. I once had a remote control four wheel drive SUV. I put a coonskin cap on it and ran it up my captain's leg while he sat at his desk."

She laughed. "And then what happened?"

"Not much," he deadpanned. "He thought he was being eaten and emptied his service weapon at it...I had to buy a new one plus fix his carpet."

She laughed harder. "You are dangerous...I like that."

"Seemed like a good idea at the time."

"So anyway, my babies, as I call 'em, are about this big." She held her index fingers apart about three inches. "They are absolutely silent in flight...have four sets of transparent wings, like dragon flies...and can record digital video and audio. I used 'em when we were searching for President Thompson down in Mexico after she got kidnapped."

"What? Kidnapped?...When did she get kidnapped? I never heard anything about it."

She smiled. "Nobody did. We got her back so quick, they developed a cover story that she had come down here to Eagle Nest for a visit."

"Who kidnapped her? That took some major balls."

"Some gun runner and human trafficker named Javier Cojone and his good friend Osama Bin Laden." She flashed another smile and licked her teeth.

Bone crossed his arms. "Now you're yanking my chain. Hey gorgeous...I was born at night, but it wasn't *last* night."

"Seriously. Ask Mickey Williams...he cut off Bin Laden's finger to ID his prints. Seems that SEAL Team Six bagged his half brother in Pakistan. Or, ask his mom...Something about same mitochondrial DNA."

"Right...Where did they try to hold up with President Thompson?"

"Oh, you should have seen it!" She leaned in as she became more animated. "Way down in Chihuahua, there is...make that *was,* an extinct volcano in the Sierra Madres...Cerro Mohinora...That guy Cojone expanded the hideout once used by Pancho Villa. He had everything in there...tanks, helos, you name it."

"And you used Heckle and Jeckle to scope it out?"

She shook her head. "No, that was up north where we first thought she was being held. I used Speedy Gonzales for the Sacred Mountain hideout."

"Speedy Gonzales?"

"A two foot, four wheel unit...had dual function HD/Infrared cameras, door penetrating thermal X-Ray, a high gain shotgun microphone and best of all...was absolutely silent."

"Uh huh...and what's Sacred Mountain?"

"That was the volcano I mentioned. The locals thought the dead spirits of the Indians the Spanish explorers had enslaved to work the mine haunted the place."

Sally returned with two drinks and left.

"So…check it out. Hannity, Trey and I are monitoring the back door lava tube…the only road into and out of the mountain. I sent Speedy in to gather all the intel we could."

"How many gigs?" Bone asked, pleased to see her begin to lighten up after they had viewed the loss of USS *Alvin York*.

"A full terabyte."

"That is a sweet setup. What did you see?"

"Lame ass guards shooting dice, then a deuce an half rolled by with a butt load of hajis…"

"Did they spot your robot?"

"No way…I put him in turtle mode…he looked like a rock. Then a Russian Shark chopper came busting down the canyon and we called in the CBUs on the surviving ragheads…"

Hours later, the two finished a fantastic meal and had regaled each other with war stories of their most kinetic exploits. Bone paid their tab with his ID card and they headed for the truck.

"My jaw is hurtin' from laughing so much." He glanced at the drop dead gorgeous Greek girl on his arm as they walked to the parking lot. Her radiant smile told him everything he wanted to know. They stopped for second and he kissed her tenderly. The sweet gesture turned into a raging brush fire of passion.

After a minute or so, they both came up for air.

Raven wrapped her arms tightly around his chest and squeezed him hard. He stood there, watching the starlight dance on the slow moving river.

Finally she looked up at his face. "I don't know what's gonna happen tomorrow when we go up against those guys...I'm more than a little nervous, to tell you the truth."

"You have a right to be...we all do."

"But there's one thing I want you to understand...If this is my last night on earth...I don't want to spend it alone."

"You won't, little darlin'...My place our yours?"

EAGLE NEST RANCH HOUSE

"Hey, Carl," Bone said to the Secret Service agent as he and Raven approached the front door.

"Evening, Bone...Miss Papadakis," he replied as he held the door open.

Upstairs in the guest suite, Bone kissed Raven as she stepped out of her high heels and stepped on the plush rug. Wasting no time whatsoever, they began to undress each other and tossed their clothes on the chest of drawers and desk.

Bone picked up the shapely naked woman like she weighed absolutely nothing and laid her down gently atop the feather and down duvet cover. He slid close beside her on the four poster bed and they kissed once more as a hoot owl called from an ancient oak tree outside the house.

Gunter and Annette had breakfast ready when Bone and Raven descended the stairs. Mickey and Maria exchanged winks and then returned to sipping their coffee. Mike tapped his foot against Jill's and tried hard to suppress a grin. His fighter pilot wife reached over and dug her fingernails into his thigh and tried to look nonplused.

Loraine's jaw hung open slightly at the sight of the two of them entering the dining room. Annette picked up the platter with the Mexican style juevos rancheros, while Gunter carried two platters, one filled with ranch cured bacon and ham slices and the other Texas toast.

"Just in time, you two," Gunter said. "Sleep well?"

"Great," Bone replied, simultaneously with Raven's, "Super nice."

"Ya'll have a seat between Lucy and Gears. Blaze must have gotten up early."

Once they were all seated, Gunter asked Annette to say grace. She did so eloquently, thanking God for all the blessing that they enjoyed, and asking Him to watch over and protect the people of earth, and especially those who were about to go in harm's way.

"Thank you, dear," Gunter said. "That was beautiful. Everybody eat up. Think we got a big day ahead of us."

The platters were passed around and talk was light and mainly about the great job Annette and Gunter had done with breakfast. The front door opened and Blaze bounded in and laid a stainless steel handgun in front of Bone.

"Here you go, big guy. You said you liked hand cannons. This is the first coil gun in a pistol. I call it the G4."

"Cool! What did you do, stay up all night?" he said as he handled it.

"Basically…I couldn't get my mind to turn off after watching all our people die onboard that ship, you know?" She hesitated and then started again, "You have thirty rounds. Chronographs at 7,300 feet per second."

"Impressive. What will that work out to in kinetic energy?"

"Over 10,000 pounds…with no recoil."

"Let me see that thing," Mickey said. "Raptors could use something like that against the Reptoids."

Bone passed the handgun down the table.

"That kinda was the idea," Blaze said. "I was hoping Lucy could get us a bunch replicated."

"How many do you want?"

"Say, sixty…plus two additional magazine battery packs combos…Is that a problem?"

"I think we can do that." She chuckled. "Send it down when you are through."

"Handles like an H&K USP," Mickey said as he passed it down the long table."

"That was the basis of it," Blaze said as she took a seat and was handed the pistol. She placed it in the center of the table in front of Lucy.

"Watch your hands," Lucy admonished as she passed the instructions to the fabricators on board the *Excalibur*. The G4 shimmered and vanished. "Would somebody please pass the Texas toast and blackberry jam?"

SECDEF STEWART'S OFFICE
Pentagon

"Percy Cooke, what are you doing here? You should have called for an appointment." The stern Executive Assistant looked over her reading glasses at the Fleet Forces Commander. She had known the four star since he was an ensign, as she did most of the line officers in the Navy's hierarchy.

"Bill, I need to see Burner. It's urgent."

She studied his face for a moment. "Sit down. I'll see if he's available."

The Admiral held his parade cover under his arm. "Yes, ma'am." He turned and took a seat in one of four solid hickory arm chairs that lined one side of the reception area.

She got to her feet and entered the thick mahogany paneled door into the Secretary's private office and closed it behind her. "Sir, BG is here to see you. Do you want me to send him back to Norfolk?"

"Damnation! What's he doing here? I told him…Ah, hell, send the old war horse in. I'll never hear the last of it if I don't see him."

"Yes, sir…I can have him cool his heels for a while in the outer office."

He let out an exasperated sigh. "No, send him in."

The ramrod straight, broad-shouldered former linebacker for the Naval Academy strode through the door, closed it behind him and stood in front of the massive cherry wood desk used by every Secretary of Defense since the first one, James Forrestal.

The SecDef—in reality the second most powerful person in the US—had occupied the office on the fifth floor of the 6,500,000 square foot building known as the Pentagon since it was dedicated on January 15, 1943. Over 28,000 military and civilian employees worked at the monstrous government office building referred to as Ground Zero during the Cold War on the presumption that it would be targeted by the Soviet Union at the outbreak of nuclear war.

"I thought we had a deal, Percy?"

Cooke's face flushed only slightly at the use of his given name. He knew his boss only used it when he was upset with him—but at this point in time, he didn't give a damn, one way or the other. "God dammit, Burner, we need to talk. Based on what I saw happen on that sat feed, I need to know what the hell's going on...Is this office secure?"

Stewart studied the chiseled face of the man in front of him and knew the old warrior didn't back down from anything or anybody. His nickname of 'Blood and Guts' was well earned. "Hell, BG, you know the Pentagon as well as I do, if not better."

"What I figured...Let's go somewhere private. I think I can help."

"You know there no place we can go to without being seen leaving the building or even going to a SKIF room...Wait a minute." The SecDef thought for a second, got to his feet and walked to the door. "Bill, we don't want to be disturbed under any circumstances. I'm going to lock the door."

She looked at him hard. *No one's ever locked the door when I was on duty before.* "As you wish, Mister Secretary."

He closed the door behind him and turned the deadbolt. "I think she got her feelings hurt."

"How's locking the door going to help?"

"You'll see." He took out what looked like a Galaxy S5 phone walked over next to the Admiral and started keying in some letters.

"You sending a God damned text...Now?"

"Not exactly...This may tickle a bit, I'm told."

"What the hell are you talking about?"

Burner held the phone up to his ear and grinned. "Always wanted to say this...Two to beam up, Scotty."

Admiral Cooke gave him a quizzical look. "What?"

There was a shimmer around the two men just before they disappeared.

"Shit!"

EAGLE NEST
BEF underground facility

Heater McElhenney and Dare sat at table going through the crew rosters and maintenance status of the BEF squadrons located at Eagle Nest. The air in the center of the room shimmered and the Secretary of Defense and Admiral Cooke materialized,

BG staggered just a bit. "Jesus H. Christ and all his disciples!" He looked around. "Heater? Dare? What the hell are you two doin' here?" He glanced around again at the completely unfamiliar surroundings. "And just where is *here*?"

McElhenney looked up. "Could ask you the same thing, BG, but, since it looks like the SecDef brought you, don't see the need...or I guess I should say Lucy brought you." The two men got to their feet and came around the desk. "Good to see you." Heater stuck out his hand. "Guess Burner filled you in?"

"Hell no! I just mentioned I thought I could help after seeing the *Alvin York* destroyed and he pulled some damned voodoo and just jerked my happy ass up...and here we are."

"I see...well, guess we better bring you up to speed." Dare keyed the intercom. "Sparkie, would you page Lucy, Blaze and Gears and have them come to the conference room? They may be in the lab."

"Yes, sir."

"Didn't know you'd be down here too, Dare. Yesterday, you were up at Denison," Burner said.

"Lucy thought it would be best to centralize down here at Eagle Nest...Especially when the Annihilator arrives."

BG looked confused. "Annihilator? Lucy?"

"You'll see...Coffee?" asked Dare.

"Got a funny feeling I may need something stronger than that."

Twenty minutes later, Blaze, Gears and Lucy arrived in the conference room.

"Have a seat. This is Admiral Cooke, Commander, US Fleet Forces Command. That was one of his ships we watched yesterday…We've pretty well brought him up to date," said Dare.

"My condolences, Admiral. They were a brave crew. Their sacrifice bought us valuable time," said Lucy.

"Yes, ma'am, thank you…I still find it hard to believe I'm really talking to someone not of this Earth…and you look just like us."

She smiled. "Actually, BG, it's you who looks like us, for you see…you are us."

He looked puzzled for a moment. "But how did you know my…Oh…Oh…I'll be damned."

"I certainly hope not," Lucy said.

"Let's get to it, shall we?" Suppose we can call this a War Council," said Burner. "Just how do you think you can help, BG?"

"Well in watching the live action yesterday, as we all did, I went back and reviewed all the recordings multiple times and those…things…"

"Reptoids," added Lucy.

"Right, Reptoids…It seemed to me that they didn't really have any defenses against our Star Killers…especially when we ripple launch."

"They did shoot down three, Admiral," said Dare.

"Yes, each ship targeted one missile…except for the fourth one…don't know what the hell they were doing. Asleep at the switch, I suppose. But, be that as it may, we took down one of

180

their big-assed ships. Son of a bitch crashed just north and east of the Transantartic Mountains…Made a hellova hole through the ice cap and into bedrock. It appears if they don't take out the missiles in flight, their shields or whatever don't seem to work against them."

"Their shields are fourth order and therefore don't affect solid matter. They are primarily designed for energy weapons…lasers and force beams," offered Blaze.

"Uh, huh…yeah, what she said," replied Cooke.

"The problem is, the *Alvin York* was lost and with it our capability to launch Star Killers…assuming we even had any more," observed Heater.

"Wrong," said BG.

EAGLE NEST RANCH HOUSE

"I don't know about you, but it's driving me crazy hanging around the house when our planet is in such peril." Annette finished wiping down the kitchen counter and looked over at her husband.

"Know what you mean, babe…" Gunter sipped from his third cup of coffee. "…considering all you've been through the last eight years…Sittin' on the sidelines ain't my style either."

"Didn't have a problem running the country and coping with all its problems, but dealing with the damn career politicians and their self-centered pork barrel agendas was what was wearing on body and soul."

"Well, what say we drive over and go down into the complex and see if there's anything we can do to help?"

"Thought you'd never bring it up, you old fart."

"Old fart? Come on woman, I'll show you old."

"Wasn't talking about that. I was talking about helping Dare and the kids." She grinned.

"So was I. Lose that apron and let's boogie, former Madam President."

EAGLE NEST
BEF underground facility

"At least part of your assumption is wrong, Heater. We have an additional twenty of them aboard the frigate, USS *Harold Baker* that was accompanying *Alvin York*. They were the last of the breed, so to speak. The Russians fought them tooth and nail under the SALT treaty, as they had nothing to compete with them. They assumed, correctly, that we could use them to take out their satellites and leave them blind in the event of a nuclear confrontation or if they got engaged with NATO forces directly in Europe."

"How did the Navy get around the limitations of the treaty? I thought the US signed another one that banned the use of space based weapons," Blaze said.

"We did…We promised not to use our missiles…now called Star Killers, against other nation's satellites…only our own and for the possible interceptions of asteroids. *Alvin York* was on a mission to do a preventative shootdown on a decaying satellite when she was engaged by the Reptoids."

"I take it the frigate is incapable of launching the missiles," Burner said.

"Right. But the canisters they are stored in are actually self-contained launch systems...my people simply transfer them to the destroyers and there is a relatively simple system to connect the capsule to the ship's fire control system. We have other ships capable of launching them, or we could fabricate mobile launchers...That part should not be too difficult."

"The physical dimensions of the missiles...outside of the canisters..." Blaze said as she closed her eyes. "...What I remember from reading a DARPA blog about them was nine meters long and one point eight meters in diameter. Is that correct, Admiral?"

"You got me young lady...I can make a call and find out."

"No," said Dare.

Blaze turned to Lucy. "If my recollection stands, I was envisioning an internal rotary launcher system like is used on the B-1 and B-2 bombers. You could build a pair of fighters big enough to carry ten internally, Lucy."

"I saw your vision immediately when you created it. It's a brilliant one. I'll contact my people with the overall concept. Four or five will be a valuable addition to the Annihilators."

"But, don't forget...we only have a total of twenty missiles," Cooke said nervously.

"Calm down, BG. You ain't seen nothin' yet," said Dare.

"If you say so. What port should the *Harold Baker* set a course for?"

Lucy smiled. "That won't be necessary, Admiral. We can teleport the canisters directly. I will have my friends onboard Excalibur make us another sixty as backups. "

BG shook his head and glanced over at Stewart. "I can see why you keep the back benchers out of the loop. Those paper shuffling FOGOs would still be crafting PowerPoint presentations for days, trying to butter up the White House for another star. These people have a war to fight. I'll get you all the tech specs you will need for the launch station controls, as well as full data on the warhead and missile range info."

"Glad you came into my office, BG…Welcome to the team." Burner smiled broadly. "Lucy, what's the ETA on the Annihilator?"

"Mister Secretary, we should plan for its arrival in six hours. One other matter…the black boxes with cloaking devices are being beamed down to the hangars as we speak. I suggest installing them on the Super Galaxies and Mantas first, and then cover the fighters and the VTOLs. My technicians estimate only a ten minute installation time per airframe."

Dare sighed. "That's a relief. My wrench benders have been chompin' at the bits to have something constructive to do. I'll pass the suggestion to Partsman…Time to get cracking."

Blaze shared a look with Dare and winked. "I suppose that's my cue to get back to work as well. Gears and I will give it our best shot to find some way to track those mother ships while they are cloaked."

"I still want to know where the hell we are," said BG just as Annette and Gunter entered the conference room.

"Madam President!…Guess I know where we are now."

***

CHAPTER TEN

BLAZE'S LAB
Eagle Nest

"Okay. We can make the model disappear, but there is way too much interference from the other equipment inside. I can't get a clean reading with all this gear running full time," Blaze grumbled.

"You're probably right, and we don't have time to build a electronic clean room just to test the model." Gears smacked his forehead. "How can we be so dumb? We have everything in the hangar to run a simulation."

"We do?"

"Of course! The modified F-15s and the Super Hornets set up in Growler configuration both have the AESA radar installed. That's the most sophisticated radar we have developed and it has sensors set up to collect any type of ECM signals it encounters. Lucy got us the cloaking devices. All we need is one of each or one and a M600 to do an airborne test."

"We turn on the cloak and see if we can register any spurious electromagnetic disturbances?...No, that won't work...the discriminating software is designed to disregard extraneous signals it encounters."

"You remember the Battlespace Innovations TACTS pods we added to try to capture the Chinese data streams from their stealth J20s and their sector AWACS and ground radar?"

"Of course."

"We program one of them to record any electromagnetic wave phenomenon it encounters."

"But that won't give us bearing and range data," Blaze replied.

"Didn't say it would. Shoot, I'd be happy if it gave us a frequency band to begin searching for."

"Gears, you are a genius!" Blaze grabbed him and placed a big kiss on his forehead, leaving a print of red lipstick. "Oops, sorry." She tried to wipe it off but only managed to smear it around a bit. "I'll call Jill and Maria and set up a test. Clean yourself up...You look ridiculous." She grinned and winked.

EAGLE NEST AIRFIELD

The klaxons inside the gigantic hangar sounded as a series of flashing amber lights announced the impending opening of the eighty foot tall steel doors. Once they were retracted to their positions outside the 520 foot by 300 foot deep building, a series of dark gray ultra-sophisticated aircraft were towed out and chocked in a row with two start carts already in place. The crew chiefs set the brakes and climbed down the ladders already hung from the canopy rails of the F-15 *Eagle* and the F-18 *Super Hornet*. A side door opened behind the left front cannard of the M600 *Black Eagle* VTOL. Once it powered up to its maximum height, the crewman climbed out of the pilot's seat and stepped down to the ramp.

Several minutes later, three of the BEF's top pilots and one WSO emerged from the hangar and walked the short distance to the flight line. Jill Hermann climbed up the ladder of the F-15, while her husband Mike and his new WSO ducked under the crew entrance gullwing door of the M600.

Maria "Double D" Williams had a stern game face on as she stepped over the canopy rail and settled into the ejection seat of the *Super Hornet*. She hooked up her lap belt as the crew chief connected her torso harness to the ejection seat—fastened her leg restraints and then looked up where her crew chief was offering her helmet.

"Thanks." She stuck her thumbs under each side and then slipped it on, but left the oxygen mask dangle from one bayonet fitting as she connected her G suit, comm and O² hoses.

He visually checked out the security of all her connections and patted her on the shoulder, giving her a thumbs-up signal. "Good luck, Double D."

She smiled and nodded.

He climbed down the five steps and stowed the narrow ladder under the chine on the side of the fuselage.

"Beta flight check in," Jill radioed from the cockpit of her F-15. She had completed her Before Engine Start Checklist and it appeared Maria had done so as well. She knew from experience the checklist was much shorter on the M600 and she expected Mike to also be ready.

"Two."

"Three."

"Copy all, clear to start engines."

Once all the aircraft in the three ship finished starting their engines, the crew chiefs ran through their routine signals for flight control checks as the other maintenance personnel disconnected the external power carts on the larger fighters and cleared the chocks from the main gear tires.

Jill grinned when the man in the black jumpsuit raised his right hand as if he was taking a solemn oath and then brought it down across his face and covered both eyes. *Let's see if the alien technology is gonna work.* She reached down and rotated the cloak selector switch from *Standby* to the *On* position. As far as she was concerned, nothing changed. She glanced at her right wingtip. It was still there, plainly visible. Jill spun around and checked out her left wingtip. Ditto.

Where the heck did Maria and Mike go? The ramp was empty except for three crew chiefs standing in a row—giving thumbs-up signs. *Oh, hell. What was it Bone had said? Things inside the cloak are visible to the people inside the cloak. Duh. Get it together, girl.* She turned the switch back to standby and her crew chief saluted her. Turning to her nine o'clock position, the F-18 and M600 had reappeared. *This is gonna take a little getting used to.*

Jill took in a deep breath and let it out. "Beta Flight, taxi."

She saluted her crew chief—he began to back away and motion her to follow him. Once the *Eagle* was rolling, he stepped quickly to the side and came to the position of attention.

The *Super Hornet* followed her F-15 in trail, offset slightly on the left side of the taxiway to avoid the *Eagle's* exhaust, while Mike in the VTOL hung back over eighty yards. Its takeoff performance could not match the twin engine fighters with afterburners.

The flight's brief had called for a formation takeoff with the jets, a 250 knot climb and an orbit at 5,000 AGL. They would allow the *Black Eagle* to set up a pass at 7,000 feet.

"Operations, Beta flight overhead at angels five. TACTS systems on, standing by for three to get into position."

Down in the underground BEF hub, Gears, Blaze, Dare and Lucy monitored the activity on the feed from the TACTS pods attached to each of the aircraft.

"Beta Three, we see you are passing angels six. Initiate your cloak and come to a heading of 180 and strangle squawk," Blaze transmitted on their secure frequency.

"Beta Three, roger." Mike turned his rotary selector switch to the *On* position and began a climbing turn to the south. Once he rolled out he turned off the IFF transponder.

Jill slid out to a fighting wing position 200 feet off Maria's starboard side and checked her radar screen. Even the highly vaunted AESA showed nothing at all, but that was not much of a surprise. The M600 was coated with a radar absorbing material that—with its small radar cross section—helped make the aircraft very stealthy even without the cloak.

At five hundred knots rate of closure, it did not take long for the three aircraft to pass each other.

"Beta Three directly overhead at this time."

"Roger that, Three. Proceed north for one minute then execute a right turn to three six zero."

Mike acknowledged the transmission and Blaze instructed Maria to make a left turn fifty seconds later. A second pass was completed with the M600 cloaked.

"Beta Three squawk 3000."

"Roger, Ops, Beta three squawkin' 3000."

The IFF icon for the cloaked craft appeared on all three radar screens.

"Well, that's a relief. I was worried we were gonna play hell trying to track our birds when they were cloaked," Dare said.

Lucy smiled. "The cloak only works in the visual spectrum and radar frequency."

"That's good to know," Blaze said. She began to transmit additional instructions to the flight. "Beta Three, kill the cloak, Descend to angels five and rejoin on Lead."

Mike rolled inverted and pulled into a tight Split-S. "Beta Three roger. Talley ho the ladies." He firewalled the throttles and the five turbine engines responded quickly bringing the modified VTOL up to its new top speed of almost 600 knots.

"Beta Two, Ops. Break right, climb to angles seven and maintain you current position."

Jill cleared the airspace at her right and tapped the *Eagle's* burners as she acknowledged the clearance. In seconds she was level at 7,000' MSL and entered tight sixty degree bank turn. She monitored the rejoin of her teammates and saw them execute the turn back toward her. Blaze had her set up her transponder and cloak to duplicate the test flown by the M600.

One last iteration flown with the F-18 cloaked completed the planned evaluation.

"Beta Flight, Ops. This concludes the test portion of the flight.

THE PLANET TYRIN

"Did the testing go satisfactorily on the *Garrin*, Kanndol?" asked Ravalan.

"Better than we had hoped, sir. The appurtenances of the new Graviton pulse generator to the Callala inertialess antigravity drive will not only enable the *Garrin* to open a singularity at any point of her choosing, but also allow her to approach the speed of light when free inside any given solar system."

"When may we lift off?" asked Garrple.

"Within three zotes, Fleet Commander. We are finishing the three fighters that Annuna requested. We have designated them the *Heracles* class. They are large enough to go to warp with their own singularity, if required. We fitted them with two of the rotary launchers holding five each of the Star Killer missiles she desired we replicate...in addition to our improved standard energy beams. Unbeknownst to her, we also included two of those multibarrel electromagnetic projectile weapons the Black Eagle Force of Tellus uses...I believe they are called G2."

"That's an odd name for a weapon of destruction," commented Garrple.

"I agree. But our weapons designing facility felt they would be devastating not only against the Reptoids, but their ships as well...if for any reason we can't use the force beams."

"You must remind me to elevate Annuna to Zone Commander when this is finished," said Ravalon.

"I agree, Supreme Overlord, she has made remarkable contributions since she returned," commented Rollân.

"Assuming we are able to fair better against the Draconians than we did when they embarked on this latest raid."

"I think with our new shields, armor, speed and hadronium enhanced energy beams, we should, Ravalon," stated Garrple.

"We still have two critical conditions to eventually overcome."

"What would that be, Rollân?" asked Ravalon.

"One, a method of detecting and locating a fourth order cloak and two, locating their home base…at long last."

EAGLE NEST
BEF Underground Mess Hall

"May I join you?" Lucy asked Padrino, Mike and Blaze.

"Sure." Mike started to get to his feet.

"Please, keep your seat, but thank you." She sat her tray on the table. "Where's Bone?"

"He and Raven are taking a walk down along Becerro Creek," said Loraine. "Hell of a time for love to be in the air."

"That's Bone," said Padrino.

Lucy smiled and nodded. "Pass the sugar, would you, Mike."

"Yes, ma'am…The real thing or synthetic?"

"Oh, the real thing. I never eat anything someone created in a lab."

"Heard that." He passed the bowl filled with little paper packets of pure cane sugar.

"We don't have sugar on Tyrin. I've grown quite attached to sweet tea in the years I lived here."

"Lucy, what's the background with the Reptoids? I mean how long has the conflict been going on?" asked Padrino.

"Goodness, eons…"

"Really? And you're still at it?"

"Wait 'til you actually see one up close and personal, Mike," commented Loraine.

"Yeah, can't wait."

Jill and Maria approached with their trays after having showered and changed flight suits.

"Room for us?"

"Sure, babe, you and D just pull up a chair...Lucy's giving us a history lesson."

"Good work today, children," she addressed the two fliers. "Now to continue. Our race...what your ancient Mesopotamian cultures called the Anunnaki, were very peaceful, but advanced. The ancient Jews referred to us as 'messengers'..."

Blaze interrupted, "Angels?" She turned to the others. "Angels in Hebrew means 'messengers'."

Lucy nodded. "They saw us coming down from the sky and assumed we were coming from Heaven when we offered suggestions or tried to help."

"Wow! You're the angels from the Bible...Who knew?" commented Bone.

She grinned. "Well, back to the Draconians or Reptoids...They would periodically raid Tyrin and harvest, if you will, back over a hundred million of your Tellurian years...We finally got tired of hiding and started developing weapons to defend ourselves." She stopped and had a couple of spoonfuls of her cabbage soup. "Love the food on your planet...Anyway, we had set up a colony on Thora...Mars."

"How could you colonize Mars? It has virtually no atmosphere...It's a dead, dry world."

"Not 85 million years ago, my dear Padrino. Then it was much as Tellus. Great rolling seas, land masses, mountains, forests and plains that teamed with life."

"Like Burroughs depicted in his novels about John Carter?"

"Somewhat, except the grass wasn't red." She smiled. "Actually this predates even the time he wrote about...Tellus was still very volcanically active and it was the time of the dinosaurs. Thora had a much better environment for our culture, plus there were several humanoid species that held great promise."

"There were humans on Mars...or Thora?" questioned Blaze.

"Not quite. As I said they were early humanoid types, but the genome was there...something we could work with. We transported some to Tellus."

Dare and Heater had overheard the conversation and got up from their adjoining table.

"Mind if we sit in, Lucy? This sounds fascinating," Dare asked. "As Sun Tzu said, 'know your enemies as you know yourself'."

"Of course not...If you don't mind if I eat while I tell the story."

"We're sorry, Lucy, we don't mean to impose..."

"Nonsense, no imposition at all...and Sun Tzu was correct." She took a couple of bites and buttered a fresh yeast roll.

"Can I get you some more ice tea?"

"No, no, I just got it where I like it...Now, we developed quite a colony that thrived for some twenty million years until the Reptoids finally found us. As I said, we had developed very powerful weapons…not the energy beams we have today, but atomic and what you call conventional weapons."

"You had atomic bombs?" asked Heater.

"And ballistic missiles…The battle lasted for several years until we finally drove the marauders off."

"I saw on the science channel recently that both of our Mars rovers, Spirit and Opportunity, picked up traces of Xenon-129 on the surface. The only known source of that is a nuclear explosion," stated Padrino.

"I think the other shoe is about to drop."

"Yep," agreed Mike.

Lucy looked at Blaze and her brother. "Yes, children. I could tell you both were jumping ahead as you could see what I was going to say."

"You mean…"

They looked at each other.

"You mean, I got the same stuff as Blaze?"

"Of course, you are full siblings. You've just not been as open to it as she."

"I'll be…"

"Are you saying he'll be able to read my mind?" asked Jill.

"Probably, but I can teach you how to shield your thoughts. It's quite easy." She winked at Mike. "Now for that other shoe…As you know, Mars lies much closer to the asteroid belt than Tellus…Shortly after the Reptoid's retreat, our scientists detected a large asteroid over four miles wide tumbling on a collision course with our orbit. Our colony was already devastated and much of the planet was very radioactive anyway, so basically my people packed up and moved back to Tyrin...Pass the rolls, please, Dare."

"Yes, ma'am."

She buttered one and took a bite. "Umm, these are so good."

"Did the asteroid strike?"

"Indeed it did, Dare. Thora, being much smaller than Tellus was almost destroyed. Several large chunks ejected out, one formed Mars' second moon...the small one you call Deimos and the other was thrown in the direction of Tellus...As it was, almost ninety percent of the Thorian atmosphere was literally burned away, effectively killing the planet."

"And the other piece of Mars that struck Earth at the edge of the Yucatan peninsula is estimated to have been over six miles in diameter and was responsible for the extinction of the dinosaurs and the converse rise of mammals...and us," Blaze added.

"A rather unique chain of events to bring us all here at this moment to face the Reptoids again, wouldn't you say?"

BLAZE'S LAB
Eagle Nest

"That was an amazing story Lucy told, wasn't it?" said Gears.

"Yes, but we have to come up with a way to get this over quickly. The Earth can't afford to get into a long war with the Reptoids, even with the help of the Tyranians. To add to Dare's quote from Sun Tzu...he also said, 'What is essential in war is victory, not prolonged operations'."

"Hit 'em hard and chase 'em all the way back to Draco."

"Just gotta give our people some better options."

"Yeah…Want some coffee, girl?"

"Please, we may be here a while."

Gears grabbed her personalized bright red ceramic oversized cup and filled it from the pot. He turned a little too quickly and sloshed almost a quarter out onto the floor. "Damn…sorry, I'll refill it."

"That's okay." She took the cup from his hand and handed him a couple of folded paper towels. "While you're up."

"Yessum." Gears knelt down, placed the towels at the edge of the spill and watched as the porous paper wicked up the spill.

Blaze put the cup to her lips as she glanced down at the cleanup operation. "Wait a minute…look at that."

"What?"

"What's the paper towel doing?"

"It's soaking up…"

"Right."

"Hey, hey, hey! That's it, Blaze!"

"We don't neutralize the disruptor beam, we wick it away…"

"Our Dragonskin armor is coated with Graphene…"

"And Graphene itself is a superconductor."

"All we have to do is ground the suit and bleed the laser pulse into the earth or suitable substrate."

"We didn't ground the top we used in the test, ergo, the steel plate took the charge and melted…Let's go test it, Mister Formby."

"As you wish, Miss Hermann."

"Worked exactly like we figured," said Gears as they walked back into the lab.

"Didn't even warm up the steel plate...Got one problem, though."

"And that would be?"

"Our boots are coated with the Lizard chromatophores over the Graphene as is the armor," Blaze pointed out.

"And?"

"The soles are not...They're normal rubber compound..."

"Not grounded."

"Exactly."

"What if we...we..." Gears paused and grabbed a yellow note pad and a pencil from his desk and started making a sketch. "You ever seen snow shoes?"

"Of course. We used to go to Colorado every winter, skiing, hiking and...Right!"

"We'll have Lucy's replicator onboard *Excalibur* make some Graphene straps that we can Velcro onto the bottom of the suits and then around the boots like this." He showed Blaze the drawing.

"Of course, the Raptors will be constantly grounded as long as any part of their suit or their boots are in contact with the earth or a suitable substrate, the disruptor charge will be wicked away like that coffee."

EAGLE NEST
Becerro Creek

Bone and Raven held hands as they walked the well-worn path along the spring-fed creek. Two hundred year old live oak trees spread out broadly and shaded the idilic path as they stopped and stared at the minnows darting in and out of the vegetation lining the near bank. A largemouth bass cruised by slowly pulsing its tail. Bone spotted a pair of limestone boulders perfectly chosen for two natural benches.

"Would you like to sit for a bit?" he asked.

"It is kind of nice in here...peaceful."

They took a seat atop the rocks. Bone studied the surface for a second. "Did you know this is fossiliferous limestone? See all those little shells? They're from back in the Cretaceous period...around eighty to sixty-six million years ago. All this part of Texas was sea bottom then."

"You surprise me...Pretty smart for a cop."

"And you're pretty gorgeous and delicious for a computer whiz." He leaned in and kissed her gently.

Raven responded with passion and then placed her head on his chest.

A large yellow and black grasshopper landed on a long skinny blade of grass sticking out of the creek bottom. The grass bent over slightly under its weight and tiny ripples spread out on the placid waters. The water exploded as the big bass reacted and engulfed the unlucky insect—droplets splattered Bone's combat boots.

"Watch it there, big guy. I think that bass is calling you out."

He grinned and used his best John Wayne imitation. "I'll sic my Kung Fu princess on him if the pilgrim wants to go a round with the champ. Wah ha."

She laughed and kissed him again.

Bone grinned for a second and then his face turned unexpectedly serious and he cocked his head.

"What's wrong?" she asked.

"Lucy wants to see us…both of us."

"Did she text you? I didn't hear any thing."

"No…kinda weird. I just heard her voice, well not really her voice…must be her telepathy." Bone got to his feet and pulled Raven close to him. He wrapped his arms around her and lifted her off the ground with a loving hug. "I'll bring you back here once we kick the Retoid's asses off our planet."

"I'll hold you to that…Now, shut up and kiss me like you mean it before I hurt you."

***

CHAPTER ELEVEN

EAGLE NEST
BEF Underground Headquarters.

Mike sauntered into the lounge to find Hollywood Stewart, Chet Ladd, Lanie Hayes, Miguel Cabrillo, Padrino and Loraine already seated in the black recliners. The big screen TV was off and the lighting was turned down considerably lower than normal.

"Hey, Lucy…you wanted to see me?"

"Have a seat. I wanted an opportunity to spend a little one on one time with each of you. We need to begin going over the systems operations of the three Heracles class fighters."

"You mean I'm not going to be flying a M600?"

"No, you are much too valuable for that."

Bone and Raven got out of the elevator and walked quickly to the lounge. They each took a seat as directed as Lucy closed the door behind them.

"It's totally different than flying your Tellus type aircraft...there are no air foils, no lift, no Gs to be concerned with. You'll be free or inertialess most of the time, but you'll have to revert to a normal state subject to Newton's laws before you land...or it won't be pleasant.

"Now just close your eyes and relax. Try not to think about anything else but your breathing...Hear the sound of the oxygen flowing into your lungs and carbon dioxide flowing out," Lucy said softly. She pictured the cockpit of the new fighter and transmitted that vision to the nine pupils.

Loraine opened her eyes, slightly disturbed by the sensation, and then her mind perceived a message from Lucy, although no words were spoken. *"Nothing will harm you. Relax and take this in. You have the capacity to send and receive, but have not developed it yet...Now is the time to learn."*

She closed her eyes once more and let the information flow—almost like a movie, but in much higher speed. Diagrams of subsystems, primary navigation instruments, and complete operating procedures of the spaceship appeared silently in her mind as it did for the other crew members. Several minutes later, the drone operating systems began to appear before her consciousness. After a few minutes the incoming flood of alien technology ceased.

"How is everyone doing?" Lucy asked telepathically. *"Try to answer without using your voice. Direct your thoughts to me...concentrate. Do not think in words, but in thought picutres. That is one reason why we're able to communicate with entities who have telepathic capability, but speak a different language."*

Bone's forehead furrowed as he did as she asked.

Lucy smiled broadly. *"No, there will not be a quiz and yes...you will actually remember almost all of what you saw."* She turned to Raven.

Raven replied using her mind. *"I'm not a pilot. Why do you want me to know all of that information?"*

"You can now operate the ship if you had to in an emergency. All crew members are required to know how to pilot the craft. I also expect you to be able to control the two drones with your mind. Any questions so far?"

She shook her head and looked over to Bone for reassurance.

He smiled and winked. *"I'm sure you can do it, doll baby,"* he said telepathically.

She flashed him a big toothy smile.

Hollywood closed his eyes to concentrate. *"Fantastic machine. Oh, my God, I don't know where to start. I got the Aviation 101 part, but when do we discus combat tactics?"*

Lucy stepped up between Mike and Hollywood. *"For this part we need to use a more complicated means. To save time, I will need to contact each of you directly."* She placed three fingers on each man's head—her thumb on their forehead, index finger on the cheek and middle finger on the temple.

Loraine looked on curiously. *"Like a Vulcan mind meld on Star Trek?"*

Lucy grinned and shot her a look as she transmitted, *"Where do you think Gene Rodnenberry got the idea?"*

"Oh."

Lucy closed her eyes and instructed the two other pilots to do as well. She took in a deep breath and appeared to be concentrating very hard. After two minutes she released contact.

"Ow," Mike said as he rubbed his temple. "That feels like a tequila hangover."

Hollywood gasped a couple of times. "Whoa…I feel dizzy."

"You'll be all right in a few minutes. I wanted you to get a feel for the basics of combat maneuvering, but we'll go over the specific tactics for Reptoid engagements in a while…I promise it won't be as bad."

"What makes me feel like I'm gonna throw up?"

"Billions of new neurosynaptic pathways have been created in a very short period of time. We increased your brain functionality a few percentage points. Ask your wife for some vitamin B supplements. You'll feel better almost immediately." She turned to the others. *"And that goes for the rest of you. Vitamin B-6 in particular will help the neural programming processes."*

BLAZE'S LAB
Eagle Nest

"My team will have everything ready by the time the Garrin and the fighters arrive later this afternoon. I've already had the first training session with the pilots and I have taken the liberty of obtaining everyone's sizes as we'll actually be replacing your existing Dragonskin armor with a combination of our spacesuits and yours. We're adding your wondrous Graphene to our own interstellar gray suits. Although almost indestructible already, the Graphene will make them more so, especially to disruptor fire.

"There is a possibility that the Annihilator and or the fighters may have to venture outside the protective shell of your atmosphere," said Lucy.

"You mean outer space?" asked Gears.

"Yes, and in that event you'll all have to be protected from solar flares, cosmic and occasional gamma rays."

"We will have suits like yours?" asked Blaze.

"Except yours will be black and have all of the equipment your people are used to, including communicators in the helmets."

"Wow! Those replicators are something," said Gears.

"I know." Lucy smiled.

"Good…Let's get back to the matters at hand and see what the TACTS pod recorded," Blaze said as she connected the hard drive to her desktop computer. She opened the file and then keyed in a few additional strokes to bring up a digital graph set up reminiscent of an oscilloscope, but square instead of round.

A third screen displayed the radar return depicting the three aircraft of Beta Flight as seen from the master control station in the Operations Center. She fast-forwarded the recording to the time corresponding to her first radio call to her older brother to turn off his IFF and initiate the Tryranian cloak. "Okay, we'll just run it and see what we get…"

Gears and Lucy looked on as the mission continued. All three looked at the oscilloscope and noted nothing out of the ordinary. The first pass went though to completion with nothing showing but a myriad of rapidly changing high PRF pulses from the two fighters' AESA radars.

"That's not exactly encouraging," Blaze said. She glanced down at the graph underneath the display and slowly shook her head. "Come on girl, you can't be that obtuse."

"What's the matter?" Gears asked.

"I'm looking in the two to ten gigahertz range…That's what wrong. I'm searching in the same frequency bands that we're transmitting in. Fourth order waves are much higher frequency." She pulled the cursor over an arrow beneath the graph and right clicked it. "What do you think, Lucy? Fifteen to twenty gigahertz to start?"

"I wouldn't skip that far ahead yet, dear. There are some 1,500 frequencies in the fourth order…at least according to Nikola Tesla…He wasn't sure how many there were in the fifth order as he was just beginning to investigate them."

"I agree," Gears said. "Try ten to fifteen first."

"Here goes." Blaze made the adjustment and ran it again with no results. The test on fifteen to twenty yielded no visible results as well.

Blaze frowned. "Maybe the TACTS pods are not as sensitive as I thought." She set the scan to the next level. "Twenty gigahertz is so much faster that any form of visible light spectrum…even ultra violet. I don't see how it could…"

The blank graph suddenly spiked at 28.8 Gigahertz point—a tiny white arrow that grew in size as the M600 flew closer. By the time it was overhead of the F-18, the arrow was slightly broader and rising almost to the top of the scale.

"Hello, my little friend…What do you guys think?"

"Looks like we have a strong suspect, Blaze. Let's check the other aircraft and confirm the same frequency."

"Sounds reasonable to me. It does appear the detection is range sensitive. Hope that's not too big a problem for us," he added.

Neither fighter cloak showed up on the next test.

"Any ideas why?" Gears asked.

"Just a hunch."

"Go with it…We don't have a lot of time," Lucy said.

"If the radius of the cloak is larger…and it would be if the aircraft was proportionally bigger…perhaps the frequency must be correspondingly higher to successfully bend light waves in a manner that is imperceptible to the human observer."

"Sounds logical. I wish I could be of more assistance from an engineering standpoint," Lucy replied.

"Won't take long to find out." She set the band width from 30 to 35 and reinitiated the scan. "Bingo! 30.05...I was right."

Gears smiled and patted his colleague on the shoulder. "It may be that if we know the size of the Reptoid vessels, we can project a operating frequency."

"That would be a huge help...assuming that the Reptoids are using fourth order shields and cloaks," Blaze said.

"If they had figured out how make a fifth order shield, your Tellurian weapons would have been of no use. Nothing can penetrate a full fifth order zone...except for thought projections."

Blaze pushed back from the desk. Her forehead was beginning to wrinkle.

Gears attempted to ask her what she was thinking, but Lucy held up a hand and shook her head. The alien fighter pilot concentrated on Blaze's thoughts of a weapon delivery system utilizing only brain waves to control it. She nodded and a smile came to her lips as Blaze envisioned a special type of missile never before seen by any species in the universe.

EAGLE NEST
BEF Underground Gymnasium

"I need three lines, people. Raptors here, crew here and aviation there," Dare directed the entire Black Eagle Force.

At one end of the basketball court—next to three large dark gray carbon composite molded cases—stood Gunter Hermann, Burner Stewart and Annette Thompson-Hermann. The lines quickly began to form in front of the three, each standing beside one of the containers.

"Secretary Stewart will call your names one at a time. You are to step forward and receive your new battlesuits for your respective divisions…Everybody nod."

For a brief moment, the gym floor looked as if it was covered with bobble-head dolls.

Dare turned to the diminutive Tyranian. "Lucy, you have the floor."

"Thank you, Dare…Members of the Black Eagle Force, these suits are custom created for each of you…personally. They are a combination of the suits we Tyranians wear and your own…and are much lighter than your Dragonskin armor. You'll note, however, that they are in two pieces…not counting the helmet…and the boots are built in and grounded against Reptoid disruptor fire. The major difference is…" She let her gaze drift around the large room. "…these suits are space worthy."

There was a murmur throughout the assemblage as they glanced at one another.

"They are completely self-contained, air conditioned and have a one hour breathing apparatus in the pouch on the left side of the utility belt."

Ten Ring—one of the Raptors—leaned over to Widowmaker Baker and whispered, "Ha! Like Batman's belt."

"Somewhat, Mister Weber, but I can assure you it contains things far more advanced that even your fantasy writers could come up with for the Caped Crusader."

James 'Ten Ring' Weber's eyes got big as saucers as he realized that she not only knew what he said, but also who he was.

Lucy grinned and winked at the former Marine gunnery sergeant sniper. "Before you ask how it works, permit me to say the suits are powered by cosmic energy stored in what is essentially a power pack on the belt." She pointed to a red disc on her own belt about that was the size of a silver dollar. "This pure ruby crystal is the face of the cosmic energy accumulator that feeds and constantly recharges the power pack. The rest of the suit repels the rays."

"Mister Secretary, you want to kick this off?"

"Can do, Dare, and with that said, you're number one."

He stepped over to Annette and she handed him his folded personal black suit and helmet.

"Thank you, Madam President. Didn't expect you to be doing quartermaster duty."

"Everyone has to serve, Dare. This is the least I can do. To paraphrase John Milton, I didn't want to serve by standing and waiting...not my style." She kissed his cheek. "Good luck and God speed."

"Thank you, ma'am."

"Heater," Burner called out as he started down the list.

Shortly, after all the BEF team had been issued their battlesuits, Lucy spoke up, "I want all the Heracles fighter crew members suited up." She turned to Bad. "Mister Poole, select three six-man Raptor teams to accompany us. Join me in the main hangar in ten minutes for an inspection, please."

"Yes, ma'am." He spun around and began pointing at individual operatives. "Widowmaker, you and Ten Ring pick your teams."

Hollywood tucked his suit under his arm. "Lucy, I think we need to name the fighters."

"Good idea...I'll call mine Guinevere. She was such a lovely thing."

"In that case, mine is obviously Lancelot."

"Guess that leaves me flyin' Galahad," Mike said. "The real hero."

His comment was greeted by groans and catcalls from the other crews.

The twelve flight crew and eighteen Raptors gathered on the large aircraft elevator that once carried fighters and helicopters aboard *USS Valley Forge*. The trip to the surface was a quick one.

"Bone, you look like a tar baby version of Chewbacca," Loraine said as she looked up at the 6' 8" black-clad warrior to the laughter of the others.

"If the shoe fits, Pard...Surprised you were able to get that top over those double whoppers. Must have put some serious super Lycra in yours and Maria's."

Mickey grinned as Loraine cuffed him behind the head.

"Watch it, Bonehead...You're treading on thin ice," she said.

Raven shot him a look. "Bone!"

He merely shrugged. "What?"

The assembled crews lined up inside the hangar doors and Lucy made her quick visual inspection of the battlesuits' individual fit. She insured the tops magnetically mated to the bottoms correctly to insure continuity of the Graphene defense systems and that all were air tight before she sent a message to the maintenance personnel to open the giant doors outside to the empty ramp.

"Hey, Lucy," Bone asked as they stepped out. "When are the fighters gonna get here?"

"They're already here." She grinned mischievously and closed her eyes, sending a signal to the three cloaked ships.

The air over the sun-baked tarmac shimmered and three iridescent silver space ships materialized. Each was roughly triangular in shape—one hundred and ten feet long and fifty feet in width. They were positioned with the four impulse engine exhausts aimed toward the hangar. Each rectangular port was six feet tall by four feet wide.

A chorus of oohs and ahhs erupted from the excited team.

"It's a lot larger than I thought it would be," Bone said.

"Those Star Killer missile rotary launchers take up a considerable amount of space," Lucy replied.

"How do we tell which is which?" Raven asked.

"One moment." Lucy blinked her eyes and sent a command to each of the ships. Photochromatic panels embedded in the skin spelled out the names in an old English font with jet black foot tall letters across the stern above the exhausts. "That's better isn't it?"

"Service with a smile," Mike said as he walked closer to the ship marked *Galahad*.

Atop each craft, a large ten foot diameter flattened red dome—made of pure ruby crystal—functioned as the cosmic energy accumulators. Beneath it lay the ring of slots from which the deadly energy beams could fire in 360 degrees. A series of dark gray windows in the cockpit bulge offered a panoramic view in the forward as well as side aspects. The ships sat on three sturdy eight foot long landing gear with three foot diameter pads instead of tires.

Mike led his crew and *Raptor* detachment underneath the ship. He looked up at the almost imperceptible line in the otherwise seamless a raknene armor where the entrance ramp was located. He turned to Lucy who was already stepping onto the padded ramp of the *Guinevere*. "Dang, it almost looks like the armor plating was sprayed on."

"You are very close to being right, Mike."

"How do we get the ramp down?"

"You know how. Use your mind," she responded wordlessly.

"Oh, yeah. Gonna take a little time to get used to that."

He stared at the belly of the *Galahad*. Without a sound, the four foot wide ramp extended to the ground. He issued another command, turning on the interior lights and life support systems in the ship. "Okay you guys, climb on up. This is gonna be interesting." He motioned to the other nine to follow.

"Step quickly, gents," Ten Ring Weber said. "Damned sure don't want to be the last one to the party."

Climbing into the ship, it was obvious that the two rotary launchers were mounted along either side of the centerline of the custom designed fighters. Exterior clamshell doors for the Star Killer missiles were flush mounted—but a full thirty-five feet long and five feet wide. Inside, the ceilings of the flight deck and *Raptor* compartments were seven feet high. Tyranian engineers created them much larger to accommodate the bigger earthlings.

Chet slipped into the copilot's seat on the right side as Mike glanced around the cabin for the drone operator and comm officer' stations. Both pilots were slightly uncomfortable with the truly alien surroundings. None of the usual accouterments of a modern fighter or transport aircraft were visible. There was no stick or yoke. No neatly stacked set of engine instruments and navigation displays cluttered the area in front of or between them.

Mike sat down in the soft gray leather arm-chaired seat and fastened the single lap belt across his waist. *This is more like a passenger belt than a pilot one, but since we'll mostly be free, should be more than adequate.* He looked up, back and beside himself for rows of circuit breakers—there were none to be seen. Actually the cockpit windscreen extended past their seats overhead giving them direct vertical views if needed. He pulled his helmet with the large almond-shaped dark tinted eyes into position and the neck band magnetically secured itself to his battlesuit top. *Here goes nothing.*

216

He moved his gloved right hand over the featureless dash board in front of him. The light gold-shaded material that resembled saddle-tanned leather suddenly became a multicolored hologram of the Eagle Nest airfield. All three ships were tiny three dimensional replicas of the real things, only with the letters *Ga, Gw, La* in red under them.

Chet waved his hand over the dash and brought up a holographic display with systems and weapons status. A quick review of the myriad of complex, but essentially automated, systems aboard told him everything he needed to know.

"All systems are go. Standing by for liftoff."

Mike nodded. *"Copy that, Guinevere, Galahad ready for departure."*

Aboard *Lancelot,* Hollywood Stewart and Blaze Hermann were going though the same process. Raven had taken her seat in the drone operator's position and Miguel Cabrillo strapped in as communications officer.

"Guinevere, Lancelot ready for departure."

Lucy smiled slightly. *"So far so good. Let's take it one step at a time until we get used to these new ships...Cloaks on."*

Using their minds only, the three aircraft commanders turned the new craft's cloaks back on and in an instant, the ramp outside the huge hangar appeared to be empty one more.

"Take it slow, now. Intertialess antigrav drive...on. Impulse power...idle, activate thrustors. Vertical liftoff to one hundred

feet." Lucy walked Mike and Hollywood through the procedures and then retracted the landing gear.

Bone heard the hydraulic pumps whine very faintly and then the reassuring clunk as the pads came flush with the ship's belly and locked into place. *"Wait a second. I haven't heard a single bit of noise from the engines. Nothing...and don't feel a thing...It's like we're still sittin' on the ramp."*

Lucy glanced up at the human copilot towering beside her. *"And you won't. They are silent. Rather peaceful, don't you think?"*

"Sure...Whatever...it just is just different than I expected."

"Relax, Bone, and enjoy the ride. Don't even think about the fact that this is your first time in this new ship, too." She grinned, but no one could see her impish little face under the helmet. *"Happy birthday, Bone...I told you we would see. I just didn't think it would be this way."*

He glanced over at her and arched one eyebrow inside his helmet. *"Yeah, me neither."*

AIRSPACE OVER EAGLE NEST

Aboard *Lancelot*, Hollywood was amazed at the rapidity of the climb to 100,000 feet. The green agricultural fields of south Texas disappeared in the haze far below—the blue waters of the Gulf of Mexico stretched as far as he could see. Above, the sky was a dark, dark blue almost black. "Incredible...Absolutely incredible."

"Beautiful," Blaze concurred. "No vibration or noise whatsoever. I always imagined what this would be like."

"I don't feel anything different. Why is it we aren't floating around like the astronauts?" asked Raven.

"You want to take that question, Blaze?" the blonde-haired fighter pilot asked.

"You bet…The reason we don't feel any different is, one we're inertialess and two, the artificial gravity installed in the floor underneath us allows us to feel pretty much the same as we did back on earth. A carefully laid out grid of gravitons in the carbon composite deck…adjusted to replicate ninety percent of the gravitational pull back home does the trick. It really comes in handy when we have to walk about the ship, drink liquids or go to the bathroom, for example."

"Gravitons? Never heard of those before…what are you talking about?" Cabrillo asked.

"Not surprised you haven't," she replied. "Gravitons are spin-2 boson particles which have no mass and no charge…but mediate gravity. Their existence was postulated for many years and they were thought to have been part of the closed string theory by our theoretical physicists. It is also believed that they interact with leptons and quarks."

"Yeah. That's kinda the way I saw it, too," Widowmaker Baker said.

Hollywood nodded his head in agreement. "What she said."

Aboard the *Guinevere*, Lucy turned to Padrino with a telepathic message. *"Have them spread out. Practice their maneuvering. I will have the Garrin send down two vehicles for each ship for the drone operators to familiarize themselves with."*

"Right away," he replied. *Finally I get to do something.*

In a moment, he received two rapid responses.

"Galahad copies."

"Lancelot, roger that."

Mike instinctively rolled *Galahad* to the left and began to wish it to the north. In a few seconds, they were almost 100 miles away. He heard Chet chuckling softly. *"What's so funny?"*

"You don't have to bank to turn any more. That's the old paradigm."

"Dang. You're right, of course. Old habits die hard."

"Let's see some rolls and loops anyway. That will tell us how maneuverable this baby is."

"You got it. Hang on, here we go."

"Don't have to say 'hang on' anymore either."

"Oh, right."

The ship remained in one spot as Mike rolled it inverted in a half second. It hung there upside down as the entire crew marveled at the eerie lack of any sensation of motion or orientation.

Lanie spoke up, "Wow that is so strange. Almost like looking at a video game when you look outside."

"Like a flight simulator without motion," Chet added. "Beats getting airsick any day."

"To remind everyone, Lucy wants us to practice our telepathy in our communication."

"Right," everyone concurred back.

Mike rolled back to the vertical and then made several slow loop-like maneuvers, but ones without the aircraft moving from its altitude. The view out the front windscreen rapidly changed from earth to sky and back. He stopped with a view of the Rio Grande river over Del Rio, Texas.

"Want to try it?" he asked Chet.

"Is a bullfrog waterproof? I have the craft."

"You have the craft." Mike crossed his arms in front of himself.

Chet concentrated on the hologram of the *Galahad* floating above his navigation display. He willed it to grow to a foot long and slipped his hand inside it. *"I thought this method of controlling it was outstanding. Every pilot knows how to hand fly."*

He moved his arm in a series of sweeping turns and rolls. The ship itself followed his movements exactly. For a minute, he practiced every aerobatic maneuver he had ever seen and invented a few more that were physically impossible for any other type of craft. *"It would be hard to hit us with moves like this."*

"Maybe with conventional weapons, but with automatic tracking pulse lasers, I'm not so sure about that," Cowboy responded. *"I'll put my money on the cloak and shields."*

"You wanna try hand flying?"

"Heck yeah. Looks like it's easier than brain power alone."

"You have the craft." Chet pulled his hand out of the hologram and Mike leaned over and slid his inside. *"I have the craft."*

"Guys, the Captain of the Garrin wants us to hold position for thirty seconds while they beam the drones down," Niki Layton relayed.

"Roger that, holding here. Standby Lanie…you get to show your stuff." The *Galahad* instantly came to a stop.

"Ready as I'll ever be."

Two cloaked drones appeared as if by magic—each five hundred yards off the port and starboard sides. A pair of holographic images of the small copies of the *Manta* URFs the BEF operated appeared on the navigation display in front of the pilots and on a similar one at Lanie's station.

"I'll take it ahead slow. Let me know when you are ready for a turn." Mike eased his hand forward. The silver Tyranian ship responded.

"Actually, Mike, I don't think it makes any difference what you do…The Galahad and my drones are totally separate and since I'm not experiencing any motion, there's no distraction…So do what you gotta do." Lanie focused on each ship and willed them to keep pace with the *Galahad*.

Tiny beads of sweat formed on the young black woman's forehead as she concentrated on the task. A minute or two later, she was pleased enough with her performance to request a heading change. *"Give me a full one-eighty, Cowboy."*

"You got it." He made a hard turn back south.

Her initiation to the concept of brain control lasted six minutes.

Mike instructed her to bring the two intergalactic drones to points two hundred feet off the mother ship's five and seven o'clock positions.

"Chet, stand by with the tractor beams. Lucy has sent us some new coordinates to fly to."

"Roger that. Tractors standing by…I have a lock on baby Mantas One and Two."

"Engage."

Chet selected twin beams—of the six the fighter had to work with—and turned them on. A pair of tractor beams captured each of the drones and simultaneously, a repellor beam locked on and kept them tethered at precisely the same distance.

"Locks are both operational. You can shut them down and take a break, Lanie."

"I heard that…Didn't know it would take so much concentration. Two at once is really hard."

"Lucy wouldn't have picked you if she didn't think it was well within your capability," Mike sent.

Lanie chuckled. *"Oh yeah? Well, tell you what…It reminds me of the old joke where the preacher told a troubled woman 'God doesn't give you any more than you can handle,' and she replied, 'That may be so, but I wish he didn't have so danged much confidence in me'."*

Mike smiled as he lay in the course to the star coordinates. The magenta line looped off the nav map. *Where the hell we goin'?* he wondered. He spread his hands apart a few inches and saw the line continue east around the globe to the mid-Atlantic. *Huh?*

He spread his hands as wide as they would go—nearly seventy-six inches—and then placed one hand over the center of the display and raised it up. The flat nav display converted instantly to the three-dimensional interstellar battlespace depiction of the entire solar system. It resembled a huge aquarium with the sun, planets, moons and the asteroid belt clearly visible.

"I see why Lucy calls it the *tank*...It does kinda resemble a fish tank."

He collapsed the display until it only showed the distance from the Earth to just past Mars. Small icons of *Excalibur* and *Garrin* indicated their positions, as well as the other two fighters. The flight path stopped at the edge of the huge asteroid belt between Mars and Jupiter. *"Holy Crap! We're gonna go there?"* He touched the magenta line. A time and distance calculation popped up. *"Jesus! 51,000,000 miles in four minutes and fifty-seven seconds."*

"What on earth?...I mean, what in the solar system?...Ay, Caramba! Why does she want to go there?" the slightly flustered Bobby asked.

"Guess she wants to do some target practice before the main event," Cowboy thought.

"Sounds like a plan to me," Chet agreed.

Mike pulled the nose of *Galahad* up sixty degrees above the horizon and began climbing and accelerating to Mach 12, the limiting speed inside the atmosphere. The craft had been maneuvering solely with the aid of thrustors that amplified the radiation pressure of an electromagnetic wave propagated through resonant waveguide assemblies located throughout the ship's exterior surface. While the small assemblies accelerated cosmic waves at the unheard of velocity of Mach 48, the magnetoplasmadynamics to obtain a propulsive momentum were certainly not capable of allowing the ship to reach velocities approaching light speed.

As the deadly fighter zipped through 250,000 feet, he selected the impulse engines *On.* All four of the huge exhausts immediately glowed a incandescent white as the immense flow of concentrated cosmic rays blasted the craft upward. Leaving the Earth's atmosphere behind, Mike followed the magenta line as the east coast of Florida passed underneath in blur. The horizon went dark as they crossed the Atlantic Ocean in mere seconds and the day turned into night as the ship outran the sun.

The curved flight path quickly straightened into the inky blackness of space as a billion stars filled the view ports and the craft leapt forward like a Thoroughbred race horse given its head. Mike checked the speed. *"Wow...186,000 miles per second almost instantly."*

The impulse engines shut down automatically as they were no longer needed at max speed. With no drag, atmospheric friction or gravity to contend with, the inertialess ship would continue on its course unimpeded and unaided. It operated in total accordance with Newton's First Law of Motion until the Callala Drive—the inertialess antigravity system created by the

High Overlord of Tyrin over three million years earlier—was shut down by Mike upon arrival at the coordinates. At that point, the *Galahad* would come to an instantaneous stop—nothing material inside the ninth magnitude inertialess elliptical field surrounding the ship held any momentum.

The vastness of space was almost impossible to comprehend. The *Galahad* was flying almost directly away from the sun on the perihelion side to reach the asteroid belt in as short a span of time as possible. Mike thought of the *Raptors* seated back at the rear of the flight deck and sent instructions to the communications operator.

"Hey, Ten Ring, you might want bring your guys up here to take a gander at this," Niki announced over the comm system installed in everyone's helmet. "We should get a quick look at Mars as we pass by…A *real* quick look."

Onboard *Lancelot*, Hollywood looked at the monitors that showed a rearward view, expecting to see the blue marble they called Earth rapidly receding in the distance.

"Hey, something's wrong. There's nothing in the rearview. It's totally black. Check the feed for the view screen, Blaze."

"Not necessary, Hollywood. What's our current speed?"

He glanced at the readout in front of him. "186,282 miles per second…the speed of light in a vacuum."

"Right, so if we're going the speed of light…which is actually electromagnetic radiation…we would not be able to visually perceive anything behind us, correct?"

"Ah…suppose that would be correct. But the stars on either side still look the same…Interesting…I'm assuming that's also why the those directly in front of us turned purple."

"Close, but not quite. Since we are traveling toward the stars, the nearest of which is Alpha Centauri at 4.3 light years, the light coming from them is traveling also 186,282 miles per second. What we are experiencing is called a Doppler shift…Think of a train coming down a railroad track. Its whistle seems to change frequency from high to low as it passes a listener…In this case, our velocity affects our perception of visual light ahead because it doubles the actual speed or closure rate and we can only perceive the highest wave length in the visible spectrum…violet."

"I'll take your word for it. I think it's a hoot that all the SyFy movies and TV shows have it all wrong."

Raven piped up, "That's show business for you. I suppose it's kind of like westerns."

"How's that?" asked Blaze.

"Their six-guns never seem to run out of bullets."

Blaze cocked her head and wrinkled her brow. *Electromagnetic radiation…visible light is 400 - 700 nanometers…Waves of the First Order. Gamma Rays are 10 to the minus sixth power nanometers and Cosmic Rays are 10 to the minus twenty…Waves of the Second Order…*

***

CHAPTER TWELVE

SOL ASTEROID BELT

"Inertialess drive off, cloaks off, maneuvering thrustors on, detectors at max range," commanded Lucy to Padrino for relay to the other two *Heracles* fighters that had halted abeam Guinevere. *"We are at the edge of the asteroid belt some two AUs or 141,000 million miles from your sun."*

"Aye-aye, Captain," responded Padrino.

"Wow! It only took us to a little under five minutes to get here from Earth."

"Yes, Bone, we travel at the speed of light when we are in free mode in the vacuum of space. That's why I restored inertia which stops us instantly."

"It's about kinetic energy. We were in inertia when the Callala Drive was kicked in and when it was turned off, we returned to the original state and stationary...Don't you see?" offered Padrino.

"Think I'm gettin' a headache again."

"Just enjoy, it, Bone. Finally...Something you don't understand or can control," Loraine projected.

"Yet, Pard, yet...Give me time."

"That's what I'm afraid of."

"Padrino, please remove my thought shield so I can give instructions to the others in hologram."

"Killing the shield. Hologram on."

Lucy's hologram appeared in the flight deck of *Galahad* and *Lancelot* as she gave the operational instructions.

"Heracles flight, we are far enough out from Tellus orbit to get in a little weapons practice. I noticed during our flight here that our fabrication team back on Tyrin added an additional weapon to our armament that you are all familiar with...Your G2 multi-barrel coil gun."

There was a saturnalian response on the other ships.

"Oorah! That's what I'm talkin' about!" said Cowboy.

"Got a weapon we already know how to use," added Hollywood.

"Be interesting to see its performance in the vacuum of outer space," said Blaze.

Farmer & Stienke

"Correct, Blaze. We'll save the G2 until just before drone practice. First, we'll start with the Star Killers. We will want to enter the field a few thousand miles to give a full 360 field of fire...Spread out...Get at least a thousand miles between ships and each of us will pick a C-type asteroid. They'll be the largest and are mainly carboniferous. Fire three missiles in rapid sequence and record the hits."

Each of the copilots flying on her wing selected a course and engaged the maneuvering thrusters to gain the needed separation.

Lucy nodded at Padrino and the hologram faded away. *"All right, Bone, your time to shine."*

"Been waitin' for this. Gonna be like shootin' beer cans off a fence rail...Captain, take us in."

"As you will." She glanced at him and grinned.

She nudged the main thrusters and threaded the *Guinevere* into the field that some scientists believe is the debris of a planet that formerly occupied an orbit between Jupiter and Mars while others think it is just the residue of planet building materials left over from the formation of the solar system some six billion years ago. Notwithstanding, it was a dangerous area to be and not a place for max speed without full shields up.

"Two thousand miles inside the field, Weapons Officer."

"Thank you, Lucy...uh, Captain. Maintain speed." Bone held his hands over the two dimensional display and spread them apart vertically causing the pictured sector of space to enlarge to the three dimensional tank. He reached inside the hologram, touched a target while his other hand passed over the

230

missile control screen. *"Ripple firing Star Killers at target Alpha...One gone, two gone, three gone."*

They watched the three missiles streak toward a rock asteroid almost a half mile wide in the display. Multiple flashes four times the size of the target, lit the hologram. After the third explosion died away, the largest piece left was no bigger than a Volkswagen.

"Good shooting, Bone," came Loraine's thought.

"Outstanding, jarhead," added Padrino.

"I know."

Lucy looked at the results from the other two ships. *Very good.* She nodded at Padrino to once again activate the hologram. "Testing complete with the Star Killers. I want you to pick a number of new silica base targets using the spectrographic sensors. S-types consist primarily of silicate anions whose charge is balanced by various cations and have a very stony appearance. Target these with your energy beam projectors in multiple directions."

"Turn left fifteen degrees, maneuver as required, increase speed to one-half thrustors," Bone directed.

"Left fifteen...maneuvering...one-half thrustors," she answered.

The powerful fighter picked up speed and unerringly wove its way through the far-flung asteroid field. Bone passed his hand over the energy beam control. Ravening purple beams of pure energy leapt out in all directions almost faster than the eye could follow from the projectors in the ring of slots just below the cosmic energy accumulator dome.

Asteroid after asteroid of the S-type turned to molten slag at just the touch of those unimaginably powerful beams of energy. Some even disintegrated into sparkling coruscating displays of incandescent brilliance.

"My sweet Jesus!" Loraine exclaimed under her breath, forgetting to use her newly acquired telepathy.

Onboard the *Galahad*, Mike initiated a similar speed and maneuvering pattern as did the *Guinevere*.

"Now, we want to check out the G2 guns on a few of the smaller M-type asteroids. These are much more dense metallic ones…composed mostly of iron and nickel and you can use your electromagnetic sensors to locate some in the ten to thirty foot diameter size…roughly the size of a Death Globe. Target them with your G2s…Finally, Loraine, Raven and Lanie, you get to do your thing with the drones. We'll rendezvous at these coordinates in thirty minutes…and don't worry about using up ammunition. We'll swing by *Excalibur* at Lagrangian Point 2 on the way back and have them transport any replacement armament items we need aboard each ship…Good shooting."

"M-type targets selected," sent Chet as he passed his hand over the operational controls for the two G2s mounted on rotating turrets between the cockpit bulge and the cosmic energy accumulator. Similar in action to the multi-directional energy beams, the six barrels of each of the deadly electromagnetic coil guns spun around and spat out twelve 7mm depleted

uranium projectiles per second at the metal-based rocks. Sparks flew from the surfaces as the dense space debris shattered, one after another.

"Yes, sir, Chet. That's the way to do it," congratulated Mike.

**EARTH'S THERMOSPHERE
SOUTH POLE**

"Report, Krrk!" thundered an agitated Fleet Commander Klsth.

"Yes, Sire. Repairs are complete to the T-Cruisers. The transporter on Captain Lssps' ship is the only equipment off-line and not repairable. Her Reapers will have to dock and physically unload," replied the maintenance officer.

"Sub-Commander, fleet status report."

"In our three remaining mother ships, we have a total of fifty-eight operational Reapers and forty-seven Death Globes standing by," reported Prlk.

"Curse that imbecile Captain Brzll. If he was not related to the Emperor, I would have never included him in this raid. The loss of his ship has cost us…Be that as it may, send out thirty Death Globes to search for concentrations of the humanoids. They are far more flavorful than the four legged creatures. Leave the seventeen remaining to serve as an expanded protection shield. Send them out to a thousand mile perimeter umbrella. We must be more cautious with these Terrestrials, however puny their weapons might be."

"Yes, Sire…We have accessed their image signals from their satellites and have noticed large gatherings in numerous locations around their planet in what the humanoids call 'stadiums' for some type of games with a sphere."

"Interesting that they should make it easy for harvesting." What could pass for laughter, rumbled from deep in his massive body. "Launch the Death Globes…It is time."

INSIDE THE ASTEROID BELT

"Dammit, stop that! Whoa…come back here," Loraine said as she fought to get the hang of controlling two drones simultaneously. One had cruised dangerously close to a jagged asteroid the size of a forty story skyscraper in New York City.

Bone glanced over his shoulder at his partner. Even without being able to see through the bulbous black helmet, he knew what her face looked like when she was frustrated. He found himself suppressing a grin, something definitely out of character for him. *"Hey, Pard…Mind if I make a suggestion?"*

"No, I don't need any of your wise-ass comments…I'm not Raven, you know. She's had practice flying two things at once, so stuff a sock in it."

He shook his head. *"Seriously…park those two flying machines for a sec. I want you to try something."*

Reluctantly, she brought one and then the other to a halt as her temperature rose slightly.

"Okay…here's the deal. You're thinking too much."

"I have to think about flying two machines in different directions at the same time. They're not on autopilot, you know."

"I'm aware of that. What I mean is you have to let each hand work independently."

"That's the dumbest advice I've ever heard," she said.

"Look, I play the guitar and you play piano...right?"

"What does that have to do with flying two drones simultaneously?"

"When you play the piano, your left hand plays the base line and the right hand plays the melody...which hand do you think about?"

"Neither one, dummy...I just play the music and...Oh."

"Right...you don't think about it you just do it. Your brain has the capacity to control each hand separately. All I want you to do is relax a little bit. You get all wrapped around the axle and try to think your way through it. Stop it...Let your hands flow with the commands...Just feel it. Take in a deep breath and then let it out slowly. Close your eyes. See what the flight paths will be and then let it happen...Look at nothing, but see everything...You can do it. I have faith."

Loraine let his suggestion sink in for a second. *The big lummox almost makes sense. "Okay. I'll give it a chance."* Once she exhaled the cleansing breath, she placed her hands over the control panels and sent both *Baby Manta's* into motion once again. The muscle tightness between her shoulders seemed to disappear and in a few minutes the drones were each circling a pair of monstrous rocks and targeting them with lasers. A smile came to Loraine's lips. *Yep, just like playing the piano.*

Lucy also joined in with her usual sage advice, *"You will never do anything well, child, until you cease to think about the manner in which you do it."*

Aboard *Lancelot*, Raven found a large carboniferous asteroid over three miles in diameter to maneuver around. After a few minutes she had one of the drones flying a ten mile radius orbit around its poles and another circumnavigating its equator as it slowly spun on its axis. Blaze and Hollywood monitored her performance.

"Doesn't look like the new drones are much of a challenge for you," he sent.

"Not much different than Heckle and Jeckle...except they can't hover and fly backward."

"I see you have the laser targeting system operations down pat as well," Blaze transmitted. *"If we get the chance to catch the Reptoids uncloaked, we'll be able to eat their lunch."*

"That's the plan, I suppose...Any more breakthroughs on the way to detect their cloak? I'm finished with what I can do here. Gonna bring the girls back and lock 'em down for the trip home."

Blaze mulled over the ideas she had been considering. *"Wish I could say yes...It's like waiting for the other shoe to drop. We know they are still out there and probably have been repairing the battle damage the navy destroyer was able to inflict. The question is when and where."*

Hollywood nodded and began to plot a course out of the asteroid field for the recovery flight to join with Lucy.

"Guenivere, Lancelot...we're almost done here. We will be returning to rendezvous coordinates in four minutes."

Lucy acknowledged the thought and directed *Galahad* to join them as soon as possible. *No sense spending any more time here than absolutely necessary. Blaze is right to worry about our enemy. They won't wait to initiate their horrendous activities.*

"Loraine, bring your drones alongside and prepare for interstellar travel."

"Copy that. I'll have them within tractor beam range in thirty seconds."

Bone monitored the seamless recovery as Loraine's hands floated over the control panels. *"Nice job, Pard."*

"Tractors and repellors locked on...cleared to maneuver as required," Loraine sent as she rolled her shoulders to lessen the muscular tension she had built up in her back.

Lucy smiled to herself. *They're coming along as expected.* *"Mister Bone, take us out of here."*

"Aye-aye, Captain." He engaged the thrustors and began to accelerate in a zigzag pattern to clear the asteroid field. Once free from the hazards to navigation, the ship zipped to the coordinates briefed for the three ships to rendezvous. He pulled a hundred miles off the *Galahad's* port side and braked to *a* stop using the nose thrustors. *"Standing by further instructions."*

The trip to resupply from *Excalibur* was uneventful. All nine replacement *Star Killer* missiles were beamed into the rotary launchers in minutes and a multitude of the G2 ferromagnetic projectiles were also subsequently resupplied. The drones were stored in their slots on either side of the cosmic accumulator dome.

"Mission accomplished," Lucy sent to all hands in the three ship. "We'd best get back into position without delay."

EAGLE NEST AIRSTRIP

The flight arrived in cloaked configuration and silently sat down outside the BEF hangar. One by one, the twelve crew members and the three Raptor detachments disembarked, walked down the ramps underneath the ships and magically appeared as they passed through the screen provided by the fourth order cloaks. The giant hangar doors were opened a few feet to allow them to enter.

Mike Hermann unlatched the magnetic lock on the flight helmet and detached it from his suit. He glanced at a large digital wall clock on the inside of the hangar as they approached the elevator. "An hour? We've only been gone an hour?"

"Not much time spent in cruise in these babies," Chet observed. "It would take forever to build up flying time in one of 'em."

"Lucky for you...I'll sign you off as combat ready with only a one point oh...total time in type."

Chet laughed. "Hey, don't do me any favors...If we can ever find the enemy, I'll be more than happy to engage them."

"I hear you."

The crews assembled on the aircraft elevator and one of the *Super Galaxy* crew chiefs pressed the green control button to send them down.

GUARAJA BEACH
SÃO PAULO, BRAZIL

The miles long white pristine beach curled around the crystal clear blue water of the ocean. The tourist magnet near São Paulo—the ninth most populous city in the world—was known as the Pearl of the Atlantic with average temperatures similar to those of Sydney and Los Angeles. The day was no exception as the beach was packed with thousands upon thousands of sun worshipers.

The air—a thousand feet above the bay just off the beach—shimmered and nineteen massive elliptical iridescent green ships materialized.

A somewhat plump American tourist turned to her retired Air Force husband. "Colonel dear, what in the world are those?" She pointed.

He pulled his hand-woven straw hat from his face, sat up in his rented beach half-chair and glanced toward the bay. "My

God in Heaven!" He jumped up and grabbed his beach towel. "Run, Mildred!"

"What are they?" She grabbed her beach bag.

"God dammit, woman, I don't know!…But they're not of this world…Now go, go!"

They sprinted as fast as they could toward the parking lot and restaurants some one hundred yards away to the north. Others on the beach just seemed to stand, awestruck or stunned, and stare at the huge alien ships.

The nineteen *Reaper* ships silently spread out along the beach and at two hundred yard intervals, teleported down ten Reptoid soldiers each. The hideous creatures took positions between the edge of the beach and the water and started herding the now thoroughly frightened people to the center in groups. Every Reptoid held a curved, double-ended, translucent metal sword in two of their four six foot long tentacles—waving the razor sharp weapons about like a ninja with nunchucks as they waddled toward the screaming humans.

SIDNEY, AUSTRALIA
ANZ Stadium

A capacity crowd of 83,500 rugby fans had gathered for the Tri-Nations contest between the Kangaroos—the Australian national team—and their rivals from New Zealand, the equally famous All Blacks. Late in the first half the score was tied at 9 all.

A blocked field goal attempt resulted in a scrum on the twenty yard line. Eight brawny men from each team lined up opposite from the other—interlocking arms in a 3-2-2-1 formation. The remaining seven players were spread out in a single wing on the same side of the field with both fullbacks holding defensive positions between the scrum and the end zone. Once they were set up appropriately, the referee rolled the chubby leather football in between the two.

Players known as hookers were supported by others called props as they kicked and clawed using their feet to try gain control of the ball. Other players behind them—two second row, two flankers, and the one called the eighth man—tried to push the opposing mass of players back and keep the ball under them until a fly half could reach down and pick it up.

Australia's scrum half gained control of the ball and pitched it quickly to the fly half who worked it out to the inside center. He tossed it underhanded in a perfect spiral past his nearest teammate to the right wing speeding along the edge of the field.

A forty-three year old stock broker from Brisbane cheered when the Kangaroos winger Robbie Coyne pitched back to outside center Terry McGregor. "Go, Terry…Go!"

The fleet-footed Aussie cut back inside the All Black defender and sprinted directly at the corner of the end zone and vaulted over the outstretched arms of the New Zealand fullback who had thrown himself horizontal in an valiant effort to tackle him.

The home crowd erupted in a thunderous roar as the flying center crossed the goal line and planted the ball firmly on the turf. He somersaulted over it and landed back on his feet before he leapt up in a joyous celebration.

"He did it! He did it! Terry scored his second bloody try!" the stockbroker yelled as he jumped up and down. He spun around a gave a kiss to his trophy girlfriend—a gorgeous tanned model who stood almost six feet and was rocking a low-cut T shirt. His buddy poked him on the shoulder.

"Mate! You and Mandy made the kiss cam!" He pointed at the large digital TV screens on either side of the stadium. Camera crews had focused on the beautiful blonde earlier and knew a photo op would be forthcoming if her team scored.

Joy for the stockbroker continued as he and his friends relished in the momentary celebrity status. He beamed a dazzling smile that matched hers for an instant.

His eyes caught motion above the stadium as a pair of strange ships suddenly materialized overhead. Sight of the alien craft dumfounded him for a moment. "What the hell is that?" The sausage-shaped metallic green ships were much too large for balloons, but they hovered silently over the stands. An intense green light beamed down from each ship—bathing the spectators in an unearthly glow.

The man's look of curiosity turned to one of stark terror as he realized what was happening at the far end of the field. The kiss cam captured his visceral reaction as he screamed and pointed upward.

Panicked spectators surged for the stadium exits, only to run into giant monsters that almost defied description. Reptoid guards, whose job was to contain the humanoids as much as possible, clacked their alligator-like jaws as they brandished their wicked blades.

The first sports fans attempting to exit screamed as they tried to stop, but the mass of terrified humanity kept pushing from behind. Scores were trampled to death—others were shoved unwillingly into the razor-sharp flashing blades.

A pair of security guards attempted to shoot the alien invaders, but their 9mm handguns were no match for the disruptors wielded by the Reptoids. Tiny holes in their massive bodies leaked a few drops of a gray liquid, but the alien weapons vaporized the security guards into atoms.

The first two *Reaper* ships quickly filled to capacity and returned to their cloaked condition as they ran the dehydration presses and sent a putrid pink mist raining down over the stadium. Two waiting ships moved into position, decloaked and turned their transportor beams on. Another two thousand rugby fans vanished in a matter of a seconds.

GUARAJA BEACH
SÃO PAULO, BRAZIL

The giant ships moved silently closer to the beach, over the groups of milling, panicked masses of humanity and the huge ravening green transportor beams went to work. Thousands went wriggling and squirming inside the deadly light to the craft overhead. Hundreds broke from the corralled groups on the beach for the ocean in a desperate attempt to swim to safety.

The *Reaper* ships began to process their grisly cargos and gallons upon gallons of blood and offal sprayed out, turning the very ocean red.

The hundreds in the water soon realized their deadly peril as the unimaginable amount of 'chum' spewing from the alien craft covered their escape route. Sharks by the score, drawn by the blood in the water, began attacking the swimmers in a feeding frenzy. Tiger sharks, bull, hammerhead, makos and the greatest killer in the ocean, the great whites—also known as the white death—began pouring into the bay for the easy feast.

BEF UNDERGROUND LOUNGE
EAGLE NEST

Lucy was fixing herself a cup of Earl Grey tea when her bracelet vibrated and Darron's voice came through from *Excalibur*, "Lucy, we're getting fourth order spikes from three different locations, all in the southern hemisphere...São Paulo, Brazil, Sydney, Australia and Mumbai, India. "Scanners show nineteen Reaper craft in São Paulo, intermittent returns on two in Australia and another nineteen in India."

"Oh, no. Notify the *Garrin* to expect transport of the BEF craft. I'll get back to you." She stepped to the base comm system on the wall and keyed a number.

"Phillips."

"Dare, Lucy...It's started. Need all personnel to their ships. Repeat, all personnel. The *Garrin* will begin transporting as soon as the first craft is up and running on the flight line. I'll be in your office to brief you in thirty seconds."

"Aye-aye, ma'am. Dare out."

The klaxons started sounding simultaneously with the red scramble rotating lights flashing above every door in the underground complex. Pilots, *Raptors* and crew quickly filled the hallways headed to their respective destinations.

"Looks like it hit the fan," Bone said to Raven as they sprinted to the flight crew ready area.

"Stay safe, you big lug. I've kinda gotten attached to you."

"Gate swings both way, Pretty…See you top side." He pecked her cheek.

They ducked into their respective locker rooms.

"Have all of your units on the line and at idle as soon as you can. I'll instruct Fleet Commander Garrple to start transporting to the three locations on your ready. We'll take Australia with *Guinevere* and send *Lancelot* to Brazil and *Galahad* to India," instructed Lucy.

"Let's continue this on the way to the elevator," said Dare.

"Of course…Based on the information I received from Darron, the stadium in Sydney is still processing per the intermittent spikes. I think we can be assured there will be protection from their Death Globes at all three locations."

"My thoughts exactly," agreed Dare. "Commander Garrple can transport Mama Bird and a squadron of 15s and 18s each. Plus we'll have our four Black Eagles…All to work with your Guinevere."

"But we have no idea how many Death Globes we'll be up against."

"I expect we will when the fur starts flying."

SÃO PAULO AIR FORCE BASE

A four ship squadron of *Gripen* single engine fighters reached altitude and streaked in echelon formation toward the nineteen giant blips showing on their PS-05/A pulse-doppler X-band multi-mode radar.

"Jesus, lead, we don't have enough missiles," said wingman two over the radio in Portuguese.

Each fighter was equipped with four ASRAAM IRIS-T HE/Fragmentation and a single 27 MM Mauser BK-27 cannon.

"Shoot what you got, then go to cannon. Maybe we'll still be around when the other unit is found and reports to base."

"Roger that," from wing two.

Two more clicks followed as the planes went to spread formation.

Lead pilot launched at fifteen miles. "Got tone…Fox one."

"Tone…Fox one," called wingman two.

The other pilots followed suit and four nine foot solid fuel missiles roared off the rails accelerating to Mach 3, each targeting a separate sausage-shaped alien *Reaper* craft.

"Break for target two," called the lead pilot.

Each *Gripen* rolled right and lined up for their second shot.

The missiles exploded one after another three miles from their targets.

"Son of a bitch!" wing four shouted. "Some kind of light came out of nowhere from above the big ships and took out each of our missiles." He swiveled his head to where the beams came from just as ten metallic green globes materialized five thousand feet above in a line along the beach.

"Fox two," called the lead.

He was quickly followed by the other pilots firing at their second targets.

"Fox two."

"Fox two."

"Fox two."

"Break away, break away! Target those green bastards on top," called the squadron leader.

Again, the four just launched IRIS-T missiles detonated in order, miles from target.

Abruptly, wingman four exploded on a ball of fire as a green pulse laser caught the fuselage just behind the cockpit.

"Attack at will...Max maneuvering!" radioed the major commanding the flight. He pulled the stick to his lap and grunted at the eight G climb. With the G suit compressing his legs and abdomen like an anaconda in a mating ritual, he fought against the onset of tunnel vision as best he could. Finally, just as the world turned gray, he unloaded a bit of back pressure and slammed the stick to the left. A bolt of green pulse laser energy blasted by his right wing tip.

He cursed the alien craft that was shooting at him and stood on the right rudder as he reversed the turn and came back almost underneath the *Death Globe*. Thumbing the switch to guns atop the stick, he pulled back until the red pipper in the HUD was centered on the Reptoid craft above. As he held the circle on the ship, he began to pull the trigger when suddenly a shaft of green light engulfed the *Gripen* fighter. It exploded into a hundred thousand tiny pieces, leaving only a dark cloud of smoke where a brave human pilot had given his all.

Number two—a seasoned captain with a wife and child—jinked higher than the closest globe and in a series of dizzying twists and turns brought his nose around as shots from several globes missed him—some by merely inches. He selected his Rheinmetal BK 27 cannon. Knowing he dare not try a stabilized lineup, he picked a sweeping high angle-off shot and squeezed the trigger as the pipper tracked across the Brazilian sky and approached the UFO. The airframe shook with the one second burst as sixteen of the aircraft's 120 cannon rounds roared out.

Eight of the nine ounce high explosive rounds made contact with the Reptoid ship and wrought havoc upon it. Being designed to be shielded from energy weapons, the *Death Globe* hull was no match for the rapid firing revolving cannon. Two rounds took out the intertialess drive. One dismembered the Reptoid pilot, allowing the mortally wounded ship to begin its free-fall 5,000 feet to the pounding surf below.

The Brazilian pilot rolled inverted and took a brief look as the UFO plummeted. His victory smile was short-lived as nine of the surviving globes targeted the two remaining *Gripen* fighters. Just seconds apart, the sound of supersonic fighters screaming over the beach ended abruptly—the echoes of their instantaneous disintegration by powerful pulse lasers faded until only the sounds of screaming sunbathers caught between the hideous Reptoids advancing along the shore and slashing attacks by frenzied sharks.

Landing in ten feet of water close to the shore, the alien ship crashed with a huge splash and crumpled the lower side. The upper half of the hull resembled a giant green jellyfish as wave after wave from the south Atlantic Ocean crashed against it.

STRATOSPHERE OVER TEXAS

"Garrin to Lancelot," called Garron.

"Lancelot, Cabrillo."

"Getting fourth order weapon spikes in Brazil, plus multiple missile launches in addition to the low magnitude emissions. Please notify when Lancelot is ready for transport. Coordinates are already set."

"Everything ready in fifteen seconds, Garrin."

"Affirmative. Lancelot will go first. Will transport Mama Bird as soon as she's on ramp after all Heracles have been transported."

"Roger that." *"You get all that, Hollywood? Blaze?"*

"Got it. Almost through with pre-fight checklist. Weapons ready, Blaze?"

"Weapons are ready."

***

CHAPTER THIRTEEN

SIDNEY, AUSTRALIA

Forty miles off shore, the air shimmered and a silver triangle craft emerged at 40,000 feet. Lucy began sending instructions to her crew. *"Shields on, cloak on. Scan three sixty."*

Her hands moved deftly over the control panel as she opened up the 3-D tank in front of her. Icons for two Reptoid *Reapers* appeared at her twelve o'clock position directly over the ANZ Stadium. *"We have contact."* She immediately sent the *Guinevere* into a shallow dive and began streaking toward her sworn enemy.

Bone had opened his tank to display the airspace over the metropolitan area and locked on the two targets instantly. He received her telepathic authorization to fire at will and—using the ring fingers on each hand—sent two annihilating purple streams of pure energy from their powerful projectors across the hulls of the uncloaked enemy ships.

Flashing with a brilliance rivaling the sun, the invader's shields failed in spectacular fashion with an incandescent flare to violet. The Tyranian energy beam cut through the outer hull of aranak as if it were cellophane and then through the exposed inner bulkheads and engine. Without power, inertialess drive and the antigravity units, the massive ships offered no resistance to the ever-present pull of Earth's gravity. They dropped like stones to the field below as *Guinevere* passed overhead.

Terrified rugby fans who had witnessed the harvesting operations cheered. They knew the stadium exits were blocked, but someone, somewhere was attempting a rescue operation.

Loraine turned on the drone's inertialess drives and unlocked the magnetic couplers holding them to the top of the fuselage. She began setting up a twenty mile orbit around the stadium searching for signs of the cloaked Reptoid fleet. *"Lucy, shall I send out the decoy missiles?"*

"Not yet. Allow our other fighters to get into position."

Fifty miles north of the stadium *Mama Bird* materialized at 30,000 feet. Her four engines were running at flight idle, but her airspeed was zero, exactly the same as when the behemoth was transported from the flight line in Texas. She began fall immediately like a runaway elevator as Aircraft Commander Gears Formby called for copilot Julio Sosa to engage the cloak, and then ran all four throttles smoothly to mil power. "Gear up."

"Cloak is on," Julio replied as reached for the gear handle. He watched the vertical velocity indicator peg at 8,000 feet per minute. "Airspeed thirty knots…Come on baby, you can do it."

The big bird slowly responded as Gears allowed the nose fall to ten degrees below the horizon. Passing 25,000 feet, the indicated airspeed rolled up through 150 knots and he began to ease back on the yoke.

Comm Specialist Sparky O'Neil gave a sigh of relief. "Whew…I thought I was gonna throw up there for a second. I never did anything like that before."

Manta One operator Richard 'Captain Midnight' Webb glanced over and grinned. "Can't say that again…You'll do fine. Just keep breathing deep."

"Manta Operators, stand by for launch."

Joe Kreimborg and Webb acknowledged the alert call from the cockpit and feverously began running the checklists. By the time the drones' turbine engines were started, Gears had the C-5M leveled off at 22,000 feet and 250 KIAS.

"Steady as she goes…cleared to launch," came the call from the AC.

"Trim set two degrees nose down, power eighty-four percent, all systems in the green band." Joe checked his scroll-down menu on the wide screen above his station. "Camera systems on, we have a good video feed. Electomagnetic locks…disengaged…"

Flash Peterman took in a deep breath as his F-15 materialized at 45,000 feet south of Sydney. *Jesus! Dead in the water.* His hand was already on the throttle and instinctively slammed it forward into burner, all the way to the stops. He let go of the throttles for a second and raised the gear handle.

His transition from the total blackness and unbelievable cold of teleportation during his four second trip from Texas to Australia was unexpected. Flash found himself breathing much faster than normal. He could hear his oxygen regulator cycling rapidly as he reached for the cloak selector and rotated it to the *On* position. Both Pratt and Whitney F-220 engines kicked in, producing 23,700 pounds of thrust.

He glanced over his right shoulder at his wingman—twin cones of fire blasted out of the titanium ringed exhaust nozzles for a moment until the aircraft's cloak was engaged. Flash eased the stick to the left and lowered the nose as the speed began to build at a tremendous pace. He monitored the integrated panel display for distance to his wingman, *Guinevere, Mama Bird* and the two *Mantas* and turned to a heading to close with them.

As he rolled out, a pair of additional *Eagles* materialized at his six o'clock, followed every few seconds by another and another.

"Launch the decoys," Lucy sent telepathically as she analyzed the disposition of incoming F-15s and F-18s. *"We've got enough assets to initiate contact."*

Loraine did as ordered, sending eight of the nine foot long missiles closing in on the target area. Each transmitted a search radar pattern similar to that of an F-16 fighter as it first climbed and then initiated a shallow descent at supersonic speeds well within the operational speed envelope of a fourth generation fighter. It didn't take long for the Reptoid *Death Globes* to respond—eight of the ten ships decloaked and began to engage the perceived threats. Intense green pulses streaked across the city of Sydney—each brighter than the sun.

Eight decoys were blasted into nothingness, but a rapid succession of purple energy beams from *Guinevere* rained down upon the closest four *Death Globes*. Three exploded instantly, while the fourth one wobbled away from the off-center impact and began to roll before it started its free fall.

Peterman made a snap judgment call to try the AESA radar for a moment to see if he could get a radar lock on the nearest globe long enough to get a pair of the AIM 120 AMRAAMs off and running.

He heart was in his throat as he fired two and called, "Eagle twelve, fox three, fox three." He pulled the stick full aft and sank deep into the ejection seat as he turned the radar back to the *standby* mode.

Three monster green laser pulses emanated from the targeted globe. Two of them destroyed the pair of Mach 4 missiles he had launched seconds earlier. A third passed 200 feet beneath him. *Holy shit! Not a good idea.* "Eagle Flight, Eagle Twelve, do not attempt slammer shots. I say again, do not attempt slammer shots."

He eased off the back pressure and snapped the cloaked fighter inverted. Flash pulled down through the horizon until the distant green globe was centered in the HUD. He thumbed the selector on the stick from missiles to guns and cross-checked his air speed—*Mach 2*. He eased the throttles back to prevent an over-speed condition as his finger tightened on the trigger.

More than dozen decoy missiles suddenly appeared on his screen as both *Mantas* from *Mama Bird* launched their contributions to the disinformation campaign. The six remaining *Death Globes* fired multiple shots with their pulse lasers.

Lucy leveled the *Guinevere* at 80,000 feet after pulling off from the first pass at the Reptoids and climbing vertically.

"Eagle Twelve guns."

"Eagle Thirteen guns."

The frequency became alive with more than a dozen *Eagles* calling in their attacks on the Reptoids. Tracers appeared out of the clear blue sky as the 20 MM Vulcan cannons roared.

Flash felt the familiar vibration as the gatling gun in the right wing root spat out a stream of HE rounds, mixed with tracers linked as every tenth one. At 6,000 rounds a minute, his burst sent 115 of the deadly shells ripping into the alien craft's hull. He could see the impacts as he followed the stream of red tracers all the way to the target.

On board the *Death Globe* that Peterman attacked, the Reptoid pilot never heard the recall order that Fleet Commander Klsth had given. The HE rounds impacted in a hellish hail of fragments and fire, ripping apart the control center and both of the alien operators in an unsurvivable shower of steel.

One of the F-18s was instantly disintegrated by a pulse laser beam aimed at a decoy miles behind him. *Eagle Eighteen* broke off his successful attack on one of the *Death Globes* only to die in a midair collision with a cloaked Reptoid *Reaper* responding to the recall order.

High above the city, another explosion was heard by terrified residents who looked up and saw a smoke cloud and witnessed two halves of a sausage-shaped green UFO plummet to a freeway leading to the stadium.

Nervous Reptoid security teams—sent to corral the spectators at the stadium—tried in vain to call the ships that had teleported them into position, but their transmissions went unanswered…

AIRSPACE OVER SYDNEY

BEF CEO and Mission Commander Heater McElhenny leaned over and checked the video feed from *Manta One*. "Midnight, can you give me a close-up of the exits to the stadium? None of the survivors seem to be leaving."

"Can do, sir." He rolled the tracking ball onto one of the arched portals and tapped the keyboard. Almost instantly the spy camera aboard the drone bought up a crystal clear image.

Heater saw two of the menacing Reptoid creatures facing a tightly packed mass of humans. Even the flashing blades wielded by their tentacles were visible. He formulated a plan quickly and reached for the intercom button. "Muddy Waters and Shadow Sidell report to the command station."

The two *Raptor* team leaders unstrapped and made their way from the gray reclining seats to the row of work stations on the port side of the highly modified *Super Galaxy's* upper deck.

Clay "Muddy" Waters and Eric "Shadow" Sidell—both seasoned operatives in their own right—glanced at each other and bumped fists.

"Time to bring it," Muddy said.

"Straight up whoop ass time, I'm thinking."

The two stopped on either side of the Mission Commander. Clay leaned over and glanced at the split screen above his station. No enemy ships were visible. The feed from the stadium showed the second portal was much like the first, except a pool of blood and dismembered human body parts showed the fate of those that had tried to rush past the alien attackers.

"What's up Heater? You pick 'em we kick 'em."

"Time for some boots on the ground. I want both squads weaponed up and ready to move in five minutes."

"We can do that, sir. HALO or M800?" Sidell asked.

"That was yesterday...Today, I want you standing up back in the aisle next to the lockers. I'll have Lucy set up a transport for you. Oh...Make sure Doc Long carries additional med supplies. Looks like the survivors down there will need his help."

"You got it."

Clay and Shadow turned and began barking orders to their respective squads.

Heater glanced over at John "Boomer" Eastman. He had been the weapons controller aboard *Sister Bird* and the best choice to take over for Blaze. His performance in Africa, the Middle East and Asia was stellar—he was highly competent.

"Boomer, can you take out a couple of those big ugly bastards on the north end of the stadium? I want the transport area to be secure for the Raptors."

"Sure thing. I can narrow the beam on the sonic cannon and use the microwave to cook their butts. I don't think any organic creature in the universe can stand as much heat as it can generate."

"Make it happen. Give me a few minutes to get the teleportation coordinated and then we'll hit 'em hard."

Lucy relayed the message telepathically. Technicians on the *Garrin* scanned the C-5 and locked onto the first twelve armed *Raptors* in position and confirmed that they were ready.

"It's a go," Heater said once her message from Padrino came through. "Try not to injure any fans if you can."

"Roger that." Boomer used his mouse and slid the power bar on the digital display. A slight humming sound permeated the upper deck of the stretched *Super Galaxy* as the weapons system's gigantic capacitors drained energy from the four engine driven generators. Within a few seconds the pitch rose perceptibly and Boomer centered the targeting crosshairs on the first of two Reptoids. A green *Ready* light illuminated on his panel. *Say bye-bye, asshole.*

Boomer squeezed the red trigger on the joystick mounted to the work station. An intense pulse of energy—an infrared laser heterodyned with a variable sonic wave set to the 2.6 Ghz range—streamed down on the intended alien target.

SIDNEY, AUSTRALIA
ANZ Stadium

One of the two snarling guards immediately looked down at his tentacles. The swords he had brandished so terrifyingly began to glow red even as his green appendages turned black from the intense heat. A scream of anguish and unimaginable pain rumbled from deep inside his gullet as his four eyes burst into flames, followed instantly by his charred upper tentacles. The red hot blades clanged to the concrete near his tree trunk sized legs. His torso split as the internal organs boiled and expanded inside him, spilling onto the pavement as smoke curled from his alligator-like snout.

Already terrified sports fans being held at bay screamed even louder at the awful sight, even as the sickening smell of the burning carnivore's flesh wafted up the exit ramp of the stadium.

The remaining Reptoid guard, unsure of why his captives were acting so agitated, turned one eye toward his compatriot. The sight of gray clotted blood dripping out of a charred upright carcass staggered him, but before he could move another muscle, the beam from the cloaked American transport aircraft began to sear into him with an intensity no carbon-based life form could survive.

Seconds later, the first team of six *Raptors* materialized in a tight circle—backs to each other—weapons at their shoulders. Another group materialized in the next portal of the stadium.

Muddy Waters radioed commands to the others. The *Raptors* began to sprint to their pre-assigned positions to engage the alien invaders.

Sight of the two black-clad warriors—both looking like a darker giant version of the Grays commonly seen in sci-fi movies—did little to calm the terrified spectators. Muddy waved for the fans to follow him clear of the stadium, but they would not budge. *What's wrong with you people?*

He glanced over at his teammate and the answer became obvious. He scanned the perimeter for threats and then set his G3 carbine on the concrete and reached up to his neck. Unfastening the helmet magnetic fasteners, he lifted it clear.

"Hey, we're here to rescue you! Get your asses out to your cars and get as far away from here as you can…Now!" He thumbed back over his shoulder toward the parking lot.

The stunned crowd didn't need a second invitation. They began jumping over the bodies of those who had fallen to the blades of the invaders and streaming out of the portal in a run—giving a wide birth to the smoldering piles of flesh that had been menacing them only a minute before.

Muddy slipped his helmet back in place and locked it down before he picked up his weapon. He stepped clear of the portal and glanced over at his teammate. Using hand signals, he pointed to Conrad and then in the direction he wanted him to go. Connie returned an okay sign.

"Cloaks on, buddy. Don't give them a chance if you can help it." Muddy slipped his hand to his wrist and activated his cloak.

"Copy that…Good luck." Connie shimmered and disappeared as a confused Rugby fan ran past and stopped for a second before shaking his head and resuming his headlong flight.

Four *Raptors* approached the next portal and immediately engaged a pair of Reptoids using their G3 carbines and G4 pistols. The hypersonic projectiles worked as advertised, sending shock waves of incredible power coursing through the alien bodies like a fluid battering ram—fracturing thick bone matter into tiny sharp crystals and turning blood and other liquids into a cell wall-shattering tsunami. A single hit from the more powerful G3 left a puddle of gray alien goo under a misty cloud of the same color. Bits of their jaws and the claws from the tips of their tentacles were all that remained recognizable of the predatory race.

Being slightly less powerful, the G4 pistol merely blasted soccer ball chunks of pulverized organ and bone from the thoracic region of the meat-eating invaders. The hideous eight footer toppled over as his tentacles went slack and the blades he had been carrying clattered to the concrete.

A raucous cheer went out from the sports fans at the unexpected sight. Some began to streak by the alien bodies without being prompted. Others followed the hand motions of the black-clad *Raptors*, taking aid from whatever the unknown creatures were that had delivered a killing blow to the Reptoids.

By the time the last *Raptors* had beamed down and reached the southernmost portals, the remaining Reptoids had been alerted by the absence of body function telemetry from their slain compatriots. One of them in each of the portals spun around to face the unknown threat that had decimated their ranks.

Dutch Offner was cloaked as he approached the next to the last portal. Spotting the alert Reptoid, he checked the line of fire to the creature and noted the heavy concrete pillar directly behind him. *That should do for a backstop.* He lined up the crosshairs on the G3 with the apparition's core, centered vertically between the four tentacles. *God, you guys are some kind of ugly.* He pulled the trigger, sending the hypersonic round across the twenty yards separating them. Gray mist and tiny body parts covered the rugby posters plastered on the walls lining the exits.

Moving a few yards forward, Dutch made visual contact with the other remaining guard. *Dammit! There must be twenty people stacked up in the line of fire behind him.*

The Reptoid nervously spun one eye stalk and then another behind himself, searching for the threat that had just disintegrated his team member.

Only one way to play this. Both of these coil weapons are way too powerful from this angle. Dutch held the G3 with his left hand and deactivated the cloak with his right.

The effect on the Reptoid was immediate—the unfamiliar black-clad warrior looked very much like his mortal enemy, the Tyranians, only far larger. He spun around and clacked his alligator jaws together in a show of fierceness as his appendages brandished the glistening metal blades in blind fury.

Awesome, dude...what kind of moron brings a knife to a gun fight? Dutch chuckled to himself. *He kinda reminds me of the Tasmanian Devil cartoon. If I can just get it to step away from the spectators...* Offner motioned for the Reptoid to come closer.

Apparently the hand gesture did not translate intergalactically as he intended. The creature stopped flailing with his two appendages and instead, raised the upper one at Dutch. An intense green pulse emanated from the silver tube attached a foot above the two finger-like growths that held on to the double-ended sword.

The beam struck the Raptor square in the chest. The black space suit instantly lit up as if struck by lightning—bolts ran all over the surface of it turning it into a brilliant suit of armor befitting a medieval knight for an instant and then dissipated harmlessly into the ground. *Damn...Blaze didn't say it was gonna tickle that much.* He laid his G3 on the ground and cupped both hands across his crotch, mocking his adversary. Using both hands, he motioned for the Reptoid to advance.

The hideous reptilian was enraged by his weapon's failure to disintegrate his enemy and the obvious insolence of the inferior species. With a resounding roar, he bent his tree-trunk size legs and sprang upward—closing rapidly the fifteen yards between himself and his smaller opponent as he arced through the air in the lighter gravity of earth.

Dutch remembered what Bone had said about the alien's ability to jump and was ready for the opportunity when it presented itself. He pushed off with his toes and fell backwards as he drew the G4 pistol like a old west gunslinger. Four shots blasted out of the coil weapon—almost soundlessly—as fast as he could pull the trigger.

The first impacted the huge creature in the crotch, blasting his legs apart at a wide angle. The next two ripped into his torso, blowing basketball sized chunks out its back before impacting harmlessly in the concrete walkway above. The fourth and final shot ripped into the almost nonexistent neck at close range, severing the Reptoid's head and sending it over Dutch's prone body and bouncing across the sidewalk leading to the stadium parking lot.

Offner tried unsuccessfully to roll out from under the rest of the falling alien mass. One heavy elephantine leg—still partially attached to the torso—landed hard across his crest, knocking the wind from him. A handful of rugby fans that had witnessed the fight rushed to his aid and tugged at the gooey remains of the carcass.

"You okay, mate?" one of the burly fans asked in a thick Australian accent. "Do you speak English?"

With the weight off his chest, Dutch was able to activate his helmet mounted speaker. He extended his hand and the burly fan helped him to his feet. "Well that didn't go exactly the way I had it planned, but it did the job. Appreciate the help...Now I suggest you get yourself and all the rest of these fine folks the hell out of here. There are still a couple more of those croc-lookin' things left."

"Good luck." The fan grabbed his girlfriend's hand and they began running for the parking lot.

Eric Sidell, who had just finished clearing the Reptoids from the previous portal saw the conflict from a distance. He jogged up as Dutch picked his G3 off the ground. "What the hell was that all about? Are you purposely trying to get yourself killed?"

"Hell...I don't what came over me, Shadow...Seemed like a good idea at the time."

"Famous last words, dummy...Get your cloak on man. We got some more of them ugly sumbitches held up at the south end of the stadium."

"Roger that." He tapped his wrist bracelet and shimmered away. The two operatives plunged through a small break in the escaping throng of Aussie and New Zealander fans and sprinted south to the next portal.

AIRSPACE OVER SYDNEY

Heater McElhenny reviewed the videos incoming from the *Mantas* while he listened to reports from the *Raptor* ground commanders.

"Negative survivors aboard either alien craft that *Guinevere* shot down," Muddy Waters relayed after the last of the of the Reptoid guards sent to corral the fans inside the stadium were dealt with. "If the missiles didn't kill the human captives, the fall from altitude certainly did."

"We were afraid of that possibility. Maybe they were already dead," Heater radioed back. "The Reaper ships had to be stopped at all costs…Break…*Guinevere, Mama Bird.*"

Padrino came up on the frequency, "*Mama Bird, Guinevere,* go ahead."

"Advise Lucy mission complete, recommend immediate recall."

The diminutive Tyranian pilot received the telepathic message from Padrino and agreed. *"Initial recall procedures. Please remind our small fighters to slow and extend their landing gear before teleporting. Bone take us back out to the beam-in coordinates. "*

"Here we go." Bone hand-flew the three dimensional model floating over the console to the point identified in the tank while Loraine recovered and docked both drones.

**WHITE HOUSE
NSC OFFICE**

"Roland, that's pretty much where we stand up to this point," said SecDef Stewart to the head of the National Security Council.

Roland Perry was the former CEO of Lockheed-Martin and Burner's boss at one time.

The stunned silver-haired senior advisor to President Carlos Benedict—Annette Henry Thompson's successor—finally spoke. "My God in Heaven, Burner. You're right, gotta keep this under wraps or we'll have a worldwide panic on our hands in addition to dealing with those aliens."

"Not to say anything about the BEF working with the Grays to fight those monstrosities. Been able to keep that little relationship quiet since Truman set up MJ-12 in '47…Misinformation is very effective. Only been two presidents since Ike allowed to have access to the UFO files…and this dickwad isn't one of them. Hell, Jimmy Carter asked the head of the CIA at the time, George H. W. Bush, if he could see the files and he was told it was on a need to know basis…and curiosity wasn't a need to know."

"Gonna take a hellova spin to cover up over twenty thousand missing people in India, Brazil and Australia…as well as the loss of USS *Alvin York*."

"Well, there's some folks up here that could almost make Hitler look like a saint. Look what they've been doing to keep our so-called Commander in Chief shiny side up…at least somewhat. They just continue rotating scandals with crises or blaming it on Thompson," said Perry.

"Would be easier, I suppose if he weren't so inept and didn't have that clown he picked for a VP. Neither one can keep their mouths shut."

"Yeah." Roland spun his chair and looked out the big bay window toward the Washington Monument for a moment and then turned back to Stewart. "You know, I thought the military-industrial game was a bucket of worms...Believe me, Burner, got nothing on DC."

"Thought you were nuts, taking this job."

Perry laughed. "I could say the same about you."

"Guilty as charged...Hell, believed I was being patriotic." Burner grinned.

Roland nodded. "Me too...Gotta keep some non-politicians in the hierarchy."

"How the hell did we get in this mess? Seems like all anyone has to do to be able to vote these days is flunk an intelligence test, be an illegal alien...or be dead."

"That too." He paused for a moment. "All right, you and the BEF keep doing your thing and here's what I'll try...I'm pretty tight with his Chief of Staff, Victoria Garnett. He'll do anything she tells him...Shouldn't be too hard, he rarely even attends his own daily briefings, much less read the data."

"What do you think? He can only play so many games of golf...Schedule some more fund raisers?"

"You got it. Seems like it's the only thing his eminence is actually good at...That or taking vacations."

"Well, whatever. Just keep him out of our hair."

"Do my best, Burner, do my best. Doesn't matter as long as we keep making him feel important."

Stewart chuckled. "He reminds me of *The Emperor's New Clothes* story."

"You think?"

***

CHAPTER FOURTEEN

BEF READY ROOM
Eagle Nest Ranch

"Report," said Dare from the front of the room. "Cowboy, you first."

"Not really much to say, Chief...we were about ten minutes late and a dollar short gettin' to Mumbai. Drone images showed massive loss of life...blood all over the marketplace. People staggering around like in a daze..."

"The blood is discharged from their harvestors during processing," offered Lucy.

"Processing?" asked Bone.

"It's our understanding that they remove all bodily fluids, eject it from their craft and then compress the remaining tissue and bone into what best could be called 'protein wafers'…It doesn't take long."

"Oh, gag," said Loraine as she turned pale.

"Hollywood?"

"Pretty much the same story, Dare…Except the Brazilians took out one of their…what do you call 'em, Lucy…Death Globes?"

She nodded. "They are the Reptoid's fighter support and the harvestors are called Reapers."

"Yeah, well there was one laying in the surf and we managed to get off a single beam on the last, uh, Reaper just as it started to cloak…Cut him in two like a scalpel…They didn't make it. Unfortunately, neither did the fourship flight from the Brazilian Air Force…Reptoids got 'em all."

"With the Death Globes and Reapers cloaked, we had no idea how many there were or even if they were still there…for that matter. The only saving grace was they couldn't see us either," said Blaze.

Dare solemnly nodded. "Lucy, looks like your *Guinevere* unit was the only one to see action."

"They were still in process of harvesting from the stadium as only two ships could operate at a time. They were, of course, uncloaked and unshielded when they were beaming up the people. We took out those two, plus two more…one accidentally when one of our F-18 pilots collided with a cloaked one…We did, however, eliminate ten of their Death Globes. They apparently have no defenses against our fighter's guns. We're not sure if ten was all they deployed. As soon as we showed up, the Reapers cloaked and presumably retreated back to their transports. Our Raptors accounted for thirty of the vile creatures on the ground with no casulties...I am sorry to report that we lost three F-18s, including the accidental one, and there was massive civilian loss...but not near as much as it could have been."

Flash Peterman spoke up, "I have to tell everybody about a decision I made...and quickly learned to regret. Our AMRAAMs are so much more powerful than the 20 MM cannon, that I took a chance to launch a couple at the first globe I engaged...Big mistake. They knocked 'em both down in a New York minute and fired a pulse where I had been a half second before. Didn't matter if I was cloaked or not...that beam was huge."

"How did you make your gun pass?" Jill asked.

"I had already made a seven G snap pull-up to separate from the missiles, so I quickly decided a high yo-yo would put me in a good position to come back down into firing range. Things happen pretty quick, ingressing at Mach 2."

Jill and the other jet pilots nodded their understanding.

"So, overall would you say the decoy missiles were effective in bringing the Reptoid fighters out of their cloaks?" Dare asked.

Flash looked around the room at the surviving pilots from the Sydney operation who were agreeing. "Yeah, damned effective this time...I wouldn't bet the ranch on it for the next engagement though. They likely will decide to change up their tactics before they try it again...Know I would."

"That's a good point," Heater added. "We'll review our options. It's always smart to not try to play the same hand every time."

Bull Gaspar stood up. "Guys, I don't want to sound like a whining bench warmer, but I felt pretty damned useless setting inside the cargo bay of *Mama Bird* during the whole engagement. I'm sure the others did, too."

He had been assigned as a M600 pilot after years flying with CEO Dare Phillips as his WSO. Dare had assigned himself to full overview of all the units from the bridge of the *Garrin*.

"Here, here," Jori 'Ice' Carter agreed. The former A-10 pilot was commanding one of the M200 VTOL fighters.

"I suppose that was my call," C-5M aircraft commander Gears Formby said. "When we transported, the Reptoids were already in position and I didn't want to slow and descend for launch."

"Why don't we have the *Garrin* transport us out in midair, like they did the Raptors? They can do that…right Lucy?"

"Of course…I'm surprised we didn't think of it before."

"Just something to try on the next engagement. I'm damned certain we could help."

"Thanks for bringing it up, Bull. The learning curve is pretty steep and we can use all the bright ideas we can generate," Dare said. "Muddy…lessons learned in ground ops with the Reptoids?"

"Boss, they aren't wearing any armor at all. G3s nearly vaporized 'em. The G4 handguns could take out a chunk the size of a watermelon…Quite effective, Blaze."

She acknowledged the complement with a blush and slight nod.

"We may want to carry some additional handguns with less penetration, due to the close proximity of the crowds. High-cap .45 H&K probably."

"Use your judgment."

Eric Sidell glanced around the room until he found Dutch Offner. He pointed over at him. "Hey, Dutch! Tell everybody about your little mano y mano with the big ugly."

Dutch shot him a quick look and then rose to his feet. "Okay, wise guy…Well, gang, it happened like this…"

"…it took ten minutes to wash the gray slime off the space suit. And that didn't do a thing about the stink…By the way, Blaze and Gears, the dissipator system did ground the disruptor pulse as advertised, but it still felt a whole lot like sticking my finger in a light socket."

Gears grinned. "We'll work on that…"

Ten Ring chuckled. "Better than the alternative, Dutchie boy."

"Dang, that would have made a great video," Bone said. "Dutch Offner doin' the Saint Vitus' dance."

Lucy listened to the exchange carefully. "Gentlemen, not withstanding the heroics demonstrated by Mister Offner, I would like to remind you all that the Reptoids are known to utilize their ability to disguise themselves by projecting a hologram similar to their victims. They can be very deceiving and still be a threat you might not immediately recognize."

Dutch frowned. "Forgot about that part…Seemed like a good idea at the time."

Shadow laughed out loud. "Yeah…right up there with hold my beer and watch this!"

Bone chuckled. "I can relate…Hell, they even duplicated Loraine and me once…Dang near got us both fired."

Raven smiled broadly. "Two of you? Now that's a thought."

"Looks like we're at a stalemate, people…we can't see them and they can't see us. Only way to engage them is when they uncloak and discontinue their shields to harvest…That's good *and* bad," said Dare.

"Without knowing when and where they will strike next, I think the next step is for the entire team to remain on full alert status twenty-four-seven. Two shifts…twelve on, twelve off for the duration." He looked around the room for any sign of disagreement, but found none. "Heater, assign the personnel to their respective shifts as you see fit.

"Folks, we have to cut our response time down to half of what we normally do…Far too many lives are at stake. I want both C5s and half the fighters outside on the ramp…cocked, locked and ready to launch in seven minutes. If you're on crew rest we'll need you to be available for a fifteen minute emergency recall. Doc Stewart, I need every member to have a go pill with them, just in case."

"I can do that," Hollywood Stewart's redheaded wife—and BEF Flight Surgeon—Kelli replied.

"Anything else…come by the office or text me. Heater, you have the floor."

He got to his feet. Dare patted him on the shoulder as he passed by on the way to his office. The CEO had a secure call to make to the SecDef and apprise him of the BEF's plans.

SECDEF STEWART'S OFFICE
The Pentagon

Burner Stewart picked up the receiver and heard a familiar voice. "I hope you have some good news for a change, Dare."

"Five Reapers and eleven Reptoid Death Globes total. Not exactly the overwhelming victory we had hoped for."

"What were our losses?"

"Three F-18s plus the Brazilian Air Force lost an alert fighter detachment…four Gripens engaged them and were able to take down one of the alien fighters."

"Jesus…I had hopes the number would have been higher."

"Unless we come up with a way to see though their cloaks, there really isn't any way to find them. They were quick to respond to radar and knocked out every decoy missile we sent, as well as a couple of slammers that Flash got off. He's damned lucky that he jinked hard after launch…Their beam weapon targeted the launch site almost immediately."

Burner frowned. He was a long time friend and admirer of the younger fighter pilot. "What effect did the M-61 cannons have on the alien craft?"

"Excellent…their standard shields cannot stop steel, thank God. All the fighter kills were with guns."

"I see…I talked with my old friend Roland Perry in the White House. He's gonna try to keep the President off our backs as long he can. Unfortunately, there are only so many fund raisers and tee times he can take before adverse public opinion forces him to act somehow."

"Even ineptocracies have their limits, I suppose."

Burner laughed. "You broke the code…What next?"

"Right now, everybody is on combat alert schedule. I'm putting the fighters and C5s out on the ramp to shorten our response times. We got to Mumbai and São Paulo too late. It all depends upon what target they hit and how many victims the Reapers can beam up at any one time."

"You can't keep going twenty-four hours a day forever. People do start making mental errors…as you know."

**BEF UNDERGROUND HEADQUARTERS
DARE'S OFFICE**

"Yeah, Burner, I know…Don't have a lot of choices. I put some of the team in crew rest, but I'll pull them right back out if I need them. This teleportation thing is different cat…You can go from cockpit alert in Texas to being in combat across the world in a matter of seconds."

Blaze walked into the office and had a seat across from Dare. "I need to speak to Burner when you're through," she mouthed.

He nodded. "Excuse me Burner, Blaze just came in and she wants to say something." He handed the phone over to his girlfriend.

"Sorry to interrupt, Mister Secretary, but I need your help."

"Not a problem at all, young lady. Just hearing your voice again gives me hope. How can I assist you?"

"I need three thermonuclear warheads. The W88 MIRV is the right size to fit in our Star Killer Missile."

Burner sat stunned for a second. He knew the brilliant scientist was not joking, but contemplated the use of the weapons over populated areas and envisioned a mushroom cloud with hundreds of thousands of civilian deaths. "Are you sure? The blast radius…"

"I know all the technical attributes of the weapons, sir. I only need your help in locating three that we can beam here for my little surprise."

EARTH'S THERMOSPHERE
SOUTH POLE

"We lost how many craft?" thundered Klsth.

Sub-Commander Prlk's tentacles waved about nervously. "Five Reapers and…eleven Death Globes, Sire."

"That was *your* mission, Prlk! I should throw you into the processor, but I am concerned your rotten carcass would spoil what little of this abominable planet's protein you were able to gather."

"Yes, Sire." All four of his eye stalks drooped as they all gazed at the deck of the ship, afraid to look at his commander's green face, tinted with the gray of fury.

Klsth stomped about the control room in a tight circle and then turned back to Prlk. "Any other craft damaged?"

"No, your excellency."

"Has all the containerized protein been transferred?"

"In two more rlls, sire. We are ferrying most of the harvest to Captain Lssps' ship due to his disabled transporter to save time on the next foray."

"Hummpf, that is the first smart thing you have done, Prlk…see that it is not the last."

"Yes, Sire…Uh, no, Sire."

"Weapons Officer Krrlp, your explanation."

"Yes, Sire. They have apparently joined forces with the hated Tyranians."

"How so?"

"We saw a new ship…unmistakably of Tyranian design but many times larger than their scout fighters. It beamed two of our Reapers as they were transporting the humanoids from the surface to their processing holds.

"They must have shown the terrestrials their cloaking technology as we could not see the actual fighter craft and could only return fire based on the launch of their weapons. They launched missiles to trick us into uncloaking and firing.

"It is also apparent they do not posses the capability of using the defensive force shields…Not so the Tyranian ship, though."

Klsth was silent for a moment. "We will send the entire fleet in tiered coverage on the next raid. The three T-Cruisers will hold cloaked and shields up at fifty kilometers in the thermosphere for top protection. They are certainly equal to anything the tiny Tyranians can bring to bear…We proved that deep space when we destroyed two of their so-called invincible Maulers."

"What about the Death Globes, excellency?" asked Fleet Science Officer Krpld.

"Thirty of our armed Reapers will layer cloaked at 50,000 feet in the troposphere and our thirty-six remaining fighters will position themselves at twenty thousand feet to closely protect the twenty-three working units close to the ground. Again, I do not want to remind anyone to remain cloaked except for the processing Reapers…is that clear?" He snapped his jaws twice for emphasis.

BLAZE'S LAB
Eagle Nest

"Voilà!" Blaze stepped back from her Elemental Magnetic Resonance Tomography unit. "Got it."

"Got what?" Gears asked as he looked up from his computer screen.

"The lens the Tyranians use for their cosmic accumulators are not rubies."

"Looks like a big flat kind of ruby."

"I just looked at the crystalline structure of the one on my bracelet." She reached in the scanner, removed it, reattached it on her wrist and tapped it. "Lucy!"

"Goodness, child, you needn't shout," she came back on the comm link.

"Sorry...But, I believe I've got a fourth order detector solution...need you back down here, please."

"I'll be right..." Lucy finished her statement as she materialized in the lab. "...there."

"You don't mess around," said Gears as he got up from his stool.

"Neither do you...talk to me girl. We and your planet will continue to suffer losses until this problem is solved."

"Well, my curiosity got the better of me and I wanted to see the inside of the bracelet...the lens is not a ruby."

"I know. We call it a seatonite. You should have asked."

"If I did, then I probably wouldn't have looked inside...A ruby is made up of hexagonal scalenohedron crystals."

"Come again?"

"A twelve-sided polyhedron, my dear Gears, and each of its faces is an identical scalene triangle, or a triangle with three different side lengths although with uneven bottom edges."

"Everybody knows that."

Lucy grinned.

"Uh huh." Blaze cocked her eyebrow. "Anyway, your crystals are all perfectly uniform and here's the key. Rather than being aligned randomly...they are perfectly aligned vertically."

"That is true, but I don't see what you're getting at," said Lucy.

"Apparently, long ago, your scientists learned to align the crystals in a vertical configuration...with the negatively charged end facing outward."

"Like an optic fiber cable to better facilitate the absorption of cosmic rays, which are waves of the second order," offered Gears.

"Right."

"I still don't..."

"I know, Lucy, it hit me like a ton of bricks."

"What? I just don't understand."

"We know that fourth order waves have at least 1500 bands. But, actually, they also have distinctive upper and lower bands too," Blaze continued.

"I didn't know that."

"Neither did I," added Gears.

"A maximum upper band fourth order zone of force is impenetrable to anything except a fifth order wave or above since they are the shortest vibrations that can be propagated through the ether...because the ether itself is *not* a continuous medium."

"I think I'm starting to see where you're going," said Lucy. "Wait, let me summon Rollân, our Chief of Science. He must hear this."

"I was just going to suggest that," added Blaze.

Lucy tapped her bracelet. "Garron, please send Rollân to these coordinates."

In less than three seconds, Rollân materialized in Blaze's lab.

"I just love that thing," said Gears.

"Please continue," Lucy said.

Blaze nodded. "Welcome, sir...Now a *zone of force* is an upper band fourth order phenomenon of the ninth magnitude. It doesn't matter if it's a lower band cloak or an upper band full shield, the fourth order wave sets up a condition of stasis in the particles composing the ether. This stasis is detectable only by a fifth order sensor."

"That is correct, child," offered Rollân. "But..."

"I'm getting there, sir. When the accumulator lens absorbs and directs the second order cosmic rays to the storage banks, it necessarily condenses and converts the energy to the fifth order similar to the way second and third order waves can be converted to different fields of force...like a white light is resolved onto colors by a prism. That's how you create your fourth order beam weapons of pure energy. In order to fully understand the fourth order, you must understand and be able to utilize the fifth order."

Rollân's eyes got large. "By the Great Obelisk! If we reverse the polarity of the seatonite crystals to positive facing outward, it becomes a fifth order projector and by its very nature, will detect and pinpoint a condition of stasis in the ether."

Blaze nodded and smiled. "I can make fifth order wave band projectors for the *Annihilator* and *Heracles* class ships to detect bands within bands...They have sufficient source power from their accumulators to operate it, but I'll need a bowl or domed-shaped seatonite crystal in order to get proper dispersion of the sensor waves. The waves would operate similarly to our radar and we could data link it to all of our BEF craft."

"We can easily create the seatonite crystals in any shape and number you wish."

"That is outstanding work, Blaze. I knew you would come up with the solution...given enough time," beamed Lucy.

"I see what you mean about this child, Annuna. This device will rank near the creation of the inertialess antigravity drive created by High Overlord Callala so long ago. Our science has become stagnant...Well done, my dear, very well done...I'm assuming you'll require one for each ship...What size would you need these *bowl shaped* crystals?"

"Actually, I see two for each craft...one for the top and one for the bottom...look up, look down coverage." She wrinkled her brow. "What I'm currently visualizing is something the size of a basketball."

Rollân glanced at Lucy. "Basketball?"

She chuckled and held her hands apart...

"There is something else I've been wondering about," Blaze added.

"Yes," Rollân replied.

"Your fourth order battle shields...What level are they?"

"Sixth magnitude...Why?"

"How many Maulers did you lose when the Reptoids broke through?"

"Two, but what are you getting at, child?"

Lucy also had a puzzled look on her face.

"Now, a ninth magnitude fourth order shield is totally impenetrable, correct?"

Rollân nodded. "Nothing can penetrate it, not even light, save and except a fifth order weapon that no one has. But our ships didn't have time to activate it before the primary shields failed."

"What if I could show you how to set up an automatic trip for activation?"

"None of our computers are fast enough to do that. Maybe in another thousand years or so…"

Blaze walked over to her keyboard and tapped in a code. "Take a look at my schematics on the screen."

They glanced up at her fifty inch monitor.

Lucy's hand went to her mouth. "Oh, my goodness, girl, what have you done?"

She pointed to a computer generated *Mauler* surrounded by concentric rings of differing intensity.

"As you can see, there are multilevels of screens from the far reaching light outer magnetic sensor and fourth order detector, to the first defensive screen of the third magnitude. If activated by any type of energy weapon, it trips the second defensive screen of the sixth magnitude which should stop anything but concentrated fire from several Reptoid ships. Behind it, is a seventh magnitude screen…Like this. I brought a prop from the house for demonstration."

She picked up a red onion from her work bench and started peeling off layers. "In the event of the seventh magnitude screen's failure by flaring into the violet, it automatically trips the impenetrable ninth magnitude *zone of force* and the ship is sealed up like a turtle. All the screens are, of course, driven by the inexhaustible power of hadronium catalyzed cosmic energy."

"They would be alive...but blind," said Gears.

"Yes and no, Gears," replied Lucy. "Alive, yes, but thought waves are of the sixth order and can penetrate a zone of force...We've just never actually been able to use it before."

Gears looked over to Rollân. "And you said a fifth order energy beam could also penetrate it?"

"So we believe. Our science has determined that the fifth order begins in the GHz range of a googol which is 10^{100}. But, before this child came along, we just didn't know enough about the fifth order to use it."

"I see," Gears said almost to himself.

"What do you call your energy force beams?"

"We've called them Z-Beams for millennia, Blaze," offered Lucy.

"Z-Beams? What does that stand for?"

"Zeus...If you'll recall from your mythology, Zeus freed the Gigantes, the Hecatonchires and the Cyclopes from their dungeon in Tartarus. As gratitude, the Cyclopes gave him the thunderbolt."

"But that's a myth."

Lucy grinned. "Is it?"

"All right, works for me." Blaze grinned, shook her head and continued with her fifth order explanation, "And since the zone of force is in the vacuum of space..."

286

"The magnetoplasmadynamics that creates a propulsive momentum could be adjusted through the resonant waveguide assemblies to open a singularity *inside* the zone of force and escape from overwhelming superior odds," interrupted Lucy.

"That's what the math says."

"May we have those schematics, my child?"

"I just sent them to the *Excalibur* a minute ago when you were talking with Gears. All of your ships can easily be retrofitted with the device."

Rollân just smiled and nodded. "We can't just call it a *device*...What if we call it the Blaze Convertor?"

"Oh, I don't really..."

"Hush, child. I think that's a marvelous idea, Rollân. The Blaze Convertor it is...Of course the Reptoids, by their very nature of using the fourth order, have a zone of force also. It could well be another stalemate. Assuming they know how to use it," said Lucy.

"Maybe, maybe not," said Blaze with the characteristic furrow between her eyes.

BEF UNDERGROUND HEADQUARTERS
Mess hall

Gears was wearing his black BEF flight suit as he came through the cafeteria line with a full meal on his dinner tray and a large Texas sized glass of iced tea. He sat alone against one of the far walls and absentmindedly removed the paper sanitary cover off his drink straw and stuck it into the tall plastic tumbler.

Something about the ruby colored plastic straw kicked his mind into overdrive. Perhaps it was the color—almost exactly like the ruby that Blaze initially mistook the seatonite crystals in the bracelets to be.

As a male, Gears was wired differently than his redheaded genius coworker. Where she often envisioned shields, screen and defensive applications of the technology they explored—just as often he seemed to be drawn to the offensive weaponry side of things. He took a long sip of the sugary sweet tea and set the glass down on the tray as the column of liquid settled back down the straw.

He pulled it from the crushed iced and blew out the few drops left in the cylinder. Gears lifted it to his face and peered through the straw like almost every child who has ever handled one. Swinging the tip around, he found Bone seated nearby in an animated conversation with Raven as they enjoyed a bite of lunch.

What the hell... Gears tore off the corner of his paper napkin and slipped in his mouth. Once it was suitably moistened, he rolled the wad tightly into a ball, stuffed it in the straw and lined it up with Bone's head. He took in a breath and wrapped his lips around the makeshift pea shooter and let fly.

Bone was regaling Raven with the tale of a dribble cup he slipped into Cross police station to torment his boss, Captain St. John, when a sloppy wet blob of paper smacked into his right ear before it fell onto his shoulder. *What the hell?* He glanced down and flicked the offending soggy little projectile from his T-shirt.

Raven looked at him with a question clearly etched on her face.

Bone shrugged and then they both started looking around the room until they focused in on Gears.

The genius pilot and engineer was grinning like a cat that ate the canary. He held up both thumbs and nodded as he said, "It works!"

***

CHAPTER FIFTEEN

BLAZE'S LAB
Eagle Nest

Gears sat the plastic bag down on his work station and handed a smaller similar one to Blaze. "Here you go, young lady. I know...you told me you weren't hungry, but I though you might be later and want a grilled chicken sandwich."

"You are so sweet...even had them put it on ciabatta bread and hold the mustard," she replied without even opening the white takeout bag. "I thought you were gonna eat yours there..."

"That was the plan. Sometimes getting away from the desk for a bit lets my mind, uh, re-engage...Question? These new fifth order projectors that the *Excalibur* is adding to herself, the *Garrin* and the three *Heracles* class fighters…can the fields be modified into shapes other than hemispheric and bubble?"

"Sure. If the emitters are correctly modulated to project other shapes, we could do beams, needle beams and even planes of force I suppose. Why do you ask?"

"Can the projectors send out a tube?"

She considered his request for a second. "Tube?"

He held up the red straw from his styrofoam container of tea. "Yeah. Like this…only bigger."

"How much bigger?"

"Big enough to fire a Star Killer through."

A huge grin crossed her face and her sea-green eyes lit up. She pushed her swivel chair back from her desk and jumped to her feet. Throwing her arms around him she gave him a huge kiss full on the lips.

"What as that for?" he asked when she stepped back.

"Gears, you're an absolute genius. I was trying to envision a means to deliver something past the Reptoid's fourth order screen while still affording our ships an impenetrable shield against their weapons. Hate to say it, but I wasn't having much luck."

Gears smiled. "Guess that's why we make such a great team. Your intellect pushes me and I like that."

EXCALIBUR
Lagrangian Point 2

Rollân viewed the simultaneous fabrication of the three Star Killer missiles through the transparent metal surrounding the work bay. Dozen of robotic 3D projectors built the component parts molecule by molecule, layer by layer, save the warheads that had been teleported from a high security nuclear storage facility at a SAC base in North Dakota.

"Sir, did Miss Hermann disclose her plan for the use of these weapons to you?" Doppek, Chief of Engineering, clad in a white space suit asked.

"No, it is one thing she is holding close to herself. I can only presume the secrecy must be absolutely inviolate, for whatever mission she has planned."

"I see. The modifications to the *Heracles* class ships have been complete. Would you like them to be returned to Tellus for their immediate use?"

"Precisely. We have no idea when the enemy will launch its next attack. Have similar modifications been completed on the *Garrin* and our own vessel?"

"Yes, sir. It is my understanding that the Captains were awaiting authorization from Miss Hermann to attempt a test of the technology. We, of course, have no experience with fifth order projectors and caution is certainly advised."

"Indeed, it is."

BEF AIRSTRIP

"We're here, where's our ships?" asked Bone as he looked up and down the flight line.

"Don't blink, Bone," Lucy said as she grinned and watched the three craft materalize.

"How do you do that?"

"Magic." She winked at him. "Blaze, this is your show."

"Well, this is new territory to me too, but I have the procedures fairly well fixed in my mind…"

"I know," said Lucy.

"Of course you do. But we still have to test out the procedures and see what else comes up. Have you notified the *Garrin* to take up a position somewhere between here and the moon?"

"I told Darron to take a position and engage his cloak and fourth order defensive shield, sixth magnitude…Where he will be positioned is up to him."

"We'll want him to go through the entire range all the way to a ninth magnitude full shield," reminded Blaze.

"He knows."

"Let's mount up, then," said Bone. He bowed to Lucy and swept his hand toward the *Guinevere*. "After you, madam."

She nodded, turned and walked toward their ship followed by her crew.

The others shook their heads and moved to their respective craft also.

Lucy broadcast her orders to the other *Heracles* units. *"Enable cloaks and shields. Go to your pre-assigned positions and engage the fifth order Blaze Convertor. We should be able to scan the system from Venus to Mars.*

"Confirm, Lancelot."

"Confirm, Galahad."

"Take us to high orbit outside the thermosphere, Bone."

"Aye-aye, Captain." He activated the inertialess drive and five seconds later he announced, *"Orbit achieved."*

"Loraine, engage our Blaze Convertor."

"Yes, Captain."

Lucy synchronized her tank with the other ships. The *Galahad* and *Lancelot* quickly followed suit. All three ship's holographic tanks were then data linked.

"I'm going to make a minor change in crew assignments. I want Loraine and Lanie to handle the sensors and screens on their respective ships along with Blaze. Your minds are more in tune with the type of projection needed to operate them telepathically."

Blaze took in a deep breath. *Here goes nothing.*

"Relax, Red...You can do it." Hollywood said.

She glanced across the cockpit at her captain and then began to concentrate on the shape she wanted the upper seatonite emitter to create. As if by some magic conjured by a modern day Merlin, an iridescent ruby red stream of pure energy began to flow upward from the bowl shaped crystal on top of the craft—a fountain of fifth order energy never before seen in the universe.

"Oh my God…That…that is gorgeous," blurted Raven

Blaze focused her mind on the control panel. The hundred foot tall fountain diverged in three hundred and sixty degrees and in doing so formed a hemispheric half dome above and around the upper half of the *Lancelot*—fading in visual intensity as the energy spread out in a thin, transparent sensor screen.

Hollywood checked his tank view of the ship and confirmed the first operation test of the upper emitter was a success. *"All systems are go for the lower unit, Blaze. See if you can complete the sphere."*

"Roger that. Here we go."

She focused on the secondary projector transmission. In a matter of seconds a lower screen matching the first one's radius and power was created.

"Nice job. Both halves mate perfectly," he sent.

"Copy that…And now for the hard part. Let's see if we can expand this puppy out to eighty million miles." As she talked, Blaze cupped one hand over the other, gloved fingers touching at the tips. Although she was controlling the machine's function with her mind, the tactile sensation of her spreading her fingers moving her hands apart matched what her mind directed the system's human interface to do.

Hollywood spread his tank out to a size big enough to see a radius of fifty million miles. A thin transparent ruby ball depicting the sensor pattern of the ship appeared to grow exponentially.

"We have a hit," announced Blaze telepathically from *Lancelot* almost immediately. *"Oh, there's another one."*

"Got 'em both," Loraine replied. *"That must be Excalibur out there at two million miles, close to Lagrangian Point 2."*

"I don't see any of the Reptoid ships," sent Lanie.

"Don't worry, girls. They're blocked by the curvature of the earth. We know they were down by the south pole earlier. This fifth order level is pretty cosmic, to coin an Earth phrase, but it's still line of sight," added Lucy. *"You ladies start manipulating and practicing with your screens and shields...size and intensity. All of your sensors will be synchronized. Just stay in your sector."*

Aboard *Lancelot,* Lanie focused on the control panel of the seatonite crystal projector. After a few seconds a small stream of ruby particles spewed forth.

Mike gazed forward through the windscreen and then glanced over at Chet. His copilot merely shrugged as the weak stream barely increased to six feet in length.

Cowboy gave his drone operator a few seconds more before he sent her a telepathic message. *"Gonna have to amp it up a bit there, Lanie, if we're gonna get any shape outta this gizmo."*

The stream of particles abruptly stopped. Lanie glared at him, but he couldn't see past her dark lenses in her helmet.

Mike chuckled. *"Hey, no need to get personal. Besides...it wouldn't fit up there anyway. Just focus and give it your best shot. Think of a bowl…a big ass bowl and make the stream do what you want it to."*

Crap. I forgot he can read my damn mind. Gotta watch my mouth…my mind. Lanie concentrated harder—blocking out all the other stimulation on the flight deck. Her anger caused a sudden surge of power that created a geyser of crimson. It quickly diverged into a vase-like cone—over a thousand feet tall. *Shit. Calm down girl.* The vase shrank in size.

"That's more like it. Visualize a flare on the lips of that thing and start bringing it around us. You can do it."

Lanie didn't acknowledge Chet's encouragement, but did try what he suggested. The one hundred foot cone began to widen from the top and soon took the shape of a shallow ice cream bowl.

"There you go, girl. Just a little deeper and you got it," Mike sent.

She closed her eyes, and envisioned a perfect half-ball. The skirts expanded down until the ship was enveloped in it.

"Beautiful. Now the lower half."

"I know." She aimed her thoughts at the control unit and a second ruby bowl began to take shape. After thirty seconds, the two halves matched. Lanie found herself panting. *Christ! This is harder than I thought.*

"Maybe so, but Lucy thinks you're the best one for the job."

"Easy for you to say, Cowboy. You and your sister are so much smarter than the rest of the team."

"Don't be so sure. I give Lucy's recommendation a lot of weight. Hey, I knew you could do it, shortcake. Now see if you

can expand the screen out to a few million miles. Maintain the shape, but bring up the power level. Okay?"

"I'll do my best."

"That's all anybody can ask of you," Niki Layton sent from her comm station.

"Hey, Pard. You're getting the hang of that thing pretty fast," Bone sent aboard *Guinevere*.

Loraine had just completed creating the first defensive shield—a third magnitude set at a mile from the ship. The Blaze Convertor automatically established the trip for the inner shields that were considerably stronger. "Thanks...we're set for now. Lucy, Do you want me to try some of the weapons?" Before she could answer, Bone broke back in. "Hey, I got an idea. Why don't we have one of the other ships shoot at us to test it?"

"What?...Have you lost your mind, Bone? If a beam broke through the shield and araknene armor, it would fry us in an instant."

"Oh, yeah...Wait a second. I thought that Blaze created multilevel screens with automatic trips."

"I'm sorry, I'm not used to having more than one screen. All we could do before was increase power...if we had time."

"Well, that was then and this is now. I'm thinkin' it's kinda like testing out a bullet proof vest," Bone replied.

"That's what dummies are for...Dummy," Loraine countered.

"Got any dummy fighters laying around, do you?"

Their silence confirmed his observation. *"Look. ladies, I'm not tryin' to get us killed. But I would suggest a controlled test at a known power level, just to see if the system works as advertised...Or, would you rather let the Reptoids be the ones to demonstrate our defensive capabilities...in combat."*

Lucy considered the options. *We've got better shields, and fifth order ones at that. Blaze says the automatic trip system will work and if it fails, I certainly would like to know that information before we engage those Reptoid transporters that destroyed two Maulers. Four feet of araknene armor? How long would it last against one of their pulses?*

"What's it gonna be, Captain? Go big or go home, I always say."

Lucy smiled. *"Bone, you are so full of it...as your partner always says. However, in this case I think that you have a valid point...Permit me to coordinate your little test. I must advise my people aboard Garrin and Excalibur. We wouldn't want anyone to believe that our own vessels had been taken over by the enemy and were actually engaging in hostile actions against us. Friendly fire is not friendly."*

"Now you're talking! Let's get 'er done."

Loraine shook her head. *How did I get stuck with the crazy one for a partner?*

Blaze was not exactly overjoyed at the suggestion to actually fire live bursts of pure forth order energy at one of the ships to test her concept, but acceded to the necessity to test the failure mode and automatic trip set she had designed. Commanders aboard the two larger Tyranian ships agreed and could not fault the logic that one of the fighters be the test guinea pig, as only a maximum of four lives were at risk, instead of possibly a whole crew of the *Garrin* and the mauler *Excalibur*. They would have to use the Tyranian pure force beams instead of a Reptoid pulse laser—either was deadly.

Blaze agreed to the test parameters Bone had suggested. *"One change to your plan, Bone. I appreciate your idea and bravery, honestly I do, but I cannot risk the life of Annuna in such a test. She is far too valuable for our coordination with the Tyranians, if for any reason my calculations fail to offer substantial protection. I therefore volunteer to have the Lancelot serve for the target vessel,"* she sent.

Mike Hermann responded immediately *"Hold on there, sis. You're the one that dreamed up this whole dang system. If anything goes wrong, your gonna be the one who has to work the bugs out of it. Besides...Lucy says you're the next step in the evolution thing and that make you pretty indispensable as well. Logic therefore dictates Galahad will be the target. I've got faith in Lanie here...and your design."*

Silence met his proposal.

"Hey! I just thought of something else...Lucy does that incoming beam have to be directed at the ship itself or just the shield to cause it to fail?"

She mulled over Mike's question before answering. *"Actually in combat, I have seen shields fail when we were maneuvering hard, and their pulse laser may not have hit us directly in those conditions."*

"*We'll there you go, Pilgrim,"* he sent in his best John Wayne characterization. *"Make the shield two thousand feet in diameter and limit the energy beam to maybe five hundred feet...A hit on the shield would still miss the ship, if you guys aim properly."*

Blaze smiled under her space helmet. *Why didn't I think of that?* "*It's a deal, Cowboy. Have Lanie set up a magnitude four shield and I'll start with a level three energy pulse to target it. We'll step up the pulse strength until shield failure."*

The first beam of pure force to impact *Galahad's* shield caused it to flare a brilliant white that rivaled the distant sun.

"We're still here," Chet said nervously.

"*So far so good. Take it up another notch, Sis."*

"*Roger that, Cowboy. Setting to magnitude four, fourth order."* She made the mental adjustment and fired a second blast at the distant target. The beam—traveling at light speed—arrived almost instantly.

The shield held once more, scintillating and flaring into crimson across half of its diameter.

"*Shield integrity down to ninety percent,"* advised Lanie.

"*Copy that,"* Mike noted. "*Ten percent degradation,"* he transmitted to his sister.

"*Roger that Cowboy, stand by."* Blaze contemplated hammering the shield four or five time more to see if it would fail, but chose the expedient method of switching to a higher level pulse. She made the necessary change and fired again.

"Jesus H!" Chet blurted when *Galahad* was enveloped in a wraparound field that went through the spectrum to violet and incandescence—even the stars and sun were blocked out for an instant as the shield failed.

"*Level three shield failure*," Lanie sent out immediately.

Mike turned to see what she was doing. "*Magnitude six force field instantly in place at nine hundred feet.*"

"*Whew…had me going there for a second, shortcake. What was the time between failure and reset?*"

Lanie studied the instrumentation. She tried to figure the exact time, but couldn't come up with an easy way to say it. "*Uh, point eight one milliseconds…with, uh, nine zeros in front of it.*"

"*Lancelot, Guinevere…did you copy that? Pretty fast trip, I'd say.*"

On board *Lancelot*, Hollywood held up his hand. "*Way to go, Red. You did it!*"

The greatly relieved Blaze Hermann smacked his gloved hand with enthusiasm. She took in a deep breath. *Thank you, Lord for keeping my brother and crew safe.*

She grabbed a rehydration container from the storage bin inset in the cockpit wall and twisted open the sealed cap. She opened the tab on the mouth seal of her helmet and exposed a small circular hole just large enough to accept the straw and took a long, refreshing sip.

I don't know how Lucy and her people can live for extended periods out in here in space...just standing guard for us. Makes me want to thank them even more.

Blaze stowed her water bottle and contemplated what they still had left to try. *"Ladies...time for us to work on the various fifth order beams...needles, planes and tubes. Slow and deliberate to start. See the shapes you want and make it so."*

EARTH'S THERMOSPHERE
SOUTH POLE

"Sire, the satellite system we have been monitoring shows streams of the humanoid creatures flowing into another of their stadium facilities," reported Fleet Science Officer Krpld as he shuffled into the control room.

"What sector?" asked Klsth.

"It's in a country they call Mexico. The satellite reports the stadium is called Azteca and is in a very populous city called Mexico City."

"Azteca, Azteca?" he mused and then roared with humor and snapped his jaws. "Aztec! Our ancestors visited a race of people who called themselves Aztecs over seven hundred of this planet's revolutions around its pitiful sun in the past. The city was known as Tenochtitlán then...They thought we were Gods." He roared and snapped his jaws again. "They referred to our leader Krrfl as Quetzalcoatl...and worshiped him. He told them he would return...Wonderful! How very fitting we should fill our larders with his subjects."

"Should we make ready to embark, Sire?" asked Sub-Commander Prlk.

"Of course, you fool! Do I have to tell you everything?"

"No, Sire. We will launch the Reapers… "

"No, the B-235 and B-237 and my own ship will launch first, idiot! We will release the Reapers and Death Globes once we are over the Pacific Ocean off Mexico's west coast. The Reapers will disembark the warriors in native hologram disguise. When all are in position…we will begin the harvest and avoid the panic of these weak creatures as before…Again, stay cloaked. Neither the humanoid military nor the Tyranians will be able to see us until it's too late."

GARRIN
Outside the Thermosphere

"Fleet Commander Garrple, I'm getting three extremely large fourth order cloak blips on the Blaze Convertor."

"Location, Lieutenant Commander Darron."

"They are moving in formation along the ninety-ninth longitude line of the planet inside the thermosphere."

"Speed?"

"One moment, sir…Mach 12. I would say it's the Reptoid T-Cruisers on the move."

"Probable destination?"

"Impossible to tell at this point, sir. They could continue due north or deviate east or west at any time. Currently they are over the Southeast Pacific Basin."

EAGLE NEST HEADQUARTERS
MEN'S SHOWER

"God, does it ever feel good to get out of that space suit," Bone said as he lathered up his hair. "I haven't felt that closed in since I had to wear the dang chem warfare suit in the desert."

"Heard that," replied Mike. "I'll never forget sweattin' like a pig in 120 degree heat. I usually lost ten to twelve pounds during the day...even after drinkin' as much as I could get my hands on."

Hollywood chuckled. "In that case, I won't bitch about havin' to wear a poopie suit in my air conditioned F-22 when we were flying from Hickam to Elmendorf."

Bone began to rinse the soap from his hair. "Ain't it funny how the grass is always greener?...Man, when I was a Marine grunt, I although thought those flyboys had the easy jobs. Now look at this...I am one and I'm already finding something to bitch..."

Klaxons began blaring an alert throughout the facility. Red flashing lights above every doorway bathed the shower with a pulsated crimson glow.

"Holy shit," Bone said as he fought to rinse the shampoo from his eyes. "That what I think it is?"

Tom Tallman's distinctive voice came over the intercom system. "Attention all personnel, attention all personnel...Red alert. All personnel report to duty stations for immediate deployment. This is not a drill...Repeat. This is not a drill."

"There's your answer," Mike said as he twisted the water handle shut. He snatched up his towel and began wiping water off his face and short military style blond hair. "Let's roll."

Dare studied at the flight path of the three alien ships on the images downlinked from the *Garrin*. The digital readout of their latitude and longitude accompanied the radar-like returns from the enemy vessels as they tracked across the empty expanses of the Southeast Pacific Basin. He marveled at the ground speed readout—9,132 miles per hour. The numbers representing the minutes and seconds of latitude scrolled by so fast, they were a blur.

His eyes fell on the longitude presentation. Curiously, it was displaying 99° 00' 00" W and appeared to be locked there. *That's odd. They are flying over open water, bypassing the southern tip of South America. I wonder what's so interesting at ninety-nine degrees west?*

Blaze had donned her black form-fitting space suit again except for the almond-eyed helmet. Her long red hair was still wet and tied back in a pony tail that dripped down her suit and had left a trail back to the women's showers.

She stopped in Dare's office to give him a good luck kiss, as she always did before they launched into harm's way. She caught the thought he was contemplating and stopped short in the doorway as the answer struck her like a bolt of lightning. "Oh my God! Eagle Nest is on the ninety-ninth meridian…They're coming after us!"

Dare spun around to face her when he heard Mike's voice from down the hallway.

"Who's comin' after us?"

"The Reptoids," Blaze turned to her brother and replied. "Look at the flight path."

They both stepped in to Dare's office. Mike looked at the present position. "How the hell could they know?"

"Well, like Shakespere said in Hamlet, 'There are more things in heaven and earth, Horatio, than are dreamt of in your philosophy'," Blaze quoted.

Mike looked at her, shook his head and did the calculations in his head almost instantly. "Yeah...We got roughly forty-four minutes until they are overhead. Plenty of time to launch and get into position...even all the reserves"

Dare nodded. "Right...Jesus...we have to get your mom and dad away from here, right now."

"Don't you think they would be safe in the underground bunkers here?" asked Mike.

Lucy stepped into the office. "The Reptoid's pulse lasers could turn the whole of Eagle Nest into a lake of seething lava if they get past us."

"We can send a M800 out with them and the Secret Service detail," offered Dare.

"That will not be necessary. I'll arrange for them to be transported to *Excalibur*. They should be safe there."

"Of course. I'll call them," Dare said.

"No. I'll attend to it in person. As Mike said, we have a little while to prepare. You see to your people and I'll take care of the President."

"Good idea…Soon as you do that, would you mind transporting me to *Garrin*?"

"Of course, Dare. I'll be back in a moment…and I'll join you two in formation," she said to Mike and Blaze as she tapped her bracelet and promptly disappeared.

***

CHAPTER SIXTEEN

EAGLE NEST RANCH HOUSE

The Secret Service agent started to reach for his weapon under his windbreaker as the light scintillated in the kitchen. Former President Annette Thompson-Hermann was placing the last of the dinner dishes in the bottom rack of the dishwasher when Lucy appeared suddenly in her gray space suit, holding her helmet under her right arm. *Dammit. I wish they would call or something before they just pop in like that. 'Bout give a man in my position a heart attack.* He released the grip on his Sig and eased his hand out from under his arm. "Evening, Miss Lucy."

"Hello, Marcus. Sorry to give you such a start like that, but it couldn't be helped." She turned to the Hermanns.

Annette was drying her hands off on a dish towel and Gunter was setting a container of iced tea in the refrigerator. He turned at the sound of her voice.

"You just missed dinner, Lucy. We have plenty of leftovers if you're still hungry."

"Thank you for the offer, Gunter, but something has come up and I'm afraid we must depart immediately."

"What's the matter?" Annette asked. "Are the children okay?"

Lucy held up her left hand. "No they are fine. Oh dear…I suppose that there is no easy way to say this, so I'll just tell you directly. The Reptoids are on the move…and their initial target appears to be Eagle's Nest."

Gunter's eyes narrowed as his hands unconsciously formed fists. *I'll get my gun.*

"That won't be necessary, Gunter."

Annette's eyes widened as she gasped slightly. "How much time do we have to prepare?"

"There is no time, unfortunately. Your protection is of utmost importance. We will transport the two of you to *Excalibur*. If anything should happen to the leadership in Washington, it would logical for you to come back and assist the recovery efforts as the immediate past President."

"That bad, huh?" Gunter asked.

She nodded. "If we cannot stop them south of here, their weapons are far too powerful for the underground facilities to protect you."

"I cannot just run away," Annette protested. "Gunter, tell her…"

He was thinking about the single beam that had destroyed USS *Alvin York*. "Sweetheart. Don't argue with her…it's time to go. You're special and a true leader…the best way I can protect you is to insist that you leave now."

Her antique gold eyes flashed for a second. "If I go, my security detail does as well…I feel I owe that to them."

Lucy quickly agreed, "We have plenty of room aboard. Marcus, have your team assemble here as quickly as possible."

"Yes, ma'am."

BEF AIRSTRIP
Eagle Nest

The crews sprinted toward their respective craft—Bone ran alongside Mike.

"Where's Lucy?" asked Bone.

"Said she was going to take care of mom and dad. Would join up later."

"How…Oh, never mind. I keep forgettin'. Guess I get to drive all by myself."

"Not much to it, just point and go." Mike grinned. "You'll do fine. Follow my lead, we'll form up a perimeter between here and Ciudad Victoria…*Garrin* is goin' ahead and transport the C5s to the coordinates so they can set up race tracks. It'll only take us about two minutes to get there."

"What about the fighters?"

"They'll go last…can't stay airborne as long as *Mama* and *Sister Bird*."

"We're not takin' any Raptors?"

"Nope, they can beam them out of the 5s as easily if not more so. Also helps if we're not jukin' around."

"Makes sense." Bone glanced over his shoulder at Loraine and Padrino just behind him. "Shake a leg kiddies, ol' Bone is behind the wheel…least 'til Lucy catches up."

"Can we wait?" Loraine asked as they climbed the ramp to *Guinevere*.

"I am truly hurt, no faith at all."

"Not that, Bone, it's just that you might decide to try some wheelies or something with *Guinevere*," said Padrino.

"Not likely. Last person I want to piss off is Lucy. Heard dynamite comes in small packages…like Raven."

"And don't you forget it," concurred Loraine.

He sent a telepathic message to the ship to close the ramp and activate the electronics as they strapped in. Forty-five seconds later Bone had engaged the Callala Inertialess Drive and *Guinevere* was streaking straight up to the thermosphere alongside *Galahad* and *Lancelot*.

WHITE HOUSE

"Secretary Stewart! Why didn't you tell me that aliens were involved in that mess down in Brazil and Australia? I had to get the information from TMZ."

"We just didn't have enough facts, sir…and actually it was included in your daily briefings."

"Facts? What the hell do I care about facts? Is there any chance they could be headed to Washington? Maybe we could negotiate with them…They're not offended at being called aliens, are they?"

"Mister President, they look upon us as a food source…their cattle."

"Oh, really now, Mister Secretary. Surely that's hearsay."

"Well, except for all the blood they expelled from their ships over Mumbi, São Paulo and Sydney, you could be right."

"Blood?"

"Yes, sir."

He turned in his high-backed leather chair and looked out the bullet proof bay window. "This is probably all Eisenhower's fault for dealing with them in the first place."

"Truman, sir."

"Whatever." He turned back to face Burner and his Chief of Staff.

"And he dealt with the Grays who are the sworn enemies of the Reptoids. They are fighting with us."

"Well, they should follow my orders."

"That's not likely…sir. We are following theirs."

"Mister President, maybe you should advance your vacation timetable and go on up to Martha's Vineyard," advised Chief of Staff Garnett.

"Did you say they were headed toward the US, Mister Secretary?"

"All we know is they are headed north along the 99th meridian, sir, which will take them into the heart of the lower forty-eight." He looked at his watch. "Within the next thirty-eight minutes...They could go east or west."

"You'd think they could find enough people in South America to fill their ships and then just head home." He turned to Victoria. "I think Hawaii sounds better this time of year. Make my arrangements."

AIRSPACE OVER TAMULIPAS, MEXICO

Lights of Ciudad Victoria shown brightly through the windscreen of the *Super Galaxy*. Gears Formby had the racetrack pattern set up in the ship's FMS with twenty mile legs running east and west. Up to the north, Monterrey—the capital of the state of Nuevo Leon—was partially obscured by a deck of low clouds that caused them to glow a light gray color. Gears had asked to be teleported to an altitude of 18,000 feet and had descended to 12,500 feet MSL to be ready to launch the two M600 and two M200 combat craft stowed on the cargo deck.

Bobby Mendez occupied the copilot's seat and Julio Sosa the jump seat in the spacious cockpit. Bobby gazed east towards the Mexican gulf coast and picked out a town in the clear night air.

"You guys ever been down to those seafood restaurants outside of Tampico? Man, they got some monster fresh shrimp...right off the boats..."

"Vera Cruz style with tomatoes, onions, jalapenos..." added Julio.

"I thought you guys ate back at Eagle Nest?" Gears said. "All ya'll ever talk about is food and women."

"What's wrong with that, gringo?" Bobby said with a big grin. "Drinkin' cerveza with my girlfriend...You know the one?"

"Cristina Aguilere? You mentioned the name a time or two..." Julio laughed. "...thousand." He cuffed Bobby on the back of the helmet. "In your dreams, amigo. She's way too good for the likes of you."

"Bite me, pendejo. Always rainin' on my parade."

"I read she's doing a big assed concert at the Azteca tonight...over a hundred and fifty thousand, if you can trust Yahoo news."

"Uh, huh. Maybe we can check it out after we take care of business."

Gears glanced down at the nav display. The max range on the screen was only 600 nautical miles. He keyed the intercom. "Weapons, AC. What's the location of the Reptoids now?"

Boomer Eastman glanced at the data linked from *Garrin* and responded immediately, "AC, Weapons, they're passing the equator as we speak...ETA ten minutes, fifty-four seconds."

Formby took the news in and acknowledged, "Mike Charlie, Alpha Charlie."

Heater McElhenny came on line. "Go ahead, AC. Getting nervous about launching the fighters?"

"It'll take two minutes to launch and we're not slowed down or depressurized yet."

"Mike Charlie copies." He contemplated his actions. *Dammit. No time left.* "AC, clear to initiate launch preparations."

"AC, roger." He spun the indicated airspeed controller on the FMS down to 200 KIAS before keying the PA system. "Attention all personnel, stand by for depressurization and launch."

The four high bypass turbofans on the big bird rolled back to flight idle as the ship began to slow. At 225 KIAS, Gears thumbed a couple of clicks of nose up trim. "Give me flaps five, and set cabin pressure system to off."

"Flaps coming to five." Bobby lifted the lever from the up position and dropped into the next lower slot. He reached over his head and turned the pressurization selector from auto to off.

In some ways, wearing the Tyranian space suits made the whole process faster. All the crewmembers already had their helmets on and were connected to the ship's oxygen system, or the systems of the smaller M200 or M600 VTOLS.

Partsman Meadows hooked a walkaround portable oxygen bottle to his safety harness and supervised the removal of the safety pins from VTOL landing gear as well as the ordinance on the M600 forward canard and rear struts. Once that was complete, the loadmaster made his way aft to the rear ramp controls and hooked the safety strap his harness. *Well, as long as the cloak works, we don't have to rig for night running anymore.*

Up in the cockpit, Bobby monitored the cabin pressure. It had risen from 2,800 when the ship was pressurized to the ambient of the launch altitude of 12,500. "Hey, boss. We're good to go."

"Roger that." He noted a pair of F-15 icons as they appeared ten miles off the port wing, but at 40,000 feet. Another pair popped up on the right side. *Looks like the shows gettin' ready to start.* He keyed the intercom. "Load, AC."

Partsman had felt the cargo deck level off slightly and had heard the hydraulic pumps kick in when the flaps were driven down to fifteen degrees. His hand was already on the rear ramp control. "AC, Load in position to launch."

"Speed 200, altitude 12,500. Clear to kick the baby birds out of the nest."

"Load copies. They're on the way." He moved the control handle to the down position, powering the outer clamshell doors open and unlocking the ramp. Once the doors were clear, it began to lower, exposing the night sky and causing the temperature inside the cargo bay to drop into the lower forties.

When the ramp approached the level position, Partsman returned the handle to off. He walked up ahead of the first M600 to launch and gave the pilots a hand signal to start their small turbine engines.

Bull Gaspar returned the gesture and spoke to the copilot. "Fire this puppy up and let's blow this pop stand."

"You betcha...Starting one and two," retired Marine Colonel Glenn "Bug" Haug replied. "All this waiting around is startin' give me the red ass."

Partsman lifted the paddle on the C-5's custom floor drive system and used a cable remote controller to bring it up flush to the VTOL's nose wheel. Both forward engines were spun up and he glanced to check the progress on the start of two of the rear mounted engines. Lacking a tilt function or louvers, the single jet between the V-tail assembly was used for max speed and was shut down for vertical takeoff and landing. The engines began to wind up and in seconds were stable at flight idle.

Bull held up four fingers and then signaled thumbs-up and brakes released.

Partsman replied with a like sign and pressed the green button on the controller. The M600 began inching backwards toward the extended ramp.

"Let's go kick some alien butt." Bull stuck out his fist.

"Yeah, buddy. Bring it." Bug bumped his fist. "Now is a good a time as any."

AIRSPACE OVER PACIFIC
Southeast of Acapulco

"Warriors!" Klsth addressed the assembled pilots on the three transports via the giant visaplate in his control room. "I have a change of operational plans for the forthcoming harvest. The thirty-six Death Globes will split into groups of twenty-six patrolling at 20,000 feet in an umbrella formation..." His four eyes looked at the three-way split screen, seemingly making contact with each and every pilot. "...and one of ten at close support level over the uncloaked and unshielded Reapers in operation at Azteca Stadium. The ten will extend their shields to protect your comrades in their most vulnerable state."

"Brilliant, Supreme Commander, brilliant strategy!" ejaculated Sub-Commander Prlk, snapping his jaws twice.

One of Klsth's eye stalks curled slightly toward his second in command. "Of course, Prlk. It's something you should have thought of."

All four of the Sub-Commander's eye stalks drooped. "Yes, Sire."

"We begin launch operations immediately. Death Globes first, to set up the two-tiered protection grid, followed by the processing Reapers and then the high level screening Reapers...You all know your jobs and responsibilities. Let us not waste time with this backward planet. We must fill our holds and be gone before the Tyranians realize where we are...Draconian power!" He held all four tentacles straight over his massive head and snapped his jaws three times.

All the Reptoids on the huge visaplate and those in the control room with Klsth repeated his movements, their clacking jaws creating an almost deafening din of sound...

AIRSPACE OVER TAMULIPAS

Flash Peterman leveled off at FL380 after the teleportation. The second time was not nearly as dramatic as the first over Sydney. He rolled into a gentle left turn as his invisible wingmen set up in a loose six ship echelon formation. "Eagle Nine coming left."

"Ten, Eleven, Twelve, Thirteen, Fourteen, Fifteen," drifted over the BEF secure voice frequency as his compatriots acknowledged the turn.

Flying in a cloaked condition made normal formation flying skills relatively useless. Midair collisions were a constant threat—400 foot lateral separation was accomplished though rapid crosscheck of the disposition of forces display fed by the data link from Blaze's seatonite detection system. Other formations began to aggregate as pairs of the *Super Hornets* and *Eagles* appeared over northern Mexico every few seconds.

Double D Williams led her two flights of F-18s forty miles to the west after they formed up. They also were assigned an altitude of 38,000 to await contact with the alien invaders. In a brief planning session, Hollywood Stewart, Jill Hermann, Flash Peterman and D had agreed to a battle strategy called El Toro—one paying homage to the territory over which the battle was expected as well as the Zulu tribe that had historically inspired its use.

The fierce African warriors had called their double envelopment plan *impondo zenkomo*—buffalo horns—after the much feared Cape buffalo native to South Africa.

Flash would lead the eastern or left "horn", while Maria would set up on the western or right "horn". The three Tyranian fighters would provide the top cover in the center with Jill Hermann's F-15s and the bulk of the BEF's fighters forming the bull's "head" and a smaller contingent, including the two C-5s and their eight VTOLs, deployed to make up the "loins" of the bull.

Hollywood checked out the disposition on the fighters miles below the three *Heracles* class Tyranian ships. *Everyone's in position. Range to target...six hundred miles. Just under four minutes now.* He glanced over at Blaze. She hadn't said a word and was keeping her thoughts to herself. *"Hey, Red. We can only do what we can do. Gotta try to relax."*

"Really? Why is it then, you have been running over alternative tactics for the last ninety seconds?"

Crap...busted. "Okay, tell me...what if they don't slow down and try to blow past us at Mach 12? We're the only aircraft that can engage the Reptoid mother ships at this altitude and speed."

"I know. We have the element of surprise...Our fifth order weapons should wreak havoc on them, but we won't know for sure until we engage them. Concentrated fighter guns can take out the Death Globes and maybe the Reapers, but I seriously doubt if they'll be a significant problem to the T-Cruisers. Those things are huge and they can gang up on any single one of ours..."

Aboard *Mama Bird*, Boomer Eastman watched the distance between the awaiting BEF contingent click off in a blur. Time seemed to stand still. The three *Reptoid* vessels passed the 550 mile mark and then...

Their northern track stopped over Acapulco instantaneously.

"That can't be right." Boomer couldn't conceive the big ships could slow from 9,125 mph to zero in an instant, but they did.

"What can't be right?" Heater asked.

"I dunno. They stopped. They're dead in the water...uh, I mean over the Mexican coastline...They just came to a halt."

"Do you think they see us?"

"How the hell should I know? I wish we had some intel on their communications or some...Hold on! I got six more blips!"

Heater pulled up his data link from the *Heracles* fighters. "Not six...ten...fifteen, still coming...Jesus, they're deploying the whole fleet, it would seem."

"Look at all of 'em..." Boomer muttered, "...lot more of them than there are of us."

Heater grinned a slightly sardonic smile. "Yeah...that's what we fighter pilots call a target rich environment." He chuckled. "I once sat in on a NATO brief and the Soviet air intel guy concluded with the statement 'but on the plus side, that means if nobody gets too greedy, we can all go home an Ace'."

For some reason, Boomer didn't quite catch the humor in that. "But where are they headed?"

GARRIN
Outside the Thermosphere

The Reptoid *T-Cruisers* had stopped line abreast about twenty miles apart. Dare studied the line of blips streaming from the three ships as they accelerated northward. *Christ...They're coming out in trail...just like a string of ducks in a shootin' gallery. What the hell kind of tactical formation is that?* He turned to his Tyranian counterpart monitoring the action. "Can you get me a height readout on those globes?"

"Most assuredly." He sent a mental signal to the sensor processor and six figure tags appeared by each of the alien craft. "Those are measured in feet for your benefit. As you can see, the highest ones are still above 300,000 feet, more or less, while the lead elements are descending though 170,000, as we speak."

"That's a lot higher than any of *my* ships can intercept."

"That is true, Dare. However, the Death Globes are still coming down at a very rapid rate."

They watched for several seconds as the lead ships in the three groups of invading aircraft passed over the town of Cuernavaca, Mexico at 95,000 feet. Visions of the ancient, but very picturesque mountain setting came back to Dare from a vacation years before. He forced himself to shed the recollection from a time long past.

Dare checked out the formation of BEF aircraft maintaining a slow 250 knot formation in the completed El Toro configuration. At forty-five miles from horn tip to tip, they would barely be able to contain the oncoming enemy fighters. "Eagle Eleven, Iron Horse."

"Iron Horse, Eagle Eleven go," Flash Peterman replied.

"Bring it left eight miles. Maintain sixty miles across the tips."

"Eagle Eleven, roger." He checked his lat/long and noted his exact longitude, before leading his flights into a shallow turn.

"Hornet One, coming right seven miles," Double D transmitted without being told.

"Iron Horse, copies…All units be advised closest enemy ships are now fifty miles south of Mexico City. Range five hundred miles and closing."

"Son of a bitch," D muttered to herself as she looked at her nav display. "Why did those pencil-neck engineers think a 180 mile range was plenty?" She knew her F-18's original radar system was never designed to pick up targets farther than that. Besides, her AIM-120D AMRAAM missiles only had a range of ninety-seven miles under optimum conditions, but that little fact didn't help assuage the frustration that was beginning to build. *Okay…calm down, girl. They'll get here when they get here and then we'll start kickin' some butt.*

Heater recounted the number of *Death Globes* that were streaming north in three columns. *Thirty-six. That's a doable number.* As he turned his attention to the stationary Reptoid *T-Cruisers*, a group of the much smaller *Reapers* appeared. *Holy crap. Over a dozen so far and they keep on coming.*

As he continued monitoring, a total of fifty-five of the elliptical ships deployed and spilt into two groups. *Those guys are armed to the teeth as well.* He looked at the small armada of BEF fighters and suddenly did not feel quite so optimistic.

GUINEVERE
Thermosphere

Lucy studied the tank as the Reptoid vessels launched from the huge transports.

"What are they up to?"

"I'm not sure, yet, Bone, but they are not headed to Eagle Nest. They're disbursing into a four level tier formation and they would not do that this far out."

"The only thing of any size between us and them is Mexico City," offered Padrino.

"We must have been a bit egotistic to think they were only after us...You think?" Bone sent to Lucy.

"So it seems..." she responded. *"...although it was a plausible supposition at the time. There must be a concentrated target in the Mexican capital tonight."*

"Guys, I see the Reptoid mother ships are on the move again," Loraine sent.

"Apparently, all their fighters and Reapers are deployed...all ninety-one of them," Bone noted.

"Look here." Lucy swept her hands to expand the tank's depiction of the airspace over Mexico City. *"The Death Globes are forming a ring low around their target. Ten ships I count. I wonder what's down there?"*

Loraine's heart skipped a beat. *"Oh my God. It's Azteca Stadium! I recognize it from when the Cowboys played the Patriots there."*

Lucy turned to Padrino. "Get me Dare on Garrin."

"Yes, ma'am...Go ahead."

"Dare, I think we know where they plan to attack. Have *Garrin* and *Excalibur* redeploy your assets around these coordinates as quickly as they can."

"Confirmed, Lucy," came the reply.

She sent the *Guinevere* surging ahead at over 9,000 miles per hour—with her two wingmen on either side.

GARRIN
Outside the Thermosphere

Dare immediately realized the double encirclement plan his pilots had created was no longer valid. His mind went from defense to offense in an instant. The warrior envisioned a huge furball over the Mexican capital—over twenty-one million residents in the metropolitan area. *Not my idea of a great place to start a fight, but we could not engage three huge ships at 300,000 feet with only the Heracles class birds.*

"All units, Iron Horse. Stand by for plan two. Maintain current formation and 250 knots...conserve your fuel. Expect teleportation to battle stations over Mexico City. Do not open fire unless fired upon...Orbit and await further instructions."

AIRSPACE OVER TAMULIPAS

Jill Hermann responded quickly when her data link message from Heater came through. *Expect to engage Death Globes at FL 270.* She hit the received button, keeping the radio clear of unnecessary chatter. *At least somebody's got a plan.* Lights from Cuidad Victoria had already passed behind her and the central highlands of Mexico looked relatively unpopulated below. To her left, the gulf coastline began to turn the east as the remaining aircraft in the El Toro "head" cruised past the city of Tampico. Starlight glistened from a myriad of distant suns, planets and constellations. Jill felt her pulse began to quicken in anticipation of the upcoming battle. Suddenly the air itself glimmered and a bone chilling cold came over her.

A moment later, Jill and *Eagles* Sixteen and Seventeen materialized at 30,000 feet sixty miles outside of Mexico City. She gasped as the shock of the teleportation wore off, but her rapid glance at the disposition of forces display was enough to cause that same physiological response. Forty of the huge *Reapers* were overhead at 50,000 feet and over three dozen of the cloaked *Death Globes* were shown to be holding position off her port wing.

Jill swallowed hard and rolled into a shallow right hand turn. Her first wingman had materialized some five mile astern. One hundred and twenty miles across the opposite side of the "wagon wheel" were four other F-15 *Eagles* at the same altitude.

Her sister-in-law, Double D, was in a slightly smaller diameter circle with a half dozen *Super Hornets* far below at 15,000 MSL, along with the *Eagles* lead by Flash Peterman. She could see a ring of ten *Death Globes* spaced equally around the stadium and the bright lights illuminating the headliner on a stage set in the center of the field. Two lines of *Reapers* running from south to north were approaching the outer perimeter of the parking lots surrounding the facility. Their altitude readout showed 9,300 feet MSL.

Dammit! We've got to get a move on! They're almost in position to begin transport…

***

CHAPTER SEVENTEEN

AIRSPACE OVER MEXICO CITY

Lucy noted the huge number of airships appearing inside the tank in front of her pilot position aboard *Guinevere*. At Heater's suggestion, the hostile Reptoid vessels had all been assigned a number by the crew aboard *Garrin*. The three *T-Cruisers* were rated the most difficult targets and given the numbers 1 through 3. Only slightly less deadly, the *Reapers* were assigned 10 through 65 and the forty-three *Death Globes* were shown as 70 through 113.

We can't wait for the rest of the fighters to be beamed in. We'll never have numerical superiority anyway.

"Lucy, I'm monitoring a series of wave emissions. They have to be the Reptoids ships sending their foot soldiers into place."

"I concur, Bone... All BEF fighters...close in to firing range. Drone operators, stand by for decoy missile launch."

MAMA BIRD

"Darron, you may begin transporting our *Raptors* to the coordinates on my signal...Three, two, one...Mark," Heater relayed to the *Garrin*.

Back on the crew deck of the big C-5M, the assembled units of the BEFs highly efficient and ultra-deadly ground troops started disappearing every half-second. The same action was taking place on *Sister Bird*. In very short order, all forty-eight of the former SEALs; Green Berets; Rangers; Recon Marines; Delta Force plus one Secret Service agent were transported to the designated areas around the huge stadium.

AZTECA STADIUM

The cloaked fighters materialized in twos all around the giant semi-covered stadium between the parking areas and the multiple entrances.

"Report," Bad Poole said into his comm unit as he studied the disposition of forces on his Helmet Display Screen.

Each man activated his status by changing his designation from 'Green' to 'Blue'.

"Team Two hot, Bad," reported Widowmaker.

"Team Three hot," came the response from Ten Ring.

"Team Four hot," was the same from Mickey Williams.

"Anybody got any idea what to look for?" asked Ten Ring.

"Lucy said they could be hologra...Hey! I got two guys just standing near entrance 'K'. Twins and dressed for all the world like *Speedy Gonzales*, you know, white peasant getup, straw sombrero and a red kerchief around their necks," said Mickey.

"Me too. I can see twins, but quads? No way," came back Bad.

"Same here," from Ten Ring.

His comment was followed by a series of clicks from the others stationed around all the entrances.

"You think they could be that stupid as to use the same hologram for all of 'em?" asked Widowmaker.

"One way to find out."

"Can't just kill 'em, Mick. What if they're for real?...Some kind of performin' group or somethin'."

"Don't intend to, Bad. We're invisible, remember?" Mickey walked over to one of the peasant garbed Mexicans standing by the gate, hit him as hard as he could in the face and jumped back.

The faux *Speedy Gonzales* vanished and one of the giant Reptoids appeared, waving dual-ended swords—held in two tentacles—all around himself.

"Jesus!" exclaimed Mickey as he drew his .44 magnum Desert Eagle and double tapped the surprised monstrosity just below the snapping jaws. "There's your answer, guys...Go get 'em."

The creature looked down at the huge holes just below his head, tried to push his mangled jaw back closed with one of his tentacles, but it flopped back down over the gaping wounds. His eye stalks wilted and he collapsed in a heap as the concert fans still streaming into the stadium in the immediate vicinity began to scream and run.

The other *Speedy Gonzales* standing nearby de-hologramed and fired his disruptor around, catching, Mickey's partner, Dutch, as well as several late arriving patrons. The beam dissipated from his Graphene space suit, but immediately vaporized four unlucky music fans.

"Ow! Damn you, not again." He shook off the effects, drew his G4 and nailed the beast, exploding his torso, dropping him where he stood. "Glad there was a concrete column behind him...I love this friggin' weapon."

AIRSPACE OVER MEXICO CITY

Jill Hermann responded to the data link target assignment with a touch on the comm panel's acknowledge button. Her dad had tasked one of the *Reapers* on the south side of the stadium to her and her wingman. "Eagle Sixteen, power," she transmitted as she pushed the twin throttles into burner and rolled in on a bearing to intercept.

Her wingman simply called back with, "Two," and pulled in behind her a thousand feet in trail.

It's gonna get real damn tight in this furball before you know it. I hope this twenty mike-mike is big enough to do some damage, she thought.

"Heracles flight, take it down to 40,000. We don't want to shoot downward with these fifth order weapons. Too many people below."

Mike and Hollywood acknowledged Lucy's command. The three cloaked silver ships moved vertically with no sensation whatsoever of a descent, thanks to their inertialess drives.

Cowboy sent a signal to Lanie. *"Be ready, girl. It's about to get real here..."*

"I'm ready. Just say when and which one." She tried to sound unafraid—and almost succeeded.

"We gonna use the pure energy weapons, too?" Chet asked.

Cowboy pondered the request for a moment. *"Don't see why not. We're only outnumbered forty to three."*

"Just get me in the middle of 'em and I'll do what I can."

"That's what I want to hear," he replied. *"Stand by."* He looked at the gaggle of alien ships above and in front of them. *Christ...I'll try not to run into one of those big mothers. Oh, hell, won't matter, we're inertialess anyway...Wonder what's gonna happen when they figure out we can see through their cloak?*

He could feel his pulse rate begin to quicken. It was nothing he was not used to. The same thing happened in college football, in the Marine Corps in Afghanistan and every other time he got into a fight for his life. He took in a deep breath and slowly let it out. The dry mix of oxygen and air made his nose itch slightly, but with the helmet on there was no way to scratch it. Curiously, that tiny limitation made him smile.

He studied the scene below. Two of the *Reapers* were crossing the south end of Azteca Stadium. Bright white searchlights positioned outside in the parking lot crisscrossed the night sky, drawing the attention of Mexico City's residents who were not already inside as the headliner took the stage.

170,000 screaming fans rose to their feet as the computer controlled laser light show atop the raised platform at midfield began to shoot red and green beams in all directions. The band cranked out the intro to one of Christina's number one hits as a dozen spotlights came together and made her sequined white jumpsuit sparkle like a billion diamonds.

Lucy watched the action below and radioed her commands from Padrino's comm station, "Launch the decoy missiles…All units cleared to engage at will."

"*Here we go,*" Hollywood sent as he pushed his hand into the 3D model of *Lancelot* floating in the tank in front of him. He thrust it forward accelerating to 1,500 miles per hour—far below its top speed. In seconds, the closest *Reaper* was coming overhead at 12 o'clock.

Blaze had a distinct furrow creasing her forehead as she formed a single plane of fifth order pure energy from the upper seatonite dome. The thin red knifelike beam reached out at least 20,000 feet as the Tyranian ship passed beneath the Reptoid sausage-shaped vessel.

Its unstoppable power rendered the ship asunder as molecule by molecule, it cut a path through the *Reaper's* shields and hull like a band saw—the fourth order shield flared for several seconds like a light bulb shorting out. The ship hung motionless for a second and then the two halves began to fall as the power storage unit and the inertialess drive system failed.

"My God! It works!" Blaze blurted as Hollywood turned to engage another one.

Raven ripped another salvo of decoy missiles above the targeted ships. Once the missiles were well away from her drones, she activated the radar systems, simulating F-16 search radars and providing a return identical to the ubiquitous fighters.

Jill Hermann slammed a quick burst of fire into the *Reaper's* transporter, rolled and then triggered another into its flight deck, as briefed from a quick survey of one of the ships brought down in Sydney. The heavy HE 20 MM rounds did a number on the bulkheads—thought to be adequate when protected by a shield.

A hundred music fans were panicked and disorientated by their abduction. They were being crowded toward the processing compactors by a pair of nervous Reptoid workers who glanced around at the series of holes in their ship.

In the cockpit, most of the crew escaped injury except for a navigation specialist and one needed for communication.

"Damage report!" thundered the captain.

"Sire, we have lost our transporter. Initial readings say…"

His report was cut short by a burst from *Eagle* Sixteen. Both elephantine legs were taken off just below the trunk.

"Helm! Get us out of here!" shouted the captain.

Venting its atmosphere from over 100 one inch diameter holes, the *Reaper* suddenly climbed fifteen thousand feet, right through the formation of *Death Globes* providing top cover.

Bull Gaspar turned in on one of the *Death Globes* on the north end of the stadium as the Reptoids fired the incredibly powerful green pulse laser weapons blindly at the F-15s and F-18s that were gunning the *Reapers* so effectively. Flash Peterman and Jill Hermann had jointly decided that the use of tracers in the ship's gatling guns was somewhat counterproductive. While tracers added in the ability to track one's gun shots, they did hinder the best elements the outclassed air breathing fighter's possessed—stealth and surprise.

Bull briefly considered the faint blue trail his G2 coil weapon created when it fired. There was nothing he could do to hide it in the clear night air, therefore, he came up with a tactic that should help. The five engines on the M600 had the invisible VTOL up to its max maneuvering speed of 625 knots.

The cloaked *Death Globe* number seventy-one grew bigger in the HUD. A green pulse that seemed to be at least ten feet across, zoomed past so fast it almost couldn't be seen. Bug Haug ducked instinctively, as if it would do any good.

"What's the matter? Too close for you?" ribbed Bull.

"Bullshit, old man...two more seconds." Bug centered the pipper on the HUD projection. Without a laser rangefinder to use on the cloaked enemy ship, he had to rely on his judgment. He pulled the trigger and held it for just one count of one Mississippi. A stream of light blue plasma followed the hypersonic depleted uranium projectiles through the fourth order shield.

"Eagle One off west," Bull announced before he could stop himself. He sucked the side stick full aft and grunted as the six G's built up. Coming through the vertical, he ran the throttles up to full power and rolled ninety degrees, continuing pulling until the aircraft was completely inverted heading 270 degrees.

Bug Haug strained his neck to look back at their target and began to grin. The rounds had ripped through the ship's propulsion and cloak mechanism and it glowed green when one of the stadium searchlights illuminated it for a moment. Like a ugly birthday party balloon, it began to slowly fall under the effects of gravity. "Hey, I think we hit it."

"Nice shootin'...old man," Bull replied sarcastically. "I see their cloak is damaged...ain't showing on the HUD." He glanced at the disposition of forces display and saw Wardog Lafavor in *Hawk* Three screaming in at treetop level on *Death Globe* number seventy-two. The smaller M200 made a gun pass and streaked over the top of the damaged alien craft by only feet. "Jesus H…that jarhead comes out of the weeds and nearly T-boned that damned globe!"

"Marines are like that," Bug replied. "Here comes Ice and Rat, with their hair on fire."

Hawk Two, another M200, made three short bursts on different targets before rocketing up to 15,000 feet and performing a rapid deceleration cobra maneuver and followed by a split S back into the fray.

"Kids…Carter and Hampshire ain't figured out the 'live to fight another day' shit yet."

"You know it," the retired Colonel replied. A furious fusillade of green pulses filled the air once more, but it was clear there were a far fewer operational Reptoid ships low over the stadium. Eight of the supporting *Globes* had already been shot down and the other two were desperately trying to retreat and streaming yellow Draconian atmosphere in their wake.

SECDEF STEWART'S OFFICE

Burner Stewart studied the frenetic action on his wide screen. Even as a seasoned professional, he had to work hard to maintain his emotional separation from the action he witnessed. He couldn't help the involuntary twisting and turning movements his body made following the action of the fighters.

His only son, Hollywood was captain of the Tyranian ship *Lancelot* and engaged in a slugfest with two other fighters against eighteen of the heavily armed *Reapers*. His live feed from the BEF via satellite did not match the brilliant display of colors as the three small ships wove their way through the interlocking fields of green pulse laser fire on pass after pass.

His executive secretary had stayed late after normal duty hours with him to watch the drama unfold. Bill saw two of the blue dots assigned to the BEF's F-15s suddenly vanish off the screen. She hesitated for a moment, and then, "Sir, when one of ours dots disappears…"

He never took his eyes off the 80 inch digital screen. "That means that they are gone…no telemetry, no survivors in this air battle, I'm afraid."

The truth about the finality of a hit from a Reptoid pulse weapon was somewhat sobering. In her years working in the Pentagon, she had numerous occasions to write letters of condolences for almost every one of her many bosses. It came with the territory, but the fact that she was, for the first time, a witness to a flier's demise and ultimate sacrifice could not help but tug at her heartstrings—a tear rolled down her cheek.

GUINEVERE

Bone glanced at the diminishing number of *Death Globes* darting about in the second tier of Reptoid craft in their umbrella coverage at 20,000 feet. *"Lucy, have ya'll ever captured one of those fighters?"*

She cast a quick look at the big man. *"No, we've always had to totally destroy them when we fought. They would rather die than surrender to us."*

"Would you like to have one?"

339

"Of course we would, but I just said they would rather ... "

"Not talkin' about surrender."

"I don't understand."

"Well, since my Pard and I are the only ones around that have ever faced those butt-ugly mothers up close and personal..."

"Are you suggesting what I think you're suggesting, Bone?" Loraine asked incredulously.

"You know me too well, Pard."

"Oh, my God."

"Lucy, can you have the Garrin transport us into that one over there at ten o'clock? Uh, number ninety-four." He pointed into the tank.

"Of course, but you would have to be crazy to go inside with those vile creatures."

"You don't know how right you are, Lucy," sent Loraine.

"We can do it...can't we, Pard?"

"Jesus. Why me?...Just hope it doesn't turn out like your driving a motorcycle across that creek on a four inch pipe."

"He did what?" asked Lucy.

"Tell you about it some other time...Well, how about it?"

Lucy shook her head and signaled Darron aboard *Garrin.* *"I'll make sure everyone else knows not to target that ship. I'd hate one of our own to shoot you down after you capture it."*

"You and me both!...Friendly fire is not...friendly. Padrino, you cover my station?"

He nodded.

"Got your .45 ready, Pard?"

"Never leave home without it." She patted the holster on her utility belt.

Bone checked the massive rounds in his 500 Smith and Wesson and then closed the cylinder. A row of custom-made speed loaders hung ready on the left side of his belt, stuffed with solid copper hollow points or more Safety Slugs. *"I'm good to go."*

"Why aren't you using the G4 coil guns?" asked Lucy.

"Go right through them and probably cause a bunch of collateral damage to the ship. Their thick bodies should stop our bullets though...We're both usin' Glasers."

"All right, be sure to activate your breathers...Are you ready?"

"Let's get back to back, girl. Won't know where they are when we materialize." They engaged their breathers and both held their weapons at the ready—he nodded at Lucy. *"Laterbye."*

The air shimmered in the center of the flight deck and the pair disappeared...

DEATH GLOBE

"Qrts, target back along that missile track, wide aperture. We can get a piece of the winged craft hiding inside its cloak."

"Aye, Captain Mrrst." The copilot slid one of his long curved claws across a touch screen.

Three yards behind them, the yellow noxious gas that replicated their own planet's toxic atmosphere distorted—two black clad warriors materialized.

"Don't think I'd do that, you horrid, loathsome piece of..."

"Why don't you say what you mean, Pard?" Bone said.

Both Reptoids spun around from their control board surprisingly fast—considering their bulk—at the voices behind them. Qrts raised a tentacle with a disruptor tube attached near the clawed tip. A green beam leapt out at Bone, scintillating when it struck him—a thousand bright white electrical bolts shot out a short distance and bounced off Loraine before bleeding down his legs to the deck of the ship.

Bone shivered like a wet mule and snapped off two quick shots at Mrrst that were almost indistinguishable from Loraine's slightly faster triple tap into Qrts' center mass. Their thick bodies shook from the obvious impact of the compressed number 12 shot cartridges. Shock waves roiled under the scaly exterior as the deafening pistol blasts echoed in the confined cockpit.

The two repulsive creatures looked down at the holes in their chests weeping a thick gray viscous fluid, and then turned all of their eye stalks to each other in surprise just before their knees went soft and they collapsed face down onto the aranak deck.

"Damn, Dutch was right...Is kinda like stickin' your finger in a light socket," Bone said after a moment.

"You okay, wild man?"

"Yep. Thought that would work…Doncha just love it when a brilliant plan comes together?" Bone cracked as he looked around and then holstered the monster stainless steel wheel gun.

"Right, Einstein…How did you know their deck was grounded?"

"Didn't."

Loraine just shook her helmeted head. "Bone, you live a charmed life…for a Neanderthal numbskull."

"What is it they say about God lookin' out for children, drunks and fools?"

"Which are you?"

"Hadn't had anythin' to drink…today. You pick."

"All right, smart ass, what now?"

"Good question. Hadn't thought that far ahead…Think you can figure out how to fly this thing?"

She looked at the plain large round flat touch screen covered with indecipherable symbols. There were no visible controls. Loraine shook her head again. "Nope…not a clue."

"Lucy?" Bone radioed back to his ship.

"Here, Bone…It went well, I assume."

"You could say that…Now what? We can't figure out the stupid controls on this thing."

He could hear Lucy chuckle over his comm. "Not to worry, Bone, we'll just lock on with a tractor beam and have the *Garrin* beam the ship aboard into a cargo hold. I'll have Darron transport you and Loraine back to *Guinevere*."

"That's cool…Better tell him to vent the atmosphere from this tub. I suspect from the yellow tint that it's pretty high in chlorine gas."

"I'm sure you are correct."

"Think I can I have it after ya'll are through playin' with it?"

"Not up to me, we'll have to take it up to the council…But I wouldn't hold my breath."

"Right, purple is not my best color."

Loraine backhanded him across the chest. "Bone, you're so full of it. Everybody knows why your eyes are brown."

"Don't hurt to ask…Figured it was worth a shot. I could take Raven on some really cool places in it."

"Sit on it, Romeo, we ain't out of this yet."

"Oh, ye of little faith." He glanced over at the two dead Reptiods, lying in an ever widening pool of their own gray blood. "By the way, Lucy, better have housekeeping bring a bucket and a mop."

Bone and Loraine vanished.

THERMOSPHERE
Over Mexico City

"All T-Crusier units, target the origination points of those blue streaks below and that red plane that just sliced through Reaper R-38," Klsth bellowed into his comm system from the Reptoid flag ship, T-233.

A barrage of green laser pulses began to rain down toward the outer edges of the two lower Reptoid formations in the general direction of the blue plasma lines they could see on their screens.

"We are firing blind, Supreme Commander!" shouted Weapons Officer Krrlp.

"I know that, fool. Something is generating those energy weapons and my instincts tell me it's the Tyranians. Keep firing. We may hit…"

The T-233 shuddered as her shields flared.

"Shields down fifteen percent, Sire!"

"Increase modulation! Take evasive action B22…Where did it come from?"

"A new type of ship, definitely Tyranian, from sector 48-60…distance three thousand kilometers. Vessel has decloaked. They've locked on to T-237 with a tractor beam."

"Only one ship? Tell Captain Lssps to shear off and fire at will. Their shields cannot stand up to our upgraded neutronium lasers. Continue targeting the area around our Reapers."

"Yes, Sire."

"Supreme Commander, the unknown vessels can see through our cloak and are targeting our ships with unerringly accurate fire," Fleet Science Officer Krpld interjected.

"Impossible! Recalibrate your findings, idiot!"

"There is no question, Sire, no matter where our ships move, they are being tracked."

"Sire! T-237 reports they cannot break from the Tyranian tractor beam!" reported Krrlp.

"Then tell that worthless Lssps to bring all his projectors on line and pound the Tyranian vessel with everything he's got.

We'll teach the Annunaki what it means to grab a dragon by the tail."

GARRIN

"Fleet Commander, we are unable to move the Reptiod T-Cruiser and he cannot shear our tractor beam…We are at a stalemate, sir," reported Chief of Engineering Davalan.

"Target their drive system with a needle beam," said Garrple.

"Yes, sir, but the Reptoid history shows they will self-destruct if they lose power. We don't know if the new automatic trips can go to a full zone of force to protect the Garrin from a complete neutronium enhanced atomic explosion in time, should they do that."

"Not a good time to test them, is it? A bit of a conundrum, wouldn't you say? We cannot let them go, cannot destroy them without killing thousands on the ground, nor can we pull them to outer space."

"It's what we call a tug-of-war back on Earth," added Dare.

"An apt description, but we are of equally powered drive systems with a virtually unlimited supply of energy from the cosmos."

GALAHAD

Hollywood turned back into the remaining sixteen *Reapers*. He noted that they were beginning to maneuver slightly farther apart from each other. *About time you lizards realize you can't just sit there in a hover. A little slow on the uptake, pea brains.*

He turned to Blaze. *"Let's try the Z-Beams on these guys. They should be more vulnerable than the T-Cruisers."*

"Let's hope you're right. It's hard to keep focused on the seatonite emitter when they start jumping around like they are."

He hand-flew the futuristic ship between three of them as she set up the upper ring emitter for auto engagement. A second later the system began to lock on and send an immensely powerful steady purple beam of pure force at the closest enemy ship.

The target's single shield flared instantly a brilliant yellow, but in the next three seconds the color turned darker as it passed through green, blue green, inky blue and violet before failing into an incandescent white. *Reaper* number fifty-one disintegrated in to a brief shower of coruscant sparkling bits that burned up in the earth's atmosphere.

"Good hit, Red," Hollywood sent as he veered to the left to engage another one. A green pulse from the new target impacted the *Galahad's* outermost shield. It flared to violet and automatically activated the inner second shield of the sixth magnitude. It, too, flared a dark blue shade, but held as the next three closely spaced laser pulses smashed into it.

Galahad's return fire blasted the *Reaper* into oblivion.

"Shield's are holding at ninety-eight percent," Raven advised.

"Copy that," Hollywood replied. *"Keep an eye on them."* He picked another enemy vessel that had begun to move away

from the intense furball and shoved the control model to pursue. *"You can run, sucker, but you can't hide...Take him Blaze."*

"On him." She shifted back to the seatonite projector and sent a needle beam a hundred miles long through the ship. With its power plant destroyed, the mortally damaged *Reaper* arced over in a high speed dive toward the uncharted jungles of the Yucatan.

Turning the *Galahad* around, Hollywood found a couple of distant targets back over the capital and plunged back into the fray.

***

CHAPTER EIGHTEEN

SINGULARITY
Outside the Moon's Orbit

In the blackness of space a distortion appeared in the very fabric of space-time. Out of its void appeared a Tyranian vessel almost a twin to the *Garrin*. The second *Annihilator*—this one christened *Thor*—laid in a course to its sister ship and accelerated quickly to light speed. Three seconds later she stopped in an instant, a mere hundred miles away. Her powerful tractor beam locked on the *T-Cruiser* already engaged by *Garrin*.

"Comander Garrple, where do you want to put this aberration?"

"Commander Ballen, nice to see you and so timely also...I think outside the Moon's orbit should do fine."

"No sooner said than...Done."

The two massive battlecruisers jerked the T-237 to the coordinates. They extended their tractor beams and backed off three thousand miles on either side and pounded the immobile *T-Cruiser* with their ravening Z-Beams.

"Modulate! Modulate the shield! Increase to maximum," yelled Captain Lssps.

"We are at maximum, Sire," replied his chief of engineering. "The combined fire is overcoming our screen. We are at twenty-seven percent."

The huge craft's fourth order shield flared through the visible electromagnetic spectrum from green to blue to indigo, and just before the screen went violet, there was a nova-like blinding explosion. The *Annihilator's* tractor beams were instantly sheared and the two Tyranian ships were hurled away at near the speed of light.

"Blaze's automatic trips to an inertialess zone of force worked."

"Apparently so, Dare. Both we and the Thor are completely unscathed, although the force of the annihilation of their neutronium core pushed us beyond the Mars orbit...Set a course back to Tellus, Davalan. We aren't finished."

"Aye, sir."

AZTECA STADIUM

A nineteen year old fan tugged at her boyfriend's arm as she watched the continuing flashes of red, green, purple and blue overhead. A multicolored star burst overhead signaled the destruction of one of the *Reapers* nine miles above them. "Manny, how do they do that?" she yelled in Spanish as the concert noise level was just below the threshold of pain.

He was totally mesmerized by the gyrations of the talented blonde singer only three rows away at the edge of the stage. Her skintight costume hugged her voluptuous figure and the deep plunge in front was working overtime on him.

"Huh?" he replied.

"How do they make it look like that?" she repeated as he bent lower to try to understand.

He shrugged. "I guess she works out a lot….Spandex, sequins and high heels…plus make-up…Definitely some make-up."

FLOATING GARDENS OF XOCHIMILCO

Miles from Azteca Stadium, the crash of one of the only *Reapers* that was actually able to teleport some of its human cargo was making a scene. News crews and police had surrounded the huge World Heritage site, but the site's attraction, over 100 miles of canals, prevented them from getting to the crash site itself until more boats were brought in.

351

The impact had been relatively gentle, as the ship had partial power and control when it hit nose first in a shallow canal and then collapsed from the unsupported weight of the fuselage.

Terrified captive humans jumped down from the containment section through huge holes in the thin exterior. They were coughing and choking from exposure to the chlorine gas inside the Reptoid ship and ran screaming toward the lights on a motorized barge a hundred and fifty yards away.

The barge operator cut the power to the Evinrude outboard and coasted to the side on the canal. "What happened?" he called out.

"Quetzalcoatl! Quetzalcoatl!" yelled one panicked man from Mexico City, referring to the Aztec feathered serpent god of early Meso America. "He's come back!"

Another young escapee from the Yucatan screamed as well. She had seen the Reptoid, but was convinced it was none other than Kulkulcán, a god to the Mayans from her region of Mexico.

One of the surviving alien crew members opened a small emergency hatch on the side of the downed *Reaper*. He stood in the opening for a moment and breathed in the oxygen-rich atmosphere. He coughed once and tumbled out the doorway, landing in the canal with a horrendous splash. He tried to swim, but that was a skill he was not capable of due to his evolutionary design. He thrashed his four tentacles furiously as the fetid, polluted waters of the canal closed in over his head.

AURORA: INVASION

THERMOSPHERE
Over Mexico City

The *Garrin* and *Thor* stopped instantly from near light speed in the outer limits of Earth's thermosphere and tractored the Reptiod *T-Cruiser*—this time it was different. The T-235 instantly fired massive laser pulses at both ships. The outer screen of *Garrin* flared to violet and collapsed back to the sixth magnitude second shield which only glowed a pale yellow, however, the fourth order shield of the *Thor* didn't fare so well. Its screen failed and she lay vulnerable to the next Reptoid pulse…

MAMA BIRD

Heater counted the remaining *Death Globes* locked in mortal combat with the BEF's air breathing fighters. *Six more to go. We still have close to forty of ours in the hunt.*

"Mama Bird, Eagle Twelve, flight of three. Guns dry…disengaging at this time. Any chance you can beam us back to base to rearm and refuel?"

"Eagle Thirteen flight, Mama Bird roger…Stand by." He switched back to intercom. "Comm, Mike Charlie. Got another three to rearm…Eagles Thirteen, Fourteen and Fifteen."

Tom Tallman responded immediately. "Copy that. Eagle Nest is ready for them. Contacting Excalibur at this time."

Looking at the altitude readouts of the remaining eleven *Reapers*, Heater came up with an idea. "Boomer, those harvesting ships have climbed out of reach for our 15s and 18s. Think you can give the three Heracles a hand with the particle beam projector?"

Eastman considered the request briefly. "Sure...I didn't want to try it earlier...that furball was way too danged tight to chance it. One hit from that bad boy could cut a fighter in two." He nodded. "Advise those folks I'm gonna crank it up...better coordinate the attack on just one or two targets."

"I'll handle that part," Heater replied.

The entire upper deck of the C-5 resonated with the low hum of the capacitors charging as Boomer prepared the TeslaPulse system and carefully completed the pre-operation checklists. By heterodyning the targeting laser—normally used for the ships sonic cannon and JDAM weapons deliveries—with a EMP generator and a molecular delivery source, Blaze Hermann had essentially duplicated Nikola Tesla's *Teleforce* weapon system he wrote about in the 1930s.

The EMP generator eliminated the need to be hooked up the a large power generating station, vacuum tubes and the ungainly Tesla coils. She had created a means to shield and protect the ship itself from the devastating effects of the pulse itself.

"Mercury valve...open." Eastman said to himself as he worked his way to the bottom on the checklist. He touched the valve icon. "Green *System Operational* light...on." He checked it and then took in a deep breath. No one had ever before used the system in combat to engage an enemy, in the air, on the sea, or on the ground. "Who's the lucky one?" he asked Heater.

"Lucy says numbers fourteen and fifty-nine are all yours. They'll try to keep the Heracles ships out of the line of fire."

"Try hard. These mercury molecules will be streaming out at Mach 48. Blaze doesn't think anything can stop 'em."

"We trust you with their lives. Do your best."

"Always," Boomer said as he used a joy stick to line the crosshairs up on the Reptoid ship almost fifty miles away. He thumbed a wheel on the side of the control to magnify the image displayed on his wide screen. The sausage-shaped ship appeared to be presenting a side profile, even though it was miles above him. *Looks the same from any angle...side, bottom or top.*

The inactive Marine sniper targeted the bottom portion he estimated to be the weapons section on the Reptoid vessel and pulled the trigger. Unlike the time he took out enemy soldiers at hundreds of yards, there was no recoil or ear shattering report—only a brief dimming of the overhead lights lining the top of the ship's fuselage.

The *Reaper*—IDed as number fourteen on his screen was indeed no match for the incredible stream of heavy molecules that had been subject to 60,000,000 volts and blasted out at almost 37,000 miles per hour. It took under five seconds for the stream to reach the Draconian ship—but it never really had a chance. The shields didn't respond at all, much as they didn't affect the 20 MM cannon shells fired from the *Eagles* and *Hornets*. Hyper velocity has a quantum effect all its own.

The mercury molecules cut like an incredibly narrow water jet through every single thing they touched—outer hull, decks, walkways, buss bars and cosmic power arrays. The pressure of the *Reaper's* cabin atmosphere pushed the two halves of the ship apart and its interior walls buckled and blew out from the immense pressure differential.

Subjected immediately to the cold and near vacuum of the extreme altitude, the crew suffered a rapid and incredibly painful demise. Gas pressure inside their intestines forced both of their stomachs up their gullet and out into their mouths. Reptoid blood—a thick gray viscous fluid and cold by human standards—boiled in their veins and cooked the tiny reptilian brains as the four eyes atop their skulls burst like rotten fruit.

"Nice shooting, Boomer. See if you can tag the other one," Heater said.

"With pleasure…It'll take the system a second to reset. Kinda hard on the Super Galaxy's generators, Gunnz tells me."

Onboard the *T-Cruiser* 233 flag ship, the weapons officer monitored the huge power surge from three hundred miles below. "Sire, we are detecting some new weapon system being deployed against our harvesting ships."

The Fleet Commander turned only one eye to his subordinate as he contemplated his next action. The tractor beam attack and subsequent destruction of *T-Cruiser* 237 had him livid and increasingly wary about the mission's outcome—T-235 was locked in battle with two of the Tyranian's new ships.

"Don't bother me with nonsense! Can you track and kill the ship that sent it? Yes or no?" Klsth thundered.

Weapons Officer Krrlp cringed at the bellicose response of his superior. "Sire, if I go to a wider beam, I can probably make contact the next time they fire. They do not have a shield to match their cloak, from what I have seen. The ship that just destroyed one of our Reapers is apparently not moving very fast. As you can see on the field detector…"

"Don't waste my time, fool! Just do it and be quick about it!"

Bowing to his commander, the technician increased the pulse weapon's diameter to 2,000 feet. *That should be big enough if I can judge their position accurately.*

"Second shot coming up in three, two, one…firing now." Boomer Eastman pulled the trigger on the retreating *Reaper*. He moved the crosshairs ahead of the maneuvering target and kept the trigger depressed. "No you don't, you slimy lizards. Ain't getting away that easy."

The ship's interior lights dimmed once again at the massive power draw as the TeslaPulse weapon drained the phone booth sized capacitors almost dry.

Heater studied the movement of the distant ship and glanced over at John's screen. "Get him, Boomer!"

"I have you now, you inferior pesks," the *T-Cruiser's* weapons officer boasted. His clawed tentacle tapped on the console screen in front of him.

From high in the thermosphere an unimaginably huge blast of green laser energy came streaming down at the speed of light—the same weapon that had destroyed USS *Alvin York* with one hit.

The cloaked C-5M almost made it clear of the danger zone. Almost only counts in horseshoes and hand grenades. The edge of the alien beam caught the entire empennage of the *Super Galaxy* in its indescribable destructive power. In a flash, the metal, wiring, hydraulic system and Graphene skin of the tail were gone. The cabin's atmospheric pressure blew out instantly creating a mini-hurricane inside the ship as the pressure fell to the same as the outside at 28,000 feet and a momentary fog appeared and dissipated.

Every crew member felt the rush of his or her life's breath explode out of their lungs in an instant—exactly as if struck in the stomach by a heavyweight boxer.

Gears caught his breath as the ship pitched over—a result of the aircraft's center of gravity suddenly shifting far forward due to the instantaneous lost weight of the tail. He pulled full aft on the yoke—no response. "Mama Bird is hit! We're going down!"

THERMOSPHERE

"Extend our shields to include the Thor, Davalan. They don't have the new equipment…" He switched to the interstellar comm system. "Commander Ballen, we've enveloped you in a sixth magnitude fifth order shield, but you can still use your tractor and Z-Beam. Let's take this Reptoid ship out to free space at light speed and on my signal, cut your beam and drive. We'll sling it out far enough that its self-destruct will not effect either of us."

"Affirimative, Garrple. Standing by."

"Engage."

The two massive Tyranian silver triangles jumped to light speed pulling the tractored *T-Cruiser* along behind them.

"Now!" ordered Garrple.

Both ships instantly came to a stop, but the T-235 did not.

"Fire!" commanded the captain of the *Garrin*.

The ravening dual purple beams leapt toward the rapidly receding Reptoid ship. A brief moment of time elapsed and a miniature sun appeared in the distance, and then winked out.

"Commander, I recommend you take the Thor to the Excalibur at Lagrangian Point 2 for repairs and have them install the new fifth order projectors."

"A capital idea, Garrple. See you there…I assume you're heading back to the fray?"

"You assume correctly, Ballen."

"Safe hunting."

The *Garrin* flashed away back toward the blue and white marble known as Earth.

GUINEVERE

Fifteen miles above, *Guinevere* circled the remaining *Reapers* as the particle beam shredded target number fifty-nine. Its shield disappeared and the ship vanished from the screens as a diagonal cut tore it apart in a slightly jagged line.

Loraine's fingers flew over the controls as she screamed out, "I got 'em! I got 'em. Slow down!"

Bone was slightly confused as Lucy brought the ship to a dead stop.

"What the hell just happened?" he sent.

"Loraine has Mama Bird locked in a tractor beam. See what I meant about her reaction time...I must contact Excalibur. The Garrin and Thor are dealing with the second T-Cruiser and cannot be of assistance."

MAMA BIRD

Gear's heart almost stopped as he glanced down at the instrument panel. The indicated airspeed was zero and the attitude indicator showed almost fifty degrees nose low. Master caution and warning lights were illuminated and the hydraulic system was a total loss—all four independent subsystems were showing zero pressure and quantities below minimum safe for continued operation.

He summoned up the courage to glance outside and back at the *Super Galaxy's* left wing. It was bent down over twenty degrees from the inboard engine to the wingtip. *Oh, my God. They're folding over due to the negative angle of incidence. Any more and they'll snap completely.*

"What the hell happened? Are we dead?" Bobby Mendez asked, his voice a full octave higher than normal.

"Not yet," Gears answered.

Julio Sosa glanced at the cabin altimeter. "Hey guys, we lost cabin pressure."

Their space suits had been hooked up to the ship's oxygen system and while they did provide protection from cosmic radiation, they were not a full pressure suit like those used by earth's astronauts and flight test pilots. Julio turned around to check on the other crew members. He could see stars in the night sky visible through past the crew seats and combat stations. "Holy crap! We lost the whole cargo ramp!"

Gears turned as well. "Lost more than that, I'm afraid…all hydraulics systems are shot to hell. Must have taken a blast that took off the T-tail as well."

THERMOSPHERE

"We got a piece of a winged craft, Commander. Our blast disabled its cloak. It is falling from the sky…No! It's stopped in mid-air…The craft has been tractored," reported Krrlp.

"Idiot! There is a cloaked Tyranian ship above it somewhere. Target aga…"

"Sire! T-235 is gone!"

361

He whirled on the communications officer. "What do you mean, 'gone'?"

"They were tractored out like 237 and they activated their self-destruct near the fifth planet."

He waved his tentacles all about causing the crew members in the control to duck and dodge the flashing talons. "Helm! Make a singularity…We head to Draco!"

The big ship moved out past the moon's orbit as a distortion appeared in front of it.

LANCELOT

"Hollywood! There is a distortion forming 300,000 miles out in front of the last T-Cruiser," reported Niki forgetting to use telepathy.

"Follow them!" sent Blaze so forcefully it almost knocked Stewart out of his seat.

The big triangle fighter spun on its axis and followed the T-233, matching its speed and direction. Blaze didn't take her eyes off the craft in her tank.

"What do you want to do?" Hollywood directed at her.

There was no response except for a deeper furrowing of the line in her forehead. A red fifth order tube just a little over ten feet in diameter leapt out from the upper projector and disappeared into the distance toward the recently formed worm hole. Down the inside, a *Star Killer* was pushed at the same speed. The tube and missile penetrated the aft section of the

T-233 just as the ship entered the distortion and disappeared in a flash of blue light.

Blaze activated the lower emitter and heterodyned her thought wave to a fifth order needle beam and directed it through the singularity behind the Reptoid craft. She manipulated the tiny spy ray inside the *T-Cruiser* and steered the missile into a storage hold almost full of the recently harvested human protein wafers from Brazil, India and Australia. She set the detonation timer at fifteen minutes and buried it deep in the grisly cargo.

EXCALIBUR

Rollân contemplated the request from his Zone Captain. "Annuna, it will be a relatively simple thing to transport your aircraft to safety. It will take a few darls to access the data stored from their last teleportation and write a program to properly integrate the files. I will put my best people on it."

MAMA BIRD

A voice came over the BEF operations frequency. "Mama Bird, Guinevere."

Tom Tallman answered, "Guinevere, Mama Bird, go ahead."

Padrino breathed a sigh of relief. "We have you in a tractor beam. Say status."

"We're still here…somehow. Standby one…AC, Comm. Padrino's on the horn."

Gears hit the transmit button. "Guinevere, Mama Bird…I guess we owe you guys our lives."

"Fast work by Loraine here…Lucy wants a status report, when you are able."

"Massive structural damage. Mama Bird has seen its last flight, I'm afraid."

"Any casualties?"

"None that I can see here on the upper deck. I'm unsure of the folks down on the lower deck."

"Guinevere copies all. Lucy says to hang on…help is on the way."

Gears chuckled, despite the dire situation. "Very funny, Padrino. That's about all we can do at this point. Mama Bird is clear at this time." *Hang on…Ha. It will be interesting to see what they come up with…* The stricken craft vanished in the dark skies.

GUINEVERE

"Hey, the tractor beam broke lock!" Loraine said with a bit of panic in her voice. She checked her screen and couldn't find a trace of the C-5M.

"It's okay, dear one," Lucy sent. *"My friends aboard Excalibur have taken over for you. Let's finish off the last two Reapers."*

"But what happened to them? Are they okay?" Bone inquired.

"All in good time, my friend. All in good time," Lucy replied somewhat cryptically.

AIRSPACE OVER MEXICO CITY

Flash Peterman and a flight of four F-15s materialized ten miles from a small cluster of remaining *Death Globes* at 20,000 feet. Almost instantly the data link from *Garrin* assigned two of them to him and his compatriots back from refueling and rearming at Eagle Nest. He touched the message acknowledgment button as he laid out a plan of attack.

"Eagle Nine flight…burners…now."

All four of the twin engine air superiority fighters went simultaneously to max burner and rocketed ahead. *Jees. Thirty seconds from liftoff in Texas and we're already in the thick of combat.* He hit the transmit button. "Eagles Eleven and Twelve plan a right break after guns. We'll go left."

Two sets of rapid clicks on the frequency told him his message had been received.

Random green pulses from the Reptoids showed they still had no clue where the next attack might come from. Flash noted a new set of blue dots transported into the battlespace at 40,000 feet. *That's Jill Herman and Fred Shore. They'll roll in from above and take out the last of 'em.*

The *Eagle's* Mach meter kept climbing as he and his wingman passed 1.7 and closed with the cloaked Draconian fighter. The distant red dot grew larger as larger in his HUD. He chanced one last quick crosschecking glance down at his nav display to gauge the distance as use of a ranging radar would have negated the flight's element of surprise.

He squeezed the trigger for a long second and a half burst as he walked the rudders slightly before increasing back pressure on the stick like a surgeon. He released the trigger, broke hard down and away as the 20 MM rounds scribed a ragged Z across the enemy ship. Another 150 rounds from his wingman ripped into the *Death Globe* as it began to plummet earthward.

AIRSPACE OVER SOUTH TEXAS

The cold was unlike any Gears had ever experienced while transporting. He hunched over involuntarily for an instant and shivered a bit as he gasped. *My God. What did they do?* As he caught his breath, he realized he was over Lake Falcon, forty miles south of the Eagle Nest airstrip. He looked over at his copilot who was looking at the systems and pressurization. No Master Caution lights were illuminated and every other mechanical parameter was normal.

"Boss! What happened?" Bobby Mendez asked. "I'm freezin' my ass off here."

Gears turned around and looked aft. Everything was normal. The ship's missing empennage was all back exactly where it had been before. *Amazing...Absolutely amazing.*

"Are we still alive, Gears? Is this some kind of dream?"

"No, Julio. You're not dreaming. Best I can tell, the Tyranians figured out a way to use their teleporter to replicate every bit of Mama Bird, just like she was the last time she transported. What an incredible amount of data to store, process and segregate in a short order."

"I take it they want us to go home and land?"

"That would be correct. Gotta check everybody out for injuries from the rapid decompression. The air battle must be well in hand...We could still fight if we had to."

"What about the VTOLs and Mantas?" Bobby asked

"I'm sure they'll bring 'em back in one piece. Hold on, guys. I gotta tell the rest of the crew what's happening..."

T-CRUISER - 233

"Commander, we were hit by one of the Tellurian missiles just as we entered the singularity! It lodged in number two cargo hold, but did not explode," reported Krrlp.

"It is apparently defective. Ignore it. The base technicians will take care of it when we reach our beautiful home world," directed Klsth.

Blaze withdrew the beam to just outside the Reptoid craft as it exited the singularity next to a monstrous yellow-green planet—almost as big as Jupiter—near an unbelievably huge white sun. *Draco*. She watched as the ship entered the noxious atmosphere and noted the rank jungles, steaming yellow seas and rugged rocky landscape. *No cities?*

The ship settled down inside a wide twisting canyon that ran alongside the base of a towering mountain range that made the Andes look like foot hills. A giant holographic mountainside wavered and disappeared revealing an opening ten miles wide and three miles high—the *T-Cruiser* floated inside and the hologram was restored, effectively camouflaging the entrance.

She directed the beam back inside the control room to catch the Fleet Commander conversing with another Reptiod on the visaplate.

"Klsth, I should have you dissected and fed to the bnths! You lost your entire fleet?" roared his eleven foot tall Emperor, Fslst.

"We had incorrect intelligence, Sire. The Tyranians were waiting for us…But my holds are full of the human protein."

LANCELOT

"Blaze?" Hollywood said aloud as his thoughts were apparently not getting through. "Hey, are you all right?

She didn't move. She hadn't moved a muscle in the last ten minutes.

"She appears to be catatonic, Hollywood," said Raven "Blaze is barely breathing. Are you sure she's okay?"

"Damn if I know, Rav…"

Blaze screamed, leapt to her feet and threw both hands to her almond-shaped lenses. "I can't see! I can't see! Oh, God!"

She frantically attempted to unconnect the magnetic

couplings attaching the helmet to the rest of her suit—Raven quickly restrained her.

Hollywood wheeled back to his control panel and the *Lancelot* jumped to light speed back to Earth as Raven continued trying to comfort her.

"Lucy! Need to transport Blaze to my wife's office at Eagle Nest immediately. She's in major pain."

EAGLE NEST
Doctor Kelli Stewart's Clinic

Two figures, one in gray and one in black, materialized in Kelli's office. The statuesque redhead in a white smock turned when she caught the movement from the corner of her eye. The smaller figure had her arm around the other's waist supporting her.

"Oh! You startled me!"

"I'm very sorry, Kelli, but there was no time to notify you. Something happened to Blaze…She is in pain."

She moved quickly and assisted Lucy to get her to an examining table. Lucy uncoupled the magnetic locks securing their helmets and removed them. Blaze immediately brought both hands back up and covered her eyes.

"My eyes, my eyes, I can't see anything!"

Kelli gently pulled them down and took out her tiny pen light. "Blaze, you have to let me take a look. Just lay back and relax."

She did as she was told and the doctor, with quick movements, flicked the light back and forth from eye to eye, taking care not to leave it on either very long.

"The pupils are almost completely closed. They're pin pricks…amazing." Kelli continued her examination. "I don't see any physical damage. She put some numbing and dilating drops in her eyes. "This should help…Can you tell me what happened?"

Blaze nodded and took a breath. "I heterodyned my mind to a fifth order needle beam and followed the Draconian ship to their planet after I had inserted a nuclear tipped Star Killer with a fifteen minute timer in her hold. It didn't occur to me that the atomic blast and subsequent chain reaction that destroyed the planet's atmosphere would hurt me, but it was unbelievably bright and it seemed to last forever…My mental projection was viewing it…I don't understand why this happened to me."

Kelli nodded. "I had an acting coach in college, Ken Farmer, tell me once, 'The body doesn't know it's acting. It only knows what the mind tells it and will therefore react physiologically.'…Your mind saw a nuclear explosion, up close and very personal…so to speak." She smiled. "Your body actually believed you were there."

"God, it seemed so real…So what you're saying it's psychosomatic that I can't see?"

"Essentially, yes. Your iris closed completely out of protection from what your mind perceived or witnessed."

"Will her condition last long?" asked Lucy.

"It shouldn't. Those drops I put in will help to relax the eye...The rest is up to her."

Blaze sat up on the table, blinked several times, and then closed both eyes for a long minute. The concentration furrow appeared in her forehead and then relaxed. When she finally opened her lids, she turned to the two standing in front of her and flashed a reassuring smile. "Well, ya'll are a little blurry, but at least I can tell you apart."

Kelli and Lucy glanced at each other, grinned and nodded.

"You are one amazing woman, Blaze. I knew I was right about you being the next stage in your species evolutionary growth," said Lucy.

Kelli looked at her with a puzzled expression.

***

EPILOGUE

EAGLE NEST
BEF Lounge

The team was gathered in the large underground lounge at the base. Services had just finished topside for the pilots lost in the confrontation with the Draconians. Present also were the Secretery of Defense, Burner Stewart, former President Annette Thompson-Hermann, Gunter, Admiral Cooke, a contingent from the Annunaki, including Lucy, Garrple, Rollân and Ravalon—Overlord of the Tyranian High Council. The mood was still somber.

The eighty inch curved screen had been turned on to FOX as it was reported that President Carlos Benedict would be making a statement.

The picture changed to a temporary podium set up at an exclusive golf club in Hawaii. The dais was flanked by United States flags and a Marine honor guard. An attractive brunette network field reporter, Andrea Faulkner, stepped into the frame.

"President Benedict requested this time to address the citizens of the world regarding the recent defeat of a fleet of marauding aliens who had invaded our Earth." She looked over her shoulder to see the president, dressed in a bright floral Hawaiian print shirt and yellow golf slacks take the podium. "Here's President Carlos Benedict now."

The camera panned to the president. "Good afternoon. I can now report to the people of the world that the operation I authorized to intercept and defeat the most heinous threat in our planet's history has been completed successfully. The vile Draconian aliens, responsible for the murder of thousands of innocent men, women and children have been routed as per my orders."

He glanced over the teleprompters until he found the red light signifying that a particular live television camera was tight on him and continued, "We know that the worst images of the slaughter of untold number of civilians in India, Brazil and Australia are too horrific to show, but I made sure my military made them pay before they could complete wreaking their havoc in Mexico.

"I was resolved to protect our world and to bring those who committed these vicious attacks to justice. I was personally incensed that those diabolical aliens would attack our world without provocation and I declared war to protect our citizens, our friends, our allies and yes, all the peoples of the world.

"Three days ago...immediately after the wanton destruction of one of our newest ships of the line...at my direction, the United States launched a full scale attack against the fleet of creatures from another planet.

"Since I took office, I've repeatedly made clear that I would take any action necessary to protect our nation, and indeed, our world...That is what I've done.

"The people of Earth did not choose this fight. It came to our world with the senseless slaughter of our people. I, as commander in chief, will personally sign letters of thanks and condolences to the families who lost a loved one in the fight to save our planet. It is a pain I will feel deeply for the rest of my life. May God bless you. And may God bless our world."

The scene cut back to the network studio anchor in New York.

"Somebody want to cut that damn thing off before I throw a chair through it?" said Bone as he got to his feet with an undisguised look of disgust.

Loraine leaned over to Dare and whispered. "Better do it. I've seen this movie before."

He pressed the remote, killing the feed. "Yep, had enough of that, myself."

"How many times did that asshat say *I* or *my* in that two minute interruption of his back nine?" asked Bone.

"Sixteen times," replied Mike.

"Worthless sonofabi..."

He was interrupted by Partsman Meadows rushing into the room. "Hey, all our cloak black boxes are gone from the planes...every one of 'em and my space suit is missing from my locker."

"All of the others are as well, Mister Meadows," said Lucy.

"Why?" asked Dare turning to the diminutive woman.

Ravalon got stately to his feet and surveyed the men and women in the room. "I first want to thank all of you for your unselfish efforts in combating our mutual enemy. We could not have defeated them without you. With their planet destroyed, possibly we are free of the malevolent creatures at long last. The only thing we do not know is if they had any additional fleets off world...We shall see." He glanced over at Lucy. "It is our considered opinion that your civilization is not quite ready for certain technologies, children. You need to learn to get along amongst yourselves..."

Lucy added, "There is a quotation I learned in my time here. 'Power corrupts...Absolute power corrupts absolutely.'"

Ravalon nodded in agreement. "You will be allowed to keep your bracelets, but they are active only for the invisibility function and communications. Annuna will remain your Watcher. She is being elevated to the rank of Zone Commander."

Lucy put her hand to face as she blushed. "Oh, my."

"The Supreme Council has implicit trust in her judgment. After all it was she who brought in the Black Eagle Force."

Dare got to his feet and stepped over to shake the regal leader's hand. "Mister Ravalon..."

"It's just Ravalon, Dare."

He nodded. "Ravalon, I'm not sure anyone of us would still exist on this planet without the Tyranians. We can never thank you enough."

"Believe me, Dare, it is mutual." He looked at Rollân. "We must go now."

"I will be along later, Overlord. I need to see Bone, Padrino and Loraine back to their homes," said Lucy.

"I understand."

"Don't suppose there's any chance I can play with that Death Globe Loraine and I captured?"

Ravalon looked at Bone—his gray eyes sparkling—slowly shook his leonine mane and gave him a very soft wry smile.

"Yeah, didn't think so."

"You never quit, do you?" whispered Loraine as she elbowed him in the side.

"How do you spell *quit*?"

The three Tyranians shimmered and disappeared.

Bone took Raven by the hand and led her outside into the hallway. They embraced and kissed passionately.

"Givin' serious thought to puttin' you in my pocket and takin' you home, pretty thing."

She looked up, gave him a seductive smile and snuggled her head to his chest. "That might work."

****

PREVIEW of the NEXT
TIMBER CREEK PRESS RELEASE

ACROSS THE RED

Fourth novel in the Bass Reeves saga

By

KEN FARMER
&
BUCK STIENKE

TIMBER CREEK PRESS

CHAPTER ONE

COOKE COUNTY, TEXAS
DELAWARE BEND

Texas Ranger Bodie Hickman instinctively ducked when he saw a puff of rifle smoke from across the Red River. Approximately one second later he heard the crack of a bullet just as it clipped the top of his gray center-creased Stetson and took it from his head—followed immediately by the boom of a big gun.

The big rawboned redhead dove from the back of his line-back dun mustang, Lakota Moon, rolled to a crouch, still holding on to the reins and tapped the horse's left front foot in the signal to lay down. Moon dropped to his knees and rolled over on his right side.

"Git down, Billy!" he shouted at the young posseman behind him as he reached over and jerked his brand new 1886 Winchester lever action rifle from its boot. The warning came too late as the second booming report of the distant big gun was followed by the sickening *twack* of the round striking flesh. Bodie turned just in time to see a cloud of red explode from Billy Malena's chest and the young man flip backwards out of his saddle and fall to the ground. His panicked horse lunged up the side of the draw and into the woods on the south.

The two lawmen had been riding single file—tracking some rustlers moving a small herd of horses—down a shallow three foot deep wet-weather wash that headed west toward an area known as the *breaks* along the Red River, still some three hundred yards away.

The heavily wooded area close to the wide but usually slow moving border river between Texas and the Indian Nations had become a sanctuary for the lawless, allowing the malefactors to head into the Chicksaw Nation if the Texas Rangers got too hot behind them.

The sweeping six square miles of the bubble-like horseshoe on the west side of the much larger Delaware Bend of the Red was ten miles directly east of Marietta, IT and twenty miles northeast—as the crow flies—from Gainesville, Texas. It had been a past haven to the likes of Charles Quantrill—the guerilla chieftain of the south—as well as the James brothers and now was a crossing point for stolen cattle and horses bound for the Nations—especially, like then, in early summer when the water level was going down

"Billy!" Bodie shouted in vain at the motionless body of his friend and brand new posseman four yards behind him in the gully. Another *boom* sounded and a slug slapped the sandy bank just above his head a half second later. "Son of a bitch!"

He raised up just enough to see over the edge of the ditch and could make out a small cloud of gunsmoke coming from atop a forty foot bluff just across the river. "Damnation! Purtnear a quarter mile...Gotta be .45-70...Got a shooter up there, Moon. Stay down, son...That bastard don't know I got surprise for him."

He belly-crawled forward—his rifle cradled across his arms—in the gully as quickly as he could about fifteen feet to a low scrub bush over the northern lip of the bank. Bodie adjusted his Lyman tang sight up to where he saw the four hundred yard range notch was marked and took a deep breath. Levering in a long .45-90 round, he brought the rifle snugly to his shoulder. He rose up slightly and found the desired sight picture on the slowly dispersing cloud of smoke in the windless morning, concentrated on the front sight, exhaled half his air and fired.

The big round, originally created for taking buffalo at long distance bucked hard, but he paid it scant heed as he quickly cranked another into the chamber and shot again. Both rounds were discharged in less than a second with the distinctive roar of the big bore echoing up and down the Red River valley. "Bet you weren't expectin' that, were you, asshole?" *Not like I had a chance of hittin' anything, but maybe I scared 'em off.*

The cloud of his own gunsmoke gradually drifted away, but not before he had smelled the pungent aroma of burnt sulfur from the black powder load. Bodie drew a pair of the cigar sized rounds out of his custom-made gun belt and shoved them past the Winchester's loading gate as he contemplated his next move.

He waited for return fire for a good five minutes—nothing. *White man...Injun would have the patience to wait me out.* Just to be safe, he crawled back to his horse. "Git up Moon."

The big mustang got to his front feet, followed quickly by his back—he shook, as horses will do after getting up from the ground. The young ranger led him over to the woods on the side near Billy's mount, ground-tied him so he could graze a bit and solemnly walked back to his friend's body.

His hat lay near Malena. He picked it up, slapped the dirt off on his thigh, stuck his index finger through the hole in the top of the crown. "Yep, .45." He jammed the Stetson firmly back on his head and knelt down beside Billy and caressed the side of his face.

"God, I'm sorry, boy...Yer first day, too...What in the world am I gonna tell yer mama?" He slipped his arms under the still warm body, easily lifted the wiry teenager and carried him over to the horses.

DEXTER, TEXAS

Bodie slowly walked Moon—leading Billy's blood bay with the young man draped across the saddle—down the dirt main street of the dying little north Texas town.

At one time, Dexter had been larger than Gainesville, the county seat, until the highly anticipated Santa Fe Railroad went south through Woodbine, instead of Dexter, to Gainesville.

He passed by Ed Stein's Sugar Hill combination store and saloon with two cowboys leaning against the porch posts smoking roll-your-owns. One—a reed-thin man in his twenties—touched the brim of his dark Montana pinch hat, gave the young ranger a surreptitious grin and blew a cloud of smoke in his direction.

The two working cowboys sported batwing chaps—as opposed to shotgun chaps preferred in Montana and Wyoming—because they were cooler and gave greater freedom of the lower leg when mounting—each wore store-bought white boiled work shirts without vests. The thin one a Colt Peacemaker strapped to his hips and his shorter, heavier friend, a Smith & Wesson Schofield in reverse grip.

Bodie noticed the two, but didn't acknowledge or even look their way. He knew who they were and would bet money they were involved in the rustling ring that was plaguing north Texas and the Indian Nations across the Red. He just couldn't prove it—yet.

Every step Lakota Moon took increased his dread, not of the two ne'er-do-wells he just rode past, but of having to tell the mother of Billy Malina what happened. *Damn, I'd rather git whipped with a wet rope...but I ain't got no choice.*

***

TIMBER CREEK PRESS